This Time We Lose

Linda Bishop

This Time we Lose copyright@2024 by Linda Bishop.
All Rights reserved.
No part of this book may be reproduced in any form or by any electronic or mechanical means including information storage and retrieval systems, without permission in writing from the author. The only exception is by a reviewer, who may quote short excerpts in a review.

This book is a work of fiction names, characters, places, and incidents either are products of the authors imagination or are used fictitiously. Any resemblance to actual persons, living or dead, events or locales is entirely coincidental.
Linda Bishop
Printed in the UK

You may forget but
let me tell you this:
someone in some future time
will think of us.

Sappho

CHAPTER 1

Landry took a tentative step forward. She welcomed the feel of her foot hitting the floor beyond. Stepping forward, she sensed immediately that she was alone. She placed her head against the wooden staging and listened intently for any evidence of people in the rest of the building. Convinced that there were none, she moved around from behind the curtain and took a moment to take it all in. The vastness of the empty stage and beyond, rows and rows of sumptuous seating. The towering drapes of the red and gold were such an extravagance. It never failed to surprise her. Her footsteps echoed as she moved to the side of the stage. She jogged to the stage door at the rear and willed it to be unlocked. The handle turned easily, and the door swung open, allowing the cool November air in. Stepping outside her auditorus were engulfed by the clamour from the road up ahead. She winced and fought the desire to step back into the void and return to the quiet of the theatre. However, Landry remained in the safety of the alley and took a moment to review her previous operations at this site. Finally, she glanced up at the shadows of movement up ahead and made her way in that direction, stepping carefully through the usual waste and detritus found at the back of a theatre.

Arriving at the threshold of Inge Street, an unfamiliar sound invaded her auditorus causing an involuntary shake of the head. Then she saw it. A public omnibus with its motors rumbling, then the hiss of the air brake release and a steady drone as the diesel engine, briefly rising in pitch, struggled to accelerate up the incline. Landry stood transfixed as the omnibus moved across her viz. She didn't see the passengers behind the glass until it was too late. She caught the eye of a young male participant. Their eyes locked in a split second before she lowered hers.

Landry let out a forced breath as a prickling sensation travelled across the back of her neck. He saw me! She replayed the interaction her mind; considered what he may have thought he saw. How she could appear to him. *She could be someone leaving the theatre after work or a cast member stepping out.* Satisfied that he wouldn't question her being there, Landry continued but pulled her cap further down over her eyes to avoid a repetition of the unwanted attention. Her training was clear. Hide in plain sight. No interaction with any participants.

Stepping to the corner of Inge Street, she welcomed seeing the distinctive H of the Hippodrome Theatre. The tall gold lettering looked gaudy to Landry, but then everything here seemed larger than life. Landry had used this theatre many times and had enjoyed its many transformations over the years. From its humble beginnings as the Assembly Rooms to the Theatre of Varieties and now to the Hippodrome Theatre. Arriving at the impressive frontage of the Theatre, she was expecting to find the distinctive flapping banners and bright, colourful adverts for the current showing of "Jesus Christ Superstar". The distinctive show title and silhouetted image of the crucifixion in the foreground with the red and purple hues behind confirmed her hopes. Unfortunately, she had never experienced the show first-hand.

Looking up the street, she observed a small group of female participants coming her way. As they came closer, Landry had to fight the urge to turn and flee. Her heart rate was escalating as her chest rose and fell and she wrestled with her anxiety as they came closer and closer. The moment came when they were almost in touching distance, but they passed by unaware of their effect upon her. She turned and merged in behind the group.

Following them at a distance, Landry could observe them more freely. They were chattering and touching each other; holding arms, and hands. She enjoyed watching them, so at ease being close to each other and being together as they walked. She heard a shared laugh as someone made a funny comment and envied their simple innocence.

Finally, Landry turned her attention away from the group and recalled her plans for the day. The sky in the east was showing the first glimmers of sunlight. She was on time and excited about what she hoped to accomplish. It had been months in the planning, and she was hopeful that this could be the chance to change everything, to change her and others' futures.

Making her way through the city streets, she began to relax. She enjoyed observing their carefree abandonment in going about their lives and the simple pleasures of living, loved to pretend, for just a moment, that she was one of them. She could spend all day watching them. The vehicles queuing in the busy morning traffic caught her attention. They were all so different, the variety of their manufacture, the number of hues and colours. However, her lungs squeezed in protest at the fumes as their engines idled in the morning air. *Such pollution just ignored? - even now?* The admiration for their naivete was quickly replaced with frustration. *Why? Why did they not act? Why did they not shout it from the rooftops?* She pressed on, her mindfulness prodding slowly at her anger as it slowly diminished.

Her attention shifted as she noted a change in the air. It was market day, and the food outlets were busy as she passed by, it hit her; a breeze of smells enticing her to stop and investigate. She passed by a doorway and almost stepped inside. It was a small café serving food products. Her nose wrinkled at the distinctive smell of smoked pork and other meat. However, it was unlawful for her to eat this and so she reluctantly continued.

As Landry entered the main road near the train transport hub, the number of commuting participants increased. They walked three or four abreast, jostling lightly but making small contacts with one another as they were funnelled toward the doors. Landry struggled against her base instinct not to touch anyone in the crowd and felt conspicuous. Being so close to people was repellent to her. She had to fight her instincts of dread and fear of being discovered. However, from previous experiences, she knew that they rarely noticed the usual, and Landry was usual in every way. It was vital for this role, that Landry was utterly forgettable in both face and form. She had been handpicked for her ability to blend in among other things. Besides her forgettability, her outfit was carefully selected although inadequate for this season. The winter wind blew chilled her, and she tugged at the woollen scarf around her neck. Its natural threads were itchy beyond belief, but it gave Landry both warmth and additional anonymity as she pulled it higher up her face.

Continuing her close quarters' march towards the transport hub, she stopped at the premises named newsagents to gain a dateline confirmation. The commuters moved around her, flowing to the station like a flock of black-coated sheep fading into the distance. Landry stepped forward towards the bright lights of the shop. A glance at one dateline on a newspaper outside confirmed it was 16/11/2015. Her success now depended on getting to Birmingham University for the presentation at 1100 hrs. But she had to remain undetected by a participant or any viz surveillance as she continued along her route.

Turning a corner into the morning sun, Landry lost her resolve for a moment. Gazing upwards, she gasped out loud. The tip of a wing and then another. Gliding high above the buildings, their wings outstretched, they rode the thermals. Landry beamed. *Birds! There were birds, maybe gulls.* She lowered her scarf, delighted in the scene developing in front of her. As one flew out of sight behind the building, she instinctively stepped out to continue her vigil. A body collided with her back, thrusting her forward.

"Sorry", a male voice muttered. He swerved around her, and he turned his face in her direction.

Her breath shattered. The physical contact. A violation. She panicked. Scenarios pulsed through Landry's brain. Her training kicked in. Pulling the back of her left hand down her back, and then down her front and both sides of her rib cage, she checked for any wounds. She studied her hand to check for blood and saw none, but noticed her hand was shaking. Looking ahead, she could see that he had already continued his path and not stopped. She continued brushing her hands over her chest, her shoulders and her back again, checking for wounds. She breathed in and out, slowing her panting breath until she could focus. *Had he robbed her? Was this a plot?* She checked around for anyone else nearby and taking her bag off her shoulder, unzipped it. The relief at finding everything intact was absolute.

"You idiot", Landry exclaimed out loud, chastising her own stupidity. *That could have been a DC 9 – full compromise. It could still be detrimental to her task.* She cursed herself under her breath and began walking again towards the University, resisting any glances into the sky.

The information boards near the entrance directed her to the science studies auditorium. Choosing the aisle seat of one of the central rows, she was pleased with her choice. However, her anxiety increased as a party of young female participants arrived and sat in her row. Now there was the possibility of having to make conversation and Landry rehearsed some of her pre-planned scripts in her head. Her concern was unfounded, however. As soon as they were seated, her seat companion turned away from Landry, facing her group of friends, and her attention stayed there. Landry listened to the conversation of the females in her row but was disappointed to find that the discussion did not include the subject of the presentation that they were about to see. What she overheard surprised Landry. They seemed to spend an enormous amount of energy on their individuality, their appearance and their opinions on the appearance of others. Their disinterest struck Landry more than anything else.

Landry had placed her notepad and pencil on her lap in the pretence of making notes. She rarely wrote anymore, using her enhanced optic as a record. Checking the status of this she held her finger against the side of her temple to pause what she had just viewed in her left optic. Lightly pulling down the finger at her temple, she played back the last few seconds and was satisfied that all was working well. She was ready. A buzz indicated the arrival of two men as they entered the room. The time had come. Landry felt settled, her pencil poised for the demonstration to begin. If only they knew why she was here and how much was riding on this. Her stomach twisted in anticipation.

CHAPTER 2

Landry turned her attention to the audience. It comprised mainly of students with some more official persons, maybe shareholders or scientists, who sat together at the front. She recognised some of their faces from the historical records. However, aware of the need to record those present, she turned her optics towards this group; this data would be analysed later. She did the same with those behind her, glancing over her shoulder into the audience, feeling her left optic automatically refocusing to record as she did so. It would appear to anyone there, that she was searching for a friend or colleague.

Dr Dana Brook began, "We are incredibly pleased to welcome as our keynote speaker today, Doctor Simon Pedersen. Simon is a research fellow at the Birmingham Institute at this University and many of you will have read his work on 'The Silent Forest." Landry scrutinised the person whose work she was so familiar with. Simon was short and over optimal weight, distinctly opposite to his colleague Dana. He held his arms behind his back and look down shyly as Dana Introduced him.

Dana continued, "He is speaking today about the current data regarding BUFR's attempts to use forest sink data to combat the effects of climate change."

Landry felt the familiar tingle of excitement at her discovery and what impact it could have on her work. Simon's forehead glistened a little under the bright lights as he began. He was a reluctant speaker, but the data was promising.

The first slide was about BUFR; the Birmingham University Forestry Research and its implications for HAFAC. Landry noted the abbreviation for the Human and Animal Fatality Assessment and Control, a foundation set up in 2006 following the Inter-government Congress on the Global Warning report, showing that climate change was a genuine threat. Landry was in admiration of HAFAC's work and a great follower of their cause.

The presentation began. The slide changed to an image of a forest. Simon turned and read directly from the slide. "Humans and forests currently take part in a mutually beneficial exchange in which trees take in and lock up carbon that would remain in the atmosphere, heating the planet."

Simon returned his attention to the audience, "We knew that this mutually symbiotic relationship that we have with trees could combat the increased levels of CO2. We want to emulate the continued increase in CO2." He gestured forward with his arm and smiled, "Travel into the future if you will." The audience chuckled and Landry smiled along with them. "Here are our initial results and I must warn you we are in the early stages of this research."

The slide changed, and he continued. "BAFR completed its second growing season under elevated carbon dioxide. It shows every sign of delivering the ground-breaking science for which we conceived it." An image of a natural woodland filled the screen. Revelling in the beauty of the fixed optic of the forest of trees with dappled sunlight streaming through, Landry sighed and took a fleeting look over the students in her row to watch their reaction. She noted boredom on most of their faces. Some were scrutinising their nails and others sketching scribbles on their note pad. 'If only they knew', she reflected. 'If only they knew that during their lifetime this would become a rare optic image to behold.' Landry felt the usual irritation with those that came before her.

Drawing her attention back as the screen slide changed, Simon specified, "Year 2 of BAFR once again saw three 30-metre-wide blocks of mature oak forest immersed in an atmosphere with elevated carbon dioxide (CO2), adding 150 ppm (parts per million) to current values of just above 400 ppm, a roughly 38% increase, which the entire globe is likely to see by about 2050. "

She smiled to herself as he revealed promising figures. Without taking her eyes off the screen, she shuffled in her seat, the anticipation of the impact of what she was recording. Feeling a shift to her left, she swiftly glanced at the females sitting next to her. She expected a comment on those facts and maybe some excitement at their findings.

"God, this is so boring," one female yawned, rolling her eyes, "I would rather be anywhere but here right now."

Landry's anger simmered, but she could find no reply. What could she say? What did God have to do with this? She shrugged her shoulders. Her gesture closed any possibility of discussion, and she returned her gaze to the presentation. As it continued, Landry felt her anger brewing at the ignorance and lack of care shown by the female. At times like this, Landry felt like shouting at all that would listen. "You should be paying attention. You should care about this. Your life will change forever soon, and you will wish you had listened, had acted, had run out of here and done everything and anything you could to fight for your world." But of course, she couldn't do that. Any conversation could compromise her assignment, or possibly worse. She knew that the female speaking would appear on her optic recording, and she was already in trouble with her supervisor.

Landry watched the rest of the presentation, which involved several slides recording the setup of BUFR's forest in the Staffordshire countryside and showing how they had come up with the initial ideas and brought them into reality. Landry avoided any gazes at her seated companion. The burning excitement that Landry felt had not diminished. She felt her optimism rise, and she recognised that this could be one of them. What they were all looking for. A true scientific discovery. A life-changing find.

Dana stepped up next to Simon. She stood for a few seconds in silence considering her words, "One of the great imponderables in climate science is how long forests will continue to buffer climate change as CO_2 levels continue to spiral. We can see that you have found a genuinely viable option for combatting the rising CO_2 on our planet, Simon." She placed her arm around Simon and mouthed 'thank you,' to him. He nodded in agreement and Dana continued, "Together, we are sharing our funding with our colleagues involved in the Spruce project, and the project to protect the peat bogs of Finland. We are pleased to invite anyone here to visit either of our research facilities and check our figures themselves."

As the presentation concluded, claps and cheers emanated from the group of science individuals near the front of the auditorium. Many of the participants showed a distinct lack of interest and almost ran down the steps in their need to leave quickly. The females sharing Landry's row stepped past her, forcing her to stand as they made their way to the end of the row and down the steps. They have already moved on, Landry thought to herself. This could be the answer to everything, and she was here to see it, but to them, it was nothing - the presentation and its implications for their future already forgotten.

Some audience members started making their way to Simon and Dana, and she saw this as her opportunity to slip past unnoticed. Clinging to the shadow of the person in front, she moved down the steps and prepared to walk past the stage. As the person in front stumbled on the last step, the gasp bought attention to them, and Simon and Landry's eyes met. She knew he had recognised her. As she moved away, he attempted to move from Dana to come after her. In slow motion, he turned to catch up with her, "Hey there," He exclaimed. At this moment, Dana grabbed his arm. The president of the committee had approached. Simon halted and turned to smile at the man but still took a glance at Landry's back, exiting through the door of the auditorium. Landry knew she had seen him speak several times, in her visits to the past. As she walked through the campus, she realised that if she was to visit him after 2015, then she would need to think about some sort of disguise.

Landry made her way back to the theatre on Inge Street. A bright winter sun had replaced the morning's coolness, which brought some warmth. The return journey was without incident, and Landry was feeling buoyed by the information that she had in her possession. She enjoyed a pleasant stroll through the city, just observing- a voyeur. Life streamed through every pore, people going about their daily lives. She arrived at her favourite place, Temple Street Science Park. Here, she could observe younger participants as well as nature. She could not waste too much time here as her optic visuals would show Kyson that there had been a detour from her designated assignment route, but she enjoyed the possibility of what she might see whilst passing through. If luck was with her, she would see a butterfly flitting between the floral growths. She loved watching their erratic flights between the tall reaching tendrils, looking for a place to land. And how their wings closed into one, poised on a leaf or flower. Looking for these and other Lepidoptera gave Landry genuine moments of joy. Today, she was not so lucky. The winter landscape was more barren. The plants and trees were in a state of hibernation. She watched as a dog began moving towards her, expectant of receiving some form of welcome. Its ears swung up and down as it lolloped in her direction. It had an adorable face and she so wanted to touch it but knew that the owner may start a conversation and she was afraid of that. With reluctance, she turned her body away, and the dog changed its route and soon became engrossed in something else.

Landry continued to the theatre; the assignment was almost complete, and Landry felt the satisfaction of a job well done. The information that she now held could easily be ground-breaking for the research authority that she worked for. She hoped this gem may even be over 70% for positive impact on Earth's past. She felt confident that what she held in her optics would be what they had been looking for.

Humming to herself, she turned the corner onto Hurst Street, enjoying the bubble of voices as people were making their way out of the theatre and onto the pavement in front, discussing the show and enjoying themselves. 'Perfect timing', Landry observed. The industry that came with the end of a live show was perfect for masking a person entering the theatre and travelling through the corridors behind the stage. Her crew member ID swung in her hand as she made her way through the blackout curtains to a small discrete part of the back wall unnoticed.

Behind the secrecy of the blackout curtain, she found the symbol on the wall, indistinguishable to anyone not looking for it. Landry placed her tattooed wrist against the symbol, and a vertical line appeared in the gloom as a doorway opened. A crack of light, the only sign that it was there. She moved towards the opening to look through. She could see the small space beyond. As she stepped onwards, hesitating, she glanced over her left shoulder, listening for any footsteps coming after her. There were none, so she entered the small space, and felt the wall closing behind her. Anyone walking past the place that she had just been would have never noticed it in the dark recess of the wall.

CHAPTER 3

Reaching back with her left hand, Landry felt for the wall behind her. The door where she had come into this space was now gone. She was back in her own time. Squinting in the gloom, she found the icon on the wall. Two small circles crossed over each other and within were the letters M and E. Holding a small tattoo on her left wrist against the icon, the wall shifted and appeared to dissolve as small blocks of black plaster broke away. These blocks moved in circular motions as if in a swarm and then dispersed. In their place emerged a green screen, approximately 30 centimetres across and on it appeared a grainy image of two spinning planets interwoven with the letters MAGERA.

The screen struggled to focus at first, the connection developing, then the symbol disappeared and was replaced with the top of a head belonging to Kyson Mullins, Landry's supervisor. Kyson did not look up and her attention remained firmly on another screen to her left. She showed little interest in Landry as she began speaking. "Welcome back, Reagan2485."

"Hey there, Kyson. How are you today?" Landry grinned up at the small static camera at the top of the screen.

"Formal protocol only Reagan2485- use your designated identity. You should know better." Kyson sighed. With no response from Landry, Kyson was forced to look up. Kyson addressed her. "You know my designation is Mullins2001, Reagan2485."

"Yes, but maybe just this once we could, you know... just talk?" Landry smiled and raised her eyebrows.

Ignoring Landry's request, the screen stuttered, and the image jumped as Kyson continued. "Reagan2485, I have confirmation date and time for you: 1948 hours on 15/06/2188. There is a no entry enforcement in place in Subdivision Sofia and Yardley Subdivision Buildings 23B- 34F. The usual curfews apply so keep to the Greenline. "

Landry's shoulders dropped. She had tried to find some common ground with Kyson on a personal level, but Kyson either wasn't interested in developing a genuine connection or she was no longer capable of doing so. Landry suspected that Kyson's disinterest resulted from her not being able to be an operative like Landry. Kyson was born with vitiligo, causing the white patches on her ebony skin. The vitiligo made Kyson too distinctive, too risky for an operative who had to be clandestine. Landry sighed.

"Thank you, Kyson for the confirmation date time and how are you today? What are your allocated cycles?" Landry glanced up at the screen, "What time do you complete your cycle today?"

Kyson stared into space and paused. *Maybe today she might talk to me?* Landry waited, staring into the static camera hopefully. With a sudden movement after the stillness, Kyson moved and folded her arms to gaze directly into the imager. "Reagan2485, your assignment download?"

Landry placed her hand against the wall next to the green screen and studied her fingers for a moment. They were slender, her nails carefully clipped, and the small lines on her knuckles. My hands are just like Kyson's, she thought. We're both human, we are the same, same beating heart, same lungs inflating and deflating with our breathing. How can we be so different? How can it be that we cannot connect as human beings? Landry reflected upon the past participants that she had witnessed in 2015. The group of female participants walking down the street, holding arms, came to mind. Close, connected and attached by some invisible thread of camaraderie. What happened to us over the century? How did we lose that connection that was so natural in 2015? Landry envied the humans of the past.

Landry shifted on her feet, "before I download my optics, I need to state that I had three non- compromising observations but- "She heard an audible gasp from Kyson, "But, but in each case, - "Landry could see Kyson's face, a grim line.

"Reagan2485 - Reconnaissance only, reconnaissance only, what do you not understand about your assignment briefs for information gathering only. "Kyson's voice rose, "This is the third time Reagan 2485." Kyson's stared directly at the camera at Landry. "The third time that you have had several compromises during a visit."

"I know," Landry exclaimed, "But there is a reason."

"There's always a reason with you, Reagan2485. Always an excuse." Kyson raised her arms and placed them behind her head, "You will have to include this in your report, and I will have to take this further!"

Landry panicked, "Look Kyson, sorry Mullins 2001. Please check out my optic visuals and the report before you take it further. At least two of them I strongly believe are non-compromising and there is NO evidence of any implications for the timeline, not even close to a 0.01. The other compromise, there was no interaction, just a possible recognition from a past participant, and I will endeavour to make sure that this doesn't happen again." Landry placed both hands on the wall next to the screen. "Look, Mullins2001, I am excited about what I have bought back. It is a pure possible predictive changer. I'm sure, if acted upon, it is an 80% positive impact on Earth's past. The highest I have ever seen."

Kyson became distracted by screen to her left again, but she continued, "Reagan2485, I have warned before you about compromising the timeline with your casual attitude. You know what happened to Scott4563. It is laziness or in your case clumsiness. "

Landry softened her tone, "Mullins2001, I believe that these are all 1's, non-compromising. The important thing here is the data that Dr Pedersen shared. In only two years of study, they had results of 38% less CO_2 released into the atmosphere. 38% in only two years! This study is exactly what Magera is looking for. You need to tell them Kyson. This is a possible actionable study. I think that this is the one." Her voice rose a few octaves, the excitement flooding through her.

"I - will- do -no- such-thing Reagan2485. You know the protocol. I will upload your feed as with any other feed received by any employee. It will be processed through the Radan system initially and then IF accepted, they will place it on the list for the Magera actionable panel." Kyson emphasised the if. "Radan will make the final decisions on any action. You know how this works. Know your place Reagan2485, you are an inexperienced stage 1 operative reconnaissance ONLY. If and I state that without confidence- if your data is what you say it is, then Radan will recognise it as an actionable find and notify us." Kyson sat back in her chair, her eyebrows knotted together, her lips pursed, and she continued, "you are a lower-ranking stage 1 operative for Magera - the Mars and Global Environmental Research Authority. You were chosen because of your somewhat questionable abilities to blend into the pre-2100 societies with ease. Being a 'lander' and born into an off-grid society is probably the only thing that separates you from many others. Be thankful that you have had this opportunity and know your place, Reagan2485. You are lucky to be allocated to this authority. Many others would take your place, given the opportunity. "Landry saw a twitch of a faint smile on Kyson's lips and she sat back. Her face softened a little, "Now please just upload your data and I will contact you later with the Radan report."

With a sigh, Landry placed her left wrist on the icon, stating "Upload234.34 Reagan2485."

"Thank you, Landry. I will contact you as soon as there is anything from Radan. I need your assignment logs by 0200 hours to find out the extent of your exposure." Landry smiled and felt a small win. *She called me Landry.* There is hope. Kyson's face faded from the screen and the symbol for Magera returned. Black swirling blocks filled the space where the screen had been. Landry turned to step back through the door that had now reappeared behind her. She paused in the darkness, her hand on the handle, the door slightly ajar. Her senses became alert, and her breath quickened as she dearly hoped that this time, she might hear a live performance in the theatre in the late 22nd century.

In 2188, however, there were no such performances. Connection with others had been outlawed following the bio-pandemic of 2170. Looking at the desolate theatre now encompassed all that they had lost. The stage was still in place but the seating beyond had not been maintained and were now just a jumble of seats with the fabric in various levels of rot. The opulence and colourful vibrancy were gone. Some seats had been removed and others folded back flat leaving empty spaces appearing as if in a mouth where teeth used to be. Cabling hung down, encrusted in years of dust and cobwebs. The silent walls echoed with past performances. She suddenly felt like an unwanted intruder, a secret visitor. The Hippodrome Theatre had survived centuries of change and although extended and modernised over the phases, it had closed its doors years earlier. Magera had purchased the building as an ideal choice for a time doorway as theatres' structure didn't change much over the millennia. Initially, universities and public buildings had been selected, however many of these had undergone significant renovations over the centuries. This caused problems for operatives. Walls or even fatal drops when moving through the doorways. Despite floods, earthquakes and bombings, many theatres stood stoically in their place through the years.

This is where Landry stood now. Backstage in the Hippodrome Theatre in Jing Division of the ration- city of Birmingham, the region of Mercia, May 2188. Home -If she could bring herself to call it that. She preferred referring it to her proper place in time.

She stood, face against the door and willed for a sound, a smell or anything signifying life. A difference, a small change, anything, something different. Nothing. Sighing, she clasped her graphino around her shoulders and zipped up the front. Landry exited the theatre placing her tattoo of the door jamb to open the lock and stepped into the alley.

The alley in 2188 was clinical, paved in regimental rows of grey brickwork and spotlessly clean. In 2015, the detritus at the back of the theatre had danced around the alley, lifting and dropping in the breeze. But the overwhelming difference was the lack of sound. The silence enveloped Landry - eerily quiet. She looked up in the direction of Inge Street. She recalled how the street looked in the early 21st century – vastly different now. The theatre was in Jing division, the once busy entertainment quarter of the city of Birmingham. The theatre now stood out amongst the residential blocks surrounding it. Truly out of place and time. The vibrant and distinctive exteriors of the various establishments framing the once busy streets were now long gone. Today, replaced with uniformity of brickwork, an absence of colour and people. A forlorn desolation. In fact, almost unrecognisable. Food or product establishments had not survived; they were no longer required. Landry lamented their loss deeply. The reality of her life hit her. It had been a rare privilege to witness the past but also a painful reminder of what she was missing. She walked up to Hurst Street. In 2015, a busy thoroughfare connecting vital parts of the city. Landry stared in vain for a small sign, a piece of evidence, an architectural feature of something signifying the once important routeway. Nothing, it was all wiped clean during the Pangacaust policy after the great fall. The forced mass movement of people into Radan selected urban zones also referred to as the centralized suburbanization act. Those entering the Radan zones were tattooed and linked directly to the grid. Some made the choice to stay outside and off-grid, but many didn't and therefore, the need for accom blocks to house the tens of thousands of migrants entering the ration city took precedence over everything else.

The road had also disappeared, replaced with what was now the Greenline. A translucent routeway meandering its way between towering buildings on either side. The green pulsing lights moving along the trackway gave it its name. Landry stepped up to a slim transparent post and waved her tattoo over it. For a moment, there was a flash of green and a blinking light throbbing at the top of her post. A vibration pulsed through the tattoo on her left wrist.

Landry stood, waiting, lifting her face to the sky, hoping to feel a breeze or wind, a movement – anything. The silence was unnerving, the sky a yawning emptiness. Nothing. No birds. No butterflies. No life. Landry's mind was filled with images of her family and the home that she grew up in. An off-grid society on the fringes of outer Maree. She pictured her younger self, running through the tall grasses– the sound of the waves crashing and the wind on her face. Wildlife still extinct there, but better than this. There was always hope however and Landry felt herself, once again, drawn to gaze up at the skies over Birmingham. A vain hope that something in the timeline may have changed and she may see life in the vast blankness. A bird maybe, a swallow dipping and soaring in the blue. Maintaining her vigil, holding her hand up to shade her eyes against the lowering sol, Landry continued, vainly sweeping her gaze back and forth. Her silent inspection ceased as her tattoo throbbed and it drew her attention to the pulsing lights on the Greenline, as they pulsed faster along the length of the track. In the distance, a transparent pod moved into view. It glided silently to her position and with a green roof light throbbing slowly; it pulled up to where Landry was standing. As the door sensor linked with her tattoo, it activated the locking mechanism and the door slid open. A toneless voice pervaded the emptiness inside, "home allocation – Reagan2485?" Landry stepped into the pod, and it lowered slightly under her weight. A padded holoseat emerged from the wall of the pod at Landry's waist height. It soon developed full substance and leaning against it for support, she replied, "Yes."

Landry's tattoo vibrated on her wrist and turned green. A voice filled her auditorus. The Radan medic's synthesised tone exuded a condescending reassurance. "Medic update-temperature- high at 37 degrees. All other systems operating at optimal frequencies – will monitor and update with any…" Landry interrupted, "No, no updates unless systems require emergency support" As an affirmation of her command Landry heard a small bong in her auditorus. The green light on the tattoo faded away.

Landry lifted her right-hand palm and said, "Video site Wynter Lund." The space above her right hand became translucent and blurred at first and then became clearer as Wynter's face appeared.

"Hi Wynter."

With the wave of her hand, Landry threw the image towards her right-hand side and a full-size holo of Wynter appeared standing in the pod next to Landry. The image was semi-transparent, but Landry could still see that she was scraping the remaining food rations from a bowl with a spoon, and in her mouth.

"Sorry, are you nourishing?" Landry asked.

"No, just finishing."

Landry watched as Wynter placed the bowl behind her and then turned, facing Landry expectantly, "successful assignment?"

"Really successful – I think at least an 80% positive impact. I'm so excited. This could be an actionable find Wynt – I'm on my way to my accom now. I can send you the visuals?"

"Wow Landry – your enthusiasm always amazes me."

"I'm waiting for confirmation from Radan services. Hopefully, I'll get this from Kyson this evening and then Magera will contact me, I am sure of it."

"It sounds promising. Let me know when you hear from Magera command. I've got some news too, Land." Landry sensed the pod slowing.

"Wait Wynter, I'm home – Can I check in with you later and we can share your news?"

Wynter nodded, "Course." Landry saw Wynter turn away, moving around her own accom. Landry closed her fist and stated, "Close VOS Wynter Lund." The image vanished as Landry reached for the door, preparing to exit the pod. Stepping off, Landry felt the pod rise and then watched it move off, gaining speed as it turned the corner ahead.

CHAPTER 4

Stepping across the Greenline, Landry looked up at her accom building. It was a simply clad Cuboid tower, identical to the others in every way. Thousands of them stretching off into the horizon. The only difference: the plaque Blg 4G, showing that it was the accom that they had assigned Landry to.

Landry instinctively moved her tattooed wrist towards the door lock, but it wasn't necessary. The sensor range was long, so the door was already opening, and she stepped into the foyer of her building.

Only the sound of her footsteps disturbed the air of funeral stillness. She was hopeful that she might see one of her neighbours today. In this time, people rarely met in person relying upon VR for communication, entertainment and socialisation. The great fall of 2150, put a stop to many things. Landry paused for a moment and considered how far society had fallen. Seeing the World in 2015 gave her a rare insight into life before 2150. It was referred to as the Great Fall by many as it was the moment when the World ceased to be one entity. A social fall from grace where lack of food internationally forced countries to turn to Radan for help. Radan was superb at redistributing resources to create maximum survival rates, at the expense of those countries with the least resources. Governments used Radan's findings as an excuse to cease supporting countries needing extra help. A Pangocaust. A World decision for countries to become insular and selfish and think only of themselves and their own needs. As a result of the great fall, the Radan ration cities grew quickly, and citizens were provided with everything that they may need for survival in these trying times.

With rationed food and essential items arriving in your accom, there was no longer a need to leave home for provisions. Those living in the ration cities had these privileges if they allowed Radan to have access to and modify certain aspects of their medical structure. Other than some workplaces clinging onto actual contact to promote creativity, many humans both worked, socialised and ate in their accom alone, in the ration cities provided by Radan.

She paused by the elevator and felt the typical tingle as it connected with her tattoo. It slid silently to the ground floor; the doors opening seamlessly. A melodic tone cut through the silence, "23F."

As the transparent elevator slipped soundlessly upwards, Landry looked at the city around her. It was early evening, and the lights from other buildings penetrated the darkening skyline. In the adjacent building, she could see lots of people. All in their accom pods standing, sitting, running or interacting with videro isomorphs of people, wildlife or just staring ahead, clearly absorbed in the latest VR experience. The sight of life around her was comforting, but Landry felt a lump in her throat. She missed people so much. Visiting the past just made her return even more painful and her loneliness came flooding in. Her family came to mind. Her parents, her brother, and the friends she left behind when she came to Birmingham to conclude her studies. Being born off- grid had given Landry a unique start in life far from the comforting umbrella of Radan Medic services where personal responsibility for survival was everything. Some called them pre-21st century traditionalists, others called them landers. They were admired by some, but many just thought them strange.

A treble tone indicated that the elevator had arrived at its destination. Stepping out between the opening doors, Landry strolled down the corridor, listening for any signs of life from her neighbours as she made her way to her home pod 23F. Nothing, no sounds. As she approached her accom door, it opened, and a voice welcomed Landry home. A small cluster of lights dimmed and then brightened in various places around her accom.

As she stepped over the threshold, Landry flicked her left wrist, commanding, "Home". A semi-translucent screen appeared in front of her. She walked straight through it and then stretching behind her, touched the bottom corner of the screen and with an exaggerated sweep of her arm threw it against the wall of her accom. The screen responded, its movement causing the pixels to break up temporarily as they flew, before re-emerging on the wall opposite. She fell into her long seat suddenly feeling tired and completed a full stretch with her arms in the air. Landry turned her face to the screen. It showed the news items for today. Pre-allocated images of various butterfly species and viz reels, special to Landry, filled the screen. They were carefully selected for her each day, and she sat in awe as a viz scope of a meadow appeared. It stimulated her auditorii first, as the cacophony of bird calls filled the soundscape. The

21st-century camera operator was focused on the tall grasses and vivid yellow floral blooms as they panned across the meadow. It was the variety of greens that intrigued Landry, then the optics zoomed in on a small Admiral butterfly twisting and turning in the air. Emotions overwhelmed her and tears welled in her eyes as she watched this tiny creature going about its daily routine. Landry stared with disbelief as the vizoptic panned back and they could hear the distinct calls of a cuckoo. There was so much life just before their very eyes, and yet they couldn't see that it would end. Landry hated the fact that these viz images generated such emotion in her and hated that they had lost it all. But she couldn't stop herself from watching them. They were like a drug to her. She gulped down her rising anger and futility of it all and commanded, "stop viz."

The images that replaced the viz were a random collection of images from her days before entering Birmingham. Today an image of her parents appeared. They stood outside Landry's home off-grid. A simple structure but one which held many happy memories for her. She turned her face away and commanded, "Magera Home."

The screen cleared and an image of Landry filled the screen. It was her official persona, used in all her identification, but it was not recent. Her mousey hair hung long and lank, framing a small face. Her large brown eyes, full of innocence, youthful. Captured at the start of her career with Magera. Her contacts came up on the left-hand side. Landry looked at Wynter Lund's Magera persona. Her blonde curly hair was in contrast with her striking blue eyes. Landry envied her Nordic beauty.

Below Wynter was the image of Karmal Rahman, another Magera operative working from Bangladesh. His expression always made Landry smile. Frowned upon in formal images, the huge grin drew all your attention. Too many upper teeth filled an enormous mouth, overlapping each other, but the warmth shone through. The smile reaching his brown eyes that were crinkled at the edges was the price to pay for living in a solar intense climate.

There were no other contacts on Landry's page. But at the bottom, a local news report running with subtitles. A VR dramascope: crime drama set in the 20th century and her recent Magera logs and communication between Magera and herself.

Landry sat forward on the chair, "Magera communication please". Using her optics, Landry scrolled down through the recent communication list. A quick blink selected the file that she wanted to see. She leant back, getting more comfortable and stated, "Communication from Mullins2001 – today."

A vidscope opened and Kyson Mullin's face appeared large on the screen as she began her message. She seemed breathless and rushed her words, "Reagan2485, Radan services has evaluated the evidence you recorded today and has assigned it 55% of positive impact on Earth's past. I know you will be disappointed. Remember your log report by 0200hrs." The screen went blank and the communication list reappeared.

Landry rubbed her temple. Never had she felt so sure about the evidence before. It confused her. Everything about today had felt right, and she was confident that the evidence she had bought back was good. To assess it as only 55% was confusing. Accessing the screen in front of her, she focussed on the faces of her colleagues, Wynter Lund and Karmal Ray. She noted that neither had a private mode spot blinking next to their persona. She needed to speak to them. "Group dialog Wynter and Karmal", she commanded.

The screen split into three showing live feeds of Wynter, Karmal and Landry. On the left split, Karmal looked poised to strike an invisible opponent, his arms raised, holding an unseen weapon. He froze at the bong indicating Landry's request and now lifted his optics to the screen. Wynter had been lounging in her long chair. She had sat up at Landry's call. There was a pause and then both smiled, as Landry stated, "Happy to visit?"

" Yes, "confirmed Wynter.

"Yeh," affirmed Karmal.

Landry turned her wrist twice and a translucent holo of Wynter and Karmal walked off the screen and sat at chairs around the small table next to the long chair. Landry missed proper company more than most and visits were always a welcome change.

"Was your action percentage high?" Wynter began.

"No – I don't understand. I was sure that it would be at least 80% positive but Radan came back with 55%!" Landry exclaimed.

"You spoke to Kyson?" Wynter replied, "She might know why Radan assessed it lower?"

All three operatives raised their optics to the screen and there was a shared look as the spinning Radan symbol in the corner of her home screen began pulsing and turned red. "Oh, I sometimes wonder why I bother!" Landry whispered, looking between her two friends, then a little louder, "If Radan has evaluated it as a 55%, then I need to accept it. Kyson will support whatever Radan Services says. She always does. She'll never question it and she certainly won't support me."

There was a knowing look that moved around the group, words unsaid but nods acknowledging its meaning.

Wynter said, "You must have overlooked something, Landry. Maybe there is evidence from previous assignments that disprove the science that you were so excited about. "

Landry continued, "You are probably right but Kar listen to this, the important thing here is the data that Dr Pedersen shared. In only a two-year period of study, they had results of 38% less CO_2 released into the atmosphere. 38% in only two years. This study is exactly what Magera is looking for…"

He nodded in agreement, "It sounds good. They have control fields as well?"

"Yes, it is a well-researched project and the results, if acted upon, could significantly impact the beginning of climate change in the 21st century. We are looking here at an 80% chance of positive impact upon change. It's what we have been looking for. This could be big Kar. If the stage three operatives could make contact, then we could be looking at a reversal of the four degrees increase in temperature, a reversal of all the events resulting in that. Kar- it could mean no freak weather events in 22nd century- no flooding Kar – This could mean no flooding in Bangladesh in 2157. "Landry stopped talking to take a breath.

"Hold on there," Wynter exclaimed, glancing across at Kar, "– Don't say that it's not fair. You don't know that. Not really."

"I'm sorry, Kar." Landry turned to face Karmal's isomorph, "I shouldn't have said that." She glanced across at Karmal. He had never known much of his family. Most of his relatives had died in the catastrophic flooding of Bangladesh in 2157.

He placed his virtual hand over Landry's, breaking into a smile, "I not miss a family that I never knew and, " He pointed at Landry, "You! You are doing everything you can to stop that flooding and maybe one day you will find it. So, I never question your motives or your drive to get there. "He paused. Wynter and Landry waited for Karmal to speak.

"Landry - I know you feel, it has happened to all of us many times." He raised his arms and his palms facing upwards in an iso embrace.

"We are not important enough to know all that Radan must do with our evidence. We are just stage1 operatives, remember." Kar raised his eyebrows and shrugged his shoulders. "Those people higher up have this World's interests at heart, we must have faith in that. Remember when we signed up as operatives, we knew risks, even to our timelines if we are success."

Landry relented, "I know. Sorry, I'm just so frustrated. Every time I come back, I'm disappointed that we are where we are and yes, I'm fully aware that if Magera are successful then we may not even be born." There was a moment of serious reflection, it was Wynter who broke the reverie.

 "Go get more evidence Land. Go back and see if you can get those percentages higher. Maybe there is something you've missed that will be everything that Magera and Radan need to see to act. They won't let anyone act unless they are sure of at least an 80% positive impact upon human life."

Karmal added, "Remember, we are talking about changing our World, it must be worth it to risk all that we have. "

"I know," Landry sighed," I just want to change what we have. Going back shows us all what we lost and who we lost. I'd do anything to change that. This isn't living, is it?" Landry spread her arms wide looking around her living pod."

Karmal chuckled, "Hey I like my twenty square metres, I can mess it in two seconds and tidy at the same time. Don't need any space for me." His isomorph stood up, and raised his arms in line with his shoulders, "look, I can touch both walls at the same time. Who would not want that?" He laughed.

Landry declared, "Hey if you live in New Dhaka, then that's what you get. Come and live in Birmingham, we have double the space." Landry spread her arms wide and glanced around her.

Wynter frowned, "Lucky you, New London isn't much better than New Dhaka!" The conversations turned to other assignments and dramascopes and finally Landry remembered her conversation with Wynter earlier.

"Hey Wynt- you had some news. You haven't shared." Wynter raised her arms above her head and stretched. "Ah my news can wait for now. I need reparation, I have another assignment in the morning."

Karmal nodded, "Me too- I go to the year 2128 today, it's now 0700 hrs here in New Dhaka. How about you, Landry?"

"I must complete my report by 0200 hrs then I am going to submit a request form to return and investigate this research again. You're right, Wynter, I may find more evidence."

Wynter's isomorph stood up and appeared to gather up papers that were invisible to Karmal and Landry. "Well, good evening to you both. No, sorry Kar- good morning to you." Wynter began walking away from Landry's table and Karmal stood up. As Landry gave a wave to her friends, she commanded, "Close group dialogue."

Both Images vanished, a double bong in her auditorus signalled their removal from the group viz and Landry was alone. She directed her optics to the screen and commanded, "Bring up report document 234.84 for Reagan2485. The Magera spinning symbol of M and E appeared on the screen, and then a blank page appeared. Landry began her dictat, "report made 0045hrs 16/06/2188, see visuals for evidence of research. Three non-compromising observations of my person. Observation 1…" As Landry spoke, the words appeared on the report on the screen. It was sometime later when Landry had finally completed her report and she received confirmation of its submission. 0100hrs Report Received Reagan2485/234.84.

Out of the corner of Landry's eye, an unexpected command appeared almost immediately. That was quick, even for Radan. It read as follows,

0101hrs Reagan2485 REPORT TO LOCAL BASE 0600hrs 16/06/2188 DISCIPLINARY MEETING.

Landry re-read the request twice. She had never had a disciplinary meeting. Maybe it was the level 1 compromise? A male past participant had walked into her, hadn't he? Landry blew air through her gritted teeth as she made her way to her sleeping pod. A disciplinary meeting was not good. She considered calling Karmal as she knew he had previously had many such meetings but changed her mind. It would be a meeting to discuss her compromises, she was sure of it. She decided to leave it until the morning. It was only five hours away, so reparation was essential and now! Landry entered her sleeping pod. As she requested the closure of her home screen, she noticed an update on the Mars Expedition from Radan News Services. The first Endeavour Scientists had reached Mars. News indeed!

CHAPTER 5

Landry made her way to the base complex for Magera at the Kallan campus of Birmingham University the next morning. She considered the reasons for the disciplinary meeting. A small part of her relished the opportunity to make her case to her supervisor Kyson, in person. She was excited by what she had found yesterday. Maybe her explanations, added to the scientific predictions, would better describe the amazing results that BFUR were having in 2015. She had prepared a presentation of her most recent findings, hoping that time to review them would be possible.

Landry knew, however, that the primary reason for the meeting would revolve around the negative compromises in her assignment yesterday. The primary goals would be at risk if the aims of Magera were ever discovered in the past or in her own time. Secrecy was uppermost and even the slim possibility of being discovered could bring Magera and its goals crashing down.

Landry ran through the compromises from her assignment in her head. First, the glance from the male past participant on the bus outside the theatre. Second, the accidental physical contact with the past participant on Inge Street when she had seen the sparrows. And third, the lead scientist for BFUR, Simon Pedersen, possibly recognising her. She considered the final compromise as the principal reason for the disciplinary meeting and began preparing her argument for this.

As she arrived at the reception desk in the Kallan building, a translucent screen appeared to her right at optic level. The text scrolled down as the melodic tones from Radan entered her Magera auditorus "Welcome Reagan2485 - you are attending a disciplinary meeting today in block 4 section 6. "

Landry felt red rising in her cheeks. She did not welcome conflict or break the rules, preferring to do everything in her power to avoid it. This was unknown territory. Landry would have felt shamed if there had been others present. But as with many public areas, there was no one else.

Landry was considering why this meeting had to be in person and not through the Viz gateway, when a thin doorway to her left slid open and a

Radan bot emerged. She could see it was an upgrade. They had maintained the medic theme from the 50's with the rounded gloss white outer casing. But on this new bot design, they had tried a humanoid face virtomorph. As it spoke, Landry placed her head forward and stared at its lips. There was a tell-tale syncing delay.

"Follow me, please." It turned and moved to the rear of the reception area. Landry noted the walking stance as it turned, its fluid-like movement of limb-like legs moving in unison. It had its back to her as it moved away, and Landry gasped as it turned its humanoid face 180 degrees to face her. An impossibility for any human being, very disconcerting, creepy. It attempted no small talk but kept a neutral facial expression, speaking when there was a need to change direction. "Left this way Reagan2485", "turn here Reagan2485." A strange commentary and completely unnecessary as she could follow its physical form easily.

They arrived at a small open doorway and Landry could see Kyson Mullins sitting at a table. Landry was immediately struck by her size. She had only ever seen Kyson's face through a screen, and she was dressed in a loose-fitting graphimo which was tighter around the rolls of her neck and the tops of her arms. It shimmered silver then black when she changed position. A large home screen bobbed on Kyson's right side, and Landry saw the Magera logo spinning.

As Landry stepped into the room, the bot followed her, positioning itself against the door as it closed. There was an empty chair opposite Kyson and Landry sat down, placing her portable memory device on the table in front of her.

As Kyson made optic contact, the screen changed. The Magera emblem span off into the distance, replaced by the Radan logo bouncing in the screen's corner. Landry looked at Kyson for reassurance, but she was busy studying the screen in front of her. Kyson's vitiligo was even more prevalent in person, and Landry caught herself staring. The mottling effect of ebony, and then white contrast on her hands were like random splashes of paint. As Kyson placed her hands in front of her, Landry noticed subtle nervous movements in her fingers as Kyson readjusted the placement of her hands. *Kyson was nervous herself.*

Landry felt her heart beating a little faster and her personal medic support confirmed this with a brief report in her auditorus, "elevated pulse - are you exercising Reagan 2485?"

Landry's tattoo glowed green as it communicated with her and Kyson seeing this stated, "Private mode only for this meeting Reagan2485. Communications or medi-support cannot interrupt you." Landry took a breath and was about to argue the point when Kyson shook her head and placed her finger on her lips. Her eyes motioned at the screen with the Radan symbol silent but expanding and contracting- Was Radan listening? Landry did as Kyson requested, lifting her tattoo to her temple and commanding "Private mode". There was a short bong in her auditorus as it acknowledged this command.

The screen moved more centrally to face Kyson. It partially obscured her face, but as it was transparent, it did not block her out completely. Landry watched it fill with a sizeable amount of text. It appeared backwards to Landry, but she attempted to read it, anyway. The text was difficult to read as it was small and moving down the screen. Landry gave up as Kyson began reading, "Disciplinary meeting for Reagan2485 0600hrs 16/06/2188. Present: Reagan2485, Mullins2001 and assisted by Radan services."

"Reagan2485, we have investigated your conduct following assignment 234.34. There are four breaches of your conduct. There are two allegations. One, you compromised yourself two times in a single visit which could have led to a significant impact, up to a 0.03 intervention upon the timeline. Two, you maintain an unprofessional manner in your references to your supervisor and your benefactor. "

Kyson moved closer to the table, "Do you have anything to say at this point?" Kyson did not allow time for a response, "I have several questions I will need to ask you. Here is a list of the questions." Kyson pushed her hand through her screen and a morphed image of a piece of paper glided out and hovered in front of Landry. She noticed that Kyson's screen changed to the identical questions. The Radan symbol remained on the side of the screen, still throbbing. "Allegation one: Reagan2485, we can see from the optic visuals of your assignment 234.34, true-time past participant scientist Pedersen showed 100% visual confirmation of you and even attempted to converse with you. In your report, you described it as a flicker of recognition on his part. I deem he recognised you from a previous assignment and if he had been successful in contacting you, he would have attempted a direct converse. In a breach of Magera regulation 6.4, a time operative will not have direct contact with any past participants;

human, computer-based life forms or animals. And regulation 7.2, a time operative must remain incognito and perform reconnaissance only."

As Kyson spoke, everything she said was being shown on the screen in front of her. Landry could see the text being added as the words were spoken. Landry considered her response before speaking, "As I stated in my report, I have already identified this issue and have declared for any assignments in the time frame after 2015, I will take measures to make sure there isn't a repeat of this recognition."

The Radan symbol turned yellow on the screen and Landry saw Kyson tilt her head slightly. She placed a finger on her left auditorus to listen to a message she was receiving. Was Radan speaking to her? After a pause, Kyson continued, "unacceptable response. I'm afraid the only way to ensure no recognition is to ban any future assignments involving that past participant after 2015." Kyson looked at Landry as she spoke.

Landry felt her defences rise, "I have centred all my research around these individuals and their research is... It's everything I have been working on. The information I brought back with me was so compelling. You must see that - "

Kyson interrupted her, "Reagan2485, you could have compromised the whole programme. You understand, don't you? We deem it as a stage 5 compromise with a 20-50% possibility of your actions altering the timeline. Your research is irrelevant. We account for all our operatives and the ultimate goals of this project."

"But I don't believe it was a stage 5 - I did not speak to him. "Landry imploring, "Look, I am so close to finding a 90% positive impact on pre-climate change Earth. This is a breakthrough. It is what they have trained me to do. To find a project that should maintain at least an 80% positive impact on Earth's history. That is what we should focus on. Not an insignificant compromise. Dr Pedersen probably hasn't even given me a second thought. This is ridiculous. "She stood up pleading with Kyson, "Kyson please- You must listen to me."

A screeching pulse caused both women to look towards the screen as the Radan symbol grew larger, taking over the whole screen and pulsing red, then blue. Both Landry and Kyson jumped as the bot moved rapidly to Landry's side.

A synthesised voice boomed, "Reagan2485, be seated. You should not be responding in this manner." Landry lowered herself back to her seat, careful not to touch the bot as it stood menacingly near her right elbow.

The neck of the bot stretched forward so the virtomorphic face was within a finger's breadth to her own; too close. Landry looked at Kyson imploring her to intervene, but Kyson looked down in embarrassment. *Or was that fear?* Landry thought.

She made furtive glances towards Kyson, but she too appeared shaken and distant. Landry knew the time to not speak. She took a moment to recover, her thoughts spinning around her head. Was she was stepping over the line? She needed to respect Radan's infallible judgement. Was Wynter right? Had she overlooked something? An AI cannot have an opinion, can it? It based all judgements upon fact. Landry was desperately trying to articulate an appropriate response. Never had she been in this position. The shame was intertwined with a sense of injustice.

Then the bot returned to its place at the door and Kyson regained her poise, "I am ready to submit the conclusions. Because you infracted regulation 6.4, you cannot plan any future assignments post-2015, in any locations where the presence of participant scientist Pederson may be present. "

Landry found her voice. "Is that it? Is the investigation complete? Can I explain what I saw?" Kyson made no reply but her eyes implored Landry to comply.

Eventually, Kyson spoke, "Please state your affirmation of the agreed findings,"

"I agree, "Landry muttered.

"And you will take all precautions in future assignments,"

Landry nodded reluctantly,

"You must state it for the record."

Landry repeated, "Yes! I will take all necessary precautions in future assignments."

The screen had returned to the previous setup with a recorded script of their conversation scrolling up the screen. She could easily read the words she had said, but she noticed the words said by Radan were missing. A small prickle of doubt ran up the back of her neck. An AI cannot lie, can it? She considered pointing out the error in the script but thought better of it. She would check things with Karmal later.

Kyson continued reading. "Now to the second allegation, Reagan2485. You have repeatedly broken code 2.3. A member of Magera must show respect for their supervisors and benefactors and treat all members equally. You have frequently spoken with over-familiarity with your supervisor and questioned your supervisor on two occasions." The screen in front of Kyson turned, and Landry saw a viz of herself speaking. Her voice flooded her auditorus. There were a variety of previously recorded visuals from Kyson's optic, and they showed Landry arguing a point with Kyson. Landry could see they were taken out of context. Yes, it appeared as if she was rude to Kyson. Landry looked at Kyson appealing to her with her eyes staring… really?

"We find this allegation justified and under this formal procedure, we suspend you from duties for 14 days and place this on your record. There was silence as what Kyson had just said filtered through Landry's brain. Then came complete bewilderment. *Why? Why were they treating her like this? Her familiarity with Kyson was her humanity, her sense of humour. Had they lost so much of their humanity? Was it so much worse than she feared?*

"Do you accept the conclusion of this second allegation Reagan 2485?" Her anger flared and thoughts scrambled. *Everything she had worked for. Everything she was trying to do. No! No! I will not accept this! This is not fair, unwarranted. She had heard other operatives doing so much worse. Why? Why her?*

Kyson tapped the table in front of Landry drawing her attention. She thought about what her father would advise her to do.

"Yes Mullins 2001, I will maintain a correct formality with all future conversations with my superiors," she proclaimed.

There was a pause as her words scrolled across the screen. Kyson began gathering up her papers and collecting her items from the desk. Landry recovered herself and took a last attempt to speak about her assignment again, "Mullins 2001, Can I talk to you about what I have discovered, What BFUR are working on? It's a breakthrough, they- "

Kyson interrupted Landry with a shake of her head and once more raised her finger to her lips to silence her. Landry's shoulders slumped. Kyson opened her mouth to speak but changed her mind. Kyson had won, but it looked to Landry as a hollow victory now. She could see Kyson was shaken by what had occurred.

"You will receive confirmation of the findings and the articles of your bans immediately. Confirm receipt of this by 1300 hours. I confirm you are now no longer a representative for Magera for the next 14 days. We will expect you to report to your station on 30/06/2188 at 0600hours as an affirmation of your return to duty."

There was no further input from Radan, and the bot swung open the door. The meeting was at an end. Landry attempted to make optic contact with Kyson, but as she left, she noticed Kyson did not look up again.

CHAPTER 6

On the way back to her accom, Landry reflected upon what had just happened. She was disappointed. She knew her over-enthusiasm sometimes erred her judgement, but how could she get it so wrong? She would speak to Wynter and Karmal.

While travelling on the Greenline, she realised she had not had a medi-update since leaving the University. A slow realisation crept through her. She was still in private mode- she had no personal record of the disciplinary meeting.

She tapped her tattoo on her temple and stated, "cancel private mode". The medi update began in her auditorus, and the soothing familiarity of the medi-voice washed over her. Landry felt her shoulders lower. She had not noticed how tense she had been.

Leaving the Greenline and walking to her accom in daylight was depressing. They built the buildings for practicality alone. She flipped her visor to reduce the blinding effect of the sunlight on her optics as it bounced off the stark concrete pathways and entrances, uninviting and devoid of colour. She glanced up at the only welcoming part of her vista. On the rooftop of each building was a lush garden of nutrient-rich trees. So beautiful in contrast to its surroundings. They were developed to provide a CO_2 sink. But with no thought as to how people would enjoy that space. There was no access to it. It was purely to produce CO_2. Quality of life considerations in the 22nd century was inefficient. Survival was the only goal.

Landry made her way up to home pod her thoughts pulled towards her parents and siblings and the life she left behind. She could cope with missing her family when she was working towards a common goal. What better goal could there be than save Earth from this empty future? But if not, what was there for her now? She swallowed a lump in her throat as she heard the treble tone of arrival at her floor. Pull yourself together, Landry It is only two weeks. She progressed down the silent corridor, and Landry was shocked as a door swung open on her left and Landry almost collided with Carter3624 as she stepped out of her pod.

"Watch it Lander!" she sneered as she stepped passed into the corridor. "Go back off-grid where you belong." and then muttering, "You come here and take our rations…"

Landry started to respond but decided against it. She didn't feel like confronting prejudice today. Carter3624 worked in the waste management service in sector 5 and was ration city born and breed.

She sighed as her door swung open and the voice in her auditorus invited her in. The homescreen appeared in front of her, stopping her in mid-step. "Welcome home Reagan2485 - you have no appointments today; you have no assignments to prepare for today following your 14-day suspension. Would you like to take part in some craft hobbies or fitness? I have prepared some - "She swung her arm through the screen, her aggression flinging it across the accom and onto the back wall. "I don't want crafts. I want nothing. Stop comments." Landry's voice rose with emotion. Even her home bot knew they had suspended her. Landry glanced up at the screen as it flashed on her left. It showed Karmal and Wynter, both blue, in private mode. Good. She wanted to recall everything they said before speaking with them. She did not have optic visuals to replay as private mode removed recordation. Landry sat quietly and replayed the meeting in her mind and made personal notes as a dictat to her home bot.

"Save note 2.34 in private, please." Landry commanded once she had finished recalling all she could of the meeting. What stood out the most was the contribution of Radan Services. She knew Magera used Radan to swift check reports from assignments and evaluate their ability to positively impact climate change. Landry never thought a supervisor would ever defer to Radan's decisions and she wondered whether that was what she saw today with her supervisor, Kyson. She concluded that she must have been mistaken about what she had seen. Her suspicions of artificial intelligence were born out of her life off-grid and her growth as a child, free of Radan. She was not thinking clearly.

Landry spent the rest of her usual work time reviewing her previous assignment notes and trying to find alternative visits to the past she could make to would prove her case for BFUR and the tree studies. After 14 days, she wanted to be ready to go again. Ready to help Magera change history. The work of Magera, the Mars and Global Environmental Research Authority could provide one moment or action in history that could change it all. If operatives could confidently act upon moments in the past, then it could be altered. All that had happened due to climate change could be reversed. Many lives could be saved. The World's ecosystems, climate and economical structure of the World could be saved. This is what Magera operatives worked towards and Landry, like many others, felt that she had a purpose in life to either find the solution or assist others in doing so. Not having this aim to strive for, left Landry feeling empty. Not everyone felt the same way. Wynter and Karmal regarded their work with Magera differently.

Later the image of Wynter appeared on her home screen with the words, accept indialogue with Wynter. Landry welcomed her friend, wanting to share what had happened and ask her opinion on the strange events of today.

Wynter did not ask, she jumped straight in. "So, they suspended you. What happened?"

"I went to the meeting this morning and Kyson suspended from duty for 14 days. It was because I am too informal with her. I don't use her allocated name and I often question her. I am not as respectful as I should to be."

"It doesn't justify a suspension from duty - What did Kyson say?" Wynter enquired further, "Kar had a stage 6 last month and didn't even have a disciplinary meeting?"

"I know, "Landry agreed, "Kyson didn't help me at all. She doesn't like the way I speak to her. "

Wynter hesitated, thinking through what Landry had just said, "Sounds like she's got it in for you - you know she is bitter. She can't be an operative because of her vitiligo. I've never heard of her suspending someone before. Was it Kyson and her supervisor, Michalle Tausz?"

"No, that's the strange thing," Landry offered, "it was only her and Radan services."

"Radan!" Wynter exclaimed, "What does Radan have to do with this? - It's a computerised database of information. A service that Magera uses."

"I know, I thought it was strange, especially when Radan spoke to me."

"Radan addressed you directly?" Wynter's face almost exploded from the screen as she moved closer, her optics wide, "I have NEVER heard of that - What did Radan say to you? What did it sound like? How did Kyson react?"

Landry froze, holding her breath as she saw it. The Radan symbol at the edge of her home screen was changing in colour from green to blue and pulsing larger then small. She thought back to the events with Radan in her meeting.

Coughing nervously, "Look Kyson was right- I deserved it. It was stupid of me to let it happen. I am fortunate to only have a suspension and I will have time to review where I am with BFUR and my research."

Wynter's face moved from confusion to affirmation, and she moved away from the screen. Landry wasn't sure if she had understood Landry's sudden change of tact, but Wynter changed the subject anyway.

"I'm going to the SAM meet-up tomorrow, in 2033 - Do you remember Land, the Survival Alliance Movement? I have talked about them before. They fit with my research into social and political pressure on environmental change. I'm going to Trafalgar Square tomorrow. If I've got the right date, then it should be a great event."

"Which doorway?" Landry asked.

"The Langham living accommodation, it's the closest I can get without getting my underwater Graphemo out! "Wynter Laughed. "Not like Britton2034 who attempted to come back through Cleopatra's needle and found himself underwater. It's difficult getting around London post-2099 when the final flood defences failed."

"Make sure you have all of your pre-assignment checks then," Landry commanded.

"I'll be careful - I promise. I'll check them again now." Wynter turned away with a wave and smile, as her image shrank to nothing on Landry's home screen. Landry's first glance was up to the Radan symbol in its usual place in the screen's corner. It now pulsed, silently. The usual green glow had returned.

CHAPTER 7

WYNTER LUND

Wynter was a child of the Radan regime, born in 2168. Raised in the nursery pods in sector 7 in the ration city, New London. A young solo who never knew her donors. Wynter had no family, no connections except for Landry and Ray and had little interest in saving the World. Her work with Magera was purely selfish. Magera gave her privileges. Her role in society required it, and Mars and Greater Earth's Research Authority was an excellent choice for her. Why not. The alternative employment opportunities were mundane; repetitive employment in the ration and medic industries in sector 2. She did have an interest in Earth's political history which began during the 5th cycle of her education, and this helped her work as a Magera operative.

Wynter, unlike Landry, had found the Magera training extremely challenging. During her training visits to Earth's past, she struggled with being severed from her Radan medi-support and taking responsibility for monitoring her own medical situation herself. It had severely hampered Wynter's initial visits, but she was developing into a valuable operative with sound results.

Wynter's lengthy observations of the Survival Alliance Movement of the 21st century was providing some promising results, and Wynter felt that with some action from Magera stage three operatives, they could impact the environmental politics. Wynter's first visits to SAM had been in the 1980s. At that time, they were a small group of students voicing their concerns about climate change. Visits to 2018 saw a growth in numbers including scientific and political backing and were having a positive impact on people's perceptions of the climate change discussion. Their movement was growing.

Wynter had made them her primary focus for assignments for over a year now. The evidence gathered on SAM was extensive, and Wynter's visits had proven extremely exciting. She admired SAM's founding members for their drive and ambition. She particularly admired Dr Robert Sanchez.

He had shown on previous visits a sound understanding of how climate change was impacting upon the many ecosystems of the Earth and Wynter enjoyed watching him speak. However, Wynter questioned why they had not become a major global driving force for climate change that they had the promise to be. She was determined to find out why.

Research evidence in their timeline showed a decline in their popularity in the middle of the 21st century, and Wynter could not find any explanation for this. The rally in Trafalgar Square in August 2019 seemed like a significant event and at the height of its popularity. She hoped that today's visit would give her the answers.

Wynter planned to travel back early on the day of the rally, as the start timings of the rally were vague in the historical references. Gathering evidence of the Survival Alliance Movement was relatively straightforward. Her optics and auditorus recorded everything that she saw, said and experienced. SAM's supporters were varied and growing each time she visited. Blending into the crowd became more challenging each time she visited and moving without have physical contact with other people was proving very difficult. Crowds were growing.

Wynter tried to put her nervousness aside as she prepared to leave 2188 behind. She heard stories about Magera operatives falling off buildings or walking into walls or even worse into chasms after a refurbishment or change of use in the buildings where the doorways were located. Few buildings kept their exact original layout through the centuries. The doorway in 2188 was in the accom block stafe 1c in the Regents district on New London. It had once been the exclusive Langham Hotel in London's Marylebone district. Pre-assignment research revealed that as with all other hotels, the Langham was reallocated as an accom block after the great fall in 2150. There were no records of any further changes to the cupboard where her doorway was located. Arriving in the basement, she found the door and she placed her tattoo onto the Magera symbol on its frame. The door shimmered and appeared to lose its solidity as square pixels expanded and shrank pulsing softly. Pushing her hand through first and feeling the slight shift in the temperature, Wynter stepped through the Langham time doorway into August 2019.

First the familiar smell from the cleaning products and the heat from the driers hit Wynter. She glanced around and found the laundry room empty of people. As she stepped past the tray holding empty dishes and a newspaper, she noted the dateline evidence that confirmed that it was 4th August 2019. Placing the Langham housekeeping Identity badge on the lanyard around her neck, Wynter stepped out of the laundry. Head down, she moved alongside her pseudo colleagues through the rabbit run of twisting and turning corridors. They were too busy rushing about their daily business to notice the new member of staff.

Wynter emerged from the back of the hotel through the service entrance and into bright sunshine. Taking a minute to re-orient herself into the 21st Century, she stood feet apart and took two deep breaths in and out while tracing her middle finger across her Radan tattoo and felt the emptiness of the loss of the connection.

As Wynter moved on towards Souls Street, her nose wrinkled with distaste. The fumes from a combustion engine burning fossil fuels caused her to place her hand over her nose. *How did they live with this?* She knew from research that London had introduced the congestion charges in 2003 and that this was better than it had been but was still uncomfortable. Walking toward a tram stop, she struggled to deal with the cacophony of sounds in the past. The whine of bus engines, horns of drivers and the people. They made so much noise, their boots hitting the pavement, their chattering laughter, shouts or squeals of delight. To Wynter, they appeared more like animals, with unbridled emotion, expressing themselves with complete freedom, showing no consideration to those around them.

As she stood waiting, she picked out the whine as the tram increased pace around the bend to where Wynter was standing. She looked towards the tram and people around her as they readied themselves for its arrival. Wynter always maintained a distance from the people, old habits of social distancing were hard to break. Wynter stepped back from the tramway edge to avoid encountering people exiting the tram. She could then observe the etiquette from a distance. At the movement of the woman in front, a gap appeared in her line of vision, and she watched a child take a step backwards, almost touching her. So close. Wynter froze. She has seen children before, but never this close. Wynter's heart contracted, and her optics widened as she took in all she could. The small delicate hand holding onto the adult's sleeve. The little head of blonde hair twisted into two intricately woven braids with two small pink plastic ties with little pink animals attached. Wynter thought they were called pigtails. Wynter reached out to touch one braid, but the movement caught the eye of the adult, and she spun her head, a piercing glare at Wynter. Wynter's hand and optics dropped to avert any compromising interaction with a past participant. She kept her gaze on the floor and smiled to appear relaxed.

Fate intercepted, and a gap opened in front of the female. She turned and followed her fellow passengers entering the tram in front of her. Wynter watched as they tapped the consort in the centre with a slim card that they had retrieved from their various wallets and pockets. Wynter had been holding the coins for her payment in her pocket. She looked for a cash payment machine by the driver and realised that there was not one. She turned and looked again towards the console where other passengers were tapping a card. Wynter hoped she had missed something. She had not. There did not appear to be anywhere to pay in cash. There was not much time. She ploughed through the various scenarios in her mind. Attempt no payment- No too compromising if caught. Leave quick before the doors closed–The only viable option. Decision made, Wynter jumped back just as the tram door closed. Inquisitive gazes from several passengers focussed on Wynter as the tram moved on. Wynter stood back on the platform, looking down instinctively to hide her face, resisting the temptation to take one more look at the child.

The moment had passed, but Wynter was shaken. She sat down on a bench and considered what had just happened. Being so close to a child had not been part of her preparation for this morning, and her reaction surprised Wynter. Regarding the lack of cash payment, she lambasted herself for her lack of research of this period. When had they become card payments only? She briefly ran through her photographic memory to find the dates for the use of cash in society in the 21st Century. She had not been prepared for this change so early in the century. A complete non-monetary society was not until 2150. She would have to add this to her report. Kyson would not be happy.

Wynter placed her hand on her fast-beating heart and once again looked to her wrist for the message from Radan medi-support. Realising her error; that it would not work in the 21st century as Radan had not been created yet in this time. The link with Radan medic services severed as soon as she left her time. A quiver of unease spread across her brow. Wynter used a breathing technique to slow down her heart and get herself back on track for her mission today.

Wynter resolved to walk or jog to the venue now. A slight change of plan, but nothing that could not be overcome. She made her way through the streets, manoeuvring through the hustle and bustle of the city centre and people out in the August sunshine. Although she did not have an accurate time for the start, she wanted to get there before the rally started to gain as much evidence as she could. As she made her way to Trafalgar Square, she began to relax She marvelled at product placements, which surrounded her on every building and on the bags that people carried. Some people carried so many bags. She could not understand how they would need all these items. The selfishness and opulence of these past participants seemed obscene to Wynter's 23rd-century values. The overheard conversations did nothing to change her mind either. They seemed to talk about such frivolous things. Where to eat, what to eat, what to buy, what they wanted. Want, want, want. She found herself confirming her opinion that past participants were ignorant, immature and self-centred; embroiled in their own lives and with no care for the lives of others.

Even before arriving at Trafalgar, Wynter heard the distinctive voice of the lead speaker of the Survival alliance Movement, Carly Albright. It had started. As Wynter sprinted up the steps into the Square, she found a crowd already gathered. Brightly coloured banners flapped in the wind and the crowd wore the distinctive blue colours of SAM. Wynter saw the familiar symbols of SAM and the various messages held high. "Love our planet–act now", Respect mother Earth, Climate change–6 years to save the planet! How could people differ so widely in their views? She gazed around at the sight, trying to keep her optics on the crowd. She had to tear her attention off the pigeons that flew around the tall buildings surrounding the square. So strange to see them for real. Their wings outstretched and many just hovering or swooping between the statues. The sadness enveloped her. She knew what the future held for those gathered here. She pushed her emotions aside and made her way to the back of the crowd to gather the evidence.

Wynter slowly scanned the crowd to attain how much the support for SAM had increased in the years between her visits. Wynter saw a mixture of society now. Gone were just students. There were groups of adults and children, maybe these were families?

Wynter marvelled at the circus atmosphere of colour and sound. She observed the children as they jumped up and down, swinging their flags and running with free abandonment. Families had bought portable chairs and staked claims to areas around the Square with their banners tied across where they communicated with ease. This movement was becoming an important find, and Wynter was starting to see it as a viable option for integration by a stage 3 operative. She stepped forward to gain a good outlook of the speakers and presentation. This rally had a large screen erected in front of the town hall and there were flashing images of the Earth, the blue planet. Wonderful images of seascapes, jungles, and deserts. Images which Wynter had seen in the archives. She thought the images were exaggerated and unreal–was Earth that beautiful once? She thought to herself. Many of those places no longer exist in her time.

The screen became blank, and Carley's voice echoed loud and clear, "We have a planetary emergency, and it is happening right now!" The crowd quietened a little as Carley continued, "To limit climate warming to 1.5 degrees and avoid extreme risks to our civilisation, burning fossil fuels needs to half in the next 10 years. What the government is not telling us is that we have a 50:50 chance of staying below that temperature. Only 50:50! Think about that. There are murmurings in the audience. "This is an emergency – This is it! It is time to come together – It is time to make a change." Wynter smiled as many in the crowd beat their drums, cattle bells and shepherd horns in response. Others clapped enthusiastically. "You are here today because you are awake to the danger. You are forthright and selfless." Another murmur and some cheers swept through the crowd. "Our government is only interested in their self-interest. If it does not save money or make money, then they will do nothing. We need to act now." Carly's voice rose at the end in defiance, and this bought a renewed banging of drums, bells and shouts of "Act now, Act now. "From the audience. "Be at the right side of history or be at the end of history." Wynter turned to watch the crowd's reaction, she was beginning to empathise a little with these people. They seemed to understand the gravity of the situation and were trying to achieve acknowledgement and government support.

Her optics fixed on the flashing images, her mind switched between the World of 2019 and the World of now. What had happened? Why had they not made the changes they needed? Wynter knew the answer herself, even as she was thinking it. Did they put it off until it was too late, or did they just think it would never happen? The actions of those in history intrigued her yet she could not understand the stupidity of those that came before her. She was keen to do more research into SAM once she returned to 2188.

Suddenly, Wynter's attention was caught by a man in the shadows behind Carly on the stage. Was it Robert? She zoomed her left optic to try to see more but he was moving, and it made it difficult. He did look younger and Wynter could see that he was fidgeting and very nervous.

Carly continued, "We need to speak with our voices as one. This government will claim scientists are exaggerating, but that is just not true. Many eminent scientists are telling us that this research is true. Carly gestured to the young man who stood beside her. Most of you know Robert Sanchez and his published work for the University of London. He has been a silent advocate from the beginning, but he has completed his studies and can now give us his support. Give us the actual picture." Many of the crowd murmured their support, "I give you Robert Sanchez– Welcome Robert." Many clapped as Robert stepped up to the microphone.

Wynter took a step towards the podium to get a better view of him. She did not need to. Suddenly, his face filled the screen behind him. He was stunning. With dominant angled features, his blonde fringe flopping over his eyes and a shy smile on his lips. Robert shifted uncomfortably and stood behind the podium, stepping towards the microphone. Wynter became irritated as part of him became obscured. She wanted to use the zoom on her optic again but knew It would be included in her vizoptics presented to Magera.

There was a pause as he leaned forward towards the microphone, and then he spoke. His voice, low and modulating. "I am sorry to be the messenger of bad news, but we are facing an ecological crisis - the mother of all crises. It is possible that 97% of wildlife on Earth will not survive." Robert paused and glanced around as he gained more confidence." A child born today will see this in their lifetime." There were murmurings in the crowd, and Robert nodded in response. "This is the reality that we are facing and that is not all. Our civilisation as we know it now is over. If we have three consecutive years of El Niño weather events, then food production will be untenable, and we will fight over a can of beans." The crowd stilled.

Wynter knew this to be a reality. The newsopics that she had seen of the riots of 2101 following the mass failure of corn yields in mid-western US, Indonesia and Brazil. In the catastrophic flooding in Bangladesh in 2157, most people didn't die in the flooding but of starvation afterwards, as countries refused medical help, water and food. Terrible times to be a human being. Wynter felt the relief. Most of these people would never have to see them.

Robert resumed, "What we choose to do today, could be the difference between life and death on Earth. We are all connected to this beautiful planet and a vital part of this huge food chain–Break it at our peril. You will have noticed that there are fewer bees and butterflies already. They will disappear forever." Landry's face flashed across Wynter's mind and Landry's love for wildlife and particularly insects. She was born at the wrong time.

Robert began to relax, "We must force the world to listen. We must force change, but we cannot do it on our own. Will you help us?"

The crowd responded as one. "Yes. Yes. Yes - Change it, change it now, change it- change it now." The crowd repeated as one and a repeated drumbeat, and other instruments joined the voices. "The petition for change that we sign today, we will take to various government departments - to set our plans for the ecological emergency that is upon us. Rallies across the World today will do the same. We can make a change together."

Wynter noticed two young girls who had stepped up behind Robert onto the stage. She was consumed by them; Were they related? Who were they? You never saw children in the late 22nd century. She was in awe of these little human beings.

Robert placed his hand on the shoulders of the younger girl as they both stepped up. In Wynter's research into 21st century and in earlier time assignments, the interaction between siblings fascinated her. In the 23rd Century new citizens were born in sector 7 and not integrated into general society until they were adults.

"I am going to stop talking now because the Survival Alliance Movement is not about me, it's not about you, it is about our future, the next generation." Robert knelt between the two girls as he spoke. A thought flashed through Wynter's mind- are they his sisters? They couldn't be his children. Robert continued, "Isabel and Esther have something they want to say." Robert looked between the two girls and whispered words of encouragement to them.

The taller child stepped up and Robert lowered the microphone for her as she unravelled a piece of paper which crackled into the microphone as she began "I dreamt I was an ocean, and no one polluted me, I dreamt I was the air and nothing blackened me, I dreamt I was a stream, and no one poisoned me." She paused as shouts and claps swept around the square in support, and with renewed confidence, her voice became more authoritative. "I dreamt I was a rainforest, and no one cut me down, I dreamt I was a polar bear and STOP! "She paused as silence ensued, "They protected my ice- they saved me!" A tremendous cry erupted. "I dreamt I was an angel fish and STOP–they stopped my ocean warming." She gave a smile as they roared again. Wynter noticed the young child pause and begin again in a quieter voice, "If you don't care about your future, care about mine."

And those of your children and grandchildren because we are looking at an uncertain future, thought Wynter. Her optics filled with tears as she watched this courageous small human being talking about her future. Shaking her head, Wynter maintained her optic on the podium.

The older of the two children stepped up, "For years governments have known about climate change, but they are slow to act. It will be OUR generation who will pick up the pieces." A cacophony of instruments, shouts, cries and singing broke out amongst the crowd. She held up her hand high into the air and her fingers clenched into a fist, "We will never stop fighting for our future, our planet's future and every living thing that calls this special place, their home."

"Thankyou." The young child started. People in the audience shouted, "no thank you!"

"If we work together, we can slow the global warming and make the World a rainbow." She held up a crude drawing of a rainbow. The crowd applauded. Robert placed both arms around the two girls. The trio stepped back to allow Carly to re-enter the stage.

"Thank you, Robert, thankyou Isobel and Esther, for coming here today and thank you for showing us we can do it." They raised many flags high as Carly continued, "In your own ways, we need to do everything that we can to make them sit up and listen. This is not about money; it is about the future of our planet." Yells and chants of "act now" rippled around the crowd, but Wynter was watching Robert and the children as they moved off the stage. She could not keep her eyes off the threesome.

Carly raised her voice above the noise, "I am going to end the rally here today with a quote from Kofi A Annan. We must face up to an inescapable reality: the challenges of sustainability simply overwhelm the adequacy of our responses. With some exceptions, our responses are too few, too few, and too late. Please do not tell me it is too late! I believe we can make the changes needed if we work together. Be on the right side of history, not at the end of history!"

The crowd clapped and stamped their feet, and the images of the planet returned to the screen. Some walked to the podium to talk to the speakers. Others moved around talking, making new friends. Many made their way to the desks, holding the petition to add their signatures.

After some time, the crowd dispersed, and Robert disappeared into the museum. Wynter wanted to follow but remembered she was here for one purpose. She jumped up onto the foot of a statue and scanned the crowd. Estimating that there were 90000 in the crowd, Wynter needed to show Magera and Radan the numbers supporting the movement. It looked to Wynter that this movement had powerful allies, so it was strange that they had failed.

She set off for her time doorway in Portland Place, she was swept up with some of her fellow activists. The selfishness of the 21st century society, not forgotten. Replaced. Enveloped with anger at their inaction. It engulfed her. Wynter suddenly felt rage for those generations that followed. Those people throughout the 21st century who sat and did nothing to stop climate change and the sorrows that followed. Wynter made her way to the Langham Hotel. She wanted to get her report entered as soon as possible.

Wynter walked down Chandos Street at the back of the hotel. With her ID lanyard around her neck, she made her way into the busy corridors behind the scenes of the prestigious hotel. The maze of narrow corridors, vastly different to the opulence in the main part of the hotel. She found the laundry and the cupboard. With the door closed behind her, Wynter placed her tattoo onto the indistinguishable symbol on the back wall and the wall shimmered and swirled in front of her eyes and the opening beckoned Wynter through. she stepped through the wall and onto the other side. As the door behind her returned to its solid-state, the green screen in front of her shimmered into life. The Magera symbol spun on the screen, and the distinctive voice of Kyson Mullins welcomed her back. "Welcome back, Lund2602."

"Thank you Mullins2001, assignment positive- I need to report a fluidity conflict," Wynter stated.

Kyson looked at the screen with interest, "What conflict is that?"

Wynter described, "social history note2345/45, 2019, London–tram transport is cashless. An oyster card is essential for transport on trams.

Implications for use of cash and how to get an oyster card. Could you check the archives for previous operatives and alternative methods?"

"Will do Lund 2062. I have a dateline and time for you. 1200 on 22/06/2188. There are no ablutions shown in your accom location to Regent's subdivision. UV is at dangerous levels, so visors are essential and underground blueline recommended. Please include all conflicts in your final report. Due at 1600 on 22/06/2188." with waning interest, she glanced to the left, the conversation was over.

Wynter looked away from the screen and it dissolved into the wall. She grabbed her graphinomo and took the mask visor from the inside pocket. As she opened the doorway into 2188, she found herself in the basement of Stafe1c, an accommodation complex in the Regents' district of New London. She reflected on the crude opulence of the Langham Hotel in 2019, compared to the primitive bare walls of the now functional accom. Living quarters that had replaced the luxury apartments and hotel rooms. Much like the Langham Hotel, London was a city much changed with time.

CHAPTER 8

WYNTER LUND

Wynter felt her optics adjust to the bright sunshine as she left the Accom complex in 2188. She considered walking back to the old entrance to Oxford Circus underground. She was in the mood to extend her visit into the past and decided to take a detour. The old tunnels were old, and today Wynter could sense the imprint of people who came before her. The SAM rally and seeing Robert and his sisters had stayed with Wynter. Even though they were all long gone, the connection for her remained. It was a strange and unfamiliar feeling.

Later, on leaving the darkness of the tunnel end, Wynter stopped abruptly and looked around her. The emptiness of New London in comparison to 21st century London was extreme. However, she had no desire to live in that time. She was not a tockhead! She could not understand why time operatives abandoned their lives and chose to live their lives in the past never returning to the present. She sat on a shelf of concrete surrounding the walkway and lifted her arm, studying her medi-support tattoo. She always felt the reassuring presence of Radan to feed her and keep her well. She commanded, "Medi update." The tattoo vibrated and then its melodic tones pervaded her auditorus, "temperature optimal, heat rate optimal, blood tests complete and optimal." The spinning stopped and her feeling of well-being returned.

Wynter began her journey to her own accom. As she crossed the security threshold, her tattoo vibrated, acknowledging her entry to the Redline underneath Portland Place, Wynter placed her tattoo on the Redline post. It pulsed once, and then a flashing beacon on the top throbbed into life. It was deathly quiet, and the silent emptiness enveloped her. She cocked her auditorus to listen. She loved the quiet of New London. Her auditorus picked up the distant sound of a pod moving towards her position. As she glanced to her left, the pulsing lights on the Redline sped up and a transparent pod with a flashing red top came into view and stopped near the post where Wynter was standing. The door opened silently and Wynter stepped inside as the tuneless voice said, "Home- Wynter Lund?"

"Yes. "She replied.

As the Redline moved rapidly through the tunnels under New London. She found herself drawn back to the rally in Trafalgar square in her assignment in 2018. Robert Sanchez stepping onto the podium with the two children. In her left optic, she replayed the crowd, immersed in their faces and their optimism and hope. Wynter was curious. She wondered what their lives would be like. She knew that in their lifetime, they would have seen significant changes. The sudden and catastrophic changes in the Earth's weather patterns. With the disappearance of vital species of mammals and insects and closer to home, the last-ditch attempts to keep the sea rises at bay with flood defences in London, Bristol and many parts of Norfolk. She wondered how being such advocates of change in 2018 had prepared them for what was to come. Did they continue to fight, or did they give up when the Earth reached its tipping point, and all seemed lost?

Wynter shook herself from her musing. It was unlike her to dwell upon these things. This was her job. Just that, nothing else. Complete the assignment, file the report. That was it. Wynter arrived underneath her accom block in phase 2 Regent's Park. Exiting the Redline pod, she took the stairs from the depths, sprinting up and up. Wynter panted as she stepped into the bright sunshine outside the entrance to the Redline. Shielding her sensitive optics with her visor, Wynter looked at the blue sky and recalled that they had built her accommodation block right in the middle of what had been Regent's Park. After the centralised suburbanization act of 2150, valuable space, needed for accommodation, made urban green spaces no longer a priority. People in the past wanted to devote leisure time outside with friends or family. With their pet animals and spend time outdoors. In 2018, it had been a vast gathering place of people of all ages. All gone now.

"It's quiet here" Wynter muttered as she turned and took in the foyer of her accom block. It was new, and although basic and designed for functionality, there had been attempts to make it a pleasant environment, with concrete seating and huge sealed greenhouses filling the rest of the space. A nod to attempts to create valuable carbon sinks across the urban areas. She scrutinised it today and could see that the plants were not looking too good Many of the leaves were brown and dry. She made a note to herself to inform the accom supervisor of her find. Without insect pollination and regular rainfall, the green spaces required intensive support to survive. Wynter knew they were a token, a frivolous decoration rather than something with a true scientific purpose. She stepped into a translucent graphene elevator, and it rose, giving Wynter a panoramic vista of New London. Many Greenline, Redline and Blueline pods zipped around the empty streets. There were giant screens interspersed across the city showing news items, community messages and advertising VR experiences and current diaramas. A message from Radan flashed up on one screen, "Carbon emissions continue to rise despite all attempts to contain it. HAFAC predict more deaths globally." Wynter sighed, and her thoughts flashed back to 2018. That was 170 years ago, and we are still talking about it?

Wynter arrived on her floor, and she exited the elevator. Her corridor was more traditional and as she approached her apartment and her door swung open. The monotone voice as she entered, "Welcome home, Wynter. Nutrition available, No.3"

"No.3. "Wynter replied.

"Thank you. Enjoy No.3", Wynter's homebot continued.

Wynter's tattoo glowed green, and her Radan medic update began, "Medical update, Lund2062. Temperature optimal, heat rate optimal, blood tests complete and optimal, UV damage of 60% recommend staying indoors for 24hrs, stomach contents…."

Wynter placed her tattoo at her temple and interrupted the update with "Lund2062 private mode." The medic voice ceased and Wynter lay back on her longchair. Today, she noticed she had bought her work home with her, and she wanted some time to review what she had witnessed. Since Wynter requested private mode, the home screen was blank except for the Radan icon on the right-hand side. She spent some time sitting, ate her nutrient ration for the day, and then completed her report for the assignment.

Sometime later, she requested an end to private mode and her home screen returned, with contacts on the left-hand side, news items on the right and a library of books and diaramas that she was following in the centre.

The main news item began scrolling and the news readers voice came through, "Radan with support from the Mars and Global Environmental

Research Authority is requesting for voluntary pioneers to be in the first wave of settlers to colonise New Earth on Mars." Images of an enormous biosphere filled the screen. Inside the sphere was an idyllic scene, of green forests, waterfalls and a lush valley with a river meandering through it. There were homes and small holdings on the edge of the valley floor connected by trackways. The voice continued, "You would need the relevant skills and applicants can expect a very prosperous life package, including extra financial bounties above and beyond necessary funding for life. The Immigration and Naturalisation Service will shortlist candidates and successful pioneers must be able to leave for Mars within 3 weeks and have an up-to-date Globalservicenumber." The newsreader continued, but Wynter's mind was already racing with what she had just heard.

"Magera communication", Wynter stated, and the spinning Magera symbol appeared on the screen, and she could see that Landry and Karmal both had no blue Private mode spots next to their images showing that they were available. "Group dialogue with Landry and Karmal." The screen split into three and Wynter could see Landry turn towards the screen as she agreed to the group dia. Karmal's apartment was in darkness, but his sleep-wrinkled face emerged through the gloom.

"Hey Wynter." He yawned, "It's early."

"Yes, but did you see the news item feed?" ignoring Kamal's complaint, "Look."

Wynter could see both of her friends watching the same news story in English and Bengali relating the same story that Wynter had seen. After studying their reactions, she asked, "What do you think?"

Karmal looked up and stated, "You will go and visit?"

Wynter turned her wrist twice and waved them to seats at the table. A wavering translucent holo of Landry appeared first, followed by an untidy-looking Karmal. They sat around Wynter's worktable.

"Interesting news," Karmal raised his eyebrows. "a Magera announcement like that would go to employees first. Had you overheard anything before today?"

"No, nothing," Landry replied, "but then I'm suspended so I may not have received it. Would you be interested, Kar?" Landry grinned and Wynter giggled.

Karmal's holo gestured with his hand as if hitting the table, "I would NOT be interested in travelling across the universe to a barren planet barely able to keep me alive. No, I would not, thank you."

"Didn't think you would," Landry stated.

"You're more of a homeboy, Kar," Wynter declared.

"Yes, Leave me in New Dhaka. I am happy here," he stated.

"I wonder who would choose to go? It's not an ideal place to live." Landry continued, "Although the extra financial support and TVR credits might appeal to some. "

Karmal leant closer as he added, "Remember, we are lucky to be Magera employees, we have more services and extra rations. Some people have only basic rations. In New Dhaka, I live like a king!" Karmal raised his arms and performed a half bow.

Wynter frowned and said, "It wouldn't matter how much they gave me; Mars is just a step too far for me. Did either of you notice the name that they gave it- New Earth! - What is that?"

Landry and Karmal both shouted as one. "I know" then Landry said, "Thought that was strange."

"I agree, it's a strange name to give a new World. New Earth? What about old Earth?" Karmal added.

"We are just stage 1 operatives, remember. Not senior enough to have an insight into Magera's plans or Radan's. Our job is to follow orders, and that's that."

Karmal's grinning face filled the screen, "I hear this about Landry Reagan being suspended because of insubordination?"

Landry blushed, "Not insubordination just some conflicts and a tiny potential timeline impact. Recognition by a past participant only. Nothing else."

"And rudeness to a superior, wasn't it?" Wynter smiled and Karmal laughed.

Landry hung her head as Karmal reassured her, "Do not worry Landry, I have been suspended many times for not following instructions." Karmal placed a holohand on Landry's shoulder as she nodded and smiled back at him.

"Thanks Kar", She said.

"Yes, Kar, but has Radan ever addressed you directly because Landry was?"

"What? The Radan bot spoke to you?" his face clouded, and Landry could see his concern. "How did the Radan sound in person?"

"It was what you'd expect, A deeper version of the medi-support." Landry confirmed.

"What did it say?"

"It just reinforced the ban on any assignments with those past participants post 2015- it was because Pedersen had recognised me. "Landry added, "It was strange though… I could see that someone was speaking to Kyson through her auditorus, and I think it shocked her too. The Radan symbol turned red, then blue, and then this voice came out."

All three couldn't resist glancing at the Radan symbol on Wynter's home screen, and the Radan symbol had pulsed red. The symbol throbbed, expanding and contracting in size. Almost like a heart beating.

"Look. Just like that!"

Karmal placed his finger on his lips and looked wide-eyed at both Landry and Wynter. He shook his head and said, "Well, what an adventure, Land. You tell us about it another day. I need to go now, but I will tell you about my next assignment when I return." He lied mouthing the word' web' several times. Both Wynter and Landry nodded, and Karmal's holo disappeared.

Wynter flicked her wrist, and Landry's image appeared on Wynter's home screen. "Try to enjoy your break from work, Landry. We'll speak soon," Landry's image reduced in size, smaller and smaller until no image remained.

Wynter performed an exaggerated yawn, observing that the Radan symbol had returned to its usual white and static. Once again requesting private mode, Wynter disconnected her auditorus and optic visualiser from the system. It provided privacy and quiet during her sleep cycle.

Once in private mode, Wynter retrieved a 21st century work pad and a small mouse device from a cupboard in her apartment. It had been a fun gift from Karmal early on when they had first begun working together. 21st century technology fascinated Landry, and he had gifted both Wynter and Landry with one each. They had had fun using the antiquated system of the dark web to communicate under the radar and search for information regarding old news items and past events not always found through the proper channels. The hardware was slow but operational and used by some off-grid groups.

The system only allowed for basic communication, however, so the threesome usually got bored quickly. Today, however, the topic was one thing.

Wynter logged into the shared chat site and watched as Landry and Karmal both entered on-screen; their names appeared on the right hand of the screen. The 21st century camera software was archaic and hard to update. Therefore, the optics were terrible; they stuttered. They froze, and they could not see clear details. The auditory system was below standard and crackly, but it had one redeeming feature. Their conversation could be truly private as it operated below the radar of any modern communication infrastructure and that included Radan services.

Karmal's face appeared in the gloom. The camera gave an almost distorted image, making Karmal look like he was in a tunnel. "Let us talk about Radan," he said. Wynter attempted to adjust to the inferior quality, and his sentence became distorted. "What did it say again?"

"Well, Radan only spoke once, but I knew that someone was talking to Kyson during the meeting. The Radan services bot that welcomed me to the meeting moved next to me when Radan spoke. I felt threatened."

"I've never heard of any meeting where Radan spoke. Kar, can it do this?"

"Radan is an AI... It is a medical AI in the 2040s to help doctors and hospitals to put the resources in the right places.

Wynter continued, "Why is Radan in a meeting with an employee of Magera?"

"There is something strange. I checked the record of the meeting and what Radan said is missing. Everything that Kyson and I said is there but no reference to what Radan said."

"But your optical visuals from the meeting will show it all."

"No, Kyson suggested I go to private mode because my medi-support kept interrupting the meeting; my heart was beating so fast."

Wynter frowned and shook her head and was about to speak when Karmal's voice came through, "I study Radan during my research on the society collapse in the early 2100's, they asked Radan to solve the lack of food production around the World and find a solution. Radan invented the ration cities. Its advice was used to make hard decisions following the collapse of corn yields in the mid-west USA, Brazil and Indonesia. It is an AI, and its primary aim is the salvation of human life. It shouldn't be involved in the Magera; except as a rapid assessor of whether our assignments are good as potential positive impacts upon climate change in the past." Both Wynter and Landry nodded.

Wynter spoke, "Yes, an AI is only there to solve problems for us, isn't it?"

"An AI can't lie and doesn't understand opinion. "Karmal leant on his hand, focussing on the screen, his expression quizzical. "It doesn't make the final decisions, so I am confused. Why are governments becoming much more reliant on Radan internationally. Look at what happens following an extreme weather phenomenon."

"What do you mean, Kar?"

"You know about my family. When they lost all things in the great flood of Bangladesh, HAFAC (Human and animal fatality assessment and control) used Radan systems suggestions and as a result, governments refused to send relief to the region. Millions of people died after the flooding. My mother said that they survived the flooding but died because of no food and water."

Neither Landry nor Wynter spoke. They had listened to Karmal talk about his family before and knew the extent to which it had affected him.

Wynter spoke first, "I understand there are instances where choices between life and death are made again and again, but how can this be Kar? How can an Artificial Intelligence formulate an aim for the salvation of human life and not opt to send relief to those in need?"

Landry's voice burst through, "My understanding of AI's is that they follow their protocols. They cannot defer from them so what we are saying is an impossibility!"

" It is true, but it doesn't seem to be possible. After the cyclone, there was a great confusion and miscommunication. It was a hard time. Maybe the need for food was greater elsewhere? An AI cannot experience emotion like us, it's all algorithms. The resources were needed elsewhere. As you all know, my mother lost all her family during that flood. I can't blame Radan. How can you blame an AI? I blame climate change and earlier generations knowing it was coming and doing nothing to stop it."

Landry nodded, "I agree Kar, so if it's all about algorithms then why are we talking about this in private mode?"

"Yes, this all seems a bit cloak and dagger, "Wynter smiled at the camera, but it faded when she saw Landry's face.

"You were not there, Wynt. It was unsettling and scary. I think seeing Kyson so ruffled was more worrying."

Karmal held up his hands. "I worry. I worry about the Radan in the work Magera. The Radan has access to our optic and auditorus communication. As part of our entry into the urbanisation Act of 2150, the zones created by the Radan, our medic tattoo allows us to receive rations, get medi packs and even medicine if we need it. The Radan tattoo controls our access to the security systems, entrance to buildings, food and transport. We rely upon the Radan for everything. It is our support and security. It keeps us healthy, but is there a darker side? What happens if we don't agree with a decision like Landry didn't?"

"Yes. But my last assignment was a definite 80% at least positive impact on climate change. But Radan assessed it as a 55%. That just is not possible. I know how good it was. I'll never be able to go back now and see if I could get more."

"You are both paranoid, Wynter exclaimed, "Radan is a programme. Nothing more. Would governments decide without questioning the ethics? I think we need to trust Magera and Radan. Why wouldn't we? It was designed to maintain human life, and it cannot choose to do anything else. It is binary code, nothing more."

There was an edge to Kars voice, "but the Radan has saved some human lives and let others die. It has no ethics, its missing from its protocols.

"I agree with everything you are saying Kar but,"

Wynter interrupted Landry, "Look, we are taking about Radan here, The saviour of the modern World. Would any of us be alive without the Ration cities? Even you could see Landry, if we had all lived off-grid like you and your family, then there wouldn't be enough food to go around. Humans, as we know it would not survive without Radan. What happened to you today Landry was strange, I agree, but questioning the motives of Radan seems a step too far. It's a computer-simulated artificial Intelligence. It does not have an opinion, so we must have faith that decisions are based upon calculated algorithms and therefore in the best interest of humankind."

Suddenly very weary, Wynter waved her hand as a farewell, "I'm going to refresh now. Sorry guys, it's been a long day."

Both Karmal and Landry raised their hands in a wave. "Speak soon." Landry smiled.

"Rest well." Karmal stated.

Wynter closed the communication device with a snap. Today had been wholly unsettling in many ways and she didn't like it.

CHAPTER 9

KARMAL RAHMAN

Karmal and Landry remained in private mode.

"Did Radan stop all the help for your mother's family, Kar?"

"Yes. My mother said that local people tried their best. Bangladesh pleaded with the outside world, and all countries for their aid, but many governments declined and said that Radan had allocated their sending of aid, as an ineffective action. "

"I cannot understand how an AI can give advice that would cause death. "Karmal nodded. "I think Radan wrongly assessed the validity of the data in my assignment. But it is playing on my mind. How could that happen? Maybe I noticed something which Radan did not, but the scientific evidence speaks for itself, Kar. You should look at my optic visuals. I think you will agree with me."

He smiled, "It will be my pleasure to look at them. Send them or I find them in the logs." Karmal paused for a moment, "Are going back Land? Get more data."

"How Kar? I am banned from going back post-2015."

"Turn off your optic and go in private mode, and then they won't see you. You cannot use what you find however." Karmal watched Landry's face. What he was proposing was against all Magera's strict policies.

Landry stared at the screen then stated, "How can you do that? How can anyone go through the doorway without an assignment checked by Radan?"

"Easy you go to two places in one assignment. I have done this. I record my proper time assignment and then I go to private mode and visit somewhere else." He chuckled as he studied the expression on Landry's face, mouth open and her eyes wide. He was interested in Landry's next words. Could she ever consider breaking the rules? He did not have to wait long.

"WHAT? You complete your assignment and then go off in private mode? Don't they know where you are? I always thought that they could monitor us."

"Landry. Give some thinking about it. You are monitored by your medi-support tattoo tracking your every move. They did not exist until 2160, so we are invisible once we go through. They only have your optic visuals and the sensor on the time doorway you used, to know you have been there."

It took a moment, but Karmal waited and watched Landry's face as realisation hit. "Lie to Magera? I don't think that I can do that Kar."

"It is not lying Land; it is not telling them everything that you do. You have never wanted to visiting places in the past or seeing something new?"

"Yes, of course, but I wouldn't dare do it. I was always aware of my optic visuals recording everything."

Karmal shifted in his seat, "Think of it as not telling the whole story. You know other people have done it. Tockheads disappear into the past."

"I have heard the stories, but it just isn't me Kar, I couldn't do it."

"Think! What could you achieve visiting more people?"

"If I am honest, you have blown my mind. I need some time to think."

"If you need to ask anything more, then I am here. But I go now. I need some reparation before my assignment this morning."

Yes, yes, of course, Kar. You have given me a lot to think about. Thank you." They both looked up at the screen. Landry waved as Karmal reached the button to exit the programme.

Both names disappeared from the screen and Karmal returned to his bed. He had a busy day ahead. He chuckled to himself and thought about Landry questioning things around her, and he liked that. Breaking the rules was part of his makeup and he was keen to influence Landry if he could. There was no harm in it. In New Dhaka, if you didn't break a rule or two, you'd never get anything done. Magera was no exception. He was a committed operative but had some personal reasons for stopping comate change as well. But this new news was concerning. The Radan acting alongside Magera? And being present in a meeting with Kyson and Landry. This was unusual. Karmal made a mental note to speak to Dipu if he got the chance in the next few days.

***

Dipu Bashir, Karmal's supervisor, nodded from the desk as Karmal walked into the Magera's office in New Dhaka later that morning.

"Subhakamana", Dipu smiled.

"Good day to you," Karmal responded. "You received my assignment brief for today?"

Dipu tapped the screen hovering just to the right of his shoulder, "Kar-all received and agreed." He read from the screen, "You are visiting 2129-presentation on Bangladesh role in preparing for extreme weather phenomena-direct result of climate change?"

Karmal nodded in agreement and began making his way towards the back of the office. Over his shoulder, he added, "I don't need any accessories or currency today as you can read in my notes."

Dipu just waved a hand; he was already distracted, absorbed in something on his screen.

The time doorway had stood in the University of Dhaka building from the early days when Magera was just ERA, the Earth Research Authority. Refurbishments had been few, and the primary structure had remained unchanged throughout its history. The doorway was in the back office. As he tapped the Magera icon with his tattoo, Karmal paused as the door lost its solidity and he stepped through. There was a rush of cooler air. It was the same month, but a century earlier. He shook his head. Karmal was shocked by how the planet had warmed. There must be a difference of at least 10 degrees! As he stepped into the empty office in 2129, Karmal placed his hand behind him and felt the door become solid again.

Karmal had been employed by Magera to identify the possibilities for more food production in his region, in its past. Lack of food had caused the greatest pangocaust in Earth's history. Tens of millions of refugees abandoned their homes to move to new areas where they could attempt to grow or find food. Karmal's role in finding alternatives for food production in the past could save lives by stopping catastrophic events that led to the great fall. Karmal admired Landry and Wynters's climate change tasks, which could save the World from the inevitable global tipping point. In comparison, Karmal held the opinion that his tasks were less significant. But even saving one life or affecting the lives of his family in the past, was his sole motivation. Karmal strode through the empty office and into the corridor beyond.

Curzon Hall had been the Faculty of Sciences for the University of Dhaka since 1904, and it was still a thriving university in 2129. This time doorway was his only official routeway into the past. The hall had changed little in the times that Karmal had visited; a building lost to time. However, the occupants of the building had changed. During the early years of its existence, the Palace housed the Governor of East Bengal and Assam. Later it housed the courthouse and the defence ministry in 1941. By 2129, it was again Dhaka University, and it was a wonderful environment for the students. Karmal, being 30 years, was not the usual student age, but with confidence, he assumed the role of a visiting lecturer. He stepped out into the corridor which ran along the veranda of the Science building. Students rushed about, full of life and mischief. Karmal enjoyed listening to their conversations as he made his way across the open Naya to the department of soil, water and environment housed in the eastern aspect of Curzon Hall. Their laughter warmed Karmal, and he envied their optimism.

Karmal waited in the corridor by the proposed meeting room. As a group of department representatives walked past, he followed in behind. His bogus ID stated he was DR Karmal Laskar–visiting researcher for Dhaka International University. He sat down with the group that he had arrived with and focussed on checking his optics to maintain his focus on the speaker during the presentation.

Dr Nadim Azam stepped up to the podium. His grave expression reflected a time when Karmal knew that climate change was a reality. Officials in Bangladesh had already experienced the consequences close to hand. The extreme weather phenomena and increased temperatures and sea rise impacted Bangladesh.

A slide introduced today's presentation, "Bangladesh- The frontline for the impact of climate change."

Karmal sighed. Past participants had sent out the message over and over. Knowing that they failed was hard to witness. The inevitable truth and his patience with Magera were waning. They would never stop this. The CEO of Magera had promised that their studies would stop climate change. They were long dead, but Karmal hoped that their work might change the fortunes of his own family. Karmal had the notion that Magera would never act. Landry's recent experience had not given Karmal any new hope. The faith he once had in Magera stopping climate change and stopping the cyclone that killed his family was being tested. Karmal recognised that this presentation would not change the world but might improve life for the people of Dhaka. Karmal sat back to watch the presentation.

"Two-thirds of Bangladesh is less than 4 metres above sea level. Current rises are forcing many farmers to abandon crops because of the salty fields and farm crabs instead. This is more profitable but produced less maize and rice for the overall population. "

A student in the audience put up their hand. "What effect does this have on drinking water?"

Dr Azam nodded, "It has a tremendous impact on drinking water. The farmers encourage more saltwater to make a higher profit, but the saltwater pollutes the groundwater and makes it difficult to access clean drinking water."

Dr Azam continued, "We have found that 33 million people are relying upon a poor source of drinking water, and we predict related health problems in the future. Four million people who live on chars are at risk, as is the mangrove forest that protects Bangladesh from cyclones becomes less. As sea levels rise, we face an impossible problem.

The image changed to local people leaving their homes and taking as much as they could carry with them, 'every day 1000-2000 people move to Dhaka.'

"That's 2000 people who are not growing food but needing to work and purchase food from others. You all know that we cannot sustain this." Dr Azam continued.

Karmal identified that what the doctor was saying was true, and when the screen changed and showed the funding provided by The World Bank and the UNDP- United Nations Development Programme funding many projects in the region, his mood darkened. He knew that in the future when countries looked to their survival, this funding will cease.

Karmal's own family died in the catastrophic floods following cyclone Zabr in 2157, but those that survived died because of starvation and lack of drinking water. The only reason that Karmal and his mother survived was that following the cyclone, they were airlifted to Dhaka. As she was heavily pregnant with Karmal, she was deemed to be a priority survivor. They were the only survivors of their entire family. No one came to his family's aid, and they died like thousands of others, trapped by their lack of support from their government and unable to leave a region devastated by the cyclone; their home. Karmal knew it was HAFAC following the advice from Radan that resulted in not sending aid due to a lack of resources Worldwide. Millions died. It was his sole motivation for joining Magera. To somehow save his family and the lives of all those lost.

What Dr Azam was sharing was insignificant compared to what was to come. This presentation would not give him the answers that he sought. He had listened to enough. The emotions surrounding the pain, sorrow and suffering that these people would experience in their future overwhelmed Karmal. He felt the prolonged frustration and the sudden personal realisation that he may not stop it.

He stood up in his place. All turned to stare, and he almost sat back down. Karmal forced others to stand as he made his way down the aisle. Dr Azam stopped talking and raised a quizzical glance at the intrusion. Karmal looked to the floor and walked across the front of the podium. He heard Dr Azam begin speaking again, and he strode across the corridor and sat on the wall of one of the large openings facing the garden outside.

He had been working for Magera for over 8 years now, and no evidence was enough. The authority wanted the perfect actionable cause, and nothing else was good enough. Today's presentation and talking to Landry last evening had touched a nerve. What would happen if they never found an actionable event and the World, and its history remained as it was? He could not comprehend that possibility. A nagging doubt was growing and becoming a complete loss of all hope.

"Private mode," he commanded, drawing the attention of two students walking past. They glanced across curiously, but Karmal realised it would not matter now as his optic and auditorus were no longer recording. He felt a lightness at the thought. He'd had enough for today. Free now, away from the prying eyes of Magera and Radan. He could do anything he wanted, and today he wanted to see those that he had lost. Previously avoiding the personal punishment of seeing his family that were lost, but today was different.

Leaving the university complex, he felt more relieved. The events leading to the disaster of 2157 hadn't happened yet. He wanted to see his family- the family he had never known. His mother had talked so much about them that Karmal felt he knew them. Would he have been a different person with his family around him? -Not just his mother? All he knew is that today, he wanted to see them.

Once outside the complex, Karmal's initial energy diminished as he thought about the enormity of what he was proposing. He had not planned for this. Reaching the university gates, he looked ahead. Mirpur was the main routeway through Dhaka and at one time clogged with the traffic of bikes, motos and pedestrians. Today in 2129 it was quite different. Cars that once filled the streets with the fumes from their engines were just abandoned. Hydrogen fuelled vehicles and small electromotors picked their way around these once treasured possessions now rusting at the side of the road.

Karmal watched for the protocol for beckoning an EV scooter driver. A hand gesture was all that was required. He lifted his hand and waited. As with all assignments, they gave operatives a small amount of local currency for emergencies. His supervisor Dipu was not so dedicated to his job, and this had allowed Karmal to store currency for this type of emergency.

An EV approached and a small, wiry man, jumped off the moto and smiled up at him. "Bahadr Sir?" he pointed to the seat at the back of his scooter.

"Bajitkha ferry?" Karmal pointed his finger back down the main road.

The man's face scrunched up in confusion and Karmal thought he had misheard him, so he repeated "Bajitkha?", simulating water with his hand back and forth.

The man's arm touched Kars, "No Bajitkha. Bajitkha gone."

The hairs stood up at the back of his neck. Karmal realised his error. The ferry terminal had gone. Of course, they lost many ferry terminals in the last decades of the 21st century, swept away by rising waters and seasonal floods. He had to think fast, anyone from Bangladesh would know that that terminal was no longer there. He noticed the man studying him.

Karmal stopped further scrutiny, hitting his forehead with his palm and exclaiming, "Of course- Patarhat Ferry not Bajitkha ferry!" The man smiled and stuck out his hand. He is going to make money from me, Karmal thought.

"Patarhat Hyam," The man stated, "500 Taka."

"450 Taka." Smiling Karmal replied. Nothing would make the man more suspicious than someone who did not barter.

"475 Taka," The man replied, getting his scooter and indicating for Karmal to go behind. The price concluded.

The journey to Parahat crossing was so different from the journey in Karmal's own time. Shanty housing still lined the route interspersed with small holdings of rice fields, maize fields with animals around the edges. It amazed Karmal. The number of fields of vegetation; lush and green and the number of animals on these. As they reached the outskirts of the city, it hit Karmal how much had changed. The lack of refugee camps.

In his own time, these camps stretched mile after mile. The centralised suburbanization act of 2150 had forced many to move to New Dhaka, but with no infrastructure to support them. The tent city surrounding the city was the result. A terrible place, but a symbol of survival. Karmal marvelled at the resilience of the Bengal people- his people. They had coped with flooding beyond comprehension year on year and watched as desperate defences were destroyed again and again. The reliance on Bangladesh as a food source for the region had elicited charitable funding for many years and the evidence of this was still apparent in 2129; The Red Cross, Action Aid, Save the children and other charity stalls littered the road's edge. It was still many years before Karmal's lifetime, but to him, the sounds, sights and colours of this region were still reminiscent of a time before cyclone Zabr changed so many lives in the region.

They arrived at Patarhat terminal as the sun was beginning its descent. After paying his driver, Karmal walked through the terminal to buy a ticket for his destination, Lakshmipur. The ferry was large, with three floors according to the class of ticket that you bought. As Karmal bought the cheapest, he found himself at the bottom of the boat sitting on a wooden bench surrounded by commuters with cages of chickens, and bushels of maize. He loved being so close to life, and people. In his daily life, encounters with other people were rare. Two brothers were teasing each other and laughing out loud. When it reached the point when their playfulness became more serious, their mother chastised them. During the journey, he saw them tire. One boy leant in under his mother's arm. The other leaned against the adult next to him and they soon fell asleep.

As the boat sped through the darkening waters, Karmal took the time to recall stories that his mother had told him about living on the farm with her family and enjoying simpler times. Not having planned this trip, he had no idea what to do once he reached his mother's home. In 2129, his mother would only be 1-year-old, but he would see his grandparents and his aunts and uncles. He wanted to see it. The life that his mother had lost, and the family lost to him after Cyclone Zabr.

The passengers collected their things together, announcing that they had arrived at their destination. He followed the main bulk as they crossed the gangplanks and onto the quayside. Karmal saw a local store selling an assortment of food, and supplies and above the sign he read, Mehendiganj. He was home. Now he just had to locate the family polder and using the visual memory created in his brain by his mother's stories, he moved on. He soon found his bearings by the health complex and walked past ancient ruins and neglected grand temples and palaces. Upon reaching the Guthia mosque, Karmal stood a short distance away and viewed the people coming out through the large wooden doorways at the side. He thought about stepping inside but knew this was a local masajida and he would be identified as a stranger. Avoiding unwanted attention, Karmal hung back in the shadows and watched as the people milled around in small groups outside, chatting.

He spotted an uncle almost immediately. He was a teenager, but the distinctive Rahman family look was all there. Family photographs of them were ingrained into his memory. His hunch was confirmed when an elder woman called to his uncle, "Suhab come here." She beckoned. Was it Ghazwan his grandmother?

Karmal studied the group and soon a family extracted themselves from the group and began making their way down the track away from the Masajida. According to his mother's description, they were going in the right direction. The road was busy with devotees and other families and workers making their way home for the evening. Karmal blended in behind them, following the Rahman family from a distance. Soon families dispersed, and the groups were thinning when Karmal watched as his family turned into a small gateway. He continued down the track, stopping behind the hedge where he could observe from a distance. He could see the Najar of their shack with the table and chairs from his location. It was a humid night and the family soon gathered outside on chairs strewn across a small patio. It was a simple dwelling and lights encouraged moths and other insects to buzz around them. Behind the silhouette of the building, Karmal could see rice fields flooded by a recent borsha and the mighty Maghna River beyond.

Karmal basked in the warmth of his mother's memories as he watched his family at ease with each other through the bushes where he sat. He saw things that his mother had shared; his uncle Ameer and Auntie Bushra arguing and teasing each other, chasing onwards to the rice field and back again. He saw his grandfather Karmal, his namesake. It felt strange as he was around the same age as himself. Then from the house walked his grandmother Ghazwan carrying a small baby. Was that his mother? His calculations made it that the baby could be his mother, Faridah. His grandmother sat, and the baby was passed to the eldest Aunt Daniyah. They fascinated him. They treated the baby, his mother, with such care and love as they passed her around the family. They all had something to say to her or a belly to poke or foot to tickle. The family scene continued into the night. The love enveloped him as he sat there seeing people, he had never met but who still meant so much to him and his mother. Pondering what a different life would have been led, had they survived the after-effects of the cyclone.

At some point, he dozed off and woke early the next morning. All was quiet in the house. As he heard the noises of a waking house; pots being filled to prepare for breakfast and the murmur of tired voices. He wanted to stay but knew that his presence here was dangerous in daylight. Reluctantly, Karmal trudged down the track away from his family home and towards the small business area. As he reached the Masajida religious place, he was compelled to go in.

He took off his shoes and moved towards the ornate marble washing basin to perform the Wadu, Karmal lowered his gaze. His family resemblance would be easy to spot. After washing, Karmal made his way upstairs to the large prayer hall and noted the men kneeling on the carpeted floor facing the Mihrab. He knelt at the back and began performing the salutation with his fellow worshippers. Following this, Karmal sat on the floor and spent some time in quiet contemplation. As with many moments of recollection, his thoughts turned to his mother and the cyclone, floods killed people, but most died after from disease and lack of food and drinking water. The aid just did not come. They had turned in on themselves and looked after themselves. This is what climate change did to the World. Made countries panic and store their resources for themselves. The previous generous societies did not send help or aid, and the poorest countries like Bangladesh just could not help themselves. Thousands died crying out for help, and Karmal knew the consequence of that. His mother often spoke about her sadness at being saved once everyone she knew had died. She told Karmal that he was the only thing that kept her going. When he was born 3 months after the cyclone, her life began again.

Karmal still visited the local masajida in his own time, but his faith was in tatters. He could not see how Allah could allow this to happen and what was happening all over the world, even in 2188. Seeing his family last night had shown him the life missed. His physical needs were being met in the life he led in 2188 in New Dhaka. He was nourished, and he had a place to sleep, but little human contact. His mother had died some years ago, and today he was more alone than he had felt for some time. An idea began growing in his mind.

Last night, the realism of his plan overwhelmed him. That morning in the masajida in Mehendiganj with his family a short distance away but close in his heart, Karmal told Allah all his plans. He left the masajida invigorated with his new plan. The journey back to Dhaka was a blur as Karmal carried out the complicated mental calculations, running scenarios like film reels in his head. By the time he returned to the time doorway, he was resolved to act. He would tell Landry and Wynter when the time was right.

Arriving back at Curzon Hall at the University of Dhaka and Karmal stood outside the cupboard in the office calculating the time frame he needed to arrive back. Since the presentation, he had been in private mode for 14 hours. Upon entering the cupboard, he changed his entry point timestamp using the keypad next to the doorway. "End private mode," Karmal commanded. He then placed his wrist on the symbol on the door frame and a screen emerged with the Magera spinning symbol on it.

Dipu's face appeared on screen. "Rahman 360 returning to 11/07/2188 at 1700hours." He nodded in agreement. The screen blinked off. "He reached through and stepped to the other side. Dipu was sitting at his desk where he left him. His manner was relaxed and as far as he was concerned Karmal had been gone only 40 minutes. They were good friends. However, Karmal was keen to get going today though. This assignment was insignificant compared to the decision that Karmal had made during this trip.

"A good report?" Dipu questioned from behind his screen.

"Yes, all good." Karmal replied, "no conflicts, just one to note. I left the presentation early, felt a little unwell." He lied.

Dipu looked up from his screen, his forehead creased, "Oh Ok, check your medic bot as soon as you are free."

Karmal reminded Dipu about contamination protocol, "remember, the door won't let anyone through if it senses disease or contamination substances."

"Yes- of course," Dipu's attention on the screen in front of him. He was already engrossed in his latest reality game.

"I'll file my report this evening by 2000 hours, ok?" Karmal continued as he walked through the office and as he reached the door Dipu called, "2000 hrs yes I'll expect it."

Karmal left University Campus in 2188 with a new sense of purpose. If Magera would not do it, then he would do it for himself.

CHAPTER 10

LANDRY REAGAN

Landry spent the next days, finding more information on the key scientists working for BAFR - Birmingham Association of forestry research. She enjoyed reading the scientific reports on their key breakthroughs and their significance to Magera. Small key projects that with further enhancement could have stopped climate change in its tracks and given birth to other alternative futures. A future where the World didn't reach the global warming tipping point and the great fall had not occurred. This was everything that Landry worked for. It's the reason that she gave up her family and the only reason that she was in Birmingham.

Following the usual work cycle break, the Magera enforced 10-day suspension stretched before her. She could continue spending the time researching BUFR, could catch up on her dioramas or go on a virtual vacation. Landry was on chapter 26 of her virtual visrama, set in Edwardian England. but, even with these distractions, Landry would be alone.

The investigation following her last assignment was still playing on her mind. Karmal's revelation of breaking Magera rules and abusing their position as operatives, stopping Landry from having good reparation. She felt weary and sluggish. The ten days stretched before her.

In the time she had been in Birmingham, Landry had never considered going back to visit her parents. They knew that her leaving could become permanent once she entered the ration city under the umbrella of Radan support. She could never risk returning. The location of off-grid societies was a guarded secret and it needed to stay that way. There was no communication between off-grid and ration city dwellers, and Landry was no exception. Her parents had supported her move enthusiastically, wanting their daughter to broaden her horizons. The reality for Landry was not everything that she expected. She often thought of her parents, brother and his family- she missed the comfort of being with actual people, not holos.

Following the great fall, Landry's parents and many others had chosen an alternative subsistence life. Radan's aims were to ensure human survival and so preferred all humans to be in the ration cities where it could safeguard their survival, control their nutritional input and medic-support. Landry's parents had been reluctant to give up their freedom, and now that Landry had lived under Radan, she could understand why they had chosen that life. It was hard physically but enriching in many ways that the ration cities were not. Ration cities were built for survival only, blank desolate places, a place that Landry was struggling to live in. She had lived the alternative. If it wasn't for her work with Magera, she would have gone back before now.

Landry hoped her parents were still near Pencal. They lived in a well-established homestead and would not have moved unless forced to do so. They had originally fled there when the centralised suburbanisation act came into force and all humans were called to the ration cities. Landry had been born in their homestead near Pencal in outer Maree and lived this life for 18 years before leaving.

She took time to consider the pros and cons of visiting them, questioning the risk it posed. Until this moment, she had never considered placing her family's choice of lifestyle at any risk. But the conversation with Karmal had lit a spark in her. His revelation had given her a new chance. She was sure that she could move in private mode; be invisible. Informing Magera of her designated rest travel time and using private mode should protect the secrecy of her family's homestead. If she was to do this, however, no one could know of her plans. Landry spent many hours considering all the possible pitfalls to her plan and when she had countered them all, she made her decision.

She informed Magera that she was to take a rest travel vacation to Edinburgh. She left messages with Karmal and Wynter informing them and started reparation with the plans swirling around in her mind. Landry awoke the next morning buoyant and excited at the prospect of leaving the city. She could choose to return at any point if she needed to.

Landry stepped onto the green line an hour later and took it to the fringes of the city. Sky trains enabled people to travel between ration cities and to cross the fortress-like expanse of these walls surrounding the cities. Landry sat on the sky train and placed the safety restraint around her as it rose high into the sky. It skirted across the wall, impenetrable and imposing, and a sense of adventure gripped Landry as she left the city. As it passed over the summit, the bio-net; a wall of blue light passed through Landry, signalling to Radan that she was leaving the city. Her rations would be suspended until she re-entered Birmingham or another Radan ration city.

Landry recalled the first time she had entered the ration city of Birmingham with her work papers and no tattoo. The customs officer had never met an off-grider, and she had been harsh in her questioning. Landry had been careful not to give away details of her family's location.

During the sky train journey to Edinburgh, Landry recalled starting her new life in Birmingham, her feeling of achievement at being selected to be part of Magera and being a time operative. She remembered how proud she felt to be part of an organisation that was involved in the possibility of rewinding history, stopping climate change, and saving countless lives. That first naivety had ebbed, but Landry was looking forward to talking to her father and describing her adventures in the past. They would be shocked to see her, and as she raced on to Edinburgh, her excitement grew.

As the sky train entered the rural outskirts, Landry could see the striking structure of the ration wall surrounding Edinburgh, dividing the ration city from its natural surroundings. Tall, stark accommodation towers dwarfed the castle once a high point of the city rose. Landry's focus shifted to the land outside the city where automaton diggers opened vast chasms in the earth in which to bury the faecal waste of the inhabitants of the city. The evidence of the consequence of the obliteration of the insects from Earth, all too clear. No insects, no breakdown of waste. The landscape outside of the city stretched before her. Forests of wind-pollinated trees breaking up the last vestiges of urbanisation and growing through the walls of the homes abandoned following the great fall.

"Magnify", Landry commanded, and her optic visuals gave her 50X magnification allowing her to see small objects. She scrutinised the waste landscape, hoping to see a grazing animal or a wild dog. She sat back abruptly, disappointed. Nothing—Was there nothing out there? She knew there could be people out there, carefully hidden and camouflaged. Landry thought about her parent's decision not to enter the ration zones created by Radan after the great fall. She had not always understood her parent's decision. As a teenager, the homestead was too small, and the cities sounded exciting. They also represented safety, good medical care and free nutritional rations.

However, after living in the city, Landry now understood their reluctance. In the ration city, established family units could share accommodation, but once entering the city, only those selected for motherhood could have children and they kept those in the matern-district of each city. Her family could have lived together, but her brother may not have been so lucky. What might have happened to her nephews and sister-in-law?

The announcement of arrival broke Landry's reverie. As they crossed the line into the ration city of Edinburgh, the blue bio wall showing the entrance to the Radan city moved through the pod. It passed through Landry, making a small beep in recognition of who she was.

As she exited the sky train, she looked to Princes Street, once the blood vein of the city. The streets were empty now, a small number of people moving between their accom, and work and the establishments closed, unnecessary in the new order of things. Walking up to the taxi sky station, Landry held her tattoo over the censor. She saw two people in her periphery optic. They were walking towards her, murmuring as she stood waiting. The two men nodded to her as they passed. Was she being paranoid? Were they talking about her? The sky taxi arrived, breaking her thoughts. She stepped inside and sat. "Pencal," she stated, and the autonomous voice replied, "Pencal. 56 seconds."

The taxi pod idled and then started its rapid ascent into the air, making its way back through the bio net. A short bong indicated she entered the space outside of the city walls. Landry sat back and lifted her right-hand and stated, "video site Wynter Lund." The space just above Landry's right hand became translucent and blurred at first, clearing as Wynter appeared. "Hey Wynter".

With the wave of her hand, Landry pushed the image to her right-hand side and a full-size image of Wynter appeared sitting in the pod next to Landry. The translucent image of Wynter looked right, then left and stated, "Where are you?"

"I'm nearly at Pencal. Wanted time away from the city."

Landry saw the rise in Wynter's eyebrows. Wynter knew about Landry's earlier life before starting her job with Magera. Landry had never divulged the exact location, even to Wynter, but she could see Wynter's brain working overtime. There was a pause before Wynter spoke, but the meaning was clear.

"Are you sure you want to go there? I've heard that it's basic. Not much to see. But you've been there before, are the locals friendly?"

"The locals are friendly and I'm sure that they may remember me."

Wynter smiled. They had talked often of Landry returning to her off-grid home before in dark web conversations, but Landry had always dismissed it as too much of a risk.

"I hope that everyone is well. How long will you be there?"

"10 days. I want to have a break, so I am going to spend time in private mode. You know... have a complete break. Rest."

Wynter nodded her head, slowly, a conspiratory smile on her face.

"Well, I will miss you but take care of yourself. You make sure that you get to see everything in Pencal. "

Landry placed her hand on Wynter's holo-arm, "Of course, I will. I'll store up my diary entries and you can watch them when I get back."

"I'll look forward to that. Contact me as soon as you are back home in Birmingham." Wynter moved and they had an unprecedented and awkward holo hug.

Landry smiled, "I will be back soon- I promise."

Wynter's holo stepped back, "I will hold you to that promise. I hope you have a great time. I am jealous."

Landry looked directly at Wynter, "I will see you in 10 days. I will contact you as soon as I return."

Wynter nodded, "Make sure you do and if you need anything while you are on a rest break then don't hesitate."

Landry smiled at Wynter, swept her hand across her holo, closed her fist and ended the vid site. Her mind was racing. She hadn't yet moved across the threshold into the off-grid landscape. She knew that the consequence for herself and her family was huge.

Off griders had no tattoo, so no medical care or rations. To Radan they were unknown humans that couldn't be scanned, and this conflicted directly with its objectives. They couldn't force them to enter ration cities but entice them with free rations, virtual credits and accommodation. If discovered, her family might have to move to a new home. Radan would not relent until they entered a ration city. But that wouldn't be necessary. Landry felt she had thought through every precaution in her planning of the visit. For herself, the breaking of her contract with Magera could cause the termination of her employment. Although she was questioning Magera's motivation. Her suspension showed that the feeling may be mutual.

The pod announced its arrival in Pencal and slowed to a stop, the door opened. The clouds blotted out the warmth from the sun and the air felt cooler. Landry pulled her grahemo closer and raised her hood, covering her auditorus. It was noticeably quiet in Pencal and Landry could see the lights in the accommodation houses blinking on as she passed them. Landry was pleased to see more family units in this urbanisation. She could see many dual occupancy units and people eating their rations together. She began looking for the temporary lodge house she had communicated with.

Landry commanded, "Find lodging house. "The voice in her auditorus stated '30 yards ahead.' She found it promptly and her tattoo vibrated as she arrived at it. She scanned the street, pleased that there were many lodging houses. Landry walked up the steps at the front of the building, scanned her tattoo on the Radan symbol, and the door opened.

A voice announced, "pod 45/2 is available for Reagan2485."

A door swung open, and Landry made her way to 45/2. As she walked down the corridor, she became aware of muffled voices coming from the other rooms. 45/2 was a pod, identical to her accom in Birmingham.

Her chosen home voice spoke, "Welcome Reagan2485, ration no. 3 available."

Landry's rations would re-route to this accom until she left the premises at the end of her rest vacation. Her plan to go off-grid meant leaving them to pile up in her absence. When she returned, she'd deal with it. She was keen to get moving before she talked herself out of this. Since the sky station in Edinburgh nothing had concerned her enough to abandon her plans.

Placing her bag straps across both of her shoulders, she stated, "Private mode." She felt the familiar tingle of the loss of medi-support. She opened the window and climbed over the threshold. Checking left and right, she taped a small sheet of paper on the sensor of the window. Dropping, her feet touched the pavement. Above her, Landry heard the window try to swing shut. Three times, Landry heard the dull thud as the window attempted to lock and finally, it was still; left open just a slit. Her plan was in motion. As she walked around the back of the property, she peeked into the window of the accom next to her own and saw the occupant in their VR pod running at speed to an unknown destination. She wouldn't be missed.

Walking through the quiet streets, Landry made her way unobserved into the trees on the outskirts of the town and began the last part of her journey. Landry stopped at the blue medi-barrier. She knew from her research that in private mode it shouldn't even detect her. But she held her breath as she stepped through and exhaled, when she was on the other side.

Taking her time, she walked through the abandoned fragments of the once lush evergreen forests, keeping off the once major roads and pathways. The old fence lines, gateways, and farm sheds were overgrown with grass and trees after decades of misuse. The remnants of past lives, long forgotten now. Fallen trees lay across each other in her path, dead and leafless but not rotten. No forms of life, no insects to decompose the dead leaves or even worse dead animals. The bodies of small rodents long passed still lay where they had fallen; with no insects to aid decomposition, there they stayed. Time had frozen them where they lay. The smell was overwhelming at first, but as she moved on, it became less invasive. She listened for any sign of life, and three or four times thought she saw an insect, a bird or movement of a creature out of the corner of her optic only to be disappointed.

Landry continued walking east, occasionally coming across abandoned homesteads she used as markers. She was on the right track. When growing up off-grid, Landry knew this area well and was reassured that she could still distinguish the tracks. In the open space, Landry could see across fields where there has once been large-scale monoculture of plant-based food products. In the early days before the great fall, when the government had attempted to use the land for the growing of food. The plants had continued to sprout, leading to untidy piles of vegetation, with tubers and rhizomes hidden beneath. Landry instinctively made a note of the location, should a party want to forage later.

The sun was setting behind her as she entered a small clearing. A sound to her right stopped her in her tracks. Something was moving through the long grass. Landry stepped backwards to hide behind a large tree trunk, as the profile of a horse came into view. She froze as a voice broke the silence, "Hey, who goes there?"

Landry rapidly collated the multitude of scenarios and escape routes. The rider, obscured by the setting sun, prodded the horse forward, making

Landry back up into the clearing. As the horse got closer, she dove under the horse's neck and began running back through the tall grass.

CHAPTER 11

LANDRY REAGAN

"Landry?" A familiar voice stopped her in her tracks, "Landry, it's Harper."

Landry stepped back into the treeline and peered through the dappled leaves. Two men on horses moved towards her. Their relaxed gait told her that they were experienced horsemen. They wore simple clothes, leather boots and coats made of animal skin. No graphene here. She glanced up at their tanned faces and the front rider came into view.

Landry saw a face she recognised, but he was too old. Was that Harper? Surely not. He was a young boy when she left. As the second rider came into view, her heart constricted, and she took in a sharp breath as he came into view. With her heart still pounding in her ears, their eyes locked for the first time in years. She smiled instantly, and he leaned forward on his saddle shaking his head slowly. His dark hair fell forward, obscuring his expression. As he eased himself off his saddle, she noted his tanned muscular forearms and his long legs with the fabric of his trousers taut against the muscle.

She left the safety of the trees and stepped forward. She tried to keep her composure as he made his way toward her. She maintained a cool exterior, placing her shaking hand behind her back and leaning casually against the tree. She was conflicted but had little time to react. Harper had dismounted and overtook the older rider. Harper had no such poise and leapt towards Landry, encircling her in an enormous hug. In his over-excitement, they both fell to the ground laughing,

"Harper, you are so tall!" Landry's voice muffled by his clothing at his shoulder, "What happened?"

"I grew up," he laughed. He moved his head back and gestured towards the second rider, "so did he. Roan. "Landry chose not to answer, and they both climbed up from the ground and looked towards Roan.

Roan moved towards Landry and there was a moment of awkwardness as they hugged. As she turned into the embrace and his shoulder hit Landry squarely in the eye.

"Ow!" she laughed.

"Sorry Land, are you ok?" He placed his hand on her face where the impact of his shoulder had made its mark. Landry's face prickled with the pain, but his warm hand on her face restored feelings long buried. Landry's face burned hot, and she babbled, "I'm fine. I'm ok." She placed her hand on his broad chest and pushed. She needed space. Her life in the ration city rarely included physical contact. She noted a small ripple of confusion on Roan's face as he stepped back, but she smiled and turned towards Harper.

"What happened to you, Harper? When I left you were only my height, but now you're a giant."

"I know Land. Did you see how I rode Comet?" Without waiting for an answer, Harper ran off towards the two horses and swung himself aloft, the smaller of the two. "I'll tell the others." Harper raced off on Comet, leaving Roan and Landry alone.

"So which track did you take?"

"I headed east along the old rail track at first and into the woods until you and Harper found me."

Roan nodded, "The best way. Very little movement in that sector."

Landry's gaze fell on Roan, "Is traffic increasing?"

"Very few raiders now. The weak have given up and entered the ration cities and the stronger groups have their own communities. We do some trading occasionally.

Glancing at the sky, he replied, "Still get occasional Radan drones. Scouting, you know." Roan stopped and looked to the ground, "Land, I never thought that I'd see you again. Didn't think that you could return once you entered the city. How did you manage to leave?"

Roan saw the Radan tattoo on her wrist and instinctively grabbed her forearm to get a better look. His touch fizzled into her skin, but she pulled against him.

"Hey. It's in private mode. It won't be sending any signal. The last download was in a guesthouse in Pencal. I've taken every precaution. Do you think I would put everyone at risk?"

He grunted and looked away. They continued in companionable silence until Landry watched as her mother ran towards them; news travelled fast.

Her throat constricted as emotions of loss flooded in. So many times, she had thought about this moment but never sure that it would ever come. Her mother had aged, she could see that her hair was all grey and her movements were a little more laboured. She was enveloped into a huge hug and for one second, she fought the human contact then leant into the overwhelming comfort of the safety of her mother's arms.

"We've missed you so much," she exclaimed in Landry's auditorus. Landry leant into the hug and relished the warm comfort of physical contact. "I've missed this."

"Oh, so have I Land, so have I. "Landry felt the tears spring into her eyes as her mothers' soft sobs reverberated through their hug. Eventually, standing back, they scrutinised each other, holding each other at an arm's length.

"Are you ok Land? It's such a surprise. It everything all right? You could have warned us, sent a message." Landry's mother shook her head whimsically and smiling softly said, "No of course you couldn't tell us you were coming."

"I'm well and gosh you look good mother, you look well."

"You look thin, Land."

Landry laughing, "Yeh rations aren't what they advertised. Not great."

"Well, let's get you inside then and have proper food."

"I need to be careful mother; my body needs time to get used to food again."

"We'll see what we can do." They both walked off towards a gateway up ahead, carefully merging into the surrounding trees.

Landry took a moment to glance back before entering her home. Roan was leaning against his horse, watching them. As she entered, she unconsciously held up her tattoo to the doorframe and then smiled to herself as she realised her error. No Radan here.

The home was as much as she had left it. Her father sat near the food preparation unit sorting seeds on a table. Her heart swelled at the sight of him, and she ran forward. His eyes crinkled with a wide smile as he stood slowly, and she immediately sensed his difficulty, as he held the table for support. He looked considerably older.

"Hey there my lovely girl."

She stepped into the familiar comfort of his arms and squeezed. They stood in silence just taking in being close. Landry noted that his frame was smaller, and her arms could easily stretch around his torso. She kissed him on the side of his face, "Hey dad."

Her mother fussed around in food preparation area and started pouring glasses of water, "Sit you two." Landry dropped her bag onto the seat in the living unit and then sat across the table from her father. Her mother joined them at the table.

"What a lovely surprise is everything ok? What has happened? How are things? How is the project?"

"Slow down, love," Dad placed his hand on her mother's arm, "Let Landry speak."

"Well, I had some time on my hands and just felt the need to visit. I miss you so much." She glanced between both her parents, a rush of emotion engulfing her.

A frown crept up her father's face, "Everything alright at Magera?"

Hesitantly Landry said, "Yes. Everything's great. I've begun finding 60% positive impact evidence. There is some research at Birmingham University in the early 21st century. Growth forests as carbon sinks that I think we could act upon."

"Sounds fantastic. So, you're here to tell us they will act on it soon and change the timeline. "He smiled, "Maybe I can give up my farming soon." He raised his arms and laughed.

"Well, no, sorry dad. They don't agree with my findings, although I am sure that they could become over 90% positive impact if they acted."

Her mother placed her hand on Landry's, "Well, you just need to tell them they're wrong. Landry can convince them, I'm sure, can't she, Ned?"

"That was what I was trying to do, and I got suspended."

She waited for the shock, but her father's face crinkled into a bemused smile, "Really? Why? I can't imagine you upsetting anyone, Land."

"Well, I got frustrated that they didn't listen to me, and I spoke to my supervisor incorrectly and so they suspended me."

"What did you say?"

"I just explained why they were wrong and that they needed to look at it again. That was the wrong thing to say."

Her father's laugh filled his face as he shook his head, chuckling to himself.

As her mother went out to share the news that she had returned, Landry sat at the table with her father, talking about her work visiting the past. It was a moment to cherish as father and daughter caught up with their news, their closeness as strong as ever. Her father listened intently as she told him news from around the World. She was just sharing the news of the urbanisation of New Earth on Mars when they were interrupted by the sounds of her brother Deren, his partner Talia, and her nephews, Honor, and Taylen arriving at the house.

The bustling chatter and warmth of her family surrounded her. There was so much to talk about. During her absence there had been many changes, great successes and some failures. They shared food-plenty together. Landry was careful not to eat too much, although it was hard as it looked and smelled so good. There was little variety; mainly root vegetables and fruit, but they were a welcome change from rations.

"What is it like? The ration city? "Deren asked, and silence descended around the table. None had ever ventured past the boundary of their homestead and were keen to hear of life in the city.

"It is not as exciting as you imagine. Its lonely. Most people never leave their accom if they don't have to and as Radan gives us everything, we need then…"

"Can you stay in your reparation comfort all day then?" Taylen's youthful voice rang out, and the adults laughed.

Landry looked at the big brown eyes of her nephew, looking up at her expectantly. "Yes, I suppose I could. If I wanted."

Talia pulled her son towards her in an embrace, "The medical care must be amazing."

Landry raised her arm and showed the tattoo on her wrist. The occupants of the table all leaned forward. Landry had their full attention. "This is where medical information from my body flows through to the medi-support provided by Radan. It enables me to get my rations and other items that I might need as well. When I am connected, it monitors my health and if I need cell reparation or vitamins, nanotech regeneration is sent straight to the tissue needing repair. There was a shared gasp from Landry's family.

Deren sighed, "It looks like your branded- like our horses. Strange. Does it feel strange? Did it hurt when your optics and audio were surgically enhanced?"

"No. I love my new optics. The enhancements mean I can see everything in such detail and my auditorus gives me 5 times natural hearing. "

Deren tapped his son's arm, laughing. "You cannot hide anything from Aunty Land, Taylen."

Landry interrupted, "I am in private mode. You can rest easy and talk normally."

"Must be peculiar, being monitored."

"At first yes but you get used to the medic updates and you can turn off the audio updates. You can never be without it though. It is how I am identified by the security bots and transport pods."

Taylen eyes wide, stated, "It's how you get to use virtual reality games and speak to people."

Talia's head snapped right, and she questioned her son, "How do you know that?"

"I heard Ark and Dese talking about ration cities and how cool they are. Can you tell me more about the VR tech so I can tell them? They've not met anyone from an actual city. They are going to be impressed."

"Not now though", Talia exclaimed, "its time you had your reparation bisec, both of you. Let's leave the adults to talk." The two boys whined, but as Talia left the table, they both took a hand and waved goodbye. The rest of the household sent their wishes for good reparation, and Landry stared after them. She had missed seeing children. Her mother moved into the food preparation area, and they left Landry with her brother and father.

"So," Deren started, "What is it like in the city? What was Earth like in the past?"

"I love the research and going back to the 21st century is so strange. It's hard to describe, but it's a lot like the images in the history books. Going back is getting easier but the people are strange. They're so selfish and only think about themselves and how much money they can earn but they're also so free. They can do what they want, eat what they want, and they just love spending time together, and sharing things. It reminds me of home.

But living in the present time and in the ration city is just terrible. I understand why Radan set them up after the Great Fall and it was necessary to make sure that there would be enough food, but they have become places full of VR addicts who spend most of their time in other realities. Most don't have to work. Radan has automated services and so they are in the city with nothing to do. It can be very lonely. I'm lucky, I have friends in Magera."

"So, we made the right decision, staying?" her father declared.

Landry nodded. "Now I've seen the cities, I think you have made the right decision."

Deren shook his head. "The physical work is tough on us. It's difficult here for us, and dad, it's hard for you." Deren glanced across at his father.

Landry's father tutted, "I'm alright. A few twinges here and there."

"A few twinges dad- you know it's more than that." Deren paused and then said, "Dad, you know you need medical attention. Landry, can you get medicine from the ration city? Dad needs it."

Landry's father placed his hand on Deren's arm, "Stop Deren. I'm fine, just getting older. "His glistening eyes met hers, but Deren was shaking his head.

Reluctantly, Landry explained. "I can't get medicine for anyone Deren, only myself and even then, I can't request it. You need a tattoo that constantly checks your body and uses nanobots or gene therapy to rectify anything. You cannot fake symptoms, some have tried. Radan's protocols are infallible. What medicine do you think you need?"

"I need nothing." Landry's father protested.

"You do, dad. You know you do." Deren's voice rose.

"We- are- not- talking- about- this -now." Landry's father's feelings on the matter were clear. The conversation was closed. They moved on to other things, but Landry made a mental note to speak to Deren again.

Deren probed further, "Are you safe though Landry?"

"Yes, completely, there are no police bots anymore. There is no crime. Even everything at the ration outlet establishments is free."

"Everything?" Deren shook his head, smiling, "Not like here then."

Landry continued, "Everything that you might need to keep you alive; rations, clothing, VR credits."

"Wow, everything free- that sounds great, doesn't it dad?" Deren looked to his father.

"No, not great." Her father exclaimed, "when everything's free, what do you value?"

Landry saw the tension between the two men. "It's not what you imagine, Deren. There are no children. Not everyone can have a child. Only those selected can be parents, and then the children are billeted in special family units. You can't just have children anymore. You may not even be able to live with Honor and Taylen."

Visibly shocked, Deren asked, "Who decides who can have a child?"

"Radan. Radan processes everything. They did not select even my friend Wynter for breeding. She would have been an exceptional mother, but she has no choice. She will never have a family because they don't deem her to be eligible to be a mother."

Landry's father became more animated. "Deren. What have I been telling you? What right has Radan got to make those decisions for us?"

"No right morally dad, but according to our government, every right. You know the history. When the government introduced the Centralised Suburbanisation Act, which caused the Pangaust Policy. Radan made selections of what urbanisations were chosen, the mass movement of people needed organisation. The Great Fall was inevitable, and after the Great Fall, Radan saved us, restored order and continues to do so. "

Landry shrugged. She could sense their indignation and was embarrassed to be defending Radan. "If you have a lack of food production and you aim to preserve human life, then you restrict the number of people being born. Its mathematics."

"It sounds rubbish to me. Can't you do something?" Deren's accusing stare riled Landry." We're only just surviving here, you know - it's hard living."

Old rivalries with her brother reasserted themselves. "We ARE doing something; we will find the key that stops the climate from warming and the Great Fall. As if it never happened so that everyone can live a life with plentiful food, and people could live as families."

Landry could feel her temper rising and her father's voice cut through, "Stop Deren. Do you think your sister isn't trying her best? The reason that she is here is that they have suspended her for insubordination."

Their father's intervention worked. "Honestly?" Her brother smiled. "Well, good for you Land. Keep fighting the fight, then." He laughed loudly and with the equilibrium restored, the rest of the evening passed uneventfully. Landry was enveloped by the love of her family and more content than she had been for some time.

Landry spent the next few days following the routines of the homestead and helping where she could. Inhabitants of the homestead had to contribute to the farming of their food and other tasks, and Landry was no exception. It had never been her favourite when she had grown up there but now returning. she relished the normal conversations of her fellow homesteaders, the human contact, and she found she enjoyed answering their questions about her new life in the city and what travelling to the past was like. Her muscles ached from the hard labour of subsistence farming but working towards a common goal refreshed her and she realised how much she had missed it.

Her father was struggling with even menial tasks, and she suspected he had asthenia as he was often fatigued and sometimes; she saw his arm muscle spasm. He must have anaemia, she thought to herself. She could see how pale he was, and she knew that the vegetarian diet required iron additives or plant-based iron ingredients. When she entered Birmingham in 2181, she was treated for anaemia within hours of entering. They were all suffering from it, but his age would make it even harder to manage.

By the third day, Landry was into the rhythm of life on the farm.

"Dad, let me do that for you." She took the paddle from his hand and helped him to lower himself onto a chair by the side of the field.

As there were no insects to pollinate most of the fruit, they had to do it, and it was a job she always enjoyed. She was busy using paddles to grab the pollen from stamen from the raspberry bushes and then transferring it to an adjacent bush when a voice stopped her in her tracks.

"You're not doing it right." Roan stood behind her and put down a barrow that he had been pushing. His tanned forearms, sprinkled with dark hairs, folded across his chest and his face gave nothing away.

"What do you mean? It was my method that we adopted." Landry turned to face Roan.

"We've improved on your method and made it more efficient. We use the two paddles and sweep back like this." He pushed her to the side and demonstrated it. She grabbed the paddles out of his hands and began following his example.

"Thank you for your help." Through gritted teeth, she hid her grimacing red face behind her long fringe and continued. The conversation was over, Landry purposely didn't glance in his direction, but she knew his eyes were on her as he stood for some time watching her using his method. Eventually, he moved away, "What is his problem?" She sighed to herself.

On the 5th day, there was always the homestead gathering. Initially, it was a method of sharing the precious foodstuffs that people grew in their small plots or foraged. The homesteaders bought what they had, and each week, one home took the responsibility of sharing the spoils. It was a gathering to share news of events outside that the watchers picked up on when talking to other homestead communities. The news of Landry's return was joyous, and the gathering had special significance. Landry had nothing to add to the feast. Rations were basic, inedible, and there was no way of gaining the extra that she could have bought with her. She wished she had broken Magera rules and bought something back from an assignment. She had seen seeds in 2015 whilst on assignment; hundreds of packets of origin seeds for a vast variety of organic food production and florals as well. Here amongst her family now, she identified the shame of not being brave enough to bring even one packet with her. With newly found brashness, she resolved that next time, she would bring seeds back.

Her move to Birmingham had been an easy one but returning now, she understood why the others stayed. Landry's hopes and dreams for her new role had kept her in the ration city. Now, she realised what she had missed. Some friends had made serious relationships with others and even had become parents themselves. She had become so wrapped up in changing the past that she hadn't considered her own future. She thought for the first time what she would do Magera were not successful and stop climate change. She put aside her thoughts of Magera for now and enjoyed the moment of being amongst friends and family.

Roan stood just outside the seating areas talking to his brother Harper and several others including some young girls, Harpers' age. Roan was an impressive figure and Landry could see the girls admired him. When Landry left the homestead, they had been close. Spending much of their time together working on the farm and exploring the woodland around the homestead. They had made a great team; they were the ones who found the wild horses and brought them into the community.

However, when Landry had gone to Birmingham, she knew that Roan hadn't agreed with her decision. As much as she had tried to bring it up, they had never spoken about it and a distance had developed between them. This distance had remained and following the conversation earlier in the day, she felt even further away from the Roan. She had expected him to be interested in her life in Birmingham and adventures. She had imagined them sitting amongst the trees or working in the fields talking about what she had seen and experienced, but no. He was distant and subdued. Landry knew he had a lot of responsibility in the community. Had he changed from the carefree boy that she had left? As the gathering was ending, Landry sat with her mother, listening to the stories of her life as a child, before the Centralised Urbanisation Act and the terrible time of the Great Fall.

As she turned to leave the gathering house, she caught Roan's eye and held his gaze. As her parents began making plans to go to their home, Landry decided it was time to talk. Roan had been a good friend, his behaviour confused her. Landry approached the group that he was with, "Can we talk somewhere?"

He turned and took a moment, "Yeh sure." They walked towards the farm wall in silence and sat on the wall looking at the fields and the distant skyline.

"I'm confused. Can you help me?" Landry turned to face him and continued, "We were friends, but since I have come back, you've barely spoken to me."

Are you staying or going back to Birmingham?" His question was abrupt.

"I'm going back, of course. Why do you ask?"

Roan stared at the sky for some time before he spoke. "When you left, it was hard. I lost my best friend. You disappeared Land ..." He flung his arm out, pointing into the distance. "I had no way of contacting you or visiting you. I did not think you'd ever return."

"I'm so sorry Ro. I didn't think about what might happen in the future. I didn't really know what I was going to be doing if I'm honest. I know you always wanted more, and I knew you would have to get on with your life without me. I was expecting to find you all settled down now and hoped that we could still be friends."

Roan shook his head. "You knew how I felt about you leaving. Why would you think those feelings would be different now? Ah what's the point," he shrugged, "You'll be going back in a few days, and I'm left here. Will you ever come back?" There was a tremor in his voice.

Her own emotions surfaced. She swallowed her tears, "I don't know the answer to that question."

Landry watched as his face contorted and then with his features set and his chin rigid, his cool anger surfaced, "Exactly, so why are we even talking?"

Landry wanted him to recognise the sense of duty that she placed upon herself. "I have work to do. Magera is committed to trying to stop the great fall. You know about this. I want to change it for everyone."

His outburst shocked Landry "You want, you want, what about what I want? Have you ever thought about me?"

"What you want? Go on, tell me then. What is it YOU want because you never tell me what you want."

Roan's head dropped and then breathing out, he looked back across the farm, "Forget it Land, just forget it. Look I get it. I know what you're trying to achieve, and I admire you so much for that but a part of me just wants you to stay here with us. I miss you Land. But we're stuck in this no-win situation, and it kills me Land. She stepped forward her arm outstretched but he wouldn't make eye contact and he stood up abruptly and strode off towards the family section.

"Roan!" Landry shouted, but he ignored her and continued to move off into the night. Her chest rising and falling with intense emotion, Landry watched as he disappeared into the distance.

CHAPTER 12

WYNTER LUND

Leaving the quiet of the laundry cupboard in the basement of the Langham Hotel, in 2033, Wynter made her way outside into the warm sunshine. It was April, and the UK was experiencing another spring heatwave. Wynter felt out of place in her long-sleeved cotton vest amid the Londoners in their short garments.

Wynter was looking forward to a constructive day following her visit in 2018. The research on SAM was vague and being here would provide information about the actual numbers and demographic of their supporters. She spotted some immediately moving through the street. Supporters trailing banners and flags in the blue colours, walking down the impressive Regent Street, singing or shouting, "Act- now, Act now" and "never too late!"

Wynter found herself caught up with a group, enjoyed watching their closeness as they walked and listened to their talk about the rally ahead. She spotted several children in the crowd and scrutinised them out of the corner of her optics. Their mannerisms fascinated her, and their language appeared so developed for their age.

Wynter reflected on the change in London in just 15 years. The once-bustling shopping in Regent Street was no longer dominated by retail establishments. Three-dimensional product placement advertising for consumers and government motive strategy messages now dwarfed the old facades. The sound and Images were an onslaught to Wynter's optics and auditorii. She struggled to watch the media messages and keep up her progress along the street. She jumped to the side as a holo-generated man blocked her path, demanding that she move forward. She stopped, startled.

"Keep moving" he shouted, sweeping his arms down both his sides.

She redirected her attention forward and kept pace with her fellow supporters. She could detect the beginnings of the changing landscape of the city, pre- the great fall. London was beginning to change merchandising units into residential properties to accommodate the influx of people into the city.

As they made their way along Regent Street, the elegant curve of the buildings came into view. A repeated security message flashed across the length of the grand facade of the Georgian buildings. "This is a peaceful demonstration. You are being monitored. Be prepared for security checks. This is a peaceful demonstration. You are being monitored. Be prepared for security checks. "Airbourne Security drones zipped in and out of the crowd scanning faces and Wynter had to resist the urge to duck as they came close. She needed to appear confident in her ambiguity.

In 2033, the security databases scrutinised the crowd for known criminals only. The personal privacy act of 2025 enabled non-criminals to move freely through the capital. She was an unknown and therefore no-criminal. There were security operatives ahead, funnelling the main surge of the crowd through gateways up towards Oxford Circus. The group that Wynter was with stepped through the scan doorway and Wynter followed tentatively. *Will my implant set off an alarm?* No lights flashed or sirens wailed as she made her way through.

The heightened presence of security was much more than she had expected. Had she underestimated the crowd size in her planning for this assignment? It was much bigger than the rally in 2018. This would provide Magera with superb evidence, and she focussed her attention on gathering as much as she could.

The crowd swelled as others joined the fray from other streets. The lights and glare of Piccadilly Circus were stunning. Wynter felt so small against the might of the crowd as she continued her watchful evidence gathering. Huge emergency drones hovered overhead, their thundering wings buzzing like giant bees, as the supporters made their way past the theatres in the Haymarket and into Pall Mall. As she turned the corner towards Trafalgar Square, she saw the Kallan Flood Towers ahead of her in the distance. They were not yet complete, but the enormity of the towers struck Wynter on the skyline of 2033 London. London, circa 2188, those same towers were dwarfed by the rising accommodation blocks which now dominated the skyline. These flood defences were far more sophisticated than the original domes that had failed in the '20s, but they were being built on top of the wonderful old buildings of the Horse Guard parade. Wynter had spent much of her time studying statistics for the flood rises in London but seeing the reality of the fight with the river was sobering.

She could hear the roars and chants from Trafalgar Square in the distance. A SAM representative was heckling the crowd, "What do we want? What do we demand? What do we want? What do we demand?" The crowd returned each question with a prompt reply of "More" and "Action now."

The Square was overrun with supporters, SAM flags hung from every available statue and sculpture, and flags encased the columns of what had been the national Gallery with the blue of the SAM flag prominent. People sat on every wall, fountain edge, and any step that they could find. Supporters had jumped up onto the plinths and were leaning against the bronze lions or sitting on the ledges.

Security drones zipped around the crowd and Wynter heard drones demanding that people allow the drone cameras to scan them. The artificial tones of the drone voices were lost amongst the buzz of the crowd. The mood was high and as Wynter made her way towards the steps of the National Gallery, people let her through, and said "Hello", or "Welcome", as she moved through them. Supporters sat in groups sharing food products, children ran through the groups holding flags and banners, and others held devices in front of them, talking into them and recording the event.

She found a good vantage point near the podium for the key presenters. She needed her optics and auditorii to have an unobstructed sound and view. Turning to scan the crowd, she attempted to record an accurate crowd number. There were several other speaker spots where supporters were denser and in other areas people were more scattered. Wynter stood in an empty spot, but she knew that this would not last once the speeches started.

Carly Albright stepped up to the podium and glancing in Wynter's direction, she then swept her gaze across the Square. It struck Wynter, how much she had aged since she had last seen her. Her eyes were ringed with black shadows and time had ravaged her. As Carley sorted through notes in front of her, a ripple of quiet made its way through the crowd and music flooded the square and images cast across the walls of the National Gallery from an immense lunar projector.

These images differed from 2018. Gone were the beautiful land and seascapes of Earth. Gone were the endless glacial scopes. The images in 2033 were foreboding, mass floods, wildfires, deforested wastelands and desertification of once lush green valleys. These images were more familiar to Wynter, yet she found they had a sobering effect on the crowd. Despite small pockets of conversation, most of the crowd turned towards the main imager and grew silent.

Carly stepped forward, raising her hands in the air and shouted," Thank you, thank you for coming today, thank you for still caring." She paused, "I planned my speech today and found myself full of despair but seeing you all gives me renewed hope. Maybe we are not too late to salvage some form of societal change. Thank you for giving light in the darkness." The crowd cheered, and individuals shouted reassurance, "There is hope", and "We can still help."

"But." Carly paused and placed both hands forward in the air in a signal to STOP and shouted, "But stop, I do not make these messages today in hope, but with the reality of the position becoming evident. No longer can we bury our heads in the sand. No longer can we think that this will not happen, the evidence is all around us, the predictions made by ourselves, and scientists are coming true, and we can no longer rely upon an alternative future than the one that faces us today."

Wynter looked around at the audience and scoffed. The human condition for hope until there was none was admirable, but it amused her. It will go wrong and when it does, how will all these people cope then?

Carly continued, "The people of the Netherlands have had to take action, their low-lying properties lost to the water." An image appeared on the screen of waterlogged communities. "However, they have been building flood-proof homes for the last decade." An image of a neighbourhood of new homes filled the screen, "This won't be enough."

Wynter saw Robert Sanchez make his way from the door of the National Gallery and stand just behind Carly and striding after him, two young women. As Carly continued, Wynter tried to keep her optic visual focused on Carly, but her attention was drawn to Robert.

Carly looked behind her at the imager before returning to her speech, "The modern cities in the Arabian deserts are reliant on solar power and need no other power sources. Amazing places where people work and live and where food products, waste measures and transport are environmentally sound." A viz image of a viewpoint of someone moving through an impressive new city appeared on the screen. "It looks wonderful, doesn't it?" The crowd murmured in agreement, "It's wonderful if you have two million pounds to live there!" The crowd gasped, and Carly paused, "But even with these cities, it's still not enough. It is not enough to stop Earth's warming. It's not enough to stop people from dying, and it's not enough to stop the disaster that is upon us."

Wynter studied Robert as he stood, glancing at his notes and fiddling with the collar of his shirt. The two young girls, Wynter presumed to be around 18years had grown and were much taller. They had changed. They had grown into beautiful young women.

The view on the imager changed to waves crashing onto the beach and waves crashing against cliffs. "Recent reports from the Inter-governmental Congress on Global Warming have stated that the collapse of the West Antarctic Ice Sheet will raise the mean sea level globally. This will affect all of us. Are we prepared to give up the coastal cities in the World?"

The audience shouted "no."

"Osaka?"

"No"

Carly continued, shouting the names of each city and the crowd responded no to each of them. "Venice? Shanghai? Alexandria? Rio de Janeiro? New York? Miami? London, Bristol, Norwich?"

She couldn't draw her attention away from him and the harder she tried the more it swung back. Wynter shouted "no" to each city, and she saw that Robert did too. In the final three, no's, their eyes met, and she saw a quizzical look in his eyes. Surely, he did not recognise her. He had aged 15 years, and she remained the same.

Carly continued, "Millions of people are going to be displaced and those cities are in poor countries in the world where governments have not informed their people of the impending disaster coming to them. The Inter-governmental Congress on Global Warming predicts a 3-degree rise at the end of this century. That far exceeds the original predictions, and so scientists are trying to work out possible new scenarios. It will be worse than we first thought."

Carly paused and let the information sink in as images of recent flooding in Bangladesh, and typhoons in the Philippines flashed across the screen.

"For us, it's going to be terrible. For the animal kingdom, it is going to be catastrophic!" Images of creatures in the sea, the land and the air, filled the imager. "It is not a pleasure for me to introduce our environmental scientist, Dr Robert Sanchez, because I know what he has to say. I need to stress to you that all that he shares today is scientific facts and current findings. Please welcome our eminent movement supporter and Hester and Isobel; both students at the London University of global sciences." Warm applause rippled through the crowd.

As he stepped up, Wynter could sense his newfound confidence. He grabbed the podium and raised his voice, reaching out to the crowd. "Imagine a world with no insects, no insect pollination of plants, no insects decomposing the waste piles of dead matter littering the Earth." Images showing barren landscapes appeared.

"No insects in the food chain, no birds, no small mammals. No small mammals, no land animals. Everything on our planet is connected by a complex system, carefully balanced and it works, doesn't it? But we are destroying the life support system of our planet. "An image of thousands of dead bison appeared, and there was a murmur of shock and distaste that swelled through the crowd in outrage. "I don't want to show you these images, but you need to see them. Burying our heads in the sand is no longer an option."

"What can we do?" someone shouted.

"Tell us what to do." someone shouted.

Robert looked towards the crowd and said, "There is nothing we can do." The crowd gasped, surely not. Wynter was shocked by the change in his approach and Robert continued, "The end has begun. Scientists have studied the effect of heat on many varieties of beetles, and the increased temperatures have already made them infertile. That research is already out of date as temperatures are hitting higher than even their research temperatures. Those of you that drive long distances, how many insects die on your windscreens now? When did you have to swat away wasps or bees? Think about it. They have been declining slowly. Most have not noticed, but we have. "Robert looked to the two younger women behind him, "We've been collating studies from around the world and the message is the same. Repeated and again, and across every continent. No habitat is immune. "

There was a hush as the crowd quietened. He had their attention.

"We are staring into the mouth of the lion, and it is the end of the World as we know it. We talk about a World changed by humans, but I want to quote E.O.Wilson, the naturalist and prophet of environmental degradation, He describes this event as the age of loneliness. When humanity survives but at the expense of all other life on this planet." A shout from the crowd, "It is not true. It cannot be true." There was a swell of noise at people all spoke at once.

Silence. Wynter wanted to shout out at the top of her lungs. It's true. Everything that he is saying is true.

Isobel, Robert's sister stepped forward, "Wait! We did not come here to scare you… Humans will survive. Some of us can live on wind-pollinated plants and the ecosystems of the oceans could survive. If the sea acidity remains tolerable and the coral lives." She raised her eyebrows. "However, current data is showing us that humankind will survive but at the expense of the animal kingdom." There were shouts from the crowd and she continued, " I think we can all agree that a world without the beauty of a snow leopard or the grace of a hawk… isn't worth living in."

Murmurs of "no," and resignation spread through the crowd, and this spurred Isobel on. With Robert's arm supporting her, she continued, "There is some small hope. If we act now, if we can halt the damage that has already been done, then we may save some species. There are plans for an international effort to create sanctuaries for many species. We are working with the Ark for de-extinction. We will attempt to save as many as we possibly can. We don't want to shock you, but we cannot lie to you either. Governments have spent too long doing that already. It is time to act." Isobel and Robert raised their fists in the air and others did the same. "Let's fight this with all that we have… Let's fight." They raised their fists again and there were claps and whoops around the crowd.

Wynter observed the change in Robert's face as soon as he left the podium. He looked deflated. Wynter fought an urge to approach him, but she knew that what she had to say would not help him. He was accurate in what he was saying, and if Magera were unsuccessful, then it would all come true. She knew it. She lived it every day. Wynter watched, as he made his way behind the podium and stood on the steps of the national gallery with the two girls standing in front of him. Their confidence and familiar closeness were like a drug to Wynter. Something that she had never experienced. She knew she was risking compromising her position and the implication for the timeline, but she was compelled to continue. She moved around the podium towards the threesome.

Carly took her position to address the crowd. "Thank you, Robert, for being so honest and telling us how it is. How long do we truly have? I'm hoping to answer that today. I want to talk to you about Hothouse Earth, where the Earth tips into a state that we cannot return from. That threshold would lead to a much higher global average temperature than any interglacial in the past 1.2 million years and sea levels higher than in recorded history. We know there is a threshold that might exist and then we could reach it. I'm here to tell that we haven't reached that stage yet, but we are close."

Shouts of "What can we do? What must happen?" came out of the crowd. It spread and people joined in the chant, "Save our Earth. Save Our Earth, Save Our Earth,"

"Government agencies around the world are working hard to reach their Inter-governmental Congress on Global Warming targets. We have done that. We have made that happen. We are going to make sure that they do not ignore us any longer – "

Carly's voice froze in her throat. There was a blinding flash, like sheet lightning and a thunderclap. Close, too close. A fireball moved forward, flattened everything and Wynter felt a 'Whump 'of physical contact as she was forced forward onto the ground. Feeling something like hot grit in her mouth and her optics, heat rushing across her back, forced her to press her face further into the dirt. Then silence.

It didn't last long. As her auditori rebooted itself, sounds were muffled, and then the volume increased until a crescendo. A howl of people screaming, shouting, the roar of walls collapsed, glass smashing. Wynter blinked, and through the twitching slit through her eyelashes, she observed the scene. From her position on the floor, she could see through the dust, enormous lumps of charred masonry. Pieces of burning paper and cloth were floating down from the sky. She attempted to lift her head. Her mouth was full of dust, and she tasted what she thought was the acrid taste of blood. She looked around her immediate area and shifted herself upwards, placing her arm underneath her and pushing into a sitting posture. Her head swam as she attempted to take in what she was seeing. Where there had been people standing, all were now on the ground. Some in the foetal position with their hands up against their ears and heads. Others splayed like rag dolls, unmoving. All covered in fine grit. She looked up towards the steps of the Gallery where she had last seen Robert. There was a huddle of bodies lying on the steps. She recognised the boots of one of them and crawled over to it. Grabbing the legs and moving up the body. It was one of Robert's sisters. Her arm was laying at an awkward angle across her body and as Wynter reached for a pulse in her neck, her emerald eyes were wide open. Lifeless. Next to her lay her sister, her auburn hair strewn, framing her face and stained with dried blood. Wynter lay her hand on her chest, hoping for it to rise or fall; nothing. She moved forward to decide if she was dead when she heard a groan just to her left. Underneath his sisters lay Robert. He was stirring and gasping for breath. Ignoring all her training Wynter moved towards him and positioned herself kneeling next to him. "Robert." She said, He didn't respond, "Robert" she shouted. His head moved in her direction, and he attempted to open his eyes. He looked up at Wynter.

"Esther?", he croaked.

"No."

"Isobel, Esther?" He attempted to place his arm next to him to push himself up. Wynter realised his shirt was covered in blood. She placed her hand on his chest and pushed him down. Panic rose inside Wynter, this was all wrong. She shouldn't be doing any of this, but her humanity wouldn't let her watch from the side-lines.

"Lie still, Robert. You need to lie still."

He became agitated, attempting to get up again. Wincing in pain, he dropped onto his back.

"Robert. You need to lie still. The medics are coming. Lie still." The blood on his chest was spreading at an alarming rate and she placed her hand where she felt the wound was to stem the flow. "Robert Sshhh. Quiet now." She felt the pulse on his wrist. It was weak.

In her panic, she grabbed his wrist looking for the Radan medic Tattoo and realising her error dropped his wrist and shouted "Medic!" Her hoarse voice tried to compete with the shrieks and cries for help around her. "Medic!"

She looked at Robert as he mouthed the names of his sisters again, Esther, Isobel.

She leant forward, "They are OK, Robert. They're getting help." Her voice broke as the lie choked her. "Just lay still, Robert. Help is coming." He stopped his attempts to get up and lay back, looking into Wynter's eyes. He was trying to say something. She leant forward and placed her auditorus close.

"Tell them I love them." He whispered.

"No, no you tell them", Wynter cried. She looked around, "Medic!" She turned back to face Robert. His chest had stopped rising, falling, and his eyes were staring straight ahead, unseeing.

CHAPTER 13

WYNTER LUND

"NOoooo!" Wynter screamed. This was wrong. This was all wrong. This shouldn't have happened. She moved closer to Robert, tilted his head back and began resuscitation. With each breath, bubbles of blood frothed through the open wound in his chest.

Placing her free hand on his chest to stop the blood. She leant forward again. "Come on, Robert," She shouted between breaths. "Stay here, Robert." She continued, her anger fuelling her forward. She began pulsing her hands upon his chest with force. The blood seemed to increase with each pulse. "No." She shouted. She heard sirens coming closer but continued. Four breaths, pause each time. Four pushes down hard on the chest. She leant forward and placed her head near to Robert's mouth, for any sign of life. "Come on, Robert." She shouted. She punched his chest hard and was about to start her next breaths for Robert when a hand wrenched at her arm and a voice, "He's gone love. I'm sorry but he's gone." Wynter looked to her left at a man in a green medic uniform.

"Help him, please," Her voice cracked. She moved aside to allow him to examine Robert. The medic spoke. "I'm sorry, but he is deceased. The wound in his chest is..."

In her confusion she almost gave herself up. "But he can be saved, you need to get a medic Bot life resuscitator here. It can save him." He stared at her quizzically.

"He is past saving I'm afraid. You did your best. He wouldn't have survived his injuries. I'm sorry. Are you ok?" His attention turned to Wynter, and started running his hands up and down her arms, placing his hand on her wrist and checking her pulse, "Did you know him?"

"N nn no. He's Dr. Sanchez. He is a ... was a scientist."

He placed his hand gently on her face and turned her attention away from Robert, "I'll take care of him now. You need to get some medical treatment yourself." He pointed to her upper arm where blood had seeped through her shirt. She stood up with his help and raising her eyes from the floor. Wynter took in the scene for the first time.

The blast had made a vast crater in the middle of the square, and on the edges of the crater lay what was left of people. They looked like the petals of a flower around the centre. Wynter averted her eyes. Even from that glance, she could see they were beyond any help. Water was running out through an opening of a damaged fountain, turning redder and redder with blood and body parts. The uniformed man moved on and Wynter's optics were drawn to Robert's sisters and Carly. They had taken the full force of the blast. Their lifeless forms lay twisted and blackened. A horrific sight. Wynter forced herself to look away.

She sat on an empty patch of rubble and took in some steady breaths. Wynter began trying to assess what had happened and what she needed to do now. Something wasn't right. This had not appeared in her pre-assignment research, and that was never wrong. How did this happen? She needed to get back to the time doorway now!

Joining the throngs of injured people drifting through the debris, Wynter began moving away from the Square. On reaching Regent Street, she picked up the pace, spurred on by her need to find out. Some past participants tried to stop her. A look of concern on their faces or for some suspicion. Her expression deterred anyone considering approaching her. She needed to get back to 2188. Get out of here and find out what had happened today. It was a bomb or explosion, but who? And why? She needed answers. Her anger simmered, as she accelerated up Chandos Street and into the back entrance of the Langham hotel. She ran straight into a cleaner coming out. Having lost her ID badge in the blast, a cleaner started to protest, then saw Wynter and her anger turned to concern. "Are you OK?" she asked. Wynter ignored her question and continued forward. Aware that the cleaner was scrutinising her as she ran down the corridor and entered the cupboard. Hands shaking, she placed her tattoo on the wall, and it shimmered into life. It was a relief that she could still travel after all that had happened. Letting out a slow, laboured breath as the Magera system activated. Wynter stepped forward and walked through into 2188.

She reached the other side and halted. The Magera symbol spun on the screen in front of her but in the distance, her auditorii picked up the distinctive wailing of the alert siren. As the screen stuttered into life,

Wynter heard the voice of Kyson Mullins, raised and agitated. "Lund2602- WHAT HAVE YOU JUST DONE?"

Wynter reeled back in alarm, "I've just done?"

"We've experienced a 0.67 timeline adjustment wave. It's swept past us fast. We studied it coming on the monitors but couldn't stop it. WHAT DID YOU DO LUND2062?"

"Nothing, I did nothing. It all happened so fast."

An medi-alarm bonged in both Wynter's and Kyson's auditorus as Wynter´s Radan medic update re-started.

"Requiring immediate attention - recommend immediate emergency medical intervention."

Kyson looked up towards the screen, "Explain. What happened?"

"An explosion, a bomb." Wynter glared at the screen defiantly. "There was a bomb blast! How did the pre-time protocols do not show a potential loss of life?"

"What assignment are you working on?" Kyson raised her voice higher.

Wynter's memory failed, and she jabbered, "the number is…. 345.5 no 345.2 sorry."

Kyson became preoccupied with her screen to the left. The siren still shrilling in both of their auditorii, "Did you follow all protocols Lund 2062? There was no reference to any bomb when your assignment brief passed through the Radan system. "

Wynter saw Kyson turn and shout to an unseen employee, "Shut off that siren, the wave has passed!" There was a relief of sudden silence and Kyson looked up at Wynter. "What happened? A 0.67 is a significant time wave variation."

Wynter's medi-support continued its vigil, and they could hear it running off the list of her injuries.

"Laceration on right upper humerus two centimetres, small lacerations in on skin on jawbone, femur, sternum, cranial contusion with bruising across 50%..."

Wynter's patience ran out, "Stop medic report! Mullins2001, all I can report is that at approximately 1500 on 12th April 2033 a bomb or some sort of explosion ripped through a large crowd of SAM supporters in Trafalgar Square, London." A sob escaped her lips and Wynter struggled to compose herself.

"Yes- we know that, but something has changed the timeline permanently. permanently LUND2062. Do you realise how serious this is?

You are a stage 1 reconnaissance only operative. You have triggered a 0.67-time wave variation. The consequences are… the consequences are… WE DON'T KNOW WHAT THE CONSEQUENCES ARE! We have yet to find that out."

Wynter had never seen Kyson so rattled, and she felt the enormity of what had just happened both in 2018 and in 2188.

"I did nothing wrong… just two, stage 4 interactions with past participants. "

Kyson shook her head, "A Stage 4 interaction does not have significant consequences for the timeline. You must have done something that impacted the timeline by 0.67. "

"Mullins2001, it was not my stage 4 interaction that changed the timeline… it was the stage 7 BOMB that interacted with the bloody timeline. A gigantic explosion… A bomb detonated in Trafalgar Square, killing and injuring hundreds of people. That is your 0.67 timeline variation wave… a bomb!"

"There is no need to become overly emotional, Lund2062. I don't know what has happened, but you are clearly upset. We are reeling here from the shock wave." She shouted over her shoulder to an unseen operative, "I want a full diagnostic of the shock wave and the time effects of this. NOW."

"Lund2062, Radan has requested a formal investigation. You are suspended pending the outcome of the investigation and will be required to take an active part. We need your full report. Full report. Do you hear me Lund2062? Every detail, however small? Due at 1600 on 23/07/2188." Kyson looked to her left as a sign that the conversation was over. Wynter could hear Kyson shouting commands across the office as the screen dissolved.

As she sat in the blueline pod on her way to her accom, Wynter was shaking. She had never witnessed anything like what she had seen today. She was in shock, and her rebooted Medic support affirmed this. "You need to attend the nearest Medi centre. Your heart rate is erratic and your injuries severe."

"I refuse to attend a Medi centre- Help where you can." She leant back in her seat in the pod as the nanotechnology surged through her veins. She scrutinised one cut on her hand and watched as the nanotech healed her skin. The buzzing in her head began. "Head injury requires specialist support." The medi- voice came through her auditorus.

"Refuse specialist support." She commanded.

"Recommend medicentre immediately."

"I refuse medical support."

"Recommend medicentre immediately."

"I refuse. Do you appreciate I can refuse? I refuse." Wynter's eyes pricked with tears.

"Recommend medicentre immediately."

"Turn off medical support," She shouted. "Turn off!" The bong in her auditorus signified that she was no longer connected the Radan medi service.

As she travelled through phase 2 of Regents Park, Wynter stared out through the glass. She could not stop the events of today replaying in her mind and the death of Carly, Robert, his sisters and so many others killed in the square.

As she exited her elevator, she looked down through the floor as she made her way towards her accom. Her optics were drawn towards the southeast where she glimpsed the top of Nelson's Column in Trafalgar Square. She stopped and stared. Her rational mind told her that this happened over 150 years ago, but as she arrived at her accommodation, she could not shake off the images.

Her door swung open, the voice of her accom broke through "Welcome home Wynter – No. 4 available." She ignored the food supplement and sat down on her chair next to the window. As the home screen news scrolled on the hovering screen in front of her, her optics once again drawn through the transparent screen to view Trafalgar Square.

She didn't know how long she had been sitting and staring, but Wynter eventually looked across at her home screen and blinking saw, "Magera communication." Searching for Landry's name first, she saw Landry was not on-virtual and, with slumping shoulders, remembered that she was off-grid. She resigned herself to talking to Karmal.

"Ind dialogue with Rahman360."

The Magera spinning symbol disappeared and that half of the screen changed. Wynter struggled at first, but Karmal came out of the dark, rubbing his face.

"Hey Wynter, everything ok?"

"No. Sorry to wake you, but I need to talk to someone. Something happened today.

I was in Trafalgar Square in and there was a bomb Kar- a bomb." Her voice broke as the emotion stopped her speaking.

He leaned in closer, "A bomb? Did you say a bomb, Wynt?"

She sobbed as her breath quickened and Karmal stepped forward, "Are you good, Wynt? Want me to visit?"

Wiping the tears from her face, "No- I'm ok. It was just such a shock."

"When was this bomb?"

"I visited a rally in 2033. Kar. I did everything right. There shouldn't have been anything. I can't understand what has happened." Wynter saw Karmal turning his head, looking to the right, his forehead creased in confusion.

"Wynt- are you telling me you experienced an explosion in 2033 that shouldn't have been there?"

"Yes! Exactly that Kar."

"Wynt, I'm sorry. How stupid of me! Are you hurt?"

"No. A few scrapes and scratches. I'm lucky. "Wynter paused, lowering her eyes, "Others weren't so..."

Karmal looked to his right and mouthed a silent prayer. This would not usually affect Wynter but today, the faces of Robert, his sisters and all those people swam into her mind.

She whispered, "Thank you, Kar. So many people died." She choked on the next words, "I... was... there... when someone died-... Robert. He died right here." She looked down at her arms in her lap, "I was with him. I couldn't save him."

"We can't save them all. Even if we would want to." Karmal was referring to his own family.

She continued, "I, I mean we, are not used to seeing death so close... Here, people go to Nivan to die, and we never see them again. I've never seen anyone die before. I've never seen so many people dead or dying. Oh, Kar, it was so terrible."

"Wynter, you are in shock... Is your Radan Medic updating you of your injuries?"

"No... I turned it off. It kept telling me to go to a medicentre."

"Be careful, Wynt... You may have injuries you don't know about."

"I know... I'll turn it back on later and I will go to a medicentre if it tells me to."

Wynter paused and she could see Karmal staring down and then he asked, "What did Kyson say?"

"She was unsympathetic Kar - she acted like it was my fault. It created a 0.67 timeline adjustment wave... the office was a mess- Something happened Kar. Something big."

Karmal whistled, "A 0.67? I've never heard of a time adjustment event that large. They must have gone crazy in Magera. You are right. Something's gone wrong. You completed all your pre-assignment checks and submitted your pre-assignment to Radan?"

"Of course, I did- I did everything right. I didn't come up with any loss of life or any danger for adjustment protocols. The protocol is there to protect us." Wynter rubbed her arm.

Karmal looked at another screen to his right, "It should have stated in the pre-time protocol. The system should pick up the danger to life?"

"I know, I thought that too, I tried to say that to Kyson, but she kept asking what I had done and that it was my fault. I don't understand. The protocol is clear and normally Radan's system would highlight anything like that- it's strange."

"This doesn't make sense, Wynt. You need to get some rest and while you are, I'll do some research into it. Give me the details."

Wynter paused, "Kar, I don't want to get anyone else into trouble. I'm already suspended pending a formal investigation."

Karmal stared into the viewer, "This is me you are talking to Wynt. Give me the details. I won't do anything. I'll check out the details, see if there is anything amiss."

"1500 on 12/04/2033–SAM movement rally, Trafalgar Square, London. I'll have a look too and see what we can come up with. I want to know who did this. There were people there who didn't deserve this.

Karmal looked up, "I understand... it's hard not to get involved when you are studying people but keep your perspective." Karmal shifted his position and made direct eye contact with Wynter, "They've been dead for over a century."

Wynter sighed, "I know, I know Kar, but I want to know why and who did this. It's important to know that."

Karmal nodded, "I'll help you in any way I can. I'll get started now. Remember what I said, turn on your Radan medic now and follow its instruction. Will you do that, Wynter?"

"Yes, I will. Thank you, Kar. Thank you for listening."

"No problem, take care of yourself. Peace be with you."

"And you, Kar."

Karmal disappeared from the screen as Wynter requested, "Turn on Radan medic."

It began its list again, "healed laceration on right upper humerus 2 cm, healed small lacerations, bruising across 50% of upper torso, cranial bruising- recommend rest mode. Pain relief to follow. Will monitor."

Wynter stretched, and reclining into a resting position, turned to face the home screen. "Magera research" The screen changed to the spinning Magera symbol and various choices appeared. "Select search data and location. "The screen responded and the Magera voice bot appeared.

"Date and location please."

"12/04/2033 Trafalgar Square, London."

The screen filled with first of many images of the explosion overlapping each other as more and more were added; people injured, services responding, photographs of the victims, newspaper reports. It was all there.

Wynter flicked her wrist towards the screen, selecting one image, a newspaper report. The headline was brief and the information thorough, but something was missing. Culpability. She continued scanning through the documents and images. She looked in vain for the admittance of liability from a subversive group or terrorist action group. Lots of speculation of who it could be, but no group taking responsibility. Her search went long into the night in vain. They never found out why or who planted the explosive device. At 0300 she gave up and with an aching head, lay down in her rest centre.

She dreamt of the time after the explosion and talking to Robert. Had she said the right thing? Could she have saved him? She relived those moments every time she closed her eyes.

***

She awoke at 0700. Her muscles screamed in pain, and she felt a raw throbbing in her head. Her tattoo circled green, and the Radan medic kicked in, "bruising to the occipital and parietal bone, surface damage bruising to 30% of upper torso, bruising on right humerus; suggest pain relief. Will follow." Wynter yawned and felt the creeping warmth as the nanotech pain relief reached her extremities.

As she stepped into the main room of her accom, she could see a silent alert on her home screen. Lund2062 is requested to attend an investigation interview regarding investigation Lund2062/2. Lund2062 must attend the interview at the Reagan building, Magera HQ, Birmingham University at 0700 25/07/2188, bring your assignment report with you as reference.

She needed to speak to Karmal.

"Open Magera communication. Ind dialogue Rahman360."

Half of the screen changed, and Karmal appeared. He was sitting by his home screen, dressed and the sun was shining through his accom lighting him. He looked up to acknowledge Wynter, but his eyes remained on his screen, to the side.

"I've spent a lot of time looking Wynt while you were in rest mode. "

"I had a look last night as well. Did you find anything?"

Karmal nodded, "Yes- it's all there. I don't know why your pre-assignment protocol failed."

Wynter nodded too. "Yes, I found it all and what I looked at was accurate. It happened as they said it did. Could you find out who did it?"

Karmal frowned, "No, it's strange, but there doesn't seem to be anyone taking credit for it. It was common in the 20th and 21st century to use publicity to further their cause. It's rare for no organisation to admit guilt."

"I suspect that too Kar. It doesn't make sense. There was nothing in the history data when I planned the assignment and why didn't Radan spot the error in the pre-assignment check."

I know. It's a mystery, you'll have to include that in your report. There may be ramifications for the Radan pre-check. Make sure you record everything you did before your visit. Have you got all your pre-assignment confirmation checks? You'll need it for the investigation. "

"They have requested that I attend the interview for my investigation tomorrow in Birmingham."

Karmal's voice rose, "What? tomorrow? And in Birmingham. That's very sudden. Are you well enough to travel?"

" I'm fine. Look, I don't mind when it is. I need to tell them what I saw and tell them about it not appearing in the pre-assignment protocol check. I'm sure they will be as confused as I am. They may have some answers for me."

"Look Wynter, be careful OK. They thought the 0.67 shock wave was because of something that you did. Make sure that your optic visuals and auditorii are all clear as evidence. "

"Yes, they were downloaded, the minute that I returned through the doorway, so they already have those. They should be able to see that my actions were noncompromising until after the explosion. I'm sure they are keen to find out for themselves. I'm sure that it can all be cleared up."

Karmal sighed, "I hope so, Wynter. You know the penalty for causing a shock wave over 0.5."

"Hey, Kar. Don't freak me out. I DID NOTHING WRONG. NOTHING.

CHAPTER 14

LANDRY REAGAN

Roan had left the homestead for a few days, scavenging in the outer lands and Landry was left trying to decipher her feelings. They had been so close when she had lived there but the Roan that she saw now was older, different.

Making her way to her parents' accom after working in the fields for another day, Landry entered the homestead and took a moment to stop in the shadows. Hearing the laughter and conversation between her parents was joyous. Landry's experience of love was limited, and relationships were not encouraged in the ration city. Partnerships were unnecessary when you could have the perfect virtual partner with TVR. Landry was envious of her parents being born before the great fall when real relationships were the norm.

Her father was commenting upon her mother's lack of patience in leaving a fallow field free. His voice rang clear, "We both know that you are not the most patient farmer, but it is the way it must be Carol- we are subsistence farmers."

"I know, but it feels wrong when we are so short of vegetables. Without insects, we must continue burying that waste. We should use human waste. It's high in phosphates!"

Landry watched as he leant forward, "but unpalatable for most people. We must keep burying the waste- for the moment."

"YOU must keep burying it, you mean. "Her mother laughed as she pulled her father into an embrace. Landry was stood in the doorway and preparing to step in when she saw the smile fade on her mother's face. "Are you going to tell her?"

"What good will it do? She can't help me. It will only cause unnecessary distress."

"She can help you. She could get the medicine. You know she would do that for you."

Landry took a small step backwards.

"Yes, Landry would get the medicine for me but Carol,"

He placed his hand at the side of her face, "At the expense of someone else. You heard her talking about Radan. It doesn't just give out medicine. She would be taking medicine from someone else to give to me. I couldn't have that on my conscience. I do not want to live at the expense of someone else."

Landry's breath quickened; her throat constricted as the tears sprang forth. She fought the urge to step forward.

"I have lived my life," He chuckled, "and it has been a glorious life, full of love. We made the right decision when we moved off grid away from that World. We did the right thing for us and the right thing for our family. Listening to Landry talk of the ration cities, that's not living, that's not a life either of us want. You know that."

Landry's mother nodded. "But I am not ready to lose you."

"Look, I need you to promise me you won't tell Landry, she will be compelled to act, I know my daughter and I don't want that for her. She has greater things to achieve." He grabbed his wife's arms and pulled her towards him. "Promise me. Promise me you will not tell her."

Landry could see her mother's shoulders rising and falling as she sobbed, "But she may never see you again. I don't think that I can live with knowing and not telling her."

"What's the alternative Carol? Forcing our daughter down a path that she will gladly travel but could ultimately be wrong for her. You know what the answer is. She must not know."

Landry saw her mother nodding slowly as she stepped backwards out of the doorway into the daylight. Their voices grew fainter as she moved away, her thoughts plagued with the enormity of what she had just heard. Her father had always been there, her inner voice when decisions had to be made. The idea of a world without him was unfathomable. The tears came slowly at first, and as she ran into the trees near to their home, the sobs sprang forth. A turmoil of emotions swarmed through her. Risk it all, save him. Respect his wishes and let him take his chosen path. Could she risk going against his wishes? What disease did he have? She knew that she could find a way to get the medicine if she knew what it was. She would have to get more information first.

When returning to the homestead later, she paused a moment at the doorway and saw that her mother was alone now in the kitchen.

"Have you seen Roan?" Her mother enquired. Landry fought the impulse to blurt out everything she had heard.

Placing a weak smile on her face Landry answered, "no- not since he stormed off at the food-plenty. He has gone off now, scavenging. I want to speak to him, and he disappears!"

Her mother raised her eyebrows and motioning to the kitchen table, "Come and sit Land."

She sat opposite her mother, noting for the first time, the crow's feet around her laughing eyes. "I don't think you realised Roan's feelings for you. Roan was hurt when you left. It hit him hard."

Landry frowned, "I missed him of course, but I thought he understood why I needed to go."

"Land- he and you were close. Have you ever considered that he wanted to make a life partnership with you? That he was torn between his feelings for you and your need to leave? I don't think he wanted to squash your dreams Land."

Landry couldn't avoid it any longer, "Like dad, mom? Like dad being ill and not wanting to tell me."

Landry's mother closed her eyes, "You heard us." Landry studied her mother as she paused, considering her response. "If you heard it all, then you will respect your father's wishes." She grabbed Landry's hands and as the tears fell, "I love your father, with all my heart and it's tempting to ask you to help us, but I agree with him. You can't help him at the expense of someone else getting that medicine."

Landry was slowly shaking her head. Her mother continued, "AND- it's not just one set of medicine, he will need more than that."

Landry found her voice, "Come back with me. Come to the ration city. You will be welcomed. You can be added to the Radan ration and medi-system. Dad will get the medicine that he needs. You will have to live in the city, but he will live."

She placed both of her hands on Landry's. "For us, that's not living Land. This is where your father wants to live, and where he wants to die."

Landry pushed her mother's hands away, "No, he is not old. He has many years left to enjoy…"

Her mother was shaking her head, "You must respect his decision. If you are your father's daughter, then you must understand his reasons."

"I WILL NOT let him die." The tears fell as Landry stood to leave. Her mother stood to stop her.

"You must Land or."

"OR What?" Landry's head snapped left.

Her mother stared up at her, her voice rang clear, "Or find another way. Go back in time and make another lifetime for him. It is what you have been trying to do. Without the great fall, we would have remained in Pencal. This off-grid life is physical. It has taken its toll on your father's health."

Landry was silent. What was her mother asking of her?

"I know that I sound selfish, but it is what you have been working for, Land. You want this for us, don't you? I want it for everyone! The World off grid or in ration cities, is not living, is it? Go back and stop global warming. Give your father the life he deserved. He was a writer before the great fall, not a farmer. You know that. Stop the catalyst to this." She swept her arms wide.

Landry stood stock still, thoughts running around her head. "Yes, I can try. I can go back. I've done the hard part; found the actionable evidence that I have been looking for. With help BUFR would be successful and maybe, just maybe, contribute to the stopping of Earth's warming. I need to follow that through until the end, whatever the result. If I can't then I could find a way of getting the medicine for him. Maybe I could go back and get it. If I know what he needs."

"Your father cannot know that you found out."

Landry let out a sob and placing her head in her hands and leaning onto the table, "I can help him."

She lay her head next to Landry's and spoke in her auditorus, "Go back, do what you must do and then come back to us. If you think you can stop this madness, then you have got to do it. We'll be waiting for you – all of us. "

There were tears in her eyes. Landry knew that her mother understood the consequences of what she was suggesting.

"You know that it could create a new timeline where some people don't exist?"

"I think that is a risk worth taking. I'm not ready to say goodbye to him or you. This may mean that I never have your father or you in my life." A sob escaped her mother's lips.

"You've got to try this Land. I know that what I am asking of you is a huge risk to everything you have worked for, but I have tried to think of another way. I don't enjoy putting this onto you Land. But your father and

I have always known that you were special." She placed her hand on her heart.

Landry's eyes pricked with tears. "But if I am unsuccessful…"

"You are Landry Reagan. Everything that you have ever put your mind to has been a success. This is what you worked so hard for." They stood up facing each other.

Landry felt a cold sensation move up her spine. "It is a huge risk mother. If I am successful, then this, "glancing around the homestead, "might not exist. In a new future, I might not find you."

Her mother placed her hands either side of Landry's face. "Look at me Landry, with even the slightest chance that you could help to do something to stop this nightmare. Change the World for everyone affected by this terrifying reality. You need to do this. Our life has been good, but it could be different. It is not just about us, is it? You've described those lifeless beings living in the ration cities. That is no life for anyone. If not for us, do it for them!"

Landry's mind was racing.

Images of the ration city flew across her mind. Those lost souls in their accoms, addicted to VR and having no life worth living. A vision of Wynter alone in her accom; not being able to be a mother because Radan deemed her unworthy. Kar without his family because of the catastrophic weather phenomena of the warming climate and the decision not to save them. They are worth saving. They all are.

Could she change the World for everyone and save her father too? She was not ready to give up on it yet. She knew she had to try and that's what she was going to do. The answers were in the past. Landry felt a renewed motivation to get started. She knew what she needed to do.

It was two days later, that Landry prepared to leave. Her father was a proud man but as they embraced, she pulled him closer. Hope surged through her and her thoughts were clear. *This will not be the last time I see you.*

"I will be home soon dad."

She hid her tears, turning to say goodbye to the others. Roan stood a distance away with his horse rein in his hand. Their eyes met and Landry could see the emotion in his eyes. Her old friend who could be so much more and she wanted that. She knew that now.

She ran up to Roan and on her tiptoes embraced him close. "I am coming home", she whispered, "I just have to do this first." The hug intensified as he too pulled her into an embrace. The energy sped through them, and the connection was intense and true. Landry found herself visibly sag as he supported her. The temptation to stay was almost overwhelming.

His speech, muffled by her hair, "I will be here. "

She stepped back and raised her eyes to his. "And I WILL return to you. I promise. "His smile was all she needed.

With tears in her eyes, she turned and strode west not daring to glance behind her. It was all too much but Landry knew that she had to leave. The images of her father and Roan etched in her mind were pulling her back towards the ration city and her destiny.

CHAPTER 15

LANDRY REAGAN

The return trip to the lodge house in Pencal was a blur. Landry's mind was filled with images of her father and the possibility that it could have been the last time that she would see him. The last time she might see them all. Her promise to Roan still rang in her ears and she was more determined than ever to find evidence to allow Magera to make the change necessary to reverse the effects of climate change. If she couldn't be successful, then she needed to find the medicine that her father needed. She wanted everyone to have a life that they chose, not one forced upon them.

The prospect of returning to Birmingham and the life that she led there was not appealing. She should be with her father, with Roan but she did have a choice. Do nothing and go back now and be with her father until the end or try to change everything. With renewed energy, she made a pact to herself. She would try all that she could and if it failed then she would get the medicine somehow, go back in time and steal it but get it somehow. Leave Magera and then go back to Pencal to live. Be with her family. But she would try the ultimate first, save them all. Her father, Karmal's family, and the other families ripped apart by the events surrounding the warming of the Earth and the Great Fall. Save herself too.

With her mind buzzing with renewed energy, she mulled over the many scenarios as she walked through the wasteland and into the streets of Pencal.

Arriving in the street where the lodging house was, she looked for movement on the street or in the house. Using the front door meant scanning her tattoo, which would reveal that she had left the accom. She needed to keep up the pretence that she had stayed inside. Satisfied that she was not being observed, she made her way around the back of the lodging house. She climbed back up to the window. The paper had allowed the window to close but not lock. Landry gently tugged at the paper which released the automatic sensor and the window swung open. She pulled herself inside, falling onto the floor on the other side.

She paused, standing in her temporary accom, taking a moment to check for any movement outside or next door, before declaring, "End private mode."

Her tattoo glowed green, and the link was established as her medic report began, "Blood pressure- normal limits, Temperature- slight elevation 37.7 degrees..." Landry looked to the ration station and the pile of cubed rations that had built up in her absence. Placing them in her travel bag, she left nothing behind. She agitated the sleeping linen. "Close diaramas 34.67. Close home screen."

Time to go.

She picked up her bag and scanned her tattoo on the doorframe as she left the accom.

As soon as she left the entrance to the accom block and began walking towards the travel pod, her right hand vibrated and became translucent and she heard Wynter's voice. "Request video call, Landry."

"Request accepted." The space just above Landry's right hand became translucent and then clearer as Wynter's face came into view. "Hey Wynter."

With the wave of her hand, Landry pushed the image towards her right-hand side and a full-size image of Wynter appeared semi-translucent and moving with Landry as she walked towards the green line station. Landry arrived at the green flashing light of the Greenline beacon, "The pod is just arriving, wait one moment Wynter."

Landry stepped into the pod, taking a seat and Wynter's holoimage stood beside her as they streamed towards Edinburgh. A tirade of babble greeted Landry.

Wynter's voice was raised, and she rushed her words, "Land – something happened. It was a bomb. An explosion. People died. I got hurt. I've got an investigation interview in Birmingham tomorrow and..."

Landry held up her hand. "Stop. Slow down. What are you saying to me? You caused an explosion?"

"No – I didn't. That's the point. I was in Trafalgar Square. SAM were having a rally and there was an explosion and so many people died and there were terrible scenes Land." Wynter's voice broke, as she choked back the tears that threatened her usual calm demeanour.

Landry struggled to comprehend what Wynter was telling her. Terrible things in history happened, but rarely when an operative was present. Magera wouldn't allow it. And a body left in the past with a Radan chip imbedded in its arm was too much of a risk. It could jeopardise everything that they stood for.

"Didn't your pre-assignment protocol checks warn you? Didn't it show up on the Radan check? I don't understand."

Wynter became anxious again, "It wasn't their Land. I did my research and there was no event in that time frame. It couldn't have passed through the Magera and Radan filters if there was an incident. It's so strange."

Landry shook her head her confused expression thoughtful. "Something must have caused it Wynt. "She looked into her eyes. "Wynt. think. Was there anything unusual that happened, anything unexpected? Did you follow your assignment plan? "

"Yes, I didn't sway from my assignment. There was an explosion, and when I came back through Kyson said that I had caused a time adjustment time wave of 0.67."

Landry couldn't hide her shock, shaking her head "0.67, 0.67. That's so high Wynt. That can't have been something you did."

"I know Land – so why are they blaming me? I'm in trouble, aren't I?" In her accom, Wynter sat down heavily and her holoimage did the same in Landry's Greenline pod.

Landry placed her arm around the back of Wynter's holo, "Wynt. You told me you did nothing wrong, so you did nothing wrong. Your optic visuals and auditorus will show them that. There must be another explanation."

"There must be! Karmal and I checked the Magera research tool, and it is there. According to historical data, there was an explosion, just as I experienced it. I think it must be a mistake at our end. The pre-assignment checks failed."

"And your own research didn't find it Wynt either? I think something has happened here, but I am not sure what. It is confusing -What did Karmal say, he's good with technical glitches? "

"Karmal's as confused as we are. He says that I need to be careful as it points to a mistake on my part."

Prickles of fear ran up the back of Landry's neck, but she didn't want to share her concerns with her friend yet. "Birmingham tomorrow Wynt, you said. Stay at my accom tonight. I will be at my accom in 2 hours. and we can go through everything before your interview tomorrow. I'm coming with you. "

"Thanks, Land- "Wynter visibly relaxed, "I'll make my way up now and meet you there. There must be a reason for it Land."

Landry suggested, "Magera may have found something in their investigation that will show us what happened."

"Yes – we might get there, and they may have solved it already."

Landry made a small sign with her right hand and stated, "close VOS Wynter Lund." The image dispersed. She shook her head. She realised she hadn't had the chance to tell Wynter about her father.

Landry spent the rest of her journey, lost in a conflict of her own thoughts. Go back, break her Magera ethical code or get the medicine that her father needs? She hadn't even noticed entering the city until the blue bio net appeared in front of her and she felt the familiar tingle as the scan passed through her.

Her thoughts moved to Wynter. Using evidence from her studies and training, she considered the scenarios that produce a 0.67 timeline adjustment, yes, a bomb would do that, which suggested that it was a new event.

As Landry entered the bionet enclosing the Birmingham ration city, there was no excitement at being home. Entering her accom building, her attention was torn as she relived her parents' homestead, the warmth of family and friends and how different it was. Her own accom, now felt empty and pointless. Her thoughts rested on Roan and her father, and what they might be doing right now.

A door bong signalled Wynter's' arrival some minutes later, and Landry greeted her warmly at the door with a hug. Landry felt Wynter stiffen at the physical contact but only increased the hug even more. Landry felt her friend relax into the comfort of a friend's hug. "Hey Wynt. It's been too long. Come in."

Both tattoos glowed blue and the Magera home screen split into two., "Welcome to Reagan2485's accom, Lund2062." The ration station kicked into life as it extended the rations for Wynter. "No.4 ration." The station chirped.

Landry and Wynter had met in person twice before, but there was still an awkwardness between them as they settled around the table. Both rarely spent time with real people from their own time. Landry had just been immersed in her previous life and felt refreshed by the human contact.

Wynter had never experienced that off grid life and human contact was rare for her. However, her discomfort soon faded as Landry's broad smile and infectious warmth enveloped her.

Landry got straight to it. "Right. Describe what happened? Tell me everything from the start."

Wynter spent a great deal of time detailing the explosion and her interaction with Robert at the end of his life and Kyson's reaction when she returned.

"I promise you, Land. I performed my pre-assignment checks. There were no warnings of danger-to-life scenarios. "

"Did it pass the Radan checking protocols?"

"Yes- it …must have. They wouldn't have let me go if it hadn't. I'm confused. We can't leave 2098 without the Radan authorization, can we? It came back as no life threat, and I received affirmation to continue. Kyson just kept repeating that I had done something. I didn't do anything Land. I've gone over it again and again and I stayed with my assignment brief. I didn't deviate from the plan."

Landry was lost for words. "Think Wynt. It could have been one compromising action, one look, one act that changed the timeline."

Wynter's voice rose, "Land, I've gone through it. I've looked through my visuals and auditorii, there were no stage 1,2,3,4,5,6 or 7 interactions UNTIL after the explosion."

Landry placed her hand on Wynter's arm. "I know it's difficult, but we need to go over it again together, we need to have the answer for the meeting tomorrow. Go through everything that happened again."

Wynter described everything that she did from leaving the doorway in the Langham Hotel, to returning later injured and distraught. They watched her visuals in high-speed mode to catch something that they had missed but they saw none. As they reached the aftermath of the explosion Landry commanded, "pause." Landry pulled Wynter's shoulder towards her, using her other arms to enclose her in a hug.

"Oh Wynt. That was an awful thing that happened to you." Landry continued holding Wynter and her small sobs pervaded the silence.

After some time, Landry sensed Wynter quieting, and she mumbled. "That's not the worst bit. He died Land. He died and I couldn't do anything to stop it. PLAY." The home screen came to life and Landry watched. Wynter kept her eyes averted as Landry watched the remaining visuals from Wynter's optics. She could hear Wynter's distress as she tried to save the scientist, Robert. Landry felt tears stinging her eyes as she glanced at Wynter, who had her arms wrapped around herself as she sobbed.

"You couldn't save him, Wynt. The medic said as much. You did everything right. It's not your fault, Wynt. It's not your fault."

Wynter pushed against Landry. Her face streaked with wet tears. "What if it is my fault? What if I did this…somehow. What am I going to do if something I did caused these people to die?"

"You did nothing. We've been over this and checked every angle. You did nothing to cause this."

Wynter looked up at Landry. "Do you believe that? Do you really think I didn't cause this? I need you to be honest with me. Was it something I did?"

"You didn't do this, Wynt and when Magera completes the investigation, they will find that too. You didn't do this."

"Who did then Landry? Who did this? And why wasn't it in the historical records before I went through that time door?" She stabbed her finger, "Why was it in the records AFTER I came back?"

"I don't know the answer to that, but there will be an answer. I'm sure this has happened before and was not the operative's fault. Maybe the system has failed. Let's find out what they share tomorrow first. There could be a simple explanation for it."

Wynter wiped her eyes and grinned at Landry. "You're right. You always are. There's no point us worrying tonight. It has taken up too much time already. I've not heard about your break away Land. How was it?"

"It was so good. Edinburgh was how I remembered it, although Princes Street had changed so much and Pencal was great. I didn't do much. Relaxed and caught up with the dioramas. Been a bit of a slob really and just relaxed."

Landry held up her tattoo and raised her eyebrows, "Private mode."

"Private mode," repeated Wynter, and their heads moved forward in collusion. Landry glanced across at the Radan symbol as it turned blue, signalling a lack of connection.

"Tell all. Was everyone well? Has the homestead changed much?"

Landry's face fell. "My parents were so pleased to be with me. But my dad, my dad is dying Wynt."

Wynter leant forward, "I'm sorry Land but they'll have to come into the ration city, now, won't they?" Wynter looked at Landry.

Slowly Landry shook her head. "No, never- It's hard to explain when you haven't lived off-grid but its magical Wynt. Growing your own food, living with your family and working together for a common goal. My father will never give that up. "

Wynter continued, "They could go to the senior comfort accom at Nirvan?"

Landry couldn't fault Wynter's reasoning. It was hard for her to visualise their life off-grid. As a child of the new state after the centralised urbanisation act. Wynter was born in the procreator programme where women were chosen for progenitor childbearing. Wynter had never known family or relationships. After being born, she never saw her progenitor again. She then moved to the infant sector where children were provided with their physical and emotional needs until at adulthood when she was reassigned to her work sector. She had seen vids and photographs of a family but struggled to understand how it would feel to have a family.

"They want to stay off-grid…even if it means dying there. It's a shared feeling of community. As a descendant of both my parents, I can see myself in them or they in me. My dad's determination is in me. My mom's eyes are my eyes and my brother, and I have the same nose and hair colour."

Landry knew Wynter had some understanding of genetics and continued. "It's more than just heredities, it's a sense that you belong to each other."

"Like they own you?"

"No," Landry struggled to explain. "No belong in a good way as you belong in the Magera family and our friendship; you would do things for me or tell me things that you wouldn't tell a stranger."

Landry could see that Wynter struggled to comprehend what she was saying. She was sorry for Wynter never having what she had growing up off-grid.

"I saw Roan."

Wynter's eyes lit.

Relationships at the end of the 22nd century were non-existent. 3D VR and holoscopes had become far enhanced versions of any actual relationship, and procreation had been taken away from everyone except for the progenitors. There was no need for personal relationships to exist in ration cities.

Trying to explain her feelings for Roan to Wynter was difficult. Especially as Landry was struggling with them herself!

"I saw Roan. He was angry with me at first."

"What do you mean? "

Landry gave some thought before answering, "He wasn't pleased to see me at first, but I still had feelings for him, and I promised him that I would go back. I can't explain it Wynt but when I touch him there's like a spark."

Wynter giggled, and Landry was always shocked at her naivety. Shaking her head, she joined her laughter.

Wynter and Landry spoke for over an hour and later they went to their rest sections. As Landry lay in her reparation station, her thoughts returned to her father. She considered the important decision that she still had to make. Keeping her dilemma from Wynter, Landry decided that she wouldn't share anything until after Wynter's interview.

CHAPTER 16

LANDRY REAGAN

Landry hid her nervousness as they travelled to Wynter's investigative meeting the following day.

"The Radan bot is unsettling when you first see it." Landry could tell that she was babbling, but Wynter remained pale-faced and subdued.

As they entered the university building, the welcome screen exploded into life. "Welcome, Lund2062. You are attending an investigation interview about your conduct on assignment 345.2. Please go to block 4 section 6. Welcome, Reagan 2485 - what is the purpose of your visit today?"

"I am attending the interview with Lund2062. "There was a pause as the bot changed colour from green to blue and pulsed, awaiting a response from the Radan mainframe.

The bot turned its face towards Landry, "You may attend the interview with Lund2062, but you may not speak. Are you in agreement with those terms?"

Landry looked across at Wynter, and they shared a nod. "Yes, I agree to those terms."

It was ominously quiet as they followed the Radan bot through the corridors of the complex. Wynter shared a smirk at Landry as she gasped at its' strange walking stance. It moved away from them, but its' head turned a full 180 degrees and faced them. An impossibility for a human. Their attempt at a humanoid face studied them as they followed it through the maze of corridors, only becoming animated when there was a change of direction, "Turn right Lund2062 and Reagan2485." Landry glanced across at Wynter and raised her eyebrows, giving Wynter a full smile, laughing at the nonsensical way that the bot was moving and speaking.

In the interview room, Wynter was greeted by Kyson sitting at the table with the large Magera symbol swirling on the screen behind her. There were two chairs opposite Kyson. They took their seat, and the bot took its position against the closed door. Landry gave Wynter a reassuring smile, and they both turned their attention to Kyson.

As with Landry's own disciplinary meeting, the Magera screen was replaced by the Radan logo. Landry found it hard not to stare, fascinated by the prominent decolourisation on Kyson's face and hands. The vitiligo was prevalent on Kyson's face with the harsh looking pale slashes and splashes around her mouth, contrasting with the darker skin around her eyes. Landry reflected on the medical protocols following the great fall and lack of medical support provided for non-life-threatening conditions such as vitiligo. Why did Kyson not feel angry at Radan for not prioritising her condition? Then Landry chastised herself. Kyson was beautiful and the vitiligo only enhanced that beauty. It just made it impossible for Kyson to ever be a Magera operative as she would stand out too much in a crowd and be easily remembered. Landry's thoughts were interrupted as Kyson started.

"Go to private mode. You cannot be interrupted by communications during this procedure."

Landry leant forward, "Can I ask why that is the case Kyson?"

"My nomination is Mullins2001. Remember that Reagan2485 AND I have been notified that you have agreed not to speak during this interview. Did not last long, did it? "Kyson pursed her lips and raised her eyebrows in her direction. Landry sensed something else in Kyson's demeanour. She was uneasy.

"Yes, I have agreed to that. However, we need a record of this meeting and our optic visuals and auditori will provide us with that record."

"Unnecessary. Evidence will be recorded, and a transcript will be available after the interview."

Wynter stared across at Landry imploring her the stop.

Landry coughed, "Ok private mode."

"Private mode", Wynter repeated. There was a short bong in their ears in response to the command and they shifted in their seats to a more relaxed sitting position. Landry stared at the pulsing Radan symbol on the screen, silently expanding and contracting.

Kyson had a translucent screen in front of her with the script flowing downwards. For Wynter and Landry, the image was backwards, and Landry attempted deciphering the backward script with little success.

Kyson studied the screen now and started speaking. "Investigative interview for Lund2062 0600 19/07/2188. Present: Reagan2485, Lund2062, Mullins2001 and assisted by Radan services."

Landry saw the Radan symbol pulse and simultaneously Kyson became distracted by something in her auditorii. It caused her to stop speaking and pause before addressing Landry. "Reason for Reagan 2485 being present at this interview?" She questioned.

Landry leant forward, keeping her eye on the Radan symbol and spoke deliberately. "Emotional support for Lund2062." Once again Kyson paused as she was conveyed a message through her auditorii.

"Reagan2485 may give emotional support but must not speak for the witness... You must not speak." Kyson looked up towards Landry for confirmation, "Reagan2485 will be removed if she interrupts the interview procedure. Is that understood?"

"Fully understood," Landry spoke deliberately and looked towards the Radan symbol. Landry glanced at Wynter and sat back.

Kyson read from her screen in front of her, "Lund2062, we are investigating your conduct during assignment 345.2. There are two allegations, one that your actions caused a stage 7 interaction timeline events resulting in a 0.67-time wave variation. "Wynter leant forward as to speak and Kyson interrupted her, "And 2, that you had two, stage 4 interactions with past participants. Do you have anything to say at this point?"

"Yes, I agree with the second allegation and have admitted to having two stage 4 interactions in my report but the first... No, I did not cause the 0.67 timewave variation. Nothing I did, could cause a stage 7 interaction. There was an explosion. I don't know what caused it, but I experienced it. If the explosive device had not gone off, then I wouldn't have had the stage 4 interaction with the past participants. I would have-"

Kyson interrupted, "Stop Lund2062. We have no evidence in the historical data that there was an explosion before you arrived in that space in time."

"Have you watched my optic visuals and auditorii? There was an explosive device ...An explosion. You must have seen it in my visuals."

"Your visuals and auditorii were corrupted when the timewave hit our mainframe... it's hard to see and hear what happened. "

"What! My visuals are in place. I observed them later when I wrote my report." She looked across at Landry and sweeping her arm towards her. "We observed them again last night - I can give you them again."

There was a pause before Kyson spoke, "The optic visuals are corrupted so we will have to rely upon your visuals 12 hours later. How do we know they haven't been tampered with?"

Kyson continued, "We will accept your account of what you believed happened at this point. If you could help us by answering the questions that we have…"

Wynter and Landry's eyes locked, and Landry, shaking her head in disbelief, gave a slight shrug to her shoulders.

Landry could see the Radan symbol pulsing. Someone was communicating with Kyson; she was sure of it. She sat back.

Kyson continued, "I have questions that I need to ask you about the two allegations." Wynter nodded, "Please speak your affirmation Lund2062."

"Yes"

"Allegation one, that your actions caused a stage 7 interaction timeline event resulting in a 0.67-time wave variation. Did you take any combustible items with you on this assignment?"

"No, absolutely not."

"Did you take any items which could cause other products to become flammable?"

"No. "

"Did you take any items which could become combustible?"

"No, no, no to these questions.", She glanced across at Landry, "I took nothing with me apart from the issued emergency pack. Unless any of those items can be combustible, then no, I took nothing combustible, flammable, ignitable, burnable or explosive. You know our filters would not let me take that through a time doorway. Why are you asking me these questions? We need to be asking, why didn't this event come up in my pre-assignment checks and protocols? It should have come up in the Radan pre-checks."

There was a pause as Kyson focused on her screen and the Radan symbol pulsed red on the large screen behind her, Kyson changed tack, "Did you procure any combustible items from a past participant in 2033?"

"No - I did not."

"Did you interact with a past participant to aid them in creating a combustible event?"

"No – I did not."

Landry whispered, "protocol."

Kyson's head whipped around, and she scrutinised Landry. Wynter made her point, "I did not aid a past participant. That would be against the Magera protocol as a stage 1 reconnaissance operative!"

There was a flurry of activity in Kyson's auditorus, Kyson placed her finger in her ear to accentuate the sound, and she read the screen in front of her. When she continued the questioning, there was a renewed edge to her tone.

"You are not speaking the truth, Lund2062. What you are telling us is not factually correct."

Wynter opened her mouth to speak and was interrupted.

"Did you follow Magera protocols? in fact, did you aid Robert Sanchez and try to revive him? Need I remind you I have your report in front of me." Kyson's hand pushed forward and a visual of Wynter's report hovered in front of her and appeared on the large screen. There were several lines highlighted.

Wynter's face froze and looking down at her lap. She replied softly, "Yes," she swallowed, "Yes I did." Landry placed her hand on Wynters.

"So, you did interact with a past participant?"

"Yes, I did. "Wynter shifted forward in her seat and placed her arm on the table, "I did, but to save his life not to create an explosive device." Wynter leant forward and raised her voice, "I could not help those people. So many dead and dying, instinct just took over me. You were not there Kyson; you would have done the same thing."

"I would not! I would not have done the same thing and I'm shocked that you would even suggest it!"

Two things happened at once. The bot moved so fast to Wynter's side that the three humans jumped. The familiar synthesised voice of Radan came from its lips. There was an attempt to move the lips in time, but it looked wrong, out of sync. The bot continued, "Lund2062, you are not able to respond in this manner. Did you break Magera regulation 6.5? A time operative will not alter the personal timeline of any past participant."

Landry could see that both Wynter and Kyson were stunned by what was happening.

Wynter with gritted teeth replied, "I did not break this regulation. He expired." Wynter lent forward, clearly upset. Landry wanted to comfort her, but the bot remained next to Wynter blocking her reach.

The voice came again, "Did you try to alter the past participant's timeline so breaking the Magera regulation 6.5? "

Wynter looked behind her towards Landry, "Yes. I attempted to save his life. Had I been successful I would have been in breach of regulation 6.5 but as it stands, I could not change his fate."

The Radan symbol glowed red, and a synthesised voice came out through the bot, "Lund2062 you breached regulation 6.5. You attempted to change the timeline of a past participant in human form. You breached a primary aim of Magera."

The bot turned and returned to its position by the exit and spoke. The voice of Radan rang out. "Mullins2001 will continue the interview."

All eyes turned to Kyson, who paled, as she read from the screen in front of her,

"Lund2485, you are in breach of regulation 6.5. Your actions could have compromised the Magera past programme. We believe you breached regulation 6.5; that is confirmed. We need more time to investigate whether you breached regulation 1.4 -A time operative will not take the life of a past participant: human, computer-based life form or animal through the assimilation and detonation of an explosive device. "

Landry instinctively thrust herself forward and was about to argue when Wynter placed her hand on Landry's arm, shaking her head, "No Landry, don't speak, I'm in enough trouble. I don't want more for you. "

She looked directly at Kyson. "I did not take a life. I attempted to save a life. I am innocent of this. I will go back and get evidence that will prove that I am innocent. It didn't come up in my pre-assignment checks. I am not in the wrong here".

The bot's voice rang out, interrupting Kyson, "We have evidence that directly links you to an event that caused a 0.67 timeline variation wave. We will complete our investigation into this event. While this investigation takes place you are confined to your accom App 23/234, Phase 2, New London as of 0600 tomorrow. You are suspended from your position as stage 1 operative, and you will attend your hearing 0700 04/08/2188. The consequence of this investigation will be decided in that hearing. Mullins2001 will explain the consequences to you."

"How can I find the information that we need if I am suspended and cannot work?" Wynter's eyes were pleading.

Kyson shook her head. "You are confined to your accom and suspended as a Magera operative until this matter is resolved. "

Wynter and Landry stared at each other and then at Kyson. Kyson was visibly uncomfortable as she listed the consequences. Her voice stuttered and was strained, "Depending upon the findings of this investigation, the consequences could be, suspension from duty for 12 months, permanent suspension from duty." Landry gasped and leant forward to protest. Kyson raised her finger to her lips and stared at Landry. Landry observed the Radan symbol pulsing red. It was communicating with Kyson.

Kyson paled, "I haven't finished the list, the third consequence is… is," she paused again and coughed averting her eyes. "Transportation to Mars." Kyson's voice wobbled.

Landry could not stop herself as protocol went out of the window. "What did you say, Kyson? What did you just say? Transportation to Mars? What is that?" As Landry continued, Kyson babbled uncomfortably, "It's written here… It's …it's what the consequence is."

The bot was quick, and it was soon at Landry's side. Landry and Kyson had simultaneously stood and turned to face it. Kyson shouted, "No Radan. No!" She looked towards the ceiling as she commanded, "Enough! This is a Magera investigative meeting with support from Radan services. Regulation 100 states that a human may refuse the support of Radan services without question." Kyson's voice shook with anger, "I am revoking the support from Radan services for the rest of this meeting."

The bot froze and everything in the room stilled. Landry held Kyson's gaze as they both slowly returned to their seats. The bot reversed and returned to its position at the door. However, the Radan symbol remained the pulsing ominously on the screen behind Kyson.

Wynter remained silent, staring straight ahead as Landry continued, "I don't care what's written there Kyson… I don't care what's written. She is not going to Mars. She made a mistake, but she is not going to Mars. What can we do Kyson? What can we do?" Landry changed tack, "What are YOU going to do Kyson. What are you going to do? Wynter has been an excellent operative for 3 years now. She has an unblemished record. This cannot happen Kyson."

Kyson looked straight ahead. Landry looked into her eyes and sensed genuine fear; the second time she had seen this. "Landry, I'm going to investigate this. If Wynter did nothing wrong, then we will find out who did. "

Landry had never heard Kyson refer to anyone by their non-operative names, and she could see that she was rattled. "We need to find out what happened Kyson. Something strange is going on here. We need to tell the directors of Magera. Kyson, do they know about this?"

"They are aware of the allegation, and they will receive the transcript of this meeting but Wynter, you need to understand that the allegations against you are severe. It has been many years since an operative has been accused of such a breach of protocol."

As Kyson rounded off the meeting, Landry's mind was buzzing with the reasons for Wynter being in the position that she was in and for the threat of transportation to Mars. Wynter was visibly shaking as they stepped through the corridors of the university building, and Landry found herself unusually silent. As they left the building Wynter spoke, "What just happened there Landry? "

Landry shook her head, "Wynter I don't know. I'm as confused as you." As they travelled back to Landry's accom, Wynter repeated what had happened from the time that she left the Langham to the time that she returned. Landry added questions to prompt any extra information that she had missed, "Did you see anyone acting suspiciously before the explosion?" Wynter held her head in her hands and closed her eyes, attempting to see her optic visuals for the event. Kyson was right. The visuals of her visit were now corrupted.

"I don't understand why the visuals are corrupted. You saw my visuals last night. They were perfect and showed everything that happened."

Landry placed her arm on Wynter's shoulder and reassured her, "Let's get back to my accom. We should talk to Kar; he'll know what to do."

"I know it wasn't me. They'll find out who did it, won't they? The evidence that proves that it wasn't me."

Landry didn't share her thoughts with Wynter. Her recent experience with Magera and Radan had been unsettling, and there was something that didn't make sense. They needed to speak privately and consult the wise head of Karmal.

On arrival in Landry's accom, Wynter and Landry requested private mode and Landry fetched the 21st-century work pad. They needed to speak to Karmal using the dark web. They were reassured that nothing that they were about to say could be heard by Radan or Magera. Landry found the chat site and could see that Karmal's icon appeared on the right-hand side. He was available.

Before requesting Karmal, her attention was drawn to Wynter, who was sitting in a chair transfixed by something on the homescreen. There was one news item flashing across the screen.

'FIRST SETTLERS MAKE PLANS TO LEAVE FOR MARS.' It was supported with visuals of humans with their possessions queuing to enter a large intergalactic transporter. These were helped by Radan work bots, and there was a festival atmosphere as the presenter, smiling and laughing, relayed the facts surrounding their journey and their new life on Mars. At the rear, Landry saw a few individuals more subdued than the others who appeared to be physically supported by the Radan bots. There was something unusual about this group as they made their way towards the transporter. As they arrived at the ramp, one individual attempted to turn and run. The screen flickered and returned to the presenter who began describing the journey to Mars.

"I'm not going to Mars." Wynter stated, glancing across at Landry, "Promise me Land, I'm not going to Mars, am I?"

CHAPTER 17

"You're not going to Mars, Wynt!"

Landry stared at the antiquated screen of the 21st century WordPad and saw that Karmal was available.

She sent her text-only message to him. 'Kar, can u talk? In pvt mde, please." She didn't want Radan listening.

There was a pause as Karmal logged in to the chat room.

Landry glanced across at Wynter, "You still in private mode?"

Wynter nodded. The screen flashed and a distorted image of Karmal appeared. The quality was poor and their auditorus took a moment to adjust.

Karmal spoke, "How did it go? Did they tell you what the problem was?"

"No. I'm here with Landry. We've just come back."

"Something's wrong Kar. It all went wrong. Wynt is being accused of a breach of the primary aim-1.4, taking the lives of past participants, and regulation-6.5, altering the timeline of a past participant in human form."

Karmal's faced crumpled into a frown, and he shook his head.

Landry continued, "They say that Wynter caused a 0.67 timeline variation wave."

"A 0.67? A 0.67? Impossible. Wynter, you cannot cause a 0.67. Unless you did assassinate the prime minister or something. "He laughed but stopped when he saw that Wynter, and Landry were not laughing.

He continued, "So they say that she, did it? I checked the historic database. It happened as Wynter said. The question is why not in her pre-assignment checks and why not found by Radan? It is so strange. I cannot fathom it and yet, there is no tampering with the data. It looks like it has always been there."

"Agreed, "Landry added, "How could something so huge get passed in the pre-assignment safety checks. It was checked by Magera and Radan. How could those protocols fail?"

"Yes, and Wynter will prove that it wasn't her. The data will show it. That permission cannot be given if it's no safe."

Wynter's voice rose, "We said that in the investigation interview Kar. They wouldn't accept it as a reason, Radan wouldn't accept it!"

Karmal's head snapped forward as he stared into the camera, "Radan? Radan spoke to you. Like in Landry's meeting?" Landry nodded and Wynter continued, "They wouldn't listen to me."

Karmal's face moved away from the screen, "If Magera won't help you, you are on your own. Go back and find out who did it. Show them who it was… Capture them on your visuals." Landry could see Karmal's head moving from side to side, plans being made, ideas explored.

"She can't Kar. She's confined to quarters; she's suspended from duty until the investigation is complete."

Landry looked across at Wynter's downcast face as they waited for Karmal's response.

He looked to the screen on his right, "They didn't have a choice. If you had caused a 0.67, it is usual that they suspend you."

Wynter leant forward and spoke into the micro. "I don't care so much for that Kar. I want to know who did it. I want to know why Carly, Robert and those people died."

Looking into the camera, his voice quiet, "I can see it Wynter but remember Gant5609, He wanted to find out what started the Doel nuclear event in 2067."

"You weren't there, either of you," Looking at Landry and Karmal, "I was there. I experienced it. It was terrible, Kar. I care about those people. They were making a difference. Someone wanted to stop them. My research last night showed that the SAM movement never recovered. Without Carly and Dr Sanchez, they lost many of the members who were the driving force. The movement wasn't the same again. I want to know why."

Landry placed her arm around Wynter's shoulder. "You care about these people."

"Yes, I think I do! I have spent a lot of time researching these people. I feel closer to them. They were looking like a workable option for action. I want to know the reason their lives were lost."

Karmal began speaking. Landry could see that he was looking at another screen on his right, "I will help you but be careful. Something is not good. You say that it wasn't there before, and Radan didn't find it and yet it happened. None of this is good…"

Wynter looked towards Landry before she spoke, "Kar, I want to go back and see what happened. There must be a way, and Landry thinks you know how."

Shaking his head, Karmal said, "You are in suspension. You cannot go back. Your Radan implant will not open the doorway Wynter."

Wynter's shoulders sank.

"Could she go through in private mode?"

"She can go into private mode, but the door won't open. You need to go through as Lund2062 and only once you are through, you go private. That is the only way."

Landry smiled, "There must be a way. Come on Kar, have you never thought about how you could do this or know someone who has?"

"It's been tried Land. Tockheads try to go through with no identity. You cannot go using Lund2062 and cannot go through with no identity."

Wynter moved forward, "Can't we use someone else's identity?"

"What are you saying, Wynter? Using someone else's implant. Do you know what you say? You got to find someone who works for Magera, who will cut out their implant and give it to you…"

Wynter and Landry paused, both lost in thought.

Landry spoke first, "When you say it like that it feels far-fetched but not impossible. Come on Kar there must be another way."

Karmal paused before answering.

"There is a way, but Wynter should not do this."

"Look Kar. Something happened to me, and I want… No, I need to go back. I must find out who set off, planted, or left the explosive device. We need to know. History should know and I need to clear my name."

"Yes, you can find that, but what you find out… you cannot do nothing with it. You cannot change it. It will cause another timeline variation. Magera will know."

"Not if Wynter doesn't act upon the information and only tells Magera. There won't be any time fluctuation if she acts in the same way as previously."

"Stop! Let's start with me trying to find out what happened. I never said anything about changing history. Have you ever felt that you just need to know something?"

Karmal sighed, "There is one way."

Karmal paused…

"What did Magera do before the Radan tattoo chip?"

"What do you mean?"

"Magera was travelling through time before Radan. "

Wynter yelped with excitement. "Yes, of course."

Landry stared quizzically at Wynter, "They had another method of going through before the Radan tattoo!"

Karmal smiled, "Yes, they had a keypad in the old doorways. The person puts the date/time/assignment number. When Radan joined Magera, they stopped using them. They were bad. Some people made mistakes, putting in wrong dates/times. It is an old way, and it is dangerous."

Wynter's excitement continued, "So old doorways will have this system. Will it still be operable?"

"They were powered by grapheme, so they may still work."

"So, I must find an old, abandoned doorway in London. That should be easy. There were many of them."

"Yes, Wynter. Look for universities, museums, hotels and old buildings that are abandoned. It will not be easy."

"I can find one, Kar. I can do this."

Karmal hesitated, shaking his head. "It is not that easy. You've got to get to the door without being seen or scanned. You cannot use transport. Magera cannot know that you left your accom."

Landry said, "I can help Wynt with that Kar. I've just been visiting my parents off-grid."

Karmal chuckled softly. "You can come up with a plan. One word as warning. Think about the consequences of what you are going to do. You could lose your employment."

"This is worth the risk Kar. If they find I am responsible for the timewave variation, then I could be on a transport to Mars…"

There was a moment of complete silence and Landry thought Karmal's connection had been lost. Then his voice came through, "Transportation to Mars! That cannot be. It is your civil choice."

"They cannot send you to Mars without your consent."

"As you said yourself Kar, in their eyes, Wynt caused a 0.67-time variation wave. She could be the person who set off the explosive device. Wynter needs to find out who did, to clear her name."

"This is wrong. This is so wrong. You must find out who did this."

Wynter smiled, rolling her eyes." That's what we've been trying to tell you."

"Did you see the news feed? The first migrants are going to Mars. I know someone who works on the transporter. He took the first settlers and the equipment to New Earth. I will ask him..." Karmal looked towards the camera, "You will not go Wynter."

"Kar, we're going to find the doorways and then let you know what we're going to do."

Karmal pleaded, "When you do Wynter ... Do not leave and not tell us. Landry and I must know your plan. Please be careful."

The three icons disappeared from the screen as they signed off from the chat room. Landry placed the laptop under the worktable, and she looked up at her home screen. She turned towards Wynter, "I can go in your place. I am happy to do this for you. I can find out everything you need."

Wynter placed her hand on Landry's, "Thank you. I know you can Land but I need to do this. I want to do this, and I don't want anyone getting into trouble for me."

"At least let me help you get organised. We've got a few hours before you need to leave."

"That's great Land. I need your help to plan this."

"Right let's start with which door. You know your London history. Which doors are pre2150 and not used anymore?"

They worked hard until the daylight faded. Soon it was time for Wynter to go back to her own accom in London. It had been a bittersweet visit, and it was with reluctance that Landry was saying goodbye to her friend. She was fearful for her.

"Do not leave before you tell me exactly where, when etc. I need to find you if it goes wrong and remember what I told you about going off-grid. You'll be great Wynt. You'll find out who did it and if you collect the evidence, they can't ignore it."

"I'm going to do this Land."

As she closed the door, Landry heard Wynter sigh as she made her way down the corridor.

CHAPTER 18

LANDRY REAGAN

Following a tough night of broken sleep, Landry had made her decision. The visit to the homestead and recent experiences with Magera had confirmed that Birmingham was not where she wanted to be. She knew one thing for sure. Radan was having a worryingly more prominent role in the work of Magera. The implications of this were not yet clear but it did not seem good.

Landry had been cocooned in her work with Magera and forgotten how if felt to be part of a family group. Her father's news was like a bulldozer pushing aside everything that came before it and her desire to be home was greater than it had ever been. She knew there was nothing for her in Birmingham, but she had a good friend in Wynter, and her predicament weighed heavy on Landry. What she had set out to achieve during her time with Magera was unfinished. She didn't know how much time her father had left. If she were to get him the medicine he needed, she needed to act now. Landry still clung to the idea that with help, she might change the lives of everyone. Find the evidence that Magera could act on that could change the world and avoid the Great Fall. This was what she felt she had found in BUFR, despite the lack of support from Magera and Radan. It was her duty to act upon that evidence in the best way that she knew how. She felt it. She was going to find evidence that was so strong that Magera and Radan could not ignore it. It was now or never.

Landry had chosen her next time assignment carefully. After the investigation into her conduct, she wasn't permitted to visit Birmingham University Forestry Research after 2018. She could not risk the past participant Dr Simon Pedersen recognising her. However, she knew that the evidence that she needed would be there somewhere. Her planned visit to 2017 coincided with the results of year one and future predictions for the Carbon Dioxide sink forestry. She was keen to get started.

Returning to work after her suspension, Landry saw Kyson for the first time since Wynter's investigation meeting. Landry retained the formality that had got her suspended in the first place and Kyson was as aloof as usual. But what shocked Landry was the dramatic change in her appearance. Her hair was falling out in tufts from the usual tight clips, and there were dark circles under her eyes. Landry wanted so much to ask her what had happened afterwards, but she wasn't given the chance.

"All assignment checks complete Reagan 2485?" Kyson looked through the screen directly at Landry. Landry didn't have time to respond. "Good, I'll take that as a yes then." And she disappeared, leaving the spinning Magera symbol bouncing on the screen. Landry's brow furrowed as she mulled over what she had just seen. She hoped that Kyson had not been reprimanded because of her outburst against Radan. Recalling that moment Landry couldn't help smiling as she placed her tattoo onto the doorframe, the door pixelated, and she stepped through to 2017.

She was stood in the dark of the cupboard behind the stage in the Theatre in Birmingham. Her heart stilled as she listened intently. She could hear music coming from the direction of the stage; a rehearsal, but what for?

The music, something familiar; string instruments and a percussion which sounded like small tinkering bells. Opening the door just enough to glance out, she saw a shadow cross the stage floor. Disguised by the thick black curtains at the back of the stage, Landry opened the doorway fully and she stood for a moment at the threshold. There was a familiar rush to the senses; sounds and smells from a theatre in 2017. She prepared herself to step out of the door and on to the stage. Her finely tuned auditorus revealed a uni plane recording, not the breadth of real musicians of course, but a limiting piece. *It was a rehearsal.* There was no sense of other people around, so grabbing a broom just in case, she made her way up to the side of the great stage. Glimpsing between the curtains, she caught a flash of the dancer as she passed by. The music rose and fell, and Landry became braver as she stood ever closer to the curtain, to improve her view.

It was a ballerina, and she was alone on the stage, moving in time with the music, leaping into the air and filling the stage with her striding launches. Landry was mesmerised. Never had she seen anything so wonderful. As the bell-like tones rippled in her auditorus, Landry watched her spin on the spot again and again as the flowing bells increased, Landry felt goosebumps on her arms and neck and a tear fell from her eye. It was so beautiful to watch, something Landry had never experienced. The future held no such visions.

The performer continued, and Landry looked around her. Gold-gilded scenery and a painted palace backdrop showed a fantasy story. The Christmas tree at the back of the stage and the music was reminiscent of a distant memory for Landry. Suddenly, the memory burst forth like a bright star in the darkness; The Nutcracker, her mother's favourite music played at Christmas, Tchaikovsky. She was hit with memories of home in the wintertime. Christmas had long since ceased to be celebrated, a commercial blasphemy to gain financials only. But Landry's family had enjoyed a winter festival where gifts were made and exchanged, and there was a harvest feast of thankfulness. Her mother always liked to listen to this music, and it was a mainstay of Landry's childhood. For the first time, Landry wished she could bring her mother here right now to witness this magnificent sight; she knew she would be overwhelmed to see it. Maybe in a new future, these performances would be available to all, and her mother could experience this wondrous sight? She felt a renewed sense of purpose as she tore herself away from the ballerina and with a soft tread made her way towards the exit at the back of the theatre.

Recent events with Radan being present at the Magera investigations were unsettling. She had never considered not following the strict protocols, but she knew now what she wanted. Had wanted all along. A future rich in togetherness for people, a sense of family and a purpose for individuals. This had been lost during the Great fall. Lost when countries turn their faces inward, when selfishness became the new currency and greed a priority over aid for others. All lost once Radan Services provided everything that you needed to survive. All who would take it. Thinking back to the ballerina, Landry considered people sharing this wonderful experience again. It had been lost somehow. She wanted people to experience risk and overcome adversity, not hide in the suffocating safety of their accom, caring less and less until there was nothing left. Talking to Karmal had led her to ponder the unique opportunity that they as Magera operatives had. It had made her more confident to explore everything in the past; more than she had done in previous visits.

She strode forward, making her way up Inge Street. The winter wind whipped through her 21st century clothes, and she crossed her arms to keep in the heat. She missed her graphemo. She pulled the scarf tighter around her neck. As with other assignments, she began with the first task, affirmation of the year. She was expecting the front of the Hippodrome to show "Aladdin" but in its place was, "The Nutcracker." It's gilded lettering was prominent across the top of the billboard. Sometimes research documents were not accurate, and Landry concluded that maybe the theatre dates were wrong. She needed to find a definitive date evidence article.

As she reached the end of Inge Street, she was struck by the immense activity, a cacophony of noise and sights' people moving up and down the street, omnibuses, articulated lorries, automobiles and small delivery wagons making their way here and there. It never ceased to impress Landry, the life that filled the 21st century. A flurry of movement with purpose. The contrast with the late 22nd century was extreme.

Recent conversations with Karmal and Wynter about their dalliances from procedure, had shocked Landry. For the first time, she considered she could use her planned assignments to conduct personal goals as well. Her father's news was devastating and as it was self-diagnosed, Landry did not know how long her father may have.

Today was for this assignment. She could not, must not compromise the evidence she was about to collect. With that in mind, she strode forward and almost walked into a past participant standing on the pavement looking at a device in his hand. She halted in time and chastised herself for her lack of alertness. He was holding a paper news spreadsheet, and she saw the date visual; 12th December 2016. The confirmation that she needed.

As Landry continued towards the train station, she walked past several food consumption emporiums and a variety of smells wafted out of the doorways. Commuters were walking out of these holding wrapped food in their hands, eating as they walked. The smells were intense. The distinct smell of animal products caused her stomach to grumble in protest. She had never experienced non synthesised meat products. However, in training, operatives had been warned about eating animal products when visiting the past. Their internal organs would struggle to adapt following years of synthesized products. Landry was the exception being a lander and having eaten some animal meat in as a child. Putting aside her hunger, she focused on the reason for being here. She needed to be at the BUFR presentation at the university. Landry stepped between the past participants and maintained a steady pace towards her goal. Stepping through a small group of trees, Landry scanned the bushes for small moths as she passed, her obsession with butterflies and her desire to see them live was hard to suppress.

Arriving at the Reagan building just before the launch started, she found herself in an atrium just outside of the lecture theatre. She attempted to mingle with the other guests, placing her fake ID around her neck in case it was needed. Participants were drinking a beverage, and she took the time to watch how they had attained it. She felt a surge of defiance as she grabbed a cup from the station where they were left already prepared and followed their example.

Sometimes it was permissible to taste the food products in history. At religious festivals or on occasions when it would be considered attention-seeking not to partake. She felt that this was such an occasion. She scrutinised it; dark, liquid, and with a bitter smell. The heat of the beverage warmed her face and blowing on it tentatively, she took a sip. Feeling the burn as the liquid reached the inside of her mouth, she fought the urge to spit it back into the cup. The taste wasn't pleasant, but she persevered and on taking further sips, a warmth spread through her body. Then Landry noticed a new sensation, a buzzing in her head and chest. She was becoming light-headed. There must be a stimulant in the drink. Landry stopped drinking the beverage ration immediately and left the cup on the table as she began making her way towards the lecture hall, concealed behind a large group of students.

Integrating successfully, she sat next to several students and waited for the presentation to start. She performed a pre-test of her optics and auditorus by holding her finger against her left temple to pause what she was seeing in her left optic; she dragged her finger down and the vizimage rewound. By moving her finger back upwards, the visuals in her left eye moved forward. The test was complete. All was in working order. She sat back, placed her notepad in front of her and waited for it to start. The aftereffects of the stimulant in the beverage were still there but diminishing and Landry was left with a feeling of comfort and wellbeing. Overall, she concluded it had been a mixed experience, both unpleasant and pleasant at the same time.

The buzz of conversations halted as two familiar people entered the room. Landry had noted several members of the press sitting on the front row and these began taking images with their devices which caused flashes that briefly interfered with Landry's optics. The illuminations stopped as Dana Brooke stepped up to the podium beneath a large presentation screen. Filling the screen was the BUFR symbol with Birmingham University Forestry Research written underneath. The symbols and writing were surrounded by a large scale visual of the branches and leaves of a tree.

Dana stepped forward, spreading her arms wide and directing her attention up and around the auditorium. "Thank you for coming today and we welcome you to the BUFR new forest launch. We'd like to welcome our shareholders and charity donors who have made this project possible. "

The screen changed, and Landry could see several logos for a variety of financial investors. "Can I thank our contributors who support our work with temperate forests across the globe, forests in Australia and the Amazon Rainforests of course." The screen changed and images of forests filled the screen. Landry gasped as the last image of the Amazon Basin in all its glory showed how far it stretched across Brazil and into Peru, Ecuador and Colombia. She knew the great fall had caused many South American countries to clear vast areas of the Amazon basin to open land for food production but had never realised how huge it truly was. Knowing that in 2017, the Earth warming tipping point had not yet been reached and that much of the Amazon Basin remained. There was hope that this time frame could be a successful action point for the halting of climate change.

Dana Brooke continued, "I cannot stress enough how important this research is going to be in taking a journey into our future." Landry's attention was fixed. "The question we have to ask ourselves is, how can we keep the vital balance between the global cycle of carbon and the planet's natural balance?" Dana paused for effect and smiling said, "We think we have found a way."

The audience clapped, and Landry did the same. "But let's learn about our Sci-fi Forest from those who understand the true science behind it. "

She gestured to the man stood to her right, "I'd like to give a warm welcome to our visionary scientist at Birmingham University. The person who has made this possible, Dr Simon Pedersen." The audience clapped again as the photographer's flashbulbs went off.

As the two presenters swapped places, Landry noted Simon pausing before beginning his presentation. Landry felt confident that this Simon Pedersen had not seen her before.

"I cannot explain to you how important this research is and how it could impact the future of this planet."

I agree, Landry thought.

Simon continued, "We know now that we are burning fossil fuels and emitting more carbon dioxide than we should be, and this causes an increase in the Earth's temperature. We are aware of the impact of that, and we know that most scientists agree that global warming is real."

On the screen appeared a graph of thermal conditions over the years. The lines were erratic, but the main trajectory was climbing.

"We are looking at a hothouse Earth tipping point in our lifetime. For those of you not familiar with the term Hothouse Earth, it is the moment where the Earth tips into a heated state from which there can be no return. " He pointed at the audience. "In your lifetime…. We will reach a point of no return."

The image changed to a road of vehicles in traffic, huge super tankers and aeroplanes. "We are not reducing our carbon dioxide emissions across the globe to avoid a hothouse Earth and we are seeing the results of this already." Images of storms, forest fires, melting glaciers and dead animals in dried-up riverbeds appeared behind Simon.

"I predict that even with every government working hard to reduce their omissions and hit their targets, we are still facing an uncertain future. A future where we lose 80% of the animal species on the planet. A future where 2 billion people will be forced to move from their homeland due to weather phenomena or lack of food. A future where there will be at least one billion deaths because of global warming. We think that this is going to happen after our lifetime." He banged his fist on the podium and there was a gasp from the audience, "It's not GOING to happen… it is happening NOW."

The screen changed and a moving visual of a scientist explaining a research project in the Amazon Basin began. The scientist was speaking into the camera and describing insect traps laid on the floor of the Amazon Rainforest in 2015. "We've laid these traps out this morning and we've come back to find evidence of the variety of species that we still find on the rainforest floor." The camera swung round to show the trap, "What can you see?" the scientist questioned. "Yes, nothing. The traps are coming up with nothing. "He looked directly into the camera and then the threw the trap to the floor and moved onto another one, "nothing" and he moved on again showing an empty trap, "Nothing." The camera focussed upon his face. "These traps in the 1970s were full! Full of an abundance of insects! There is a severe shortage of what we find in the most species-rich rainforest on the planet. If we are finding this here, then what's happening in other regions around the Earth?" The camera panned to the empty traps on the floor and then reverse zoomed and paused.

Simon stepped forward, "It's happening now… it's not 'going to happen' …it is happening now so what can we do to stop it? Is there anything we can do?"

Simon paused, and Landry had to fight the familiar desire to reveal herself and her task. To stop herself from shouting that she knew it all and telling them what she had seen and what had happened to the Earth. Shaking her head, she grimaced and then a thought popped into her head. If this solution is proven, then why didn't they have the impact that they wanted to have? They must have failed. She sat back, defeated, her mind full of the possibilities for their lack of success.

"Right enough of the negative," Simon smiled, "Let me tell you what we are planning and what we predict will result from our research."

The screen showed a visual of a forest with tall towers emanating above it. Gas billowed out from the towers.

"We know we are now living on a planet of 406 parts per million of CO_2. Going back in time in 1979 it was 336 ppm; pre-industrialisation was 278ppm and the ice age was 185ppm. The situation now is that we believe it will rise to 550ppm by 2050. 1 in every 3 molecules of CO_2 released by us because of fossil fuels burning is taken back into the atmosphere and into the land surface by trees. We know this, but what we don't know is if the increase in CO_2 emissions could be returned to the land through the growing of more trees."

Simon's voice rose, "We at Birmingham University are excited to be entrusted to make this brave new scientific adventure, a reality. What we are trying to do here is move forward in the future. To the year 2100. "

Excitement filled the room.

"We have created an atmosphere in a forest that could be a reality in 2100 and are recording how the forest performs under those conditions. We predict the forest will absorb more CO_2. We need to show if the trees will plateau in their absorption rates or continue rising."

The image of the Amazon rainforest appeared behind Simon. "With your support, our project has begun in forests around the world. It will give us much-needed results to prove that what we have is workable. We trust we can prove that trees will not only cope with absorbing the increased CO2, but they will become more efficient as carbon sinks as a result. We speculate this will turn the tide of hothouse Earth, but we need this to become an international effort and we need your support. I'm going to pass back to Dana Brookes to explain our research dreams."

The audience clapped as Dana stepped up to the podium. She swung her arm towards the image on the screen, an image of a forest far into the distance.

"Right, everyone, if you go away from here today with nothing, then remember this one fact… forests are the solar powered hoovers of C02. The temperate forests across the planet will be a sink for the C02 produced by the EU annually. Good news?" A few members of the audience cheered and clapped.

Raising her hand Dana halted the clapping "Stop! If every square inch of the United States of America is made into a forest, then it would create a carbon sink large enough to reduce the current C02 emissions for the entire planet." The audience stilled as the realisation hit them and some groaned. Dana laughed, "I'm not expecting to convince the government of the United States to cover their shores with forests, but vast swathes of the planet could support forest growth. In pre-history and during the history of man's time on this planet there were 400 billion forests. We recognise this, we must educate the World into knowing it too. If we can work together and keep the forests that we have and grow forests in inhospitable places, it would make the difference. "

The screen behind switched to an image of what appeared to be a forest in the basin of a river. "This forest is in India. They've been planting trees since 1979 to halt the land being eroded every time the river floods during the monsoon. Elephants, rhinos, deer, tigers and vultures use the forest. Wonderful, isn't it?" The audience murmured in affirmation, "The greatest threat to this forest?" Dana paused, "The greatest threat is humans… wanting to cut down the forest for economic gain."

Another image appeared, the screen split in two with a similar image on both sides, a desert with a forest at its edge. Text written at the bottom of each image read, Egypt and Israel. "Can you grow a forest in the desert?" Dana waved her hand across the screen and looked towards the audience, "Yes. The answer is yes you can. For both projects to conserve precious stores of freshwater, the researchers used low-quality recycled sewage water and saltwater. The by-product of desalination plants. They searched for a plant species hardy enough to grow in desert conditions. This is happening now. In the Arava — a section of the Great Rift Valley running from the southern end of the Sea of Galilee past the Dead Sea to the Gulf of Aqaba near Eilat — they planted 150 different varieties of Tamarix." Dana paused. "These are projects internationally involved in the reforestation of our planet, but these projects are isolated from each other both physically and in the scientific sense too. We need a global recognition. But wait…"

The next image caused a jolt to move around the audience. An image of a forest with lorries and workers cutting down and processing trees. Dana continued, "With funding, we can mitigate to stop this from continuing. The UN currently funds many projects in Paraguay, Ecuador, Chile and Brazil and for the work we do building forests, we MUST stop any economic gain from the destruction of those forests that we still have. This can be achieved only by the continued work of the UN Climate fund but also with our partners in universities around the globe where their sole task is to fund alternative climate-resilient crops so reforestation can occur. "

Dana stepped from behind the podium and walked towards the audience. "The science isn't wrong; the science tells us what we must do…. hundreds of projects, people, and communities are doing the right thing. The forest is our friend," She chuckled, "but on a serious note, the forests are our future, our salvation. The lives of every one of us in here and out there, rely upon these forests. We've achieved the hard part. We've found the answer and now we need everyone to know about it. Now, we need funds to help us spread the message and to convince countries, communities and companies to come along with us. "

A shout from the audience, "How much do you need?"

Dana looked up towards the woman. "Thank you." She pointed her finger at her, "Thank you for asking. Unfortunately, I can't answer that. But I know education for reforestation is key. If we can spread the word and gain people's confidence in our results, we're halfway there. With funding, we can visit people face to face, we can set up similar projects around the world and we can build momentum in this. That's what we need rapid momentum because trees take time to grow…" She smiled up at the audience, "What I am saying is- It is not too late, but this time we could lose. "

Her attention moved to the fleet of press associates in front of her. "Do you want a headline? I'll give you a headline. Plant a tree, they are the lungs of our planet, plant a forest and save our planet! She looked up again at the audience. "Spread the word, please." She placed her palms together, curling her fingers around her hands and closing her eyes. "Thank you for coming today. Thankyou Simon. Thankyou press. We are available for the next few minutes, should you have questions."

Several of the audience including those close to Landry stood up, clapping and talking. Landry was filled with renewed hope. Maybe people would act. Once the applause faded, some began making their way towards the presenters. The students in Landry's line began making their way out. Landry followed them, contemplating the actual sphere of influence that Magera would be willing to have upon past events to avoid the climate chaos of the future. She made her way out of the Reagan building onto the campus. Would Magera give money to this project? She was uncertain whether this fresh evidence was strong enough to make Magera reconsider their decision not to act.

As Landry made her way back through Birmingham in 2017, she tried to imagine a world full of forests. This world. In her proper time 2188, at the top of each accom tower, were biospheres full of trees, but these were too little too late, these recycled the oxygen usage in each accom block. Not enough to combat the high levels of carbon dioxide in the World. She kept coming back to the same conclusion again and again. Why didn't the World listen? The science was crucially basic in its principle, so why wasn't it successful?

As Landry approached the Hippodrome Theatre once again, she came to a reluctant conclusion. BUFR needed money, but would Magera agree to pay for a new future by funding the past? Landry was excited to try, but even before she stepped into the cupboard at the back of the theatre, she resigned herself to an answer she felt would come. She knew the presentation, however inspiring, had little additional evidence that would add to her previous findings. This wouldn't be enough, but she wasn't going to tell them. She would run it through the Radan system check again and hope to gain a different result.

She entered the small, enclosed space and lent against the back wall, placing the tattoo on her left wrist against the small Magera icon. The green screen came to life and Landry watched the two spheres interwoven with the Magera lettering. Kyson Mullins's face appeared on the screen. Landry considered whether to try to speak to Kyson again.

"Welcome back Reagan2485." Kyson looked directly at Landry; she had her full attention.

Landry coughed, "Hello Mullins2001."

A small look of triumph moved across Kyson's face as Landry used her formal nomination. She smiled briefly and then continued. "Reagan2485, I have confirmation of date and time for you; 1500 hours on 28/07/2188. 3 entry enforcement positions in place for subdivision Sofia and subdivision Carlton, Phase 6. You'll need to enter through enforcement position B at Phase 6 subdivision Carlton, I'm afraid. Normal curfews apply after 1700 hours."

"Reason for the enforcement position?" Landry was concerned; it was near her accom.

"Fugitives from the Mars re-development programme." Kyson's face contorted as she realised her error.

Landry couldn't resist, "Are these other people who are being forced to go to Mars? If it's such a wonderful proposition, then why are people running to avoid it?" She waited and watched as Kyson took a moment to choose her words.

"Many of the first waves of permanent settlers are thrilled to be moving and looking forward to an outstanding quality of life. There are offenders needed to support systems that bots cannot be requisitioned for. These are reluctant migrants. "

Landry interrupted Kyson. "Reluctant, are they? So reluctant that they risk everything to not go there. Wynter doesn't want to go either... she's terrified that she may be sent there!"

Kyson coughed, clearly embarrassed. "I really don't think that will happen Reagan2485. Now I need your download please."

Landry clucked her tongue and blew her breath out between her lips. "OK Mullins2001, I had 1 stage 2 - non-compromising interaction."

Kyson's attention stayed on the screen to her left. "I'll look at the visoptics. You must include it in your report."

Landry placed her left wrist again on the symbol and exclaimed, "upload236.3 Reagan2485." And leant forward towards the screen, "I'm excited about Radan checking this one Mullins2001. I believe this information adds to the early evidence that was an 80% positive impact upon Earth's history. If you look at the first-year results and if that continues, it is a climate change positive event. We act upon 80% positive impact ripples and this solution is an 80%."

Kyson's face was fixed. "Make sure your report is well-written and ON TIME Reagan2485, 0600 28/07/2188."

The screen closed, and the blank space returned. Landry stepped through the second door into the darkness of the stage in 2188. With no performance planned, all was quiet. On making her way through the theatre, Landry knew the rear door would be open. She stepped through it into her home city, unseen and insignificant.

CHAPTER 19

WYNTER LUND

Wynter had reduced her list of unmonitored doorways to two. This was the pre-Radan system for time travel that Karmal had suggested. But it relied upon her finding the keypads and getting the complex coding right.

The Playhouse Theatre in 21st century London had not met the requirements for the 2093 buildings act, allowing buildings of historical significance to be moved inland. As a result, it was not saved from the rising tide of the Thames. The Playhouse had been privately owned for more than a century when the act came into force and so its ineligibility for free movement was a death knell for the once-loved theatre. The owners couldn't afford the phenomenal costs and the popularity of live theatre was already waning. It was abandoned in 2088 and the building fenced off, but Wynter´s research found that much of the ground floor had remained intact. Magera records showed a time doorway in a small staff room, off the corridor backstage.

In Wynter's own time of 2188, tours could be arranged through the London historic building society. These were conducted during low tide and the advertisements promised that much of the theatre was still accessible. Wynter was confident of finding the abandoned doorway, but the small keypad was a different matter. Karmal had said that it should still be operational. Grapheme power did not deteriorate with time.

Another possible doorway was in the Corinthia Hotel, previously named the Metropole and commandeered by the British army in the 2nd World War because of its underground tunnels which used to lead to the government offices. The Corinthia had met the requirements for the historic buildings act, but it was located just inside the Thames tide cordon, only the principal building had been moved inland. The annexe left in 2098 was now service accom and offices. Wynter's research had shown that there was an office in the location where the time doorway used to be. The problem was that the office where the doorway was located required a Radan tattoo to enter. Wynter's presence would be revealed as soon as she entered the room, and so would have to be her emergency exit only.

Soon, she was ready to go back to 2033 and find out what had happened on the day of the explosion. As promised, Wynter kept to her word and told Landry and Karmal the detail of her plans in the secret web chatroom.

Wynter was keen to get started. "Right, I'm going to spend the day in 2033 tomorrow… or for as long as it takes. Thank you, Kar, for your ideas. I've found a doorway in the Playhouse Theatre, Near Embankment. It was abandoned in 2098 when the Thames water penetrated the ground floor."

Karmal laughed. "Your feet will be wet then?"

"Yep…but other than that it's ideal, abandoned but still semi-open for tourists. If I can find the door, I should be OK."

Landry didn't share their levity. Holding up her hand she exclaimed, "Wait Wynt- you're going into a flooded building?"

"Please don't worry Land. I've researched it well. There are still tours of the building, so it's accessible."

"Just remember, the Thames is a tidal river."

"What happens if you misjudge your return and it's full of water? Karmal said that the reason they stopped using the old doorway keypads was because of the high risk of human error. You might not make it back?"

"Hey, have faith! I've completed my checks. High tide is still only up to my chest so if I misjudge the time that I return, I'll get wet but it's still passable."

"If you can open a doorway with the water pushing against you. This is a terrible choice, Wynt. There must be others?" Landry had moved closer to her screen.

Wynter looked away from the screen. "The quality doorways were transferred to the Radan tattoo system after the Great Fall, so whatever door I choose comes with risks. You both know that."

"She's right Land, all doorways not claimed by Radan will have issues. Just in a bad case, do you have an emergency second?"

"Yes, the Corinthia hotel service buildings, Northumberland Avenue, just off Whitehall Place. The Corinthia was moved after the historic buildings' act of 2093, but the annexe next door remains, and they are now offices and accoms."

Landry brightened. "That sounds like a much better choice?"

"I agree, use that one."

Wynter's face screwed into a frown. "The problem is the Radan access locks. The only way to get to the time door is through a Radan locked door. I can't go when the offices are open, the Radan system would detect me the moment I enter."

There was a pause as the three operatives took time to weigh up Wynter's options and it was Karmal who spoke first, "You are right Wynt, the wet way is the best choice."

Landry scowled, "I'm not happy Wynt."

"I know. I know the risks. I'm sending the details of the date/time of the explosion and my route from the door."

"And if you don't come back?"

"I'll come back. This is reconnaissance only. I want to clear my name." Wynter held both hands up.

"I'll come after you if you are not back by the 3rd day."

"No Land, if I'm not back, don't come after me. I promise you. I'm going back to find those responsible. If I don't come back, then something terrible has happened."

Landry's raised her voice, "You can't ask us that Wynt. You can't ask us to leave you somewhere. No!"

Karmal shook his head. "She is right. You cannot ask us to do that. It would be different if you wanted to stay."

"Look, it's my problem, and it's my assignment. I need to do this. You can't come after me."

"Ok Wynter, I will back off, but have you considered a human error. Think of the scenario... You put the wrong date on the keypad, for example. As Karmal said, they got rid of the keypads because of the high risk of human error when keying in the dates."

Karmal moved closer and his usual wide smile filled the camera. "I can help with that. I can use old software to find old events at the doorway. If it goes wrongly then we can see the dates of most recent travellers."

"Kar, You kept that quiet. Can you find data for all doorways?"

His smile broadening, "I have many talents."

"Are we in agreement? I will return, but if not, I permit Kar to check the last time/date index for the doorway in the playhouse. Remember, if I go to the wrong day/time then I can key in the right one."

"Yes, of course, the keypad works with a digi-date transfer. An example, 21.07.2188/0300. That's 21 days in the month of July in 2188. The time indicator is the same. 0300. If you go wrong, then place the new digi-date transfer in and step back through."

Landry interrupted him, "As long as you can key in a new digi-date. Be careful with your dates, Wynt. You don't want to go back too far."

"Yes, be with care. The keypad in the past could look different. If that happens, keep looking; it will be there."

"I'm nervous for you, Wynt. With no access to the Radan system, it will be scary. How did the first travellers do it?"

"You of all people should be OK with this. You were born off-grid. Your life until 4 years ago was with no direct link to medic or Radan. You lived and cared for yourself with no help at all."

"I know Wynt, but I feel edgy about this. I was never alone with no help nearby."

"I appreciate your concern, Land, but I need to do this, and I want to do this. I can look after myself. You've both been good friends and I understand your concerns, but I'm doing this."

Karmal nodded. "You do what is right. There is another way. You could agree that Magera and Radan are right and face the consequence."

"I know I didn't do this, and I need to find the evidence of that and show it to Kyson."

"Please take care and think about all steps. Do not rush it."

Wynter's smile returned. "Yes, here's my list. Number 1, private mode, number 2, leave the building without using my tattoo and number 3, avoid secure Bot areas and transport. "

"Remember to do what I did in Pencal. Have a record somewhere of you staying at home in the time that you are absent. Radan won't question you staying in your accom."

"Yes, I'll vidchat you before I leave my accom telling you I'm staying a home."

"That should be enough. Remember, everything that we've talked about."

Karmal mimed writing on his hand, "Remember to write your digi-dates to carry with you."

Wynter let out a long breath. "Right. Thank you, guys, so much. You've been so good at helping me." Her smile broadened as she stared at her companions. Their body language mirrored hers.

Karmal serious face returned, "Happiness in your travels Wynt."

Landry held up both of her hands, "Good Luck." She chuckled, "It means that I am wishing you every success and I hope you succeed."

"I will succeed. Thank you Land and Kar."

Wynter's icon disappeared from the chatroom open page. Followed by both Landry's and Karmal's.

CHAPTER 20

WYNTER LUND

As the Earth rose, the sky darkened and Wynter completed her last preparations. As she would be disconnected from her Radan optics, she had prepared a portable optic to take information that would prove her innocence. She'd deal with the fact that she had defied the restrictions of the investigation later. She had already vidi-chatted with Landry and delivered the fake narrative that she was planning on staying in her accom.

Wynter knew that her neighbour, Mrs Burrows, stepped outside most evenings around 1900 hours and so she timed her exit to coincide with her. She had already gone into private mode, turning off her link to Radan before leaving her accom. Making her way down the stairway to the ground floor, she arrived before 1900. She waited as the elevator descended from the 34th floor, her heart beating in her chest. The doors opened and a stooped figure shuffled out into the foyer.

"Good evening, Mrs Burrows."

"Evening Miss Lund."

"Going outside?"

She nodded in reply and Mrs Burrows turned and began making her slow way towards the door to leave their building. Wynter resisted the temptation to step in front of her neighbour but remained behind, making small talk as they went; It was tediously slow but necessary.

"I don't see anyone anymore, Miss Lund. I can see them from the outside, all sitting staring at the screen or running on those machines or talking to themselves."

Wynter murmured in agreement, "It is more entertaining to watch diaramas or Virtual reality visits."

"People don't speak to each other unless it's through those blasted screens. It's like they're not there at all or half there. Not like it used to be. There is no family time anymore. Where have all the families gone?"

"I'm surprised that you're still living here, Mrs Burrows. Don't you want to live in the senior comfort accoms in Nirvan? Be with people of your age?"

She stopped walking to scrutinise Wynter. "I'm not going there. They kill you off, you know. I'm a leach to society. Radan doesn't like ancient ones."

"Don't be silly, Mrs Burrows. Radan doesn't kill people. Its purpose is to save life, not to end it."

Tutting, she turned away from Wynter. It felt like an eternity, but she finally arrived at the door to the outside. Her auditorus volume was so high, Wynter could hear the reassuring bong as Mrs Burrow's tattoo unlocked the accom door. Aware that the door was now open, Wynter stepped in front of her. As she got through the open door, Wynter turned and held out her arm. "Need help to get down the rampway, Mrs Burrows?"

She batted her hand away. "No, I can manage. You go ahead."

Walking away, Wynter said over her shoulder. "See you soon, Mrs Burrows." She heard no reply, so wasn't sure if she had heard her. Wynter was elated. Her last link to Radan would now be in her accom and, according to Radan, that was where would remain.

She moved through the walkways between the accom blocks and this route enabled her to get to the Playhouse well before curfew. The streets were relatively empty apart from the familiar sound of redline pods zipping back and forth. Wynter could hear them approach in the distance. She stepped into the shadows of the accoms as they zipped past.

Her greatest threat was the crime enforcement representatives. In her research, she had placed importance on knowing where they were located and at what times. If she came across one of them, she would have to end her private mode to reveal her identity. The problem with taking a route lacking in crime enforcement representatives was that it would not be as safe as other areas.

She focussed on the walk ahead as she made her way down Carriage Drive, glancing inside the accoms as she passed. As Mrs Burrows had said, in every window, people were mainly alone and interacting with the screen in front of them. During Wynter´s assignments into the mid-22nd century she had observed families but had never really understood the notion of family; having been kept in the infant accoms until adulthood. The privilege of visiting the past gave Wynter an insight into what had been, and until recently, she had felt no loss for that former life.

The journey passed quickly and with no events to note. Only one enforcement vehicle had overtaken her at great speed as she walked towards constitution Hill. Her breath faltered but the vehicle did not stop, busy after someone else. Her planned route made her approach to the Playhouse from a quiet street and not down the mall, which in comparison was busy with pods. There were two flood protection gates to cross, and she paused at the first gate at the top of Craven Street. She placed her grapheme hood up and extended her footwear up her leg to provide a waterproof barrier. She knew that until this point, she could name many reasons to be here. Beyond was the area of greatest risk. There was no justification to be past flood barriers in the evening and therefore she would likely be detained if discovered.

The high sided exclusion fencing had sensors cross each support post, so Wynter chose carefully where to make her way up and over the fence. She had little trouble reaching the top and swinging her legs over, jumping to the ground on the other side. The height of the fence made her invisible to the main street behind and she now turned on her lightweight illuminator fixed to the cap that she wore. She was careful to keep the beam down as she moved through the waste ground between the first and second flood fences. It was eerily quiet as Wynter cautiously stepped across a ground strewn with building materials, partially submerged in the water which lapped across the top of her feet. As she made her way towards the second gateway, the water became deeper and her way more difficult as the bricks and materials under the water, were difficult to spot. On a couple of occasions, she almost lost her footing, the splashing water seeming loud in the evening's silence. Several times she stopped, listening intently for any movement in the street.

The second barrier was more solid, needing to keep the rising water at bay, and Wynter struggled to get traction as she scaled it. This was reinforced as a double barricade, and as she reached the top, Wynter needed to breach a gap between the two. For the second that she sat on the top, she looked towards the Thames itself and the accom blocks at the distant shore. The lights in the accoms sparkling like regimented stars in the distance. Silhouetted against this were the remains of the Playhouse, partially demolished now and ominously dark compared to the brightness beyond.

As she jumped to safety on the other side, her beam shone across the walls of the Playhouse. Wynter turned her head slowly left and then right, looking for the gap between the debris where the historic tours enter the building. She found it, a slight change in the shadows, hardly distinguishable. She made her way towards it, wading through the rising waters and using old fence lines and low walls as supports. Wynter eventually arrived at the threshold to the back of the theatre. Peering inside, she could see where the water had entered the building. The roof was now gone, replaced by the night sky. The historical stucco features were gone, taken away at some point, but Wynter could still sense the grandeur of the building's past.

She had memorised the layout. But as she entered the building, Wynter became more distracted by the maze of backstage corridors, which had once echoed with music and laughter. There was an eeriness to the empty building in the darkness, with the sounds of water lapping against the walls. She found the corridor where the room should be. There were many doors and they all looked identical. She moved along, opening each door, pushing against the resistance of the water and fighting the fear of finding something unwelcome on the other side. She had to force open many doors before she found the right one.

As she stepped inside, the darkness enveloped her. She stilled her breathing as she turned a full circle in the small room. She studied the walls. Ripped Posters, torn signs and frayed photographs leapt out from the darkness as the glow from Wynter's illuminator reached them. Karmal had told her that the keypad would be hidden in plain sight, and about eye level. With shoulders hunched, Wynter took her 4th turn around the room and no keypad appeared in her beam. Was she in the wrong room? She considered her options and tried to imagine what could have happened. Maybe they had removed it? With a last attempt, Wynter took her time to move around the room's edge, using her hands to press the wall as she did so. As she reached the last wall before coming back to the doorway, her fingers fell upon a small part that flexed to her touch. It was not solid as the surrounding wall. She pulled at the wallpaper with her fingertips. They brushed on thicker card, covering an object in the wall. As she prized the card away, she saw a glint of metal. She had found it. Relief surged through her as she removed the rest of the card, revealing the keypad buttons. Karmal had explained where the power button would be found and what to expect.

With slight hesitation and a small wish, Wynter held down the keypad power button and counted to 10. At first, there was no response, then the keypad buttons sprang into life, a red glow appearing behind each key number in order, 1,2,3,4 until all the numbers were illuminated. The last sign that power was on came when the visual screen came to life and throbbed red in anticipation.

Wynter pulled her vispad out of the pocket of her graphemo. It held the all-important date indexes she had carefully prepared with Karmal's help. She worked her way methodically through the instructions that he had given her. Pressing buttons was antiquated, and it took some time for Wynter to learn how much pressure was needed to apply to select a particular number. There was no room for complacency. She checked and double-checked the date index on the small visual screen many times before pressing the enter button to activate the doorway.

The wall to her left shimmered and the ERA symbol appeared, spinning in the centre. The name ERA- Environmental Research Authority was the original name of Magera. It was pre-Radan and before the coalition between ERA and Radan. It hit Wynter like the chill of icy wind. The Environmental Research authority had now become the Mars and Greater Earth Research Authority; Had Mars been the plan all along?

Wynter took a moment to prepare for what she may encounter as she entered through an unfamiliar doorway. She reviewed her plan in her head. Once she entered 2033, she had to be ready to face anything. She had never used this doorway so didn't know what to expect. She took her portable optic visual from the breast pocket of her graphemo.

"Begin optic viz evidence for 120433." She felt the lens focus as the visual recording began. She began stepping through the doorway into 2033, a blinding light hit her optics, blocking out everything for an instance.

CHAPTER 21

WYNTER LUND

A strong smell of perfume engulfed Wynter as her optic adjusted to a blinding light. It was coming from a mirror. In the reflection, a young girl was sitting at the dressing table, makeup brush frozen in her hand. Her mouth wide open, a scream threatening to invade the quiet.

Wynter made no noise. She didn't even look towards the young girl who had just seen Wynter walk directly through the wall behind her.

Heart racing, Wynter fought the urge to speak as she strode through the open door of the dressing room and, turning, ran down the corridor towards the main exit. A delayed scream pierced the quietness, and Wynter glanced behind her. The girl had made her way to the door of the dressing room and was leaning around the doorway. Holding her head at a 90-degree angle, astonishment on her face. Wynter chuckled. Had she just been the source of another theatre ghost story?

Still smiling, Wynter stepped into the street behind the theatre. The exhilaration of being on her own and out from under the radar of Magera was liberating. She wouldn't need to complete a report for this assignment. She wouldn't have to inform them of any stage 3 compromises. These feelings of freedom increased as she made her way with the crowds towards Trafalgar Square. She felt a lightness that she had never experienced before. Wynter had planned to arrive at 0800 on the morning of the rally in 2033. It would give her plenty of time to study the section of the square where the blast had occurred.

Like her first visit to this day, Wynter soon became pulled into the excitement of the SAM crowd as they moved through Northumberland Avenue. This route differed from her first visit to 2033. The doorway in the playhouse was closer to Trafalgar square however, the streets remained just as busy. She stopped at a street corner and took the time to gain her bearings. In her time, this area of New London had been lost to the Thames, so the surrounding buildings were lost, moved, or abandoned.

Her attention was dragged to the repetitive banging coming from the pile drivers building the Kallan Towers flood defences behind her. Evidence of London's battle with the water that was yet to come. At least these towers would save some of the older buildings for New London.

Taking a deep breath and stepping off the pavement to position herself behind a group, Wynter Lund disappeared into 2033 London. Fighting her phobia, she maintained the slightest distance from herself and the group as they jostled their way through the streets. She was focused upon maintaining her own space when her attention was drawn to a public house on the righthand side, The Sherlock Holmes. It was a sunny, warm morning and people were spilling out from the inside of the establishment, holding glasses of alcohol. In her time, the prohibition of alcohol came after the Great Fall along with many non-essential commodities, making it illegal to get or consume. In her new feeling of freedom, Wynter was tempted to try it for the first time. Then someone in front of her moved aside revealing Nelson's column standing proud against the blue sky. Her levity vanished. Seeing the column still intact, she was instantly taken back to her last experience at this site. The public house forgotten, she forged ahead.

Looking up, she saw the familiar Trafalgar manned security barriers. The airborne security drones swarming like bees; dropping into the crowd, forcing people to stop and stare at the camera as they scanned their faces. As with her previous visit, she felt no threat from these drones. As of 2033, they would only have access to faces of known offenders and therefore unknown faces would be presumed to be innocents. But surely, one person here today was not innocent. For the first time, she considered how the terrorist had breached the gauntlet of security?

Her focus shifted to the task at hand. It was painful knowing what was about to happen and knowing that she couldn't stop it. She must not stop it. Even if she found the culprit, she knew there had already been a 0.67-time intervention wave. She must observe and not change anything. The damage was already too great. She just needed to know who it was, for Magera to accept that it wasn't her.

The familiar chanting of the crowd enveloped Wynter, as she made her way to her new vantage point. She could not under any circumstance, meet her earlier-self. It would cause a huge new time wave adjustment. Her need to blend in was more important than ever. She zipped her jacket up high onto her face and hid her blonde hair in the back of the hood.

Her first task was to scrutinise the space where she estimated the explosion was centred. It could not have been far from the curved edge of the closer of the Lutyens fountains. The height of the fountain edge made it a perfect perch for a seat. Parents sat on the edge and bags were stacked along the side as children ran around wielding SAM flags and jumping on and off the rim. Wynter squeezed her optics tightly closed, banishing the image of the aftermath of the explosion. She knew she couldn't save them and change history, but she so wanted to. She focussed on the area of the fountain, looking for anything or anyone that looked suspicious. Sitting on the steps, her attention remained on the fountain, the portable optic in her pocket capturing it.

Carly began her welcome speech and Wynter scanned the crowd as they cheered and shouted, "We can do it" and "There is hope." When Robert stepped forward next to Carly at the podium, Wynter's attention on the fountain rim briefly waned as she turned to look at Robert. The difference from the last time she had seen him; dying on the floor was telling. Her heart constricted as tears filled her eyes. Carly listed the cities that would be affected by the global sea rise and the crowd responded "No" to each. "Are we able to give up on these cities?" Carly began listing them. When she reached the end of the long list, Wynter saw Robert's attention fix on a figure that Wynter could see out of the corner of her eye. It was herself in the earlier time assignment. The strangeness of being able to watch herself was a rare privilege. She studied her own face and saw something in her expression that she couldn't place. His gaze remained on Wynter's previous self. She could see their eyes locked, and he didn't look away until Carly introduced Robert to speak.

Wynter felt compelled to return her gaze to the fountain area to watch for anything unusual. She saw nothing which would cause her any alarm. Robert began speaking and Wynter could hear his voice but kept her attention on the families near to the fountain where the source of the explosion was. When Carly began her concluding comments regarding Hothouse Earth and the point of no return for the temperature of the planet, Wynter knew that the time was near.

She turned her body straight on to the fountain rim, focussing her portable optic on the area of interest. Zipping up her graphemo to the top, she placed the hood over her head. Tying her graphene neck scarf around the lower part of her face, she placed her sunshades over her optics for full protection. She must have looked strange wearing a scarf on such a sunny day, but Wynter knew better. She wouldn't normally bring this clothing through the doorway but knew that she needed it today. The graphene cloth was a thin a silk but as strong as steel with an interlocking honeycomb structure which could stop a bullet. She needed to have every chance of watching the source of the explosion right until the last second. She began scanning the crowd for movement, looking for something out of the ordinary, something overlooked, maybe a lone suicide bomber. Above all else, she knew she couldn't stop the explosion; however, she felt her pulse rise as the time came closer. Her anxiety reached its peak as Carly reached the last sentence she had spoken.

Two things happened at once. Carly's final words describing the Inter-Governmental congress in global warming targets rang across the square. Wynter took that as her cue to look at the point of explosion. Instinctively shielding her face from the blast by pulling her hood low over her face whilst still frantically scanning the crowd. She saw no one.

The blast knocked Wynter onto her back, a fireball flattening her against the ground. Her auditorus was temporarily affected and there was a moment of silence and then a rush of sounds, shrieks and cries. Her optics were more protected this time, and she looked in front of her to check the source of the explosion. She tried to pinpoint the exact location as she attempted to move towards it. Just like previously, the bodies, body parts, clothing and bags were strewn like petals from the source. She saw the children and adults that had been sitting on the rim of the fountain. Some had been blown across into the fountain and ripples of red began coursing into the water. Seeing the lifeless children, small feet in boots and toys and flags strewn around, was horrific. Wynter felt an attachment to these small people, and a jolt of responsibility for not saving them. She could so easily have spoken to the parents or moved them onto another part of the Square, but to what end? To have them replaced by yet other people and cause another time variation. No, she knew she had to distance herself from them. But it was difficult. She wasn't a war operative and the first time it had happened; she had attempted to deal with the emotions of shock and disgust. But to experience it again was a different matter. She wasn't made for this. She couldn't isolate her feelings from what she was experiencing. She wasn't immune to her reactions to seeing those people die again.

The source had been in the centre of the group that she had observed before, but the creeping possibility that one of those adults was to blame was unfathomable to Wynter. Which of those parents could kill themselves and their children? She knew from history that belief in a cause made people do things you would think impossible. But she had seen nothing in the mannerisms of anyone in the group that gave credence to this theory. She'd found the source, now she needed to find the individual or individuals. As she moved towards the source the smell of burning engulfed her and she raised her hand to cover her nose and mouth. The hole that the explosion had created was huge and if Wynter had hoped to find any clues there, she was disappointed. There was nothing left of many of the items and people who one moment ago had been enjoying the April sunshine. Wynter took the portable optic from her pocket and rewound the blast, scrutinising every frame, looking for that unusual movement in that group but there were none.

She turned towards Robert and his sisters and saw her past-self groping her way towards them. Wynter was the reluctant voyeur as she watched everything happen the same as before. She saw her past-self checking Robert's sisters; felt the emotion rip through her. He was stirring and gasping for breath. She watched as her past-self knelt next to him as he looked at her. She had to resist the urge to move closer, push herself aside, and attempt to save him all over again. He tried to push himself up, and she watched herself place her arm gently on his chest and push him back to a lying position. Wynter couldn't turn her face away. It was a tender moment and watching it from outside, Wynter could see the gentle way that her past-self was speaking to him and the emotion on her face. "Lie still Robert. You need to lie still. The medics are coming." She saw the blood spreading across his chest and her past-self place both hands on the wound to apply pressure. Watching herself bought everything into focus. The feelings that she had for Robert were unlike anything she had ever felt before. She knew she should move away, but her feet were rooted to the spot.

She saw his mouth moving, Robert was asking about his sisters again and becoming agitated and as before, she saw her past-self leaning forward, murmuring to him and she saw his body relax and his breath leave his body for the last time.

She watched her past-self scream, an agonising scream. After attempting resuscitation, beating his chest, shouting Robert's name again and again. Wynter saw the medic approach, observed him check Robert's pulse and whisper to her past self. She scrutinised her face as the emotion washed over her. What she saw shook her to her core, an undeniable pain and suffering. She watched as the tears fell freely down her past-self's face. She felt it again, this renewed sense of affection, tenderness towards Robert. Wynter couldn't watch anymore. She turned her head to hide her face as her past-self walked past her and she watched as she made her way through the rubble, stumbling out of the square and past the ambulances stationed there.

She made her way over to Robert. The medic had moved onto other survivors. Wynter placed her hand over his eyes, closing them. His face was cold to the touch. "Goodbye Robert. I wished I could have known you. I think we would have liked each other." Wynter was shocked for the second time at the rawness of this new emotion. She couldn't identify why she felt so connected to Dr Robert Sanchez. She continued to sit there for some time with Robert, planning what she would do next.

A medic made her way towards Wynter and crouched down in front of her, scrutinising her face. "Did you know him?" she enquired softly, glancing across at Robert. Wynter nodded as the medic began squeezing her arms and brushing her hands across her jacket, checking for injuries. "We cannot help him, but we can help you." The medic had a quizzical look on her face. "Were you involved in the explosion? Where were you standing? Are you hurt?" Wynter brushed her hand away. She knew her graphemo had significantly protected her. "Yes. No, I'm fine. I was further up the steps." She indicated with her chin the space behind the podium up the gallery steps.

"You're not feeling unwell at all? No pain?"

Wynter slowly shook her head and smiled tentatively.

The medic, satisfied with her answer, moved on. Raising to stand, she turned and speaking over her shoulder, "Make sure you get checked over at the ambulance station before you go." Wynter's attention moved back to Robert. She couldn't save him, she knew that, but she had failed in her mission as well. However much she didn't want to, she needed to go through it all over again. Looking at him lying by her side, she wished there was a way to save him. The nanotechnology of her time would have. But Wynter knew that there was no possibility of doing that.

Finally, she knew she needed to get up and get back to the doorway. With a last look at Robert, she turned and began making her way through the debris to the cordon created by the emergency services. Taking her scarf and hood down and opening her graphene coat, she blended in with the crowds being moved away from the area by security personnel. Her route back to the Playhouse was significantly different; the joviality of the crowds gone now, replaced with fear and grief.

As the theatre came into view, she could hear the dull throbbing of music inside. The matinee in full swing. Walking back down the corridor to the dressing room where the doorway was located, she hoped the cast would all be on or near the stage. As she pushed open the dressing room door, she prepared for the worst. She had spent some time thinking of what to say to the young girl. She had bought a journalist ID badge she had used on a previous assignment as an emergency identity. She now had that on a lanyard around her neck, but she would still have some explaining to do. On turning the handle and opening the door, she breathed a sigh of relief. The dressing room was empty. Stepping inside, she quickly closed the door behind her.

Her relief turned to panic as Wynter attempted to find the keypad on this side of the doorway. She hadn't been able to search for it this morning, as the young girl had forced her to leave quickly. She tried to imagine the mirror room in 2188. But the room had looked different, in darkness and devoid of furniture. Now her anxiety increased with every minute that she stayed there and couldn't find the keypad. She paused and breathed out slowly. Think! Wynter checked all around the doorframe, behind the mirror and under the dressing table. Nothing. She felt it must be close to the doorway, much as it was in the future. Had they changed the layout? Had the walls moved? Did she have the right room? The feeling of dread increased. The longer she stayed there, the more likely the risk of being seen. She crouched down, studying the space. Thinking back to where she had found it on the other side, she turned slowly and suddenly, there it was. Surely not! Staring at her all this time. The perfect size. The light switch. Its surround stood apart from the wall, but Wynter noticed it looked more pronounced than the others. She placed her thumb and fingers around the light unit and pulled. She was ecstatic when the front cover came off in her hand. Behind it was the keypad with vis display. Wynter was quick to place the time/day index into the keypad but took a few seconds to check it; Karmal's caution ringing in her auditorus. After double-checking, she pressed enter, and the wall shimmered into life. Placing the cover back on the light switch and not waiting for the Era symbol to appear, Wynter stepped forward, pressed her fingertips against the wall and walked through to the other side.

She was struck by the contrast between the two places. The inky blackness of the abandoned building enveloped her as her optics adjusted to the intensity of change. She felt the water seeping through her shoes.

She quickly reset the keypad in 2188 to take her straight back again to the same day. She made a slight alteration with the time arriving at 0700 hours hoping to avoid the young girl in the changing room and her second previous self. She placed her finger on the inside collar of her graphemo and stated, "green." The graphene fabric shimmered and changed to a dark green colour. She did the same with her graphene scarf. Tapping the enter button on the keypad, the integrity of the wall changed, and she stepped back into 2033.

Wynter was relieved to find the room empty. She made her way unhindered, aware that she was ahead of her second past self. No stopping this time straight on her path to the Square. She reviewed everything that she had learnt already and quickly came to only one conclusion. With a heavy heart, she knew she would need to watch those parents carefully to find out which one had detonated a device.

CHAPTER 22

WYNTER LUND

It took two more visits, two times to relive moments of death and destruction and two times to discover that the parents were not personally responsible. Watching Robert, his sisters and the parents and children, die in 2033 and the pressure of avoiding the duplications of her past selves were having a toll on Wynter. She was slipping into traumatic shock as the adrenalin built up in her body.

She had ruled out the parents sitting on the edge of the fountain but was successful in identifying a black bag that she thought could hold a device. It had been left under the pile of rucksacks, next to the mountain of toys, clothing, food and flags bought by the group sat next to the fountain. From previous visits, she saw that there was one bag that no one had opened or touched. Scrutinising the members of that group arriving at different times, Wynter could see how the bag had been overlooked; each family thinking that it belonged to someone else. She would not criticise the group for their recklessness in not seeing the bag. There had not been a terrorist incident in Britain since Cardiff 2025. The only thing Wynter did not know was who was responsible for the bag?

For this final visit, she moved the timeframe much earlier. She was determined to arrive before the bag was hidden. As she made her way down Northumberland Avenue, the sun was only just throwing slim shadows onto the pavement. At this time in the morning, there were very few SAM supporters and although Wynter could see the security drones in the distance, they were focussed upon Trafalgar Square as the organisers set up for the rally. She walked past the Sherlock Holmes public house and was surprised to find people inside. She could hear their raucous laughter and intoxicated singing. Some sat outside smoking nicotine enhanced products. It was 0500. Wynter did not know that people would still be in a public house. Wynter had long ago come to believe that past participants were selfish and hedonistic in their lifestyle appearing to have no worries or cares.

As she entered Trafalgar Square, her first glance was to the lip of the fountain edge, and she saw that there was no black bag there. Elation and relief overcame her. She would see who put it there. She would find her terrorist. She made her way to a secluded vantage point and sat down behind the edge of a pillar. She held up her portable optic and checked the viewfinder. It gave Wynter a sniper-like view of the small space that interested her. This was it. Excitement welled up inside her. Taking in a long breath, she took a moment of calm, slowed down her breathing, and waited.

It was almost one hour before any movement came into view. She saw a family that she recognised to make their way slowly over to the area under scrutiny. She watched as they took their time taking out various paraphernalia. Claiming that area by the fountain edge. In each visit to this day, Wynter had turned over and over in her mind the implication of telling the people to move. To move to another area of the square or to tell them to leave; anything to save them from their inevitable fate. But with all Wynter's imagined scenarios, she had come to an impossible conclusion. She couldn't tell them, even if she wanted to. She couldn't change their future and the inescapable future of those people whose lives would be changed as a result. The timewave alteration would not only signal her presence at that location but also affect countless future timelines. The wave could be larger than the original blast, larger than 0.67. She was torn and in an untenable situation. Knowing the fate of all those people, including Robert, was the curse of a time operative. She didn't like it, but she knew she could do nothing, and she also knew that Karmal and Landry would say the same thing.

Her thoughts stilled. There was a new movement by the fountain. A tall man wearing a hooded coat had just moved past her zoomed optic as another group appeared at the fountain edge. He was at the rear of the group. They were in high spirits and were talking and laughing. They didn't notice the person at close quarters behind them. Placing their bags with those already there, the parents began moving them around, taking out items for the rally, chatting to the other families sat there. The hooded individual unobserved by the excited group deposited the black bag under several others, and then continued forward, not breaking their stride. Wynter quickly checked the pile, zooming in with her portable optic to confirm if she was correct in what she had just seen. Yes, there it was, just peeking out from the bottom. She had found the terrorist! Now she had to find out who they were.

Wynter glanced in the direction of travel and saw the black hooded jacket and the back of the assailant. The person had a slow fluid gait and a casual manner which made catching up with them easy for Wynter. As she followed at a distance, she tapped the portable optic, each time gaining additional still images of the individual, should she need them later. She hoped he would enter a building or a vehicle, which would give Wynter some method of identifying him. Maybe even follow him to his accom? Anything of information that she could then share with Magera.

As she made her way through the glare of the billboards in Piccadilly Circus, the crowds coming towards them increased and the scrutiny of the security drones intensified. Despite the pushing crowds and the frenzy of the scene, the target was easy to follow. Both herself and her prey were the only people moving away from the rally. He was very tall and thin and had a fixed walking movement, making no rapid turns and not once glancing behind him. Wynter slowed as they neared the security gateways at the top of Oxford Circus, and past several officials in uniform. She expected her assailant to avoid them or become more guarded on approaching the security gate, but with supreme confidence, he walked through without hesitation. She was also waved through without a glance. She could see that the focus was on those supporters going to the rally, not away.

Moving into Regent Street, the funnelling effect of the crowds made the pursuit more challenging. However, Wynter and her target got into a steady rhythm as they made their way up the busy street. At first, she was cautious, but she soon noted that her target never looked over his shoulder, obviously not concerned about being followed. Wynter was elated. It was going so well. She was sure of success and finding some valuable intelligence once they reached his destination. As All Souls Church came into view, everything changed.

The concentration of people had lessened, and Wynter had been forced to create more distance between them to remain hidden. With less people clouding her view, Wynter observed that the gait of her target was unusual. The movement of his legs looked like he was skating on ice, and this sparked a previous memory. A chill rippled up her spine. *No. Could it be?*

It was as she stepped out from behind the corner of the building that everything changed.

A shout came from behind, as a large dog running at speed, past Wynter's left side and streaked up the pavement towards her target. As the dog reached him, it moved to overtake but then lost control skidding to a stop and turning its body to face him.

With ears flat against its head, the dog dropped onto its front legs and began baring its teeth and snarling. Her target slowed, turned his head, and pitched forward, scrutinising the dog with interest. The dog's demeanour changed. It had begun barking, a high anxious yapping but this stopped and there was a sudden hush. The dog began shaking its head, in strange jerky movements, backing away. The owner had caught up and scrambled for the dog's lead. She turned towards the target; an apology ready on her lips but all Wynter heard was a muffled cry as she too backed away, yanking at the dog's lead as she repeated its name. Wynter could see that it was now foaming at the mouth and whimpering. As the pair slowly made their way down the opposite pavement, she saw the owner turn several times to glance back.

Wynter was disturbed by what she had just seen, but what happened next stopped her in her tracks. He was still facing away from her, but as he slowly raised his head, she saw him freeze. *Had he sensed her watching?* She shrank behind a column but from her position, she could still study him. He stood stock-still. He began to turn his head slowly. The flesh at the neck strained as his head continued to turn and continued until it had turned a full 180 degrees so that his face was facing fully backwards. An impossible act for a human being. Suddenly she knew him. The ashen face, so familiar to her. It's neutral expression, neither a smile nor a grimace. The face from the future. The face of Radan!

Wynter panicked recoiling further back into the shadows and trying to regulate her rapid breaths. Whilst fighting the questions raging through her head. But first, *had it seen her?* She strained to listen for footsteps coming her way. She couldn't look yet and held back listening intently. Then Wynter let out a long breath as she heard the tapping's of its distinct footstep, lessening as the distance between them increased. She pinned both hands against the column and with a slow movement tilted her head just a little to get a view up the street. Her breath stilled as she saw the bot making its way away from her and up towards the church in the distance.

Her thoughts were a tumbling torrent of rage and terror. *Why would Radan kill people? How can an AI kill people? How could a Radan bot be a terrorist? It's not possible. An AI cannot cause death. How can a Radan bot go through a time doorway?* She was overwhelmed with the information she now had. Everything that she had come to know was now under question.

Wynter quickly concluded that she needed to act and get definite proof. Something was wrong with the Radan matrix, surely. Magera needed to know, and she needed concrete evidence to show them. She checked that her portable optic was still running and veered out from behind the column. The bot was fading into the distance. She followed cautiously as she saw the bot entered the back of the Langham Hotel. Following it inside, Wynter prepared herself in case she was met by any hotel employees. There were none. She leant against the wall and steadied her portable optic on the corner edge. Angling its viewer down the corridor, she took several still shots of the bot as it opened the cupboard door. There was no exit from that cupboard so she knew the bot could only be going to one place. The time doorway. Wynter waited. It would either come back out or it must have passed through the time doorway back to the 23rd century. Wynter stood waiting for some time and then made her way towards the closed cupboard door. As she reached for the door handle, she breathed out slowly, readying herself with what she might face. With a surge of energy, she pulled at the door handle, opening it wide and stopped the open door with her foot, her arms up in a defensive position. The cupboard was empty. Her projections were correct, and the bot had used the time doorway. She tapped the optic three times, taking three stills of the empty cupboard, and then released the door, moving her foot. It closed with a soft click.

She needed to get back to her time but couldn't use this door, as she would be exposed. She left the Langham Hotel, keen to get back to her doorway in the Playhouse Theatre. She ran, taking long strides, unaware of everything around her, her mind full of what she had just discovered. It was only as she entered the back of the theatre and walked towards the dressing room that she heard the rumble of the distant explosion in the square. She froze as the ground shook causing fine particles of plaster to float down from the ceiling above. There was a roar of rushing air and then a tangle of sirens as all emergency vehicles began making their way to one location.

Radan had murdered Robert and all those innocent people. *But why?* Her thoughts were with Robert, as she punched the time key number into the keypad and made her way back to the 23rd Century. She had to speak to Landry and Karmal.

CHAPTER 23

KARMAL RAHMAN

The Bhola Cyclone of 1970 had killed 300 000 people, relief efforts were poor, and President Khan had shown a lack of understanding of the magnitude of the deadliest tropical cyclone on record. It was a significant time in the history of Dhaka and because of lack of support; the government was accused of gross neglect, callous and utter indifference.

With the University student protests in November 1971 and the resulting civil unrest leading to the creation of Bangladesh as a republic, it was a time of great upheaval. Interesting for historians, but as an environmental scientist, for Karmal it was a significant time of social change. His role in Magera was to observe events in history when food production was affected by physical or social events. Karmal knew that his studies were not as valuable as Landry and Wynters', but he played his part and hoped that his work would enhance their studies and be celebrated by some. His motivation for visiting 1971 today however, was for none of these reasons.

This period was one of the most turbulent in the history of Bangladesh and the land was cheap and people desperate. It was significant as after independence Bangladesh was divided into 11 sectors, each commanded by leaders from forces of the Bengali army. Many Bengal Hindus abandoned land and made their way to the borders with Pakistan and India. Karmal felt opportunity.

As he entered the Magera office in New Dhaka in 2188, Karmal greeted Dipu, his young supervisor "Alsalam ealayk Dipu."

"Hey alsalam ealaykum eami, Kemon Achen?"

"Yes, I'm well." Karmal replied.

Dipu gave Karmal a large pile of documents." A change of identity name for this visit?"

Karmal keeping his voice casual. "Yeh, I need an identity from 1971. I expect to be asked for identity papers if the army stop me."

"Very wise Kar. Here you are." They went through each document checking the details and Karmal signed off each item, birth certificate, travel papers along with others.

With all checks complete, the tension in Karmal's shoulders began to dissipate. He stood up and holding the papers to his chest, he looked across at Dipu.

"Checks complete?"

Dipu was squinting at his screen "Yes - pre-assignment protocols complete." Reading from the screen, "Attending the press conference led by the S force on food relief. Be aware of roadblocks throughout Dacca."

Karmal raised his arm and shook the documents. "I have prepared."

Dipu didn't reply. He was fixated by something on the screen.

Karmal was walking towards the storage cupboard when Dipu called to him, "Hey Kar, come see this." Dipu's lips were set in a grim line.

Karmal froze. "Something wrong with the assignment?"

"No, you are good but come look at this."

Karmal shook his head. "I'll look when I get back." He was nearly at the door and eager to go.

There was no response from Dipu, who was still scrutinising what was on the screen. Karmal closed the cupboard door and placed his tattoo onto the small symbol in front of him. The wall rippled and Karmal paused before stepping through. What he was planning was a significant risk. He hoped that he had considered all the consequences of what he was about to do. He stepped through into 1971.

Karmal was always prepared to greet whoever might use the office on the Curzon Hall campus, but as with previous visits, no one was present. The desk and chair were in their usual place, but the office was empty. The smells of 21st century Dacca filled his senses, A mixture of spices and diesel fuel. He paused for a moment to get his bearings; something wasn't right. He opened the door onto the open veranda and prepared to join the rush of students. There were none. It was quiet, too quiet. He felt very conspicuous as he made his way around the building. He stepped down from the veranda at the main entrance and walked up the long driveway towards the city street. With his optics and auditorus in normal mode, Karmal followed his planned route.

On reaching the main street, he saw the first people. Their heads were down, and they were making their way here and there. But their manner was hurried and uncharacteristically aloof. In the distance, he could hear muffled gunfire and rumbles of explosions.

His planned route was to avoid public squares and open spaces where he knew people would gather and use the back streets. It was whilst going down one of these that his identity papers were first tested. Karmal was relieved that it was in a quiet location and only one guard approached him. Karmal kept his stride purposeful and slowed his breathing.

"Paricayapatra!" the guard barked, holding out his hand. Karmal placed his identity card in the guard's hand. "Forhad Rahman?" The guard read the name on the identity card. Karmal nodded. "Licence?" the guard requested. Karmal began sorting through the sizeable amount of paperwork in his hand, aware of the guard's eyes on him with his hand outstretched in anticipation. It felt like an eternity before Karmal found the travel licence.

"Ekhane," Karmal stated as he placed the document in the guard's outstretched hand. Karmal tried to maintain a relaxed gaze as it was inspected. The guard took his time, occasionally looking up at Karmal, appearing to assess him.

Finally, the guard satisfied gave Karmal back his papers. He stepped back to allow Karmal to continue down the street. As he tidied the papers, he noticed that his hands were shaking.

It was a turbulent time for Dacca and Karmal knew from history reports that his presence anywhere near the university could place him in a difficult position. The forces from Pakistan had massacred teachers and students during the uprising for the independence of Bangladesh. Karmal had chosen a date after this time, but tensions were still high in the city. He was relieved when he reached the parliamentary building near the airport. With his journalist badge firmly clipped to his collar, Karmal was led into an opulent oak-panelled room for the presentation from Bengali forces.

The commander stepped forward and Karmal followed many of the newspaper journalists next to him, maintaining the appearance of making notes using his paper pad and pencil. He didn't need this, of course, as he would have the optic visuals that he could rerun and viz later. As the presentation began, he struggled to keep up, shielding his badly written notes from prying eyes.

The commander of the National liberation army talked of lifting martial law and the strict curfews because of the Pakistan surrender and that he was hoping to invite the exiled Provisional Government of Bangladesh to return from Calcutta within the week.

Karmal felt the importance of such a statement travel around the room, and he was mindful of what his fellow citizens had been through in the last months. The most harrowing period in his country's history. He felt a rush of nationalism and pride at the resolute way the commander conducted himself and was surprised at the extent to which the citizens of Dacca were considered and supported by the troops. Karmal recorded that foreign aid played a huge part in the resurrection of Dacca, but the will and determination of the people to get the crops harvested had not been recorded in the historical data. The army using their vehicles to bring grain and rice from the outlying areas and on the city street corners was significant. Karmal took a moment to think about his own family being part of this tremendous effort to help each other. Karmal found his attention drifting and his family filled his thoughts. Karmal began working through what he was about to do next.

The commander concluded his talk by sharing current numbers of wounded and dead and allocated no-go areas across the city.

Later Karmal was making his way back to the University, Karmal felt an uplifting of relief. He knew that within months Bangladesh would be recognised as a sovereign nation and begin its journey into independence. It was a stark contrast to Karmal's usual assignments following flooding, cyclones or periods of great mourning.

On reaching the office where the time doorway was located at the University, he was not worried about being observed. The university was empty.

He looked at the Magera symbol on the side of the door and he lingered for a moment. This was it. He was about to go against everything that Magera stood for. He had flouted protocol before, but nothing like what he was about to do. Placing his tattoo on his temple, he requested, "Private mode" and felt the familiar tremor as the optic viz and auditorus closed. Turning his back to the time doorway, he walked back out of the office and back onto the veranda in 1971, now severed from Magera and Radan.

Karmal had set in motion a personal assignment that he had been planning for some time. Although Bangladesh was on the eve of independence from Pakistan, the rupee was still the currency in 1971 and Karmal had been squirrelling away rupees for some time. His supervisor

Dipu was not thorough, and his lack of detail had allowed Karmal to attain quite a considerable amount of rupees. Karmal needed them all to carry out his plan.

Arriving at the Tohasil land office, Karmal opened the door to the street and was surprised to find a narrow wooden staircase leading up to office door of Resna Shiktar. Knocking on the door, Karmal was greeted by a small man wearing a traditional hijab of blue cotton. He smiled as Karmal entered, they clasped hands and Resna leant forward to kiss Karmal on both cheeks. It was a usual greeting in Dacca, but Karmal was out of practice. This greeting was outlawed following the Variola-Virus in the 2150s and Karmal had to resist the urge to pull back. He was not medically neurotic, but old practices were hard to lose. He looked Saab Shiktar in the eyes as he stepped back in the reassurance of his piety.

"Assalamoe `alaykum," Karmal stated.

Resna replied, "wa`alaykum assalam," raising his arm and gestured towards a chair opposite his own. Karmal took the seat in front of the desk.

"I have the deed of transfer for you to sign Saab Rahman. Can I confirm the location of the land first? I have it as a Khas in sector 22. Agricultural farm with accommodation buildings."

Karnal nodded and Resna passed across the paperwork. Karmal took his time to read all the details. It needed to be right.

"A pen please," Karmal requested.

Using the identity of his six times great grandfather, Forhad Rahman, Karmal signed the purchase document and the deeds of transfer. Karmal sat back and breathed out slowly. He retrieved a large roll of rupees from his pocket and placed it in front of Resna. "Saab Shiktar, does this conclude the sale?"

Resna nodded, "I am pleased to present you with the Khaitan and now we can deal with the custodian of the land, yes?" Resna glanced at his watch as he spoke and coughed nervously before continuing, "It is unusual Saab Rahman to have a custodian and specifically to have the additional conditions that you have requested. Very unusual."

Karmal smiled and he could see that Resna was relieved to not offend with his question. "Yes Saab Shiktar, it is strange of me not to want to live on this land. It is for my family's future. The custodian, my brother will farm the land until the two families can be joined." Resna nodded in agreement. The additional conditions ensured it stayed on that side of the family, left to each son and that at any point in the future, it could be shared. Karmal had composed his family tree with care. He knew that the two sides of the family had never met so that his falsehood would be complete. Karmal could not leave the land to his branch of the family, as then they would leave their home in Perahat, and his parents would never have met. He knew the risks of the paradox and he needed to make sure that he would be part of their future. That he would get the family life that was taken from him. He would act in the last moment to ensure that he was safe in his mother's womb. Careful planning would be necessary, and he knew the risks. At least now he had this option, should he need it.

At the arranged time, there was a timid knocking at the door and a stooping man stepped cautiously through it. Dressed in the lower-class hijab and looking very out of place in Resna's office, Karmal could feel Refat's anxiety as he looked to the floor and bowed repeatedly.

Karmal quickly rose and placed both hands in Refat's, pulling him towards him and kissing both of his cheeks without the previous reticence. "Brother, brother." Smiling broadly, his actions put Refat at ease and he held Karmal's gaze, "Forhad?"

"Yes, brother. It is I Forhad," Karmal stated. Karmal could see the family resemblance immediately and he hoped that enough time had passed since their childhood, that Refat would not question the imposter in front of him. Why should he?

Resna invited both men to sit and Karmal pulled a new chair next to his own, "Sit, sit brother." Karmal watched as Refat hesitantly lowered himself into the fine armchair.

Resna took control of the meeting. "I know that you have some idea why you have been asked to come here today. The letter gave some information?" Refat nodded and grabbed Karmal's hand. It was a slight gesture, but Karmal felt the emotion of being close to a family member cut across him in a wave. "Your elder brother," indicating to Karmal, "has been successful in business and wished to buy some land for his family and that includes you." Karmal had known from family records that the brothers had become estranged by distance and war when they were young men, so knew that they would have had little contact since then. Also, Forhad was the eldest and Refat the youngest son so that added to their distance.

Karmal was pondering his loss of growing up with his family and the emptiness that it bought when Saab Shiktar addressed them both. "We have confirmed the location of the land. Saab Rahman and Refat knows the land well." Karmal glanced across at Refat and saw his forehead crumple.

"Can I speak?" Refat's low voice pierced the air. Astonishment flew across both Karmal's and Resna's faces.

"Of course, of course, Saab Rahman."

"Why? Why are you doing us this great honour brother? It is a prize indeed, but why?" Karmal thought carefully before answering. He knew these words would be passed down by the generations and had a desire to get it right.

"I am a business owner, brother. A successful one. I wish to help you and my family. I wish to buy this land and farm it for profit but have no desire to live on it now. You have a smallholding in the south, so you are the perfect family member to do this for me. It is good land, is it not?

Refat nodded vigorously. "Oh yes. It is very good land. Much profit can be made. This will change our family fortunes for the better."

"Oh, I am pleased so pleased," Karmal smiled at Refat.

Refat joined with a wide smile of his own, "Bless you brother, bless you for this."

"We need to discuss the special circumstance that you have requested Saab Rahman."

"Oh yes, of course, please go ahead."

"Refat Rahman, there some special conditions that are attached to this land." Refat nodded. "You can never sell it. It must be passed down to a son on the death of the eldest."

"Of course, but I am still fit and healthy." Refat raised his arms in a stance of strength.

Karmal and Resna chuckled. "Yes, we can see that."

Resna continued, "Will you abide by this condition? You must leave the land to a son of yours and he must also leave it to his son. This cannot be broken."

"Why of course, this will be done." Refat nodded at both Karmal and Resna.

Resna continued his brows knitted, "You will be the owner in name and have all the profits from this land but there will be a time when you will invite Forhad Rahman's family to come and join you at the farm and share in the good fortune. "

"But of course," Refat smiled and spread his arms wide, "the land is vast. We will need their help to farm it. When can they come? Are they coming from Parahat now? It would be wonderful to see them..."

Karmal interrupted, "No, brother. We are staying there for now. We enjoy good profits on our farm."

"Then you will come for the next growing season?"

"No, we will not."

Karmal could see the confusion in Refat's face. Resna stepped in. "Saab Rahman, your family will be treasured caretakers of the land from now and for many years into the future. Maybe even after you are dead. This is a business investment by your brother and in the future, his sons will come and claim their stake in the land. But not now." Resna looked enquiringly at Refat to see if he understood. Refat blinked slowly and looked down. Karmal could see that he was disappointed.

Refat's voice was gravelly as he spoke, nodding slowly. "A business enterprise. I see."

Karmal felt a rush of sympathy and shock at his six times great uncle's reaction and the lie was out if his mouth before he could stop it, "Oh brother, we will try to come soon. We have a lot to do for us to all move here. It may take time."

Refat's face brightened. "Oh yes, I understand. We will get the land ready for you. You will see. My sons are hard workers, they will take no time to make a profit and we will build houses for us to live in."

Karmal felt the lie die in his throat, and he struggled to speak. Resna saved him. "Refat Rahman, you must make sure that when you leave the land, your sons and their sons must know about this day and what has been agreed. It is important. Whenever Forhad's family come to join you, you must be ready to welcome them with open arms. "

"Of course, it will be done. All that you have said." He grabbed Karmal's arms in his. "You will see brother; we will make you proud. "

Resna began sorting the papers on his desk, "Therefore Refat Rahman, it leaves two things to be done. One, to give you the khatian- proof of ownership, with the conditions added. Please sign."

Karmal watched as his relative clasped the pen clumsily and drew a large cross over the place as a signature. "Sorry- I know not how to write Saab."

"Do not worry yourself, Refat. Your mark is enough. Put you mark on this one."

Refat added his cross again and rattled on in excitement. "I am still in shock at what has happened. How will I explain this to my Seema and my sons?"

Resna's calming voice broke through, "Show them the papers Saab, your sons can read a little I think and tell them the story of everything we have done today."

Refat looked across at Karmal. "Will you come and tell my family? It will be better from you I think." Karmal was torn. He would desperately like to see his family and share the joy of the impact of what he had done, but common sense made him stop. He had taken tremendous risks already; he was concerned that this might cause a time alteration and to meet and converse with his family could be catastrophic. He was disappointed, but he had to decline.

Karmal swallowed his emotion down as he spoke, "I will come but not today brother, I have other business with Saab Shiktar and may come on another day. You understand?"

Refat stood and pulled Karmal into an embrace. "Thank you, brother. What you have done here today for my family is… I know not why we have been so graciously chosen but thank you. Family is everything and I thank you for all my family."

"Peace be with you brother," Karmal's voice was muffled, and he was grateful for the fabric of Rafet's hijab as tears fell from his eyes. He knew they would never meet again.

"If we cannot come now or for years maybe, know that we will always think of you and wish you well."

"And you brother and you," Refat rose and looked at Karmal's face with tears also running down his own. He patted Karmal on the back. "I will do everything that you have asked of me. Goodbye. Peace be with you and your family brother. We will see each other soon. I know it."

With that, he turned, nodded at Resna, "Thankyou Saab." Clutching the papers to his chest, he left the room. Only once his footsteps faded away down the stairs and they heard the door close did Resna speak.

"Well Saab Rahman, what a strange day this has been for me. "

"And for me." Karmal agreed. "Thank you, Saab Shiktar. You will ensure my wishes are met?"

Suddenly unreserved, Resna grabbed Karmal's hand and shook it. "It will be my pleasure Saab."

It was time to go. Karmal had a desire to get back.

"As-salāmu ʿalaykum- Peace be with you."

Resna replied, "waʿalaykumu as-salām- and to you."

Karmal waved his hand as he exited through the door and bounded down the stairs into the street outside. He was shocked to find that the sun was fading, and darkness was setting in. He needed to get back to the doorway before the curfew.

He arrived at the university building unhindered by checks. Finding his way along the veranda in the dark was difficult, and Karmal fully expected the office to be locked. He reached for the handle and was relieved to find that it remained open. As expected, it was empty. He placed his tattoo on the symbol on the doorframe, he stated, "manual date override. 22.07.2188 1300." The door turned into a shimmering mass, and Karmal was about to step through when he halted. Attempting to slow his heart rate, he paused then, "end private mode" He felt a tiny change in his optic as it turned back on as he stepped forward and into 2188.

In the office in 2188, It was as if he had just walked back through the door a few seconds later. Dipu was still scrutinising something on his screen as Karmal had left him hours earlier. Only a few seconds ago for Dipu. Karmal's brain was filled with the emotions and excitement of what he had achieved today. But this was quickly forgotten as Dipu spoke.

"You have to see this Kar." Dipu looked across at Karmal, his face pale and gaunt.

CHAPTER 24

KARMAL RAHMAN

Dipu broke protocol himself and commanded, "Go to private mode."
"Private mode?" Karmal said.
Dipu nodded.
They had enjoyed a mutual friendship as colleagues for some years. Dipu was not a great supervisor, but he always conducted their working relationship in line with Magera's strict procedures. Karmal felt uncomfortable with this new arrangement. He wasn't ready to share. His demeanour was relaxed, but inside, his thoughts were racing. Had Dipu discovered his deceit?
Dipu was busy studying at an image on his screen. "What am I looking at?" Karmal sighed. The viz image on the screen looked like the embryo pods used at the Radan birth centres, but these were different. They were adults. A bag of translucent liquid suspended from above, and tubes ran into the liquid from the top and out of the bottom. The woman in the image was naked. A tube ran from just below her stomach area and out of the sac of fluid. Another led into her mouth and a mask was secured over her eyes. In the image, she looked like she was running. It looked macabre.
"I told you about my friend, the engineer on the transport vessels to Mars. He sent this to me via his private file."
Karmal stepped closer. "Is it a medic facility? Is she hurt?"
"Wait, there's more." Dipu switched to another image, taken from a distance. Karmal counted at least 100 identical pods in rows and columns. It looked like an apartment block with its walls removed. Each person was in a fluid sac and had a tube leading from their lower abdomen and another into their mouth just as the first, but each person seemed to be in a different position. Some upright, some lying down, some looked frozen like they were doing some sort of physical movement.
"Are they sick? What has happened to them?"

Dipu paused. "I trust my friend. He's taking a big risk sending this to me."

"What am I looking at Dip?"

"My friend has no reason to lie." Dipu pulled his hands down his face, breathing out as he did so.

"What Dipu? What's happened? Are these people injured?"

Dipu looked straight at Karmal as he spoke. "This is Mars, Kar. Not a medic facility. Mars. This is what those pioneers are going to Kar. My friend said that they are taken straight from interstellar space stasis to this."

Karmal was blinking at Dipu, but not speaking. His mind filled with questions and the fundamental one was, why?

"You mean they are in this stasis until the biodomes and living landscapes are complete? Are they behind schedule with the city infrastructure?"

"No THIS IS MARS." Dipu's eyes pierced into Karmal's as he made his point again.

"What are you saying, Dip? That this is deliberate? Is Radan putting all this effort into getting people onto spaceships and sending them to a life on Mars, this?"

Dipu paused considering what Karmal was saying, "Well, that's what my friend is saying, yes."

"But why Dipu? This makes no sense."

"I don't know, Kar. I'm as confused as you are. I can't take in what I am seeing."

"Can you send this to me? A private file of course."

"Yeah sure. Look, Kar, we need to be careful. It's dangerous. My friend is scared, Kar."

"Why is he scared?"

"He's scared of Radan. He's scared that Radan will find out."

"I'll be careful with this, Dipu. I understand."

Karmal turned to leave, his mind full of what he had just seen. As he was about to step outside, he turned to Dipu.

"Answer me this Dipu. Who else is involved here? This can't be just Radan. Radan was created to help us. Keep us healthy not …" And pointing at the image, "this!"

Dipu shook his head. "I can't answer that Kar, but my friend. Something is not right with Mars."

Karmal blew through his lips, "Take care Dipu."

"And you." Dipu's voice faded as Karmal made his way out of the office.

His route back to his accom flew by, his mind agitated over what Dipu had just shown him and the implications for those pioneers. The idea of Wynter being sent there spiralled through his mind in a repeated loop. Before seeing the images, he had been determined to help Wynter, but now fear drove him on, fear for her and for the future.

He cancelled private mode to enter his accom building. Arriving in the corridor by the door to his accom, his door opened, and he heard the ping of his home screen kicking into life. "Welcome home Rahman, No. 7 ration available."

"No ration." He stated as he turned. The home screen hovered just on his left side, the Radan symbol pulsing in the corner. His tattoo glowed green and began medic updates," Rahman2135, temperature optimal, heat rate optimal No medic messages." He studied the Radan symbol for a moment and considered what it was doing now. Its reassuring presence had been part of his life for many years. It had always been a symbol of hope.

He saw that Wynter had attempted a Magera group dialogue on three occasions, the last being 3 minutes ago. It was 1900 hrs in Dhaka, which meant 1300 hrs in London. Wynter had left a vis and Karmal requested it to be played.

Her face filled the screen, and he stepped forward hearing an edge to her voice. "When you return, can you contact me? We need to have vis or optic chat. "

She looked tired and unkempt. There was a desperation in her manner, and this was mirrored in her eyes. He knew he had to share what he had just discovered and took a moment to plan his words. Maybe he needed confirmation that it was true before sharing, but why lie? Who benefitted from it? He decided that Wynter and Landry should be told even if it proved later to be false.

This conversation had to be away from the listening presence of Radan, and so he reached for the 21st - century Word pad and mouse device and logged into the dark web.

"Private mode," Karmal stated. For the first time in his life, he glanced across at the Radan symbol on his home screen before continuing. It had turned white and appeared frozen, pulsing no longer- just as it should be in private mode.

Karmal logged into the shared site and found no avatars for Wynter or Landry. They were not logged on. He glanced across at his home screen.

"Cancel private mode. Magera Communication." The Magera spinning symbol filled the screen and the names of operatives scrolling down. Karmal could see both Wynter and Landry had blue spots next to their names. They were home.

"Group dialogue with Lund2200 and Reagan2485." The screen split into three and he could see himself and at first only Landry as she stepped closer to the screen. Wynter's screen remained blurred, as she had not yet acknowledged the dialogue.

"Hey Landry. Are you ok?" Her face looked pinched, and her smile strained.

"We've got news, important news, "Landry stated. "It's about Wynter…" Landry stopped speaking as Wynter appeared on the screen. Karmal was shocked by her appearance. He saw she was sweating, and her movements were rigid and jerky. "You alright Wynt?"

"No." She paused. "I'm tired. I need reparation I'm going to block out the daylight and go dark." Her manner had changed, and she now stood staring into the camera. To Karmal, this message was obvious. She was staring straight at him.

"You too Land? Going dark?"

"Yep, you should too, you look tired," Landry lied.

They disappeared one at a time as each requested private mode and reached for their Wordpad and mouse. The dark web, a solace and a place to share secrets. Now more than ever, they had some to share.

The strange bongs as the outdated chatroom connected repeated for a time and Karmal stared blankly at the empty screen. He was pleased that Landry came through first, and Wynter's screen box remained empty.

"Hey Landry," He glanced up at the camera at the top of the Wordpad and smiled at the image as Landry began speaking; her viz and audit were out of sync. "Is Wynt ok?"

There was a pause as his audit reached Landry. "No, not really. It's bad Kar, bad."

"What has happened?"

"She went back to find out about the explosion at the SAM rally. Remember?"

"Yes of course. Did she find the terrorist? Can she clear her name?"

Landry paused. "She has found the terrorist yes but..." the audit stopped but Landry's image remained, and her lips were still moving.

"Did not hear that Land. Did not hear the end of that."

"She can tell you herself." Landry nodded to the side as Wynter's face appeared in her screen box.

Wynter's hair was askew, and her lips set in a grim line. Landry was leaning forward with her left auditorus facing the screen.

Karmal spoke first. "What did you find Wynt? Did you find the terrorist?"

"Yes... well I think so, yes." He noted she was looking to her right, recalling something. "Now I am back here, it's hard to believe what I saw."

"Just tell us what you saw… don't question. Start from the beginning."

She leant her elbows on the desk in front of her and began, "It was terrible, Kar… I had to watch those people die so many times. Robert, Carly and the children die over and over again." Her body convulsed in sobs, and he heard her catch her breath as the wails left her body.

Landry's face crumpled. "I know Wynt. I know." She placed her hand on the screen, her palm filling the lower corner.

Wynter shook her head, wiping the tears from her face with the sleeve of her nightwear. "Look, I'm ok. A bit shook up. You know."

Karmal nodded, his face grim.

Wynter continued, "So I found the bomber. I found that the bag had been left much earlier in the morning."

"Who was it? We're they from a known group." Karmal questioned. Wynter looked up.

"I'll get to that. I followed the terrorist to see who he was. He was wearing a hooded garment, so it was difficult to see. You know. I followed him." Wynter paused and looked at the camera. "I followed him to the Langham Hotel."

"Kar", prompted Wynter. "He went into the Langham Hotel." Karmal had not yet found the connection.

Wynter's voice rose in frustration. "THE Langham Hotel Kar." There was a pause as Wynt and Landry smiled at his ignorance, and then the sudden realisation hit Karmal.

"What!" Karmal exclaimed." You mean THE Langham hotel? The time door? A Magera operative then?"

"Not an operative Kar. But they came through the doorway.... I know this because there's more."

Karmal's mind was racing. He glanced up to Landry for a reaction. There was none. A Magera operative from the future going back to murder people in the past. Not possible. These thoughts were on the tip of his tongue when Wynter continued. "There's more Kar. As the operative approached the hotel, there was a stage 3 compromise with a dog. The dog ran across the road and interacted aggressively with the operative. As the dog was dragged away, the operative looked behind him. His head turned a full 180 degrees, Kar." Wynter looked straight into the camera, "180 degrees Kar, inhuman."

It looked like the chatroom viz had frozen as no one moved or spoke for what felt like minutes.

Karmal fell back in his chair and placed his hand over his mouth. A small voice emanated from between his fingers. "Wait." He put his hand up, palm facing the screen. "Wynter, are you saying a Radan bot went back to 2033 to kill people in Trafalgar square? Are you telling me something that is impossible and wait Wynter. Are you telling me that Magera colluded with this? Is this what you're telling me? Land, is this what she's telling me?"

Both women were silent, nodding their heads.

"Could you be wrong?"

"I saw it, as clearly as I see you now. The bot turned its head to face behind without moving its body, and the way it walked was wrong. I have visuals of it."

Karmal had placed his face in his hands. "Ok. Before you show me, tell me this, Wynt. Tell me Land. Why then? Why did Radan kill those people? HOW could Radan kill those people?"

Landry stepped forward, "That we don't know yet, but I think I know how it can do it."

"You mean how Radan, an AI built to save lives, can take lives?" Karmal asked.

"Yes. You both know that I have been researching Radan's beginnings and developments."

"Go on." Karmal instructed.

"According to my research, Radan was created by a student, Luke White, at Birmingham City University in 2022 for his PHD. It was designed originally as an AI to allocate medical resources to the greatest need. A successful programme which ultimately saved the National Health Service in the UK."

Karmal stated, "We know this, and it was safeguarded by its main constitution to save lives so as an AI, it cannot take lives."

"Yes, it can." Landry stared into the screen. "It can and it has."

"Impossible! This goes against everything we know." Karmal was animated.

"Listen, its primary constitution is, to allocate resources to preserve human life. Yes?"

Both Karmal and Wynter nodded slowly. "Yes."

"So why during the Variola Virus of 2099, when Radan began being used by governments across the World, did Radan halt the distribution of resources that would have saved thousands in Nigeria?"

Karmal argued, "It didn't stop those. There were not enough masks, gloves, medical gowns. There was a world shortage. "

"I've looked at this carefully in the last few days. Radan recommended the halt of resources being sent to Nigeria because of the low-quality provision of the hospitals. Radan argued resources were better assigned to Europe where more people would be saved. The objectivity of the AI concluded resources were better delivered to a First World context. A greater likelihood of survival. In Radan's terms, more people survive. Better than wasting resources in an antiquated system where survival was deemed unlikely."

"No Radan saves lives," Karmal said.

"It's algorithms, simple." Landry sat back in her chair, folded her arms and waited.

Wynter sat up. "So, when Radan was adopted across the World. When food production became low, its programme was enhanced?"

"It looks that way, yes, although the original protocols were not touched. They just asked it to add food allocation protocols to save lives, in addition to the medical supplies. "

" Land, this doesn't explain why Radan killed those people in Trafalgar Square. It cannot. It is in its constitution; thou shall not kill?"

"Kar, you are right. It is but its primary aim, to allocate resources to preserve human life, will always override this. It doesn't say, you can't kill someone, it says you must maintain human life. It doesn't tell it how. We know that in the battlefields of the three World Wars, tough choices had to be made, like in Nigeria in 2129. You place the resources in the place of greatest potential success. I'm sorry to bring this up Kar but this happened after Cyclone Zabr to your family in Bangladesh."

Landry leant forward with sympathy in her eyes "I'm so sorry Kar, the decision was made to not send aid to the region after the cyclone. It is a zone of extreme weather phenomenon and with the effect of climate change, this region was unstable. I believe that the decision to not send aid was made following advice from Radan. "

Karmal cried out, "They tried to send aid, but they couldn't get through."

Landry continued, "Think Kar. An artificial intelligence with no feelings uses algorithms; numbers and statistics to make the decision. That resources would be wasted being sent to a region because next year or the year after or the years after, it will happen again. The decision is, do you waste resources again or do you save those resources for somewhere else? It's unethical I know but ethics don't come into it."

Wynter sat back. The toll of the last few days was making it difficult to stay focused on what Landry was saying.

"Go on Land. I will listen."

"It's simple maths Kar. Take from one to save many. That shows that Radan could justify its actions. Following the great fall, after the government alliances collapsed and countries looked to themselves only, Radan gave the first world countries an excuse to keep their resources and not share. They slowly became more reliant on Radan and, by introducing rationing, Radan became all-encompassing. This AI could organise, arrange and allocate everything needed to save us, and they welcomed it with open arms. Once the ration cities were established, Radan began working independently of the government. With the extension package of medical services, it became what it is today."

Wynter seemed to wake up. "Radan refused me as a surrogate mother because someone in my bloodline had experienced a miscarriage."

"There, an example of algorithms. Why risk using you, when there were other surrogates without that risk?"

"So that decision which changed my life was made just like that." Wynter clicked her fingers, "No dilemma or feelings of guilt?"

"You're right Wynt. From what I can see, there were no ethical sub-routines added to the original programming. No ethics at all."

Karmal finally looked up, "So my family died so that others might live?"

Landry's face softened. "I'm sorry, but yes, Kar. It's pure numbers and it's the same today."

The vizimage from Mars flashed across Karmal's consciousness. "Now. It is happening now! Give me a minute."

Karmal dropped the chatroom down onto the taskbar and opened his private message files. He opened the vizimages that Dipu had sent and looked at them again with renewed understanding. He considered what this image could do to Wynter but pushed that concern aside. It was too late to preserve her innocence. She needed all the information.

He clicked on the chatroom icon and saw that Landry and Wynter had continued their discussion. Their faces were solemn and pinched.

"I was shown something about Radan, and I try to make sense of it. There is no reason not to believe it and from what you say today Wynt, it is true."

"What is it?"

Karmal was trying to delay, "Wynt, it is about Mars. It is not good."

"What is it?" Wynter's voice rose.

Landry moved forward, her face filling the screen, "Look whatever it is Kar, we'll deal with it and Wynter, we'll deal with it ok?"

Karmal took a deep breath, "Dipu showed me this vizimage this morning," as he continued, the first vizimage filled the screen, "his friend works for interstellar transports and he says that people are not going to Eden that was promised, he says that they stay in stasis."

Karmal split his screen so that he could re-evaluate the image and view both Wynter and Landry. The impact of vizimage had not lessened with a second viewing, and Karmal watched as their reaction was much the same as his own.

Landry was strangely silent, and Wynter showed a similar naivety to Karmal. "Is she unwell?"

"No, wait. There is more." A new image flashed up where the previous image had been.

He heard a sharp intake of breath from Landry, and Wynter continued, "Are they unwell? Is there an epidemic?"

"No, Dipu's friend is saying, they are well. Too well. This is Mars, Wynter. There is no biosphere, no trees, valleys, homesteads. These are the pioneers that went there. This is their reality."

Landry's voice broke through, "Radan... its Radan's doing. But why?" and then she answered her question, "Oh my God Radan is doing what it was programmed to do, allocate resources to maintain human life. Oh my God!"

"What's Radan doing?" Wynter shouted, "what are you saying, Land?"

Karmal was impressed at how quickly Landry got it. "Land, you have researched Radan, why would it be better to have people in stasis living out their lives like this than living in a Martian city, working, eating, living a full life."

Karmal waited for Landry's response. "Less risk this way. When you work and walk, there's a risk of harm. If you work and live in virtual reality, then no risk to life. I'm guessing Dipu's friend is sharing that they are in a virtual reality that is all-encompassing, so they don't know that they're not living the life they expected on Mars. You know how easy it is to become addicted to VR. Look around you, at your accom neighbours. How many of them never leave their accom? It would be easy to create a VR for Mars and for those people to believe that they are living it. Radan is still fulfilling its primary constitution."

Karmal saw the realisation on Wynter's face. "How much do you trust these vizimages Kar?"

"I trust Dipu and his friend has taken much risk sending these."

There was a moment of silence from all three friends as they assimilated what they were seeing and hearing today.

This was broken by Wynter as she laughed manically. "Well, that's it. I'm not going to Mars. I can't go. "

"No, absolutely not but we need time I think." Landry said.

"I'm not attending my investigation meeting, either. Why would I? I am going to get the blame for the bomb. Even with the evidence, Magera won't possibly believe me. They will think the same as us. How could Radan do this? They'll think I doctored the optic image. I'm not going?"

Landry nodded, "No you can't go, not until we can get this evidence to the right people."

Wynter began moving around her accom, walking back and forth, "I might have to disappear, I have to go..."

Landry interrupted her, "You can go to my parents off-grid."

Wynter spread her arms wide and smiled. "Do I look like an off-grid girl?"

The recent tension was broken as both Karmal and Landry smiled, "No, Wynt. I don't suppose you are?"

"Tockhead life feels appealing at the moment."

"What! Going back and stay in the past?"

"No, no Wynt, there is something we can do." Landry shook her head, looking up at Wynter.

"Tell me, Kar. What's my other option?"

"Stop! "Landry interrupted them both. "Look, I don't know about you, but I've been blown away by what we have found out today. I need to take this on board and think about it. I think we need time."

"I completely agree."

"Yes, a good plan Landry," Karmal stated. "But we don't have lots of time. Wynt, when is your investigation meeting?"

"04.08.2188" Wynter sucked in her breath as she spoke.

"We have a week then. I will go and find more on Mars. We can speak this time tomorrow?"

"Yes, I'm not thinking straight. I need sleep." Wynter announced.

They both look towards Landry who was already deep in thought. Landry waved absently, and they ended with goodbyes and reassuring smiles. Karmal logged out and sat back, exhausted. His first thoughts were with Wynter and his own recognition that things were happening too quickly.

CHAPTER 25

Ensuring that they were in private mode, they connected through the dark web at 1300 hrs on the 30th of July, five days before Wynter's Investigation deadline. Landry was eager to share her ideas with the others. However, it was Wynter who began the discussion. The archaic system stuttered in places, but it was private. Landry saw the dark circles under Wynter's eyes, and her face was pale and grim.

"All in private mode?" Wynter asked. Both Landry and Karmal confirmed they were. "Right, I've been busy trying to contact Magera directly and share the information that I have, and I was successful. I provided them with images of the bot entering the Langham Hotel, time-coded and everything. I also gave them the vizimage of the same bot leaving the bag by the fountain in Trafalgar Square. "The image froze in place as the connection stuttered. Landry hadn't noticed that she was holding her breath until the screen unfroze and Wynter, still speaking, said. "They would not accept them as evidence."

"Why did you do that Wynt? They will know that you went back." Karmal looked visibly shaken.

"What did you expect me to do? It's my life on the line here."

"Stop both of you. It is done. We can't change that. Did you speak to Kyson?"

"Yes, I've been contacting everyone that I could. I sent the whole vizoptic of the visit so that they could see that it wasn't me."

Wynter paused. "They are saying it was an illegal visit. They said the image could have been created by anyone. They are more concerned that I took an unauthorized trip. Magera are threatening to take out my Radan tattoo chip. Take my rights away. Send me straight to Mars. It was Kyson who helped me. She convinced the senior director to give me until the hearing on the 4th of August. Told her that I have an exemplary record. But that's all I've got. "Wynter's voice shook. "I need to do something before that meeting."

Landry was shocked "Look, Wynt, we will make plans. We'll sort something out. I've got some ideas."

Karmal looked down, paused, and then spoke. "I have been speaking to Dipu and some others that I know. I am sorry but the vizimage of Mars is real. It's all true. The reasons are not clear though." Landry saw the muscles in Wynter's face tighten.

Landry studied the notes that she had made for the meeting and began, "Kar, Wynt, I've spent most of the hours gathering more information about the formation of Radan and demands that the NHS made upon Luke White. It was an AI created to organise resources only. It was never coded to be as far-reaching."

Karmal's tone rose and frowning he said. "We know that so why Mars? Why keep people like that? Why not let them have the life they expected? I cannot see why."

"Yes. "Wynter joined Kar. "It makes little sense. We all know that Radan saves lives."

"Exactly, saving lives…" Landry stressed, "not enhancing lives, not improving the quality of life but just saving lives at all costs. I've spent time thinking about just that. Keeping people in a virtual life, Radan IS saving lives. People in this stasis can be kept to the optimal temperature, be constantly monitored. Think of it from an objective point of view. More people will survive with this plan. It's not morally correct but from the perspective of an AI, it is fulfilling its role." Landry attempted to curb her excitement.

Wynter leant forward. "We talk about what governments will do when they find out what Radan is doing. They need to know, don't they?"

Karmal and Landry both frowned and talked at once, their voices cancelling each other out. Karmal's voice rose above, "We can't show anyone this, the man that took the image will be in danger."

"I hate to say this, but I'm not sure the government will believe this. If Magera isn't willing to listen, then what makes you think that the government will. "

Wynter raised her hands in the air and slammed them down again. "We've got to try, haven't we? "Pointing her finger into her chest. "For my sake and all those people being duped into this Mars nightmare. This is not what Radan promised of New Earth. Going backwards in time to kill people is not right!"

Landry responded, irritated "What do you think Radan will say? When we've exposed it, what will its' answer be? I know. It could say, there are delays on Mars, that building works are only late, they have come across some unexpected problems that are taking longer. The World has become so reliant on Radan that they will believe anything that it says. They won't question it. Think about it. Why would they? Radan has people's best interests at heart. It keeps us all alive every day. Its algorithms have saved lives. Continues to sustain lives."

"Not everyone. Not my family. They were not worthy of being saved. They lived in a part of the World not important enough. Radan must not be allowed to do this anymore."

"Yes, I agree Kar. But no one is interested in holding Radan to account. They've had many opportunities. Several times in our history, Radan has removed support for nations in peril, but what happened as a result? Nothing. When you look carefully, it places support where there is a high likelihood of saving the most lives. This is how artificial intelligence deals with failure to preserve lives; it looks at the bigger picture and decides based upon the mathematical probability of saving most lives. There is no emotion involved. It is doing what it was coded to do. By being there at those moments, I believe that climate change helped Radan to become more powerful."

"But why suddenly go back and change the past? "

Karmal's excited voice burst through, "suddenly? Is this only the first time or the only time that someone has noticed? "

Silence as all three contemplated the idea that Radan had done it before.

Karmal was first, "Other Magera operatives have been suspended before because of big timeline alterations. Some said that they were innocent. What if…. It was Radan."

Landry's head snapped up as she checked that the Radan symbol on her Home Screen was white, and that she was in private mode. Fear rippled up and down her spine and her hair follicles tingled as a cold dread swept through her. What were they up against? All three operatives were looking forward, eyes wide unblinking. For the second time in days, the reality that they knew lurched forward into a new unrecognisable one.

"Right, what are we saying here? That Radan changes things in the past to save lives…. By murdering people?"

Karmal took his time to answer Wynter. "Why would Radan kill people who could stop climate change? Climate change has killed millions of people."

Landry slowly, selecting her words as she spoke,

"Radan became more powerful – because climate change happened-without climate change – Radan was not responsible for the lives of the World. It can only fulfil its aims because of the control it has now…not before." Landry let out a slow breath.

Wynter and Karmal nodded as Landry continued,

"In those times when the World tipped into chaos after the Great Fall, what was the stabling influence? Radan. When food production across the world declined as the Earth warmed, we didn't notice because of Radan. It appeared to save us. Global Warming made the governments rely on Radan more and more. Radan gave them an excuse to be self-centred. Its policies made governments more and more reliant. Even myself, growing up off-grid, I saw my family's reasons for staying as personal, but moving in a ration city, I see how lazy I have become. Now I'm used to being provided with everything I need. The idea of doing without Radan is frightening for people and governments. You, Wynt, find it difficult not being connected to the medi-support. Think about the World without Radan? It runs everything, every system, every policy flows through Radan directives. No government could be without it now. We've inadvertently invited a monster into our lives, but can we survive now without Radan?"

Karmal shook his head. "People would be scared. There would be fear and chaos in many cities. We couldn't cope without Radan now. "

Landry spoke quickly. "We must travel back. Change the timeline. Halt climate change and stop Radan. That's the only option open to us."

All three friends considered what she had just said. No one spoke. Not ready to share their hidden thoughts. Then Wynter sighed. "Well, this discussion makes my decision easier. I've given it a lot of thought. I'm travelling back to Trafalgar."

"To do what Wynt?" Karmal's face came closer to the screen.

"I'm going back to stop the explosion." Wynter's face appeared to have frozen, lips set in a firm line and her arms folded, a goading challenge in her eyes.

Landry attempted to think of the many time implications of what Wynt was suggesting and then Karmal spoke, "Think about your training Wynt, time paradox? You can stop it once, but Radan will go back and do it again?" Wynter's shoulders dropped.

Landry had the same thought." I'm sorry to say it, but Kar's right. The timeline won't be changed enough. Radan will just change it back. We must stop Radan."

Karmal's face crumpled. "You cannot stop the bot from doing it again. Didn't I just say that?"

Landry hammered her point home. "I mean STOP Radan, Stop Radan for good! Not just stop the blast, stop Radan, the whole thing, everything associated with Radan. I've been giving this a lot of thought in the last 36 hrs."

"Land, it's time paradox again. How are you going to stop Radan? Have you thought about all the people that Radan saved?"

Landry spoke her most secret thoughts. "What I am talking about, is changing Radan. If I go back to the beginning. If I work back to the creation of Radan and change its constitution, change Radan's timeline then I can make sure that Radan cannot become as influential ever again."

Wynter and Karmal's faces crumpled in confusion. "How can you do that?"

Landry sat forward in her seat. "We know the reason that Radan is what it is today is because of its primary constitution- to allocate resources to preserve human life. If we added ethics which include empathy, quality of existence. Maybe humanitarianism, if they are not conflicting with saving of life…, Landry paused, frowning, "I haven't fully thought it through yet."

"You are right, you have not. What are you going to do? Speak to the AI creators in the past and make them change Radan just like that?"

"Well, yes, that was my first thought."

Wynter hadn't responded, but when she did, it surprised Landry. "I think your idea has got merit, but you'll only get one chance at this Land. If you are even remotely successful, then it will vary the timeline irreparably. Have you considered that?"

Karmal interrupted, "Landry, you could make a 1.3-time wave. Everything changes; we may not be born. It's a risk to us all."

Wynter was smiling "Well, I've got nothing to lose. Do you think you could make a difference?"

"I do, yes Wynt, I do, but Kar is right, it's an enormous risk."

"I think you wrong Landry. You change Radan in history, you change the World. You risk it all."

Landry walked back out of the shot and began pacing up and down in her accom. Returning to the wordpad viewer, she peered into the camera. "I didn't start working with Magera for it to end like this. I wanted to end the great fall and change the climate of the world for everyone. Avoiding

Hothouse Earth was my original aim, but the actions of recent weeks have shown us we need to do more. We need to go after Radan." She could see Karmal shaking his head. "Why do you work with Magera Kar?"

There was a pause as Kar pulled his hands down his face, resting his chin on them before speaking. "Because I want to save my family. I want those that I lost."

"So not to help the food production in your region. Not to find that hidden source of food that everyone else overlooked. Not to take care of people in Bangladesh and Pakistan?" Landry knew she was being confrontational.

Karmal stared into the WordPad. His eyes narrowed, and Wynter's face crumpled into a frown. She cared for her friends but depending upon how they responded would be the difference between doing it together or going it alone. Landry had already decided and changing her father's life was the extra motivation. She was going ahead, with or without them.

Karmal walked away from the WordPad and Landry could see him walking around his accom and going to his ration station.

Wynter spoke in a whisper. "A bit of a low blow Land."

"But it's the truth, isn't it? If there was ever an occasion for the truth, then it is now." Landry held her breath.

Karmal came back round to the screen. "It is time to be honest. I ashamed to admit but my family is everything to me. I think about them always. I want to right that wrong."

Landry straightened her shoulders and then looked at Wynter. "Your turn Wynter, why do you work for Magera?"

Wynter considered her answer. "If I'm honest, I was assigned here after my application for the motherhood programme was refused. I never knew parents like you and Kar. I didn't care about being an operative when I first started. Exploring the past has changed how I feel about my future. I wish the world hadn't changed as much as it has. When I visit the past, the people are so full of life and have such a purpose in their lives. Climate change and the great fall killed our planet in so many ways. It's killed us really. The choices that they can make in the past are not available to us. Watching Carly and Robert speak at the SAM meetings has made me angry. I'm furious with all those people who knew that this was going to happen and did not stop it. I'm angry with governments who turned their back on their people, all thinking that it was someone else's problem or blaming others."

Landry looked directly into the small viz camera as she began, "I'm angry too Wynt and I've got ideas buzzing around my head. Changes that I really believe might avoid the Earth falling into the climate change abyss. You both know why I am working for Magera.

Having grown up with my parents and siblings off-grid, I can tell you Kar and Wynt that I think you both missed out. Having family, roots you firmly in your past and your future. I left my family thinking that I was helping Magera to change the World. I gave up my family to save the world but if I can't do that, then I'm going back there. I can't stay here. I need to be with my father." Landry spread her hands wide. "I can't stay in this prison, in this faceless city surrounded by soulless people. I just can't do it anymore. "

She paused, and they waited. "I might be naïve, but I want everyone to have what I have had. The great fall was the loss of our humanity. It caused the formation of the ration cities which forced families like mine to go underground. Going back in time, I can see that it changed us as human beings. Made us scared of taking risks. Made us need Radan for everything. "

She was at full force now. A tide of thoughts that she had wanted to unleash flooded out. "My greatest desire was to go back and make changes that would stop the great fall. Magera promised me. Find the moments in history that might save us and bring them back. That's what they told me to do, and I did that. With every desire in my being, I did that.

My father is dying because of the life that he has been forced to live. He's too young to die. I MUST change that. If it means that I no longer exist, then so be it. In 2188, life isn't living at all, it is existing. I'm happy to risk it all, hoping I just might make that variation that would stop all this from happening. I've been thinking about this since my visit home. My father deserves more from this life. Wynt- your investigation and the bombing have just given us a deadline.

I see Radan as a dangerous child. Radan can't understand what it has lost in its attempts to preserve our lives. But is it worth being saved if the future for humans is Mars? No no-no. It's not worth it. "She paused and before either could speak, she said it. "I'm doing this with you or without you. I'd rather do it together and maybe then we can ensure that we all can get what we want but I'm doing it."

Landry sat back in her seat and waited for the onslaught. It felt like an eternity, and then she heard and saw Wynter clapping. Slowly at first, but then louder. Landry stared at the screen and saw that she was smiling at her. Karmal joined in too.

Karmal exclaimed. "I knew you were special Landry. It will be a success or a fatal failure- for all of us.

"I know what I am asking, and I know I don't know everything, but I wouldn't suggest this unless I believed it could be a success."

"We can work together on this. If we all work as one, we may have a better chance. It's easier for me." She laughed." The prospect of the 'no' life on Mars is enough to spur me forward. What about you Kar?"

"If I can help my family, I will do anything. I have plans of my own."

Landry smiled, "You're a dark horse, Karmal Rahman."

" Yes." Karmal smiled. "And I have some knowledge of changing timelines."

"Go ahead Kar."

"Study the timings. If one of us acts before the other, then it will alter time and affect us. We must plan. "

"Agreed," Wynter said.

"Agreed," Landry repeated.

They spent that day talking excitedly about what they were about to attempt. Karmal told them stories his mother had shared about his family. Landry shared memories of her childhood that she hadn't thought about for years. Wynter even shared her confusion over her feelings for Robert. It felt like everything that it was. Friends chatting about their lives. Friends who wanted to prolong the talking as their time to share was ending.

Finally, they made plans for the next day. They proposed to find their time doorways, make their final preparations and say their goodbyes. They were on a tight timeframe due to Wynter's Investigation meeting. Land couldn't contact her family but truly hoped that she would see them again. Wynter and Karmal had no contacts to speak to.

It was early morning on the 1st day of August when they spoke for the last time. It was strained with nervousness.

"Wynt, Kar? Are you happy with the timings?"

"Yes, but you must keep to time once you have passed through the doorway. We have a lot to do. One of us lose track and it is over."

Wynter was hesitant "Are we ready to do this? We have so little experience and haven't had much time to plan? "

"We have fate on our side. We can do this. "Karmal's face was now solemn as he spoke. "Land and Wynt, it is a pleasure having time with you. I am praying for great fortitude and success."

Landry replied, "We do not need luck Kar. We are doing what is right. If we are successful, we will likely have never met. But know that we did what we needed to do and in the end success or failure, we tried."

Wynter's eyes welled up. "We are not going to see each other again, are we?"

Karmal shook his head slowly and Landry spoke, "Not if we're successful Wynt."

"I am grateful to have your friendship. Thank you. Thank you for everything. I feel responsible for what we are about to do."

Landry shook her head, "The moment that Radan interfered with the timeline was the moment that I knew, everything had changed."

Karmal nodded. "If Magera had been stronger, it would be different. Not your fault."

All three were reluctant to sign off, but eventually, their names disappeared from the chat list as they closed their word pads for the last time. Landry stared at the WordPad and considered a new future. A future where secrecy would not be necessary, and her family and many others could live where they wanted to. She hoped she would never need the WordPad again.

CHAPTER 26

KARMAL RAHMAN

He had spent years planning this moment, but as he reached the time to act, he hesitated. He'd wanted it for so long and had wished for it with all his heart, but it was a selfish desire, wasn't it? A huge risk. What they were all proposing was a risk to all of humanity. That their efforts could make it worse had crossed his mind. His actions would benefit himself and his family, but the actions of his friends might benefit everyone- he hoped.

The shadow of resentment that he carried over the death of his family was always there. They were not killed by the cyclone but killed by human frailty, selfishness and Radan's deductions. Whatever it had been, his family had died of starvation and disease in their small homestead. He had spent hours replaying their suffering at the end; each watching the other die with no support coming and no hope.

As a boy, this had seethed through his body, pushing him forward, pushing him to join Magera; to change the World. As a man, the anger dissipated to a reminiscence of a missed life, of a family that he never knew and a life he yearned for.

The recent actions of Radan had driven them all to act, but this was his only chance. Wynter and Landry's actions could change the timeline drastically. There was no other opportunity to save them. Staring this possibility in the face, Karmal felt the shame of his self-centred plan. It went against the beliefs of Islam; not self, but many. He didn't have much time but could he do it? If Landry was not successful and the great fall still took place, then at least he could try to save more by his actions. The Early warning storm system created following cyclone Zabr in 2157 was a simple one. As were the cyclone shelters, the strengthening of embankments, created because of the tragedy that killed Karmal's family. These interventions, if enforced earlier, may have saved thousands of lives. Could he save more than just his family?

He had developed a friendly relationship with his Magera supervisor Dipu over several years. A trusting relationship. As a young man, Dipu regarded the older Karmal as a harmless visionary. His laziness and trusting nature had already allowed Karmal to squirrel away enough rupees to purchase the land in Dhaka. Now Karmal needed more for this final trip.

He hadn't seen Dipu since the discovery of the viz images from Mars, so that topic of conversation was at the forefront as Karmal sat on the edge of Dipu's desk. Karmal always enjoyed their conversations, and today was no different. They had both glanced up at the Magera homescreen as he entered and stated, "Private mode." Their collusion was complete.

"Dipu, those images …." Shaking his head Karmal blew air through his closed lips.

"My friend will get reassigned. He wants nothing to do with it."

"Are you sure, it is not temporary or because of unpreparedness?"

"My friend doesn't think so. He has said that no building works have even begun. No new London, No New Tokyo. No cities at all, just the complex that you saw in the viz."

Karmal nodded." Are you going to share it with anyone else?"

Dipu shifted in his chair. "You mean Magera don't you?" He hesitated, "I have thought about it, I have thought about sending it to everyone." Reaching for his forehead. "But I made a promise to my friend. Not until he can get away. The met data in the viz leads straight back to him. I made a promise."

Karmal nodded slowly and Dipu continued, "Maybe once my friend is away, you can help me decide what to do…" The muscles in Dipu's face tightened." We cannot ignore it but what can we do?"

"Do nothing Dipu. This is bigger than any of us. leave it for now. Until your friend is safe."

Dipu let out the breath that he had been holding. Karmal felt the urge to share everything with Dipu. All that Wynter had discovered and his collaboration with them both. It might reassure Dipu, but he knew he couldn't. He did not know what was going to happen to the timeline. Glancing up at the homescreen, Karmal was shocked by the time. He needed to get through the doorway if he was going to set his plans in motion before Wynter and Landry acted. He cancelled private mode and Dipu did the same.

"Did you receive my assignment brief and pre- protocol checks?"

"Oh yes, Kar." Looking at his screen, Dipu became engrossed in the assignment brief. "Yes, you sent it late last night. I do have to perform some last-minute checks. Do you have to go today?"

Keeping his demeanour casual, Karmal glanced towards the inventory cupboard. "I tell you what. I'll speed you up. While you're doing that, I can get the operative pack ready."

"Ok." Dipu nodded focussing on his screen. He reached behind him and fetched the security fob off the hook, and passing it across the desk, "Yeh Karmal, you go ahead."

As Karmal scanned the fob on the locking mechanism and entered the operative money safe, he paused. What he was about to do could end his career and damage his integrity forever. He needed to be sure that he was doing it for the right reasons. He considered the plans made by his two friends and quickly concluded that if he didn't act, then it would be taken out of his hands, anyway.

Grabbing bundles of American dollars, he placed them in the very bottom compartment of the bag. He already had several contraband documents on him, and he needed to hide those as well. He knew Dipu wouldn't check, but just in case, on top of these, he placed the usual operative pack. Closing the zip of the bag, he locked the door and made his way back to Dipu. With all protocols ticked off, it was time for Karmal to leave. He could not predict how the changes to the timeline might affect people like Dipu. Karmal stopped himself from raising his arms and embracing Dipu for what could be the last time.

Karmal smiled, "Back in a minute." He succumbed to their shared joke.

Laughing Dipu replied, "Don't be late."

As Karmal entered the cupboard where the time doorway was located, he couldn't resist a glance back at Dipu, who was already engrossed with something on his screen.

"Goodbye," Karmal whispered.

Waving his Radan tattoo across the door frame, the door glowed and losing its solidity he stepped through. In 2150, the office was empty. He listened for any voices nearby. There were none. He needed to locate the old pre-Radan keypad that he would need later. It took time to find it but at last he spotted what looked like a socket for electrical items. Tugging hard, the front panel came free, and he could see the keypad hidden behind. Placing the cover back in place he turned to leave the office. There was a distant ringing of the bell, and he could hear the students making their way to lessons, doors banging, the busyness of Curzon Hall. He waited patiently until much of the noise had ceased, then stating, "Private mode", he turned the handle to the outside world.

The smells hit him. The heady spices mingled with the humidity of a summer day in Dhaka. A food stall at the entrance to the university would sell Jhalmuri, Kathi Rolls and Ghugni. His mouth watered at the idea of them. In New Dhaka in 2150, the Radan ration city plans, had not been completed yet. He hoped that after today, it never would be a ration city. He walked along the open veranda, admiring the botanical obelisks and turquoise water pools as he made his way towards the university gates.

He set the timer on his optic for three hours. The time he predicted he had, before the timeline changed irreparably. He had a lot to do.

The city was such a different place from his last visit. The streets were full of hawkers and motos screamed up and down the streets overloaded with goods and people.

He soon reached his first destination, the Tohasil Land office, which now also housed The Shiktar Group of solicitors. On approaching the offices, he saw they were more prosperous than when he had visited in 1971, with new smart signage outside. However, Karmal chuckled when he saw that the small narrow staircase leading up to the office was just the same. On reaching the top of the stairs, he was greeted by a distinguished-looking man in a suit. The greeting had changed now, with a shake of the hand replacing the kiss on each cheek. The more commercial English greeting of "Good morning. I am Mahbubul Shiktar. Pleased to meet you, Mr?"

"Mr Raham, Mr Shaffiullah Rahman." Karmal had desperately wanted to use his father's name, Emran, but he would have only been 13yrs old, so Karmal had been forced to use the identity of his grandfather, Shaffiullah.

"Yes Saab Raham, I have been expecting you." He signalled to the chair before his desk, "Please sit." Karmal studied the desk and was contemplating if it was indeed the same desk from 1971 when Mahbubul spoke. "Do you have the document key with you?"

"Yes, of course." He opened his bag and began rooting around for the document key he required. Having found it, he placed it on the table. The solicitor swept his hand across it, and the document appeared in front of him. As Mahbubul studied the document, Karmal had the first opportunity to look around the office. He instantly saw the transformation from 1971. Gone were the stacks of paperwork on the desks and the antiquated filing system filling the shelves along the back wall. This office was clean, dust-free, with every surface empty and spotless. He wondered where his purchase agreement from 1971 would be. Did they even still exist, or were they transferred years before?

His reflections were halted by Mahbubul speaking. "Well, Mr Rahman, it is certainly a formal document and the stipulations that you are asking of the Centre of Environmental Services, the CESB, are rigorous. You are sure that you only donate the sum if they agree to this timeline. I mean, the building of cyclone shelters, the cyclone early warning system and the bunkers of medicine and food products is a huge undertaking. The Mehendignj region is remote, prone to flooding and an area of extreme weather patterns. This makes it a difficult region to work in."

"But not impossible, Mr Shiktar. I just have plans and am impatient for them to be completed before 2157."

Mahbubul's manner changed, holding up his hands, "Saab Rahman, this document from my point of view is watertight, I am merely questioning if the CESB will agree to these terms."

"If they want my funding for it, then why shouldn't they?"

Mahbubul nodded in agreement, "Yes, you are doing a wonderful thing, Saab Rahman. To donate so much for the benefit of others. A truly noble thing. But don't you want the pleasure of meeting with them yourself? "He flicked through to the 4th page of the document. "You wish to remain anonymous? You do not wish to be acknowledged for the good that you are doing."

"Mr Shiktar." Karmal raised his hands to the ceiling, "It is for Allah and for the people that I do this, not for myself." Karmal knew that this was an outdated religious gesture in 2150 but Mahbubul smiled.

"Of course, Saab Rahman." He put the palms of his hands together and raising them slightly, "Peace be with you Saab Rahman."

Karmal mirrored him. "And with you Saab Shiktar. I leave this secret in your capable hands and this document once shared with the CESB, it will be placed with you for safekeeping."

Mahbubul nodded, "Yes of course Saab Rahman." He extended his right hand to shake Kamal's. "Shall we do business?"

Karmal shook his hand vigorously, nodding.

"How shall you transfer the funds?"

In a realisation of panic, Karmal cursed his lack of time to research this right. He only had a bank card. He paled. It was too late; he was committed. He placed the card on the desk and saw Mahbubul's face drop immediately.

"Saab Rahman. This is extremely unusual. The laws regarding card purchases..."

"I know Saab Shiktar, City coin transfer would be more ideal, but my grandfather has this old account that he had been paying into. It is his life savings." Karmal lied, "I have told him he should have changed this years ago, but he is a very old man, a very stubborn old man. It is a large sum." Karmal continued, "I am happy for you to take a substantial handling fee. It is a lot of extra work for you, I know. "

Mahbubul held his hands up. "It would need to be a considerable fee for handling such an old account. "

Karmal nodded. Mahbubul rang a bell on his desk and a young man appeared in a suit just like Mahbubul's. "Fetch the old card processor."

He turned to Karmal, "Do you mind if my son, Arfin, is present for the transaction? This is highly unusual. You must understand."

It took some time but later when Karmal left the office, Karmal felt his spirits lift as he thought about the impact on the people of the Mehendiganj district. He could stop there, but he couldn't leave it to chance. He'd done his best for all those people whose lives were changed by the cyclone. His thoughts turned to his family. It was time to move them out of the path of the cyclone.

As he walked down the road towards the university, Karmal didn't see the timewave variation thundering towards him. Back in the Magera office, Dipu did. It was not small. The result of Karmal's donation changed the timeline significantly. Dipu watched it coming and heard the alarm sounding.

In the Magera office in Birmingham, Kyson Mullins saw and heard the same alarm. It read as a 0.23 timewave variation, not catastrophic but still not good. It swept from the doorway of the office in Curzon Hall and through the Magera office where Dipu was sitting. He heard it first, like a rush of wind coming towards him. It felt like the temperature dropped a few degrees as a blurry line passed through Dipu and his desk and out through the opposite door. All in Magera winced a little as the time variation passed through them.

Once it had, they had no personal recollection that it had occurred, but their screens told them otherwise. Their first thoughts were who and where? Locating the answer to this would be difficult, as at this moment three operatives were moving under their radar in private mode. It would be impossible to find them.

Karmal didn't hear the wind coming behind him but felt the tug of his insides as the invisible line passed through him. He froze and as his brain registered what was happening it was already over. Karmal continued on his way with no knowledge of anything having happened. This Karmal was already walking in an altered timeline with no recollection of the old one.

Once back at the empty office in Curzon Hall, Karmal located the old keypad from the pre-Radan system and typed in 12.05.2157.0900. He was going back to Dhaka, two months before Cyclone Zabr was due to sweep through. The room shuddered as the key number was entered and Karmal felt a ripple rush through him as the time frame changed.

As he left the University complex, Karmal noted that the buildings in Dhaka were a little more well-kept, the streets a little cleaner and the refugee camps less of a drain on the city than previously. The cyclone shelters were already having a positive impact.

Returning to the offices of The Shiktar Group now 7 years later, he was disappointed to find Mahbubul's name absent and his son Arfin's, in his place. Karmal had been looking forward to seeing Mahbubul again. On stepping up the narrow staircase, Karmal was mindful that in his time, he had only just left them at their office, but in their timeline, it had been 7 years. He didn't expect Arfin to remember him. 7 years was a long time, and they had met only briefly. He was wrong. The donation had bought much credence to their establishment and because they had kept the anonymity of the donation, had benefited them. Business had been good.

Arfin's eyes lit up as soon as he entered and he was greeted with a familiarity, shaking his hand vigorously. "Welcome Saab Rahman. You are very welcome. You are looking very well." He almost bowed, simpering in gratitude and showing him to the usual chair.

"Please sit." Arfin rang the bell and a younger man thundered up the stairs. "Refreshments for our guest."

Turning to Arfin, Karmal immediately asked after his father.

"My father? He is still working, but he is less in the office and more with our family. A retirement of sorts. But Saab Rahman, I am sure that I can assist you today." He leaned back in his chair and waited.

"It is regarding a land purchase in 1971, I believe when your relative Resna Shiktar ran the business."

Arfin frowned. "1971, that is centuries ago! With all respect Saab Rahman, how can you have business from 1971?"

"Not myself, of course, but my family, yes. Can I provide you with copies of the document? My family has kept our copy for years. I have placed it on a document key if you would rather study it there?"

"Saab Rahman, it is rare to handle such an old document, even as a copy of the original. I have a fascination with these document forms, especially from the 20th Century, rare indeed."

Arfin took out a pair of white gloves to enable him to examine the paper copy, and Karmal reverently passed it across the desk. Karmal had to age the document himself and he hoped he had done a good job. The joy on Arfin's face said it all. He was thrilled.

It took Arfin some time to read through the land purchase agreement and Karmal noted that several times he carefully turned the pages back to check previous points. While he waited, Karmal glanced at his timer several times, and thoughts moved to Wynter and Landry and their progress. He hoped he was still in time before their actions impacted the timeline.

Finally, Arfin looked up, "And you have a full genealogy confirmation, DNA affirmation and the documents proving that you are indeed the descendant of Resna Rahman?"

"Of course." Karmal placed a document key in front of Arfin. With a sweep of his hand, he opened the key, and the translucent images of the documents flew up in front of both, bouncing expectantly. Arfin swept some documents aside and scrutinised others while Karmal continued to wait.

"Well, Saab Rahman, it all appears to be here." Karmal let out his breath steadily and for the first time felt an excitement rippling through him. He smiled at Arfin.

Arfin leant forward, looked to the left and right and lowered his voice, "I have to say Saab Rahman, in the years that I have known you, you have visited only twice." He paused, holding up his two fingers in V-sign. "On both occasions, the business that has ensued has been the most unusual that I have ever come across." He smiled and Karmal reciprocated. "I hope this doesn't offend you, Saab Rahman. "

"No offence taken, Saab Shiktar. "

Arfin looked again at the document. "I believe your ancestor was just like you." He pointed at the land purchase agreement. "This is a strange way to purchase land, Saab Rahman. Maybe strange business runs in the family." He chuckled, shaking his head.

"You will act on my behalf, Saab Shiktar?"

"Yes, with pleasure, but first…" He sat back. "I need to find the original in our document library. It was probably copied to the library in the late 2060s and notarized. I need to find this before I can act."

Karmal's shoulders slumped. "I understand, but once this is found, you will contact the various parties. "

Arfin placed his gloved fingers together in a pyramid shape, leaning his elbows on his desk, "Of course, I can contact the Rahman's living on the land purchased in 1971. They are easy to find. I know the land well. I will inform them of the enactment of the clause." He paused as he referred again to the document, "Clause 13.2, that you are requested to invite the family of Forhad Rahman and or his descendants to join in farming the land and sharing the profits."

Arfin frowned. "But Saab Rahman, Shaffiullah Rahman, you are a direct descendant of Forhad Rahman. You can bring your family to this land. You need no invite. You are here! "He swept his arms in front of him, palms up.

Karmal sat up, smiling. "As you have said yourself, Saab Shiktar, this is indeed a strange business." He hesitated, "I believe that my ancestor, Forhad, stated a need for an invitation and was specific in his language, don't you agree?" Arfin pursed his lips and nodded. Karmal continued, "I want to respect the wishes of my six times grandfather. He wanted the family invited to come and share the land that he purchased and so that is how it should happen. I feel strongly about this."

Arfin was resigned. "Yes, of course, Saab Rahman." He fixed his palms together. "For our usual fee, we will ensure the wishes of your ancestors are met. This business is incomprehensible, but I am not here to question, only to serve." Arfin swept aside the floating documents and with a twist of his wrist, a screen appeared between them. Karmal could see the same as Arfin, but to him, it appeared backwards. Arfin commanded, "Contact Father." There was a pause as the connection was made, and then Karmal saw Mahbubul Shiktar appear on the screen. Karmal was briefly shocked by his aged appearance remained composed.

Arfin began talking, "Father, you will not believe who I have with me today… Saab Rahman has once again visited us."

Karmal saw Mahbubul's face creased into a wide smile. "Saab Rahman, are you pleased with our work? Your shelters and cyclone systems have reached completion and are already saving lives. We have watched the work with great interest as have you, I am sure."

"Yes." Karmal was careful not to elaborate. "I have been pleased with the progress. "

"Oh Saab Rahman, the environmental services wanted your identity, but we kept your anonymity, as were your wishes. We are a loyal firm."

"Thank you, Saab Shiktar."

"Father," Arfin interrupted, "We have more business with Saab Rahman and it involves a document from 1971. Do you know where those doc notaries may be stored?"

Mahbubul placed his hand on his chin. "Now, let me see. 1971 you say, we would have copied these documents in 2085, when I first took over the business. "His face broke into a smile of satisfaction, "They would be stored in the first library files in the archives. Library files 2085. Do you have the reference number?"

"Yes, I do, "Karmal began, "it's L67685.2."

"Right Arfin, search that library, the reference number should take you there." His father commanded, "If you do not find it, then contact me. There may be another way. "

Arfin closed the communication screen and verbally commanded access to the document library as per his father's instructions. The document was found after some perseverance.

"We have everything we need Saab Rahman. I will inform the custodians of the land that it is time for the clause to be implemented. It shouldn't take much time to reach out to the family. A matter of hours."

Karmal gathered up his copy of the document and his doc key, and shaking his hand said, "thank you Saab Shiktar."

"It is always a pleasure to do business with you. I hope to see you soon."

Karmal hoped that they would not meet again as he stepped into a bright sunny day.

The weather suited his mood, and he felt for the first moment that his plan for his family's past and future was assured. With everything in place, Karmal took his time strolling back towards the University campus. His plans hadn't stretched beyond saving his family, so he did not know what might happen next.

Arfin was busy putting things in motion, contacting Karmal's relatives and giving them the good news. They were to share a prime piece of agricultural land on the outskirts of Dhaka with their extended family. It couldn't have come at a better time, as Faridah Rahman was due to give birth to their first son. As soon as Arfin ended his conversation with Karmal's relatives, the timeline shifted.

The timeline variation was considerable for Karmal. It was a 0.33 and the time variation line thundered towards Karmal, whipping up leaves and waste along with it. To Karmal it appeared as a wall of shimmering air hastening towards him. He knew what it was. He had heard about them. He stopped in the street and stood with his feet braced against the pavement, his face raised to the sun and his eyes closed. Waiting expectantly for the wave to pass, he took a moment to enjoy the last moments on this timeline on Earth.

People passing later described a wall of air passing down the street. As it reached the man, stood with his face towards the sky, there was a distinct popping sensation in their ears and when they looked again, he had gone.

Dipu saw the wave coming. The wailing alarm directed him to a second wave. He watched the time wave on the screen build as it approached. It was increasing the closer it came to 2188. It swept through the office and again Dipu braced himself for its impact. After it passed through, he had no recollection of the old timeline, and the only evidence that it had happened was on his screen.

Dipu never questioned why Karmal didn't return through the doorway that day. In the new timeline Karmal Rahman and Dipu Chandra had never met.

It's January 21st, 2148, a child's first cry echoes through the corridors of the New Dhaka General hospital, Mother and father share a smile.

"Have a nama? "The nurse asks.

"Yes, we do, welcome to the World Karmal Rahman." There is pride in his eyes as the father Emran leans forward to kiss his first-born son.

CHAPTER 27

WYNTER LUND

Wynter had not worked out how she could stop the explosion. She packed her time assignment bag mentally listing everything that she might need. She must take her nanotech clothing for protection but couldn't decide which identity to take. Grabbing all her previous identities, she thrust them in her bag. If the authorities caught her with these, she would need an explanation. If the plan was a success, then she might not be returning to her accom ever again, and she spent some time considering what other items she might need. She had downloaded as much research into climate change that she could find and had placed it in a secure data storage device that she could access in the 21st century. The realisation that she had nothing of any personal value to take with her weighed heavily. With no family in 2188, she was leaving nothing behind.

With private mode requested and the exit from her accom undetected, Wynter made her way to the unused time door in the flooded Playhouse Theatre. It gave Wynter an unmonitored route through to the past. To wait until nightfall before entering was her first choice. But that would mean waiting around while Landry and Karmal were acting on their plans. She couldn't afford to waste that precious time and so needed to move during daylight. The London History society led fortnightly tours and Wynter could see that they would pass close enough to the time doorway. Booked on the tour beginning at 1300hrs, Wynter had to slip away from her escort when the moment was right; she hoped the group was large.

Striding towards the theatre, Wynter avoided public transport and the security bots that buzzed up and down the streets. In a positive mood and buoyed by her plans for today, Wynter felt the tension of the last few days ebbing away. The relief of removing herself from the brooding cloud of Mars and her investigation with Magera was palpable.

She was purposely late to ensure the briefest of communication with the tour guide. The group was standing at the first security gate when she arrived and as predicted, her tardiness irritated him. He was keen to begin, and as she predicted, didn't check her booking or scan her tattoo. She made no eye contact and remained aloof, reducing any need for interaction.

"Please increase the depth of your footwear before we enter the water," the guide instructed as he placed his wrist on the first gate. Wynter remained at the back, and the tour started.

"Although it is low tide, please be very careful in placing your feet through this section. There are building materials that have fallen from the structure. We don't want anyone requiring medic-support, so take your time." The guide stopped just beyond the second gate and began speaking of the building's history. "Built in 1907 by F. H Fowler and Hill and with a seating capacity of 1200." A low murmur rippled through, and Wynter smiled to herself. She enjoyed the history of buildings and would enjoy seeing it in all its grandeur soon. However, today she had to keep her focus on getting to the right section of the building and slipping away.

As they arrived inside, he described the impressive structures and where they had once been. The Greek Stucco facades, the carved balustrades, and the blank walls where gigantic murals once were. Seeing it in daylight, a feeling of great sadness struck Wynter. The guide was proud to share the stories of a once magnificent place, but all Wynter could feel was regret that they had abandoned it to this fate.

She focused her attention to where in the building they were. They walked behind the stage and passed the corridor Wynter needed to go down. The guide's tone had changed as he described the inner workings of the stage. When he started talking about the substage machinery. Wynter took her moment. The group had to walk in single file through the narrow doorway. Wynter maintained her distance at the rear. While the two people in front of her went straight forward, she turned to the left and waded through the water, rushing to make it through the doorway in time before they missed her.

Wynter entered the room, closing the door behind her. She heard a commotion as the guide pushed through the group and began running down the corridor, calling her name. Rushing to the keypad that she'd used on her previous visit she entered the ten-digit time code that would deliver her to the past. 12th April 2033 at 10.00hrs. His shouts intensified as he came closer. Wynter began to panic. Karmal's warning echoed in her mind, and she took a few seconds to check the numbers before pressing enter. The doorway shimmered in front of her as the ERA symbol bounced across the opening surface. She heard him struggling to open the door another room and breathed a sigh of relief as she crossed the threshold into 2033.

She prepared herself for the young girl from before but saw that the room was empty. For just a fleeting moment, Wynter heard the echoes of the guide's voice as he shouted her name in 2188.

Tapping her graphino Wynter stated, "green." The jacket's darkness rippled away, and a vivid green replaced it. Wynter tapped three more times, "0.1 darker 0.2 darker, 0.3 darker." Satisfied with the colour of her graphino, she opened the door and entered the corridor leading to the back entrance. The pounding of feet on the stage above was deafening, and she instinctively jumped back against the wall. Small particles of dust were falling rhythmically from the ceiling to the beat of the music. "I'm surprised any of it is still standing," she muttered to herself as she strode into the morning sunshine.

Wynter had visited this day so many times and the over-stimulus of sounds and people had felt overwhelming every time but today her heart was racing, and her smile beamed. She had never had a home in the traditional sense, but the streets and views of London were starting to feel familiar to her.

She was happily pulled through Northumberland Avenue with her fellow SAM supporters and for only the second time, felt that she could enjoy the procession; she was going to save them all today. She just hoped that she was successful. Shading her eyes from the sun, she stopped on a street corner and looked up at the decorated roofs. She gasped as she spotted birds; some taking flight, others clinging to the edge, calling to each other. Her smile broadened as her thoughts turned to Landry.

She followed the traffic of humanity, moving towards the square, sharing the excitement of the moment. A growing emotion filling her as their hope pulled her forward. They believed they could save the World. Oh, how she wished they could. The future she knew could not compare to the abundance of life she saw before her. The repeated thump of the pile drivers for the construction of the Kallan Tower flood defences behind her reminded her that action was being taken to save this London, but she knew that this was not enough.

Enjoying her journey today, Wynter passed through the landmarks now so familiar to her. The Sherlock Holmes public house was now full of revellers, and she made a promise to herself to visit there after her plans had been complete.

As with her earlier visits, the airborne security drones seeped through the crowd, pausing at individuals and scanning their faces. As she turned, one appeared just above her." Look into the lens." The command broke her stride, but she followed the instruction. Her identity was not on any wanted list in 2033. The drone took an eternity to process her image, and people filed past her as she stood there waiting. Could Radan have discovered their plan? Could it be coming back to stop her? Stop them? The wait was terrifying, and her pulse raced in her ears. Finally, the drone spoke, "Proceed." Almost stumbling, she started walking, relief spurring her forward.

She entered the square and felt the embrace of the chanting crowds, banners and general delight of people sharing this moment in time. However, her interest was firmly on one item. She approached the fountain rim where the families gathered, being careful to avoid any of her previous selves. She soon spotted it and saw that it lay where she expected it to be undisturbed. Now, what to do now?

Wynter had taken a considerable time checking the security protocols for explosive threats in this period. Terror plots before 2033 mainly centred around Islamic extremists using weapons or vehicles to kill people. The last successful politically motivated explosion had been in 2017 when a suicide bomber detonated a bomb on an underground train at Parsons Green station. The last threat came in 2024, with the discovery of an undetonated bomb in a car outside the offices of a prominent news agency on Carter Street. By 2024, the city of London had banned unauthorised cars in central London. On this occasion, the authorities had removed the car and later found the bomb. Until 2033, there had not been an explosive device in London for many years. The drones were checking for activists known to them. Homeland security was strict and unrelenting. The parents at the fountain felt very safe under this security regime.

Wynter had made her plan of action based upon the current protocols. She planned to have as little involvement as possible. As the organisers were still setting up and the square filling with supporters, Wynter took out the ID that she felt looked the most official, placed the brimmed cap on her head and approached group by the fountain. Her heart was pounding in her chest, but she knew that she needed to get this right. The parents were busy establishing their places to view the proceedings. As she reached them, she flashed her badge at the nearest adult.

"Added security measures. You must not leave baggage and personal items unattended. We will treat any unattended items found as suspicious. "

Wynter pointed at the pile of bags and belongings, "This cannot stay like this. You need to claim your belongings and put them near you."

The man was reluctant to act. Wynter could see him pause, but then he turned and addressed the others, "Come on you guys, we have to take our own bags and carry them with us."

She saw him scrutinise her badge again, but she turned her shoulder away in the guise of helping the adults by holding up bags, passing them out and asking for ownership. "Yours? Please take it, madam. Is this your flag? Can you keep it with you, please?"

She stopped as she noticed the edge of the black bag appear from under the mountain of colourful items and stepped back and watched. Ready to step in should anyone touch the bag. She waited patiently. The black bag came into view and to Wynter's relief, he pointed and shouted, "Is this anyone's?" On hearing no reply, he repeated the question. A murmur spread around the group, and he moved forward to lift it.

Wynter jumped forward shouting, "No!" The group froze and stopped talking, many turning to look at her. With a wave of her hand, "Leave it. Don't touch it." She turned to to the man again. "You! Tell security. Tell them you have suspicions of a bag left unattended." Wynter watched as he made his way to the security gate, waving his arms to get their attention. She relieved as Several security operatives ran forward, and Wynter stepped into the shadows behind a pillar and observed from a distance.

The security forces soon gathered and moved through the crowd telling them to make their way out of Trafalgar square. There was a great reluctance and Wynter felt their disappointment as they all slowly left the square. Wynter wasn't disappointed. She was elated. A bubble of uncontrollable relieve and happiness welled from inside her. So, this is what it feels like. Saving all of those people was worth everything that had happened before. This was joy! No one was going to die today, and she had done that. A small trickle of doubt crept into her subconscious. If Landry wasn't successful, then this could all have been for nothing. Radan could come back again but she looked around. Would it have already happened?

She turned, her sole on the inner sanctum of the SAM group as she watched Robert, Carly and the others being escorted to safety by police officers. She smiled to herself. That was such an amazing sight.

Wynter had her back to the timeline variation as it travelled through the Square picking up litter and leaves in a wave. She felt the wind pass through her back and has a strange feeling of her insides being pulled along with the wind. It took with it all of the anxiety and stress of recent days. To Wynter it felt like a new day. Different somehow.

As she caught up the group and Robert turned,

"Do I know you?"

Wynter beamed.

"I know this is strange, but could we talk?"

CHAPTER 28

LANDRY REAGAN

"I don't understand the rush, Reagan2485. Time waits for..."

"I know. I know. Time waits for us all." Landry drawled. "I've had two weeks rest, and I'm keen to get started. "

Landry felt the agreed timeline with Wynter and Karmal pressing on her. She needed to reach her primary goal before Wynter acted.

Kyson stared into the optic, the exasperation in her voice. "I understand Reagan2485 - I know how impatient you are. Let me check the progress of your report." Kyson started scanning the screen to her left. "Yes, almost complete." She sighed, "You could return in one hour and it should be ready."

"Mullins2001, I'll wait here. "

"Or you could come back tomorrow."

Landry knew that tomorrow would be too late. She instantly regretted her decision to go through the official Magera time doorway. She paused, recalculating if she could run to an unused doorway in New Street, but her regular one in the Hippodrome Theatre was closer to her goal on the other side, and so she waited.

"I'll wait, Mullins2001. I'll wait here. There are no scheduled performances now. "She slid into a seated position at the rear of the theatre. It was a quiet place, secluded, with layer upon layer of set curtains and scenery. She took the time to review her plans. Her last day of travel through time. Enveloped by the darkness, Landry's thoughts swung to the beginning of the end.

How did we get it so wrong? The planet ravaged by war, famine, financial greed, pandemic and ultimately the death of everything. But why? Humans are resourceful and resilient, and so how did they miss something as damaging as climate change? She knew the answer. It was greed. She imagined how the new world might look if they were successful. A world where the Earth and everything on it had equal value. Where her beloved animals were still a vital part of it. Her thoughts turned to her family and the life that they might have if the great fall hadn't happened, where her father may not need to perform the physical work. Her stomach twisted; the nerves began.

The screen above her came alive with the distinctive voice of Kyson Mullins. "Reagan2485? Reagan?"

Landry stood up and stared at the screen.

"Reagan2485, I've done a few things for you myself and you can now go through and fulfil your assignment."

Landry smiled at the screen, "Thank you Mullins2001, Thankyou Kyson." This time, Kyson didn't chastise her.

Landry wasn't sure if she would see her again. What they were planning would change everything. As she tapped her tattoo onto the symbol, and the horizontal crack of light opened on the back wall, Landry turned to face Kyson on the screen.

"Goodbye Kyson." There was a quiet seriousness in her tone.

Turning, Landry heard her name repeated by Kyson and becoming more distant as she stepped into 2013.

Multiple drums exploded in her auditorus, beating a repeated rhythm and loud. Landry expected singing. She had seen the Lion King on history reels from that period, but it didn't prepare her for the intensity as voices joined in chorus. Landry listened intently for any movement behind the scenes. Seeing or hearing no one, she strode across the back of the stage.

Once outside, Landry was surprised by a wet, dreary afternoon. She sheltered under the awning at the stage door watching the rain bouncing off the pavement and making its own symphony of sounds on various receptacles left in the alleyway. She needed to keep to time and she was already late. Placing her hood over her head, she shouted, "Private mode", as she leapt through the collected puddles and taking shelter where she could. Her attention was directed on avoiding the commuters. With hoods up or carrying umbrellas, people passed by, swerving deep puddles or jumping from the edge of the kerb where water collected against the roadside.

Landry stepped up to the newsagent's shop that she had passed many times before and never dared venture in. She had never talked to a past participant and wasn't looking forward to it. People were naturally gregarious, but suspicions arose if someone spoke differently or used unfamiliar words. She was worried that her language would be out of time.

Historical data showed that the Birmingham of the 21st century was a thriving multi-cultural city with a reputation for warmth and friendliness to immigrants and refugees. These positives, she kept in her mind as she crossed the threshold into the premises.

She almost stepped straight back out! The floor was dirty. Brown streaks of mud mingled with the rainwater, creating a slippery soup. Horrified, she just managed to fight her revulsion and jumped across the infected area. She had never considered that floors were not self-cleaning, and she forced herself to not exclaim out loud at how dangerous it was.

She was so motivated to avoid any water and mud that she hadn't noticed that she was being studied by the shop worker. Ducking behind a shelf, she walked down the narrow aisles and pretended to be engrossed in the products on the shelves. The shop worker's attention moved elsewhere, and Landry relaxed. This was an alien world to her, and the sheer volume of products on display, overwhelming. Landry wondered how anyone made a choice when there was so much variety. The bright colours hurt her eyes.

Landry needed to focus on her reason for being there today. She was looking for a lottery station. She had watched vizoptics of them; a place to take a form and record lottery numbers. It was at the end of the counter where the worker stood talking to a customer.

"Terrible weather," he exclaimed.

The customer responded. "Yes, but they said on the TV that it'll stop later and tomorrow, should be fine."

Landry stepped up to the station. Taking out the paper from her pocket, she scrutinised the dates and numbers that she wanted to record. She had chosen special weeks where there were no winners referred to in the 21st century as rollovers. Landry knew it what she was doing could result in a reduction in the amount won by the winners in the weeks following. But felt justified; she was saving the World after all. She took the first long sheet and held the pencil provided. Although she had seen a viz of how to complete the card it was far more complicated than she remembered. This added to the pressure to get it right. She only had one chance at this.

The customer had left, and she noticed the shop worker watching her. She froze, staring at the card.

"Can I help you?" The worker moved from behind the counter and towards Landry. Unconsciously, Landry took a step backwards to create a distance between them. He stopped, her body language speaking volumes and held up his hands, "sorry - just want to help."

Landry took a breath and fought her instinct to flee.

Turning to him, she smiled, "Sorry- I haven't done this for a while."

"You don't need to fill out the card, just tell me your numbers." He pointed to a large grey box. You can tell me the numbers and I'll put them through.

"Can I?" Landry stepped up to the counter with the paper in her hand., "Right, I want to buy a ticket for Wednesday 13th June."

"Wednesday," He said as he tapped the keypad in front of him, "and the numbers?"

Landry held up the paper and read out the numbers, "2,5,31,33,34,20."

On entering the last number, the machine kicked into life, making a loud crunching sound as it belched out the ticket. Landry was fascinated. So noisy and antiquated. He took the ticket and passed it to her, "That's two pounds please."

"Oh, yes." in the excitement, Landry had forgotten to pay. She took a handful of coins from her pocket and searched the horde, aware that he was studying her. It felt like an inordinate amount of time before she found the two one-pound coins. Placing them on the counter, Landry took the ticket in her hand and felt her excitement bubble.

The shop worker moved to the space behind the counter and began arranging the merchandise there.

Landry leant forward. "I wish to buy another. Another six."

The worker looked up. "Which round is the next ticket for?" Landry was confused, "Round?"

"Which date is the ticket for?" The shop worker explained, "There are two rounds each week."

Landry looked at her paper and began, "right, ticket number two is for Saturday 23rd June and the numbers are..."

"Wait." He was looking at her paper. "It may be quicker if you give me your paper with the dates and numbers on it?" He held out his hand expectantly.

Landry hesitated, holding the paper in her hand. It represented so much to her; she was reluctant to give it away.

"I will take care of it." He declared, placing his hand on his chest and holding her gaze. Grudgingly, Landry held up the paper, and he took it from her. She watched the muscles in his face tighten as he scrutinised the figures.

Landry had prepared an explanation for the dates of the tickets. She felt compelled to share. "They are presents for my friends' days of birth.... birth's days." She attempted to correct herself. He did not reply, and instead started typing in the relevant dates and numbers, and soon the machine churned out six more tickets. Landry gathered a further twelve one-pound coins to buy the tickets. He smiled as he handed them over, swiping the coins from the counter into his palm and depositing them into the till. Landry had a pound coin leftover and buoyed by her success; she saw a small packet of confectionary placed temptingly in front of her. "I'll take those please."

"Of course." He held out his palm, and she dropped the pound coin into it. Landry took the tickets and confectionary, placing them in her bag.

As Landry turned to leave, he stopped her. "Wait, your change." Landry held out her hand, and he deposited a pile of coins into it. She avoided stopping and scrutinising them there and instead walked casually out the door.

As she moved out into the falling rain, she heard him in a singsong voice shout, "Good Luck."

Landry smiled. She didn't need luck; she knew they were winning numbers. Walking with renewed confidence, Landry considered how the shop worker would feel with so many winning numbers coming from his shop. Would it boost his sales? She hoped so. He seemed to be a friendly person. The rainfall had stopped, and she removed her hood as she entered the Birmingham University Campus.

Landry picked this date, as it had been the first BUFR presentation. The start of the forest Earth project, now so familiar to her. Placing her press badge on her collar, she entered the smaller auditorium where the presentation was being held. She was early and pleased to see Dr Simon Pedersen preparing for the presentation and alone.

He turned towards her. "I'm afraid you are very early. "He hesitated before adding, "but you're welcome to stay, of course." He pointed to the seats and returned his attention to the WordPad in front of him.

"Dr Pedersen, it's you I came to speak to and by coming early I was hoping to find you here." He stopped what he was doing and asked, "Are you interested in forestry research Miss...?" He stepped forward and read her press badge. "Miss Reagan."

"Oh yes Doctor, I have been following your work and I'm very excited about your study..." She corrected herself, "up-and-coming studies." Landry stumbled with her words. She had been so eager to speak to him.

"Do you think it has merit? The venture into trees as carbon sinks?"

"Oh yes. I do. I think you are going to prove new scientific developments in forestry research Dr Pedersen."

She watched as he studied more carefully at her press badge. "World Science Today? Never heard of that publication."

"We are new. We specialise in scientific projects, which may positively reduce global warming. Your press release introducing the work of BUFR came onto my desk. But today, I have something else I wish to discuss with you." He nodded, encouraging Landry to continue.

"I've checked out your income and you gain a large percentage from the university and small pockets of funding from forestry charities such as England Forestry Commission and forest for the World."

Nodding he said, "These are insignificant compared to what we need to support an effective inquiry, one which will change our perspective of forests of the World. This study will prove that we can reverse climate warming using forests as carbon sinks. The results are promising. We need to prove that forests can cope and even thrive with the added carbon dioxide." He gestured wildly with his hands as he became more animated.

Landry swallowed and then spoke, "They will, and not only do they cope with the added CO2, but they will thrive, and you prove it works on a large scale. This could be the key to the hothouse Earth problem."

Landry noticed he was staring at her, his mouth slack. Before he could speak.

"Dr Pedersen, I'd like to give you something. A donation of sorts." Landry passed the envelope to him. It was open and she could see the pink of the tickets upright inside. He stared at them, flicking them with his finger. "Are you a gambling man, Dr Pedersen?"

He pushed the envelope towards her, his protest firm. "No, absolutely not... what is this? Is this from your magazine? There are proper channels for funding." He swept his arm in agitation, and it connected with Landry's. She placed her hand on the envelope and pushed it back towards him.

"We have allocated our donation budget for this year. I know that lottery tickets must seem a strange donation but sometimes you must have faith in things that are not scientific. What's the harm in seeing what happens?"

"Who are you? Are you serious? "

Landry stood firm, looked him directly in the eye, and spoke. "No joke, Dr Pedersen. "She pointed her finger towards him. "You need financial support... this could be it. This could represent two hundred million pounds or more." She'd lost him. She felt it.

"Go away and stop wasting my time. This is not funny." He shifted away from Landry and looked at his WordPad. She knew that she may have to break protocol, but she'd try one more thing first. She spouted his results back at him.

"Right Dr Pedersen, in 2016 you prove that a forest does cope with 550ppm of CO2. Your prediction for 2050." He attempted to interrupt her, astonished by what she was saying. She raised her voice, "Not only will you prove that the forest can cope, but that it becomes MORE efficient. "

He stared at Landry. "In 2016, the forest will prove to the world that CO2 emissions caused by burning fossil fuels are offset by the growth of trees."

Landry stopped.

Simon Pedersen broke the silence and quietly said, "Who are you? You are quoting my scientific targets back at me. Things I haven't shared with anyone."

Landry turned to face him. "I am your friend Simon. You won't get there without this," she held up the lottery tickets, "is your funding. It may be unorthodox, but it's still what you need. What have you got to lose? If these tickets give you nothing, then you've lost nothing. If they give you something, then you've gained everything."

Landry held the envelope out to him once more, and he took it. "Please don't lose them Dr Pedersen. They could fund an abundance of trees. I believe in your research, and I believe that this project could impact climate change. Well." She swung her arm towards him. "You know it will. You know the figures work and when you prove it, with this funding, you can get your message out to the world... save the rainforests and grow more. We require a landmass, the size of the USA, don't we? "

She smiled at the astonishment on his face. She stepped backwards, aware that she had said too much. As she reached the doorway, she turned. "Please, please check those tickets, Dr Pedersen. I cannot stress that enough. There's a lovely man in a shop on Hurst Street waiting to congratulate you on your winnings. "

As she pushed the door into the corridor, she heard him shout, "Miss Reagan. Wait. Miss Reagan."

She set off at a jog and increased her speed as his voice rose behind her. Running through the reception hall, she was satisfied that he hadn't followed her. She stepped outside. Th3 clouds had cleared, and the sun shone proud in the sky. Her heart swelled with pride in what she hoped she had just achieved.

In the Magera office in Birmingham 2188, Kyson's assistant yelled, "Another one," One second before the shrilling alarm began "We've got a 0.58 coming our way... it's coming from 2013. It's riding high." There was a pause as the officers ran to their stations.

Kyson shouted over the din. "Stop that blasted alarm."

Several voices rose at once. "It's increasing... the time variance is increasing as it comes into the 22nd century!" There was a flurry of questions and exclamations, "How can it increase?"

"What would cause a wave this high? "

"Whose out in time now?"

Their alerts became louder as more joined the throng. The timewave continued its rapid journey. As it came closer, Kyson shouted, "Brace yourselves." She held onto her desk, genuinely scared that this time wave could sweep her away. As the wave passed through the office, Kyson watched as two science officers disappear with a pop as the wave passed over. The second this happened however, it erased Kyson's memory of events before this instant. The only thing that remained of the two operatives' presence was their empty desks. Kyson and the staff, unaware of any variation, continued quietly working as if nothing had happened. The only proof that any time variation had happened lay in the historic data recorded on Magera's time mainframe.

CHAPTER 29

LANDRY REAGAN

Landry checked her watch, satisfied that she was working to time. Traffic was lighter, and commuters were at work. Her route back to the Hippodrome Theatre was a joy. The birds had come out following the rain, and she twice stopped in her tracks to watch them swooping across the sky. It amazed her to see birds flying together as one. This was such a privilege for her, and she watched as the past participants didn't even give them a second glance. She chastised herself for getting frustrated with them. They did not know what the future held. Mistakes were made and still being made.

She pushed forward towards the rear door of the Hippodrome and replayed her plans in her head. Would saving the World from Climate change and the great fall change it? It could become worse.

Reaching the back wall, the stillness of the confined dark space was welcome. Relieved to find the stage deserted, she now had to find the original keypad. She wasn't planning on returning to 2188 just yet; she had more to do first. Landry slid her hand along the uneven surface of the wall in the dim light, trying to find anything that might conceal a keypad. It took a long time, but she found it. Located inside an electrical box at the edge of the back wall, it looked like an abandoned light activation system for the stage. Karmal's instructions ran through her head as she keyed in the dateline 16.05.2018.1300. The back wall sizzled, and bricks melted away, revealing the emblem of ERA, the earlier time university, the Earth Research Authority.

Her arm out in front of her, Landry touched the shimmering wall and saw as her fingers disappeared through the area of the wall where the icon span. She stepped forward through the wall and into 2018. Once again, the stage was empty, and she repeated her journey down the corridor towards the rear of the Theatre and stepped outside. It was 1o'clock in the afternoon and except for the omnibuses trundling up and down Inge

Street, it was quiet. Little had changed since 2016 and Landry couldn't resist glancing inside the newsagents as she walked by. She saw the shop worker, chatting to customers and leaning against the counter. Behind him, she was thrilled to see the sign, 'Two lottery winners in one year. This is the place to buy them!' Landry was so tempted to go inside but knew that she couldn't.

She walked down New Street and heard a new sound; a sliding, screeching rumble towards her and as she reached the bottom of the street, was thrilled to see the tram slide by. Trams were re-entering the city! There was some pleasure in knowing that they were attempting to make strides towards reducing the carbon footprint of Birmingham's citizens, but was it enough?

Landry had changed her usual route as she was visiting a different University. Birmingham City University; a new modern complex in the city centre and the birthplace of Radan. Entering through the glass doors, she looked for the information desk. She had prepared what she needed to say, but Landry hoped that it would easy. At the desk was a receptionist eagerly waiting. She looked like a student at the university.

"Can I help you, I am Carol," She declared.

"Yes, you can. I am looking for a student here completing his PhD. I believe he uses an office on the second floor."

Carol's attention turned to the monitor in front of her, "What is his name, please?"

"Luke White."

"He works in room 23.2. I will call the office and see if he is there." Carol picked up a device and pressed a key on the pad in front of her, raising the handset to her ear. It still fascinated Landry although she had seen people communicate like this in Vizdramas. Such an archaic system of communication but so nostalgic.

Landry watched as Carol listened to the ringing tone at the other end. Landry sensed a change in tone and heard a voice and then a beep.

Carol spoke into the device, "Hello, this is a message for Luke White. Please contact the reception. You have a visitor waiting for you. "Landry almost laughed out loud, she was leaving a message for him to find later. How inefficient a system was this? Landry questioned how they ever conducted any business in the past. Carol was apologising, "I don't have any record of a mobile phone so all I can do is leave a message I'm afraid. You could wait in the student refectory, get yourself a coffee and when he returns the call, I'll send him your way." Carol was clicking an object on the desk and looking at the screen in front of her, "He's in the building somewhere, he scanned in this morning. He might be in the refectory, getting lunch."

Landry tried to assimilate all that Carol had just said quickly. There was a pause as Carol expected a response.

"I'll go to the refectory then?" Landry's questioning tone gained another smile from Carol.

"Yes, if you go to the refectory, then if he rings back, I'll tell him where you'll be. What's your name please?"

"Landry Reagan."

"Ok Miss Reagan, do you have a mobile that I can ring you on when he returns the call?"

Landry froze, "No, I don't have that device." Landry felt her heat rising on her face as Carol studied her. Landry looked expectantly at Carol.

"OK, You-go--to-the-refectory-and -I- will-send-Mr-White-to-you." Carol spoke deliberately slowly. Landry could see that Carol was frustrated.

"Yes, of course," Landry pointed behind her with her thumb and began walking backwards, "I'll go to the refectory."

Landry moved toward a wall map on the left, feeling Carol's gaze bore into her back. She knew that Carol was watching her. Identifying the route to the refectory, she stopped before the doors to count how much money she had. She wasn't keen to buy anything, but she thought she would look strange if she bought nothing. She clipped her student union ID badge onto the pocket of her shirt.

As she arrived at the refectory door, she took out the vizimage of Luke White from her pocket, a pale blonde haired young man with distinctive blue eyes. If he was in there hopefully, he would be easy to spot. Landry pushed open the doors. There was a buzz of activity in the room, with noises coming from the food preparation area. On the right was a metal rail and she saw students sliding trays along it. They put items on their tray as they passed them and swiping a credit card on a scan unit at the end.

Landry turned her attention to the rest of the room and instantly saw a young person sitting alone in the far corner, fitting the description from the vizimage. Could she be that lucky?

She moved toward him and saw that he had a tray of leftover wrappers and food items on the table and a red beverage can in front of him. He looked up as she got closer and she could see it was Luke White, the student she was looking for. Her first thoughts were, now don't mess this up. She had prepared her speech carefully, but she couldn't be sure how he might react.

She smiled as they made eye contact, "Luke? Luke White?" He nodded. "Would you mind if I sat with you?" She suddenly felt a nervousness at being the company of the creator of Radan. Would he be able to listen to what she had to say?

"No, go ahead." He said in a low, quiet voice and indicated to the chair in front, "you are?"

"Landry, Landry Reagan."

She was surprised when he raised his hand to shake hers. She pushed down her feelings of anxiety at human contact and took his hand gingerly. The awkward handshake ended quickly, and she sat down and studied his features. There was nothing noticeably special about the creator of Radan in front of her. She felt no sign of malice or even guile. He was waiting for her to talk.

"Hi Luke, I am a master's student completing my MSC in data science and business analytics. I read your recent paper on the extent to which the five applications of data inform our decision making."

He smiled, "And do you agree with my conclusions?" Landry felt under pressure but could be nothing but honest.

"Honestly, no, I didn't agree with your fifth point, that the filtering of data in recommender systems is infallible." Luke raised his eyebrows, smiling. He didn't rise to the discussion and sat quietly. It was difficult for Landry, usually a great talker, but this conversation was such an important one that she suddenly fell quiet. She was surprised when he offered to buy her a drink. She nodded and studied him as he went to the counter. She watched him choose the can from the refrigeration unit and then take it to where the lady stood. Cash exchanged hands and Landry dipped her head as he returned to the table.

He placed the aluminium can in front of her and she immediately felt the pressure of his gaze. She had examined the open can while he was away, so she knew that the opening was at the top. Taking a pen from her bag, she attempted to stab the top of the can and got in several stabs before Luke reached out to stop her. She saw his expression, absolute amazement. She watched as he placed his finger under the metal ring and raised it, Landry heard a hiss as the opening appeared.

"Thank you." she was flustered, "they don't have this type where I live."
Luke interrupted her, "Yes where are you from?"
Before she could answer, she took a sip. The liquid bubbled and tickled as it reached her tongue. It went up her nose and she snorted loudly. She wanted to spit it out. There was an incredibly high sugar content, and it hurt her teeth. Why would anyone want to drink something so sweet? Radan controlled her intake in the ration city, and they had prohibited high sugar products for over a century in her time. It felt like it was eating the plaque away from her teeth. Luke smiled politely as she placed the can firmly down on the table.

She knew that she wasn't making a good impression. However, Luke seemed to be unperturbed, and he waited for her to respond to his question.

"Where ARE you from?"

"I live in a small homestead in Scotland, and we only eat what we can grow or make." Luke nodded slowly. "I am completing my dissertation on the extent to which ethics is incorporated into artificial intelligence, and my tutor Dr Brown suggested you would be the person to speak to about this. A leader in the field." She raised her eyebrow in challenge.

Luke looked down clearly feeling uncomfortable, "Well- I wouldn't say leader, but I've been reading a lot of research for my PhD and your Dr Brown is right, I have a lot of information that might help you."

Landry took this as a sign to carry on and reached for a notebook and pencil. "Would you mind Mr White? It would help me a great deal."

"No problem, call me Luke though please."

Landry nodded and reflected on how amenable and mature he seemed. Wow, if only he knew what his creation would become.

"Right, I've got some questions. Can ethics be an integral part of a medical artificial intelligence, filtering system to decide which person to treat first?"

His expression froze. Was her question too advanced? "I mean, in a military situation, medics make these decisions every day. In such a situation, can an AI decide who to treat first?" She saw him relax a little. She knew that Luke was in the early stages of planning the Radan algorithms. He could be reluctant to discuss his ideas with anyone at this stage.

He took some time before answering. "The simple answer is no. An AI cannot have the ethics of compassion or empathy. "

He sat forward animated, "so given your example, two wounded soldiers on a battlefield. A quick decision is vital. The first algorithm considers who has the greatest chance of surviving?" He grabbed Landry's pad and pencil and started drawing decision keys as he spoke, "first the AI would check for the strength of life signs, age, which injuries? It would quickly search for recoverability from such injuries and with a combination of other lesser condition checks, it would decide who had the greatest odds for survival."

Landry interrupted, "Or which needed treating first, had the most extensive injuries, was more likely to die first?"

"No," Luke shook his head, "No, the greatest chance of life. Even human doctors know that if you treat the person closest to death first, then you risk losing both."

Landry understood his reasoning. "So, we leave the other to his fate? "

"Sadly, yes. Utilitarianism, for example, holds that morality is determined by the consequences of actions, and we should strive to always create the best chance for the maximum number of people. It is only in times of crisis or a time of warfare that tough decisions are required. Read up on the work of Alex Sandron, a director at Birmingham University for ethics and policy. He has written detailed papers on this very issue. It would help your research."

Landry continued, "On the other hand, a deontologist would start with a justice argument: every individual is valuable and should have the same chance in life."

"Yes," Luke said, "Of course, and when you might have optimal resources, optimal medics and everything in your favour then everyone is saved. But you ask a health care professional how many decisions they must make every day that means a difference between life and death. Ask them. Wouldn't it be better if the AI could give the reassurance that their decision was the right one?" He sat back, and Landry smiled.

Things were going well, but she needed to keep the conversation rolling. "For the sake of argument, let's say that the AI on my battlefield has empathy for the soldiers. "

Luke shook his head, "Ok, give it a list of algorithms for empathy, care, patience for example, and what will you get?"

Landry didn't respond. Luke continued, "You'll get a slower decision-making process because the AI will attempt to feel what they feel. But it won't change the outcome. "

He began drawing visuals on her pad again. Giving an AI empathy for the patient will not increase their chance of survival. Quick decisions will increase the chances for the many. You use the resources you have to the greatest effect to save as many lives as possible."

"I see," Landry nodded slowly," yes, I see. Just humour me. Explain again why you cannot add the deontologist algorithm to the army medic AI, that each person has the same value individually?"

Luke laughed, "Do you know what would happen if you did that?" He stood up and held up both his hands at shoulder height. "The AI would assess all the medical information for each soldier, and then the ethnicity of the individual would kick in and the decision would overwhelm it. It would go around and around in circles until it would force its programme to shut down. It could not make the decision we require it to make."

He sat back down, satisfied with his explanation. "I agree you shouldn't be discriminatory against age or sex. In certain cases, an older person's chances of survival are greater than those of a young person. But adding algorithms of deontology – the value of an individual – it cannot be."

She nodded in agreement, "I understand Luke- Thank you for explaining it to me."

Luke rubbed his hands up and down his face, "I have a similar dilemma, Landry. My PhD is being funded by the National Health Service." He glanced around, "They have asked me to create an AI that will help them allocate resources geographically in times of crisis but also within hospitals and health centres – a more efficient system for them."

Landry nodded, "Wow- what an amazing project."

"Yes, but what they need is a Utilitarian AI, a bit like your soldier medic but on a larger scale. I am struggling with the lack of ethics too because like yourself I am a little uncomfortable with an AI making decisions on who gets resources and who does not. The NHS is funding my entire PhD and they need productivity, not empathy- it just won't work."

Landry shifted in her seat, her excitement growing. They were getting to the core of what she wanted to speak about.

"It just sounds so soulless Luke; the AI could deny a person the resource that could save them, but human determination is so strong. Some people survive against the odds."

Luke clicked his fingers, "Exactly Landry, and there's evidence that 5% of patients survive purely on the tenacity of the health care professionals. I am deeply concerned that this will remove that, and they will stop fighting for a patient because an algorithm says so. I'm in a difficult position." Landry felt sympathy for him.

"There must be something you can do to combat this?" Thoughts of Karmal's family in Bangladesh whirled around her head as they both were lost in their own reflections.

"Come on Luke, there must be a way of adding a never-give-up objective to an AI."

Luke shook his head slowly, "It will reduce its ability to make that ultimate choice between two patients. Where there is a tie-breaking situation, there must be a deciding factor. For instance, if there were an epidemic, and doctors had to decide who got treatment, then the clinical factors would be used in assessing a patient's likelihood of survival. Yes?"

"Yes," Landry agreed.

"The doctor has no choice if a tie-break occurs between two patients, and usually the age is a deciding factor, for example, children under 17 are given priority over an adult only if there is a tie-break clinically. I can't give an AI that dilemma, the algorithms won't allow that function."

Landry understood Luke's argument and felt sick to her stomach. Sitting forward in her seat, "You've got to find a way, Luke. I cannot stress how important this will be. In the future, people will look back at your AI and examine its algorithms."

"No pressure then." He laughed nervously and leaning back in his chair, stretched his legs out in front of him.

"Luke, think about everything you have read. There must be some theories in adding quality-of-life factors or changing the clinical factors to include tenacity to save lives."

He stopped and looked towards her, and she feared that she may have overstepped herself. She saw him studying her quizzically.

"I need a drink." He said standing.

As he walked away, Landry focussed on her next step. She needed to persuade him somehow. This tact was not going anywhere. She felt she was making statements he had already considered and rejected. She had a decision to make. Go against every protocol of time and tell him her real purpose. Risk the wrath of Magera and Radan. Risk all their plans. If she told the truth and he still made no changes to Radan, then it was all over. Radan would be able to come through time and stop this anyway if she didn't act now.

She'd made her decision. Now, how do I tell a past participant that time travel exists?

He returned with the water, and Landry was aghast to see plastic bottles in front of her.

"It's disgusting what we are doing to the planet, don't you think?" Landry's mind was clear.

"I couldn't agree more Luke, it's why I'm here today." His brow furrowed, and he sat back in his chair.

"You're a scientist Luke."

"Well, a scientific analyst, I suppose."

"Are you into space, the stars?"

His face lit up, "Love it! I spend most weekends glued to my telescope."

"Great," Landry continued, "So you believe in the creation of our planet, the big bang, the universe is increasing in size, global warming destroying the planet blah blah."

"Yes of course, but how does this relate to my AI?"

Landry took in a deep breath, "Ok, do you believe in the theory of the 4th dimension, that time can be altered?"

Luke scoffed, "In theory yes but..."

Landry looked at Luke directly.

"Do you believe that at some time in the future someone will find a way to travel through time?"

"Yes of course, but..." He stopped speaking and he stared at the can of Coca Cola with the marks where she had tried to stab it.

Studying her more closely, he said "What are you saying?"

"Luke, you are the creator of Radan, an amazing medical AI. An AI which saves lives efficiently distributes resources to support medical practitioners, and aids governments in times of crisis to make those hard decisions and predict the impact of those decisions."

Shaking his head, "But how do you know its name? I have told no one ...." He stopped speaking and paused, "Who are you?"

She took a deep breath and breathed out slowly. There is no going back from this moment.

"I work for the Mars and Earth Greater Research Authority. I am working for that authority, and my primary aims are..." She paused, "are to travel back in time to find projects with support that could positively impact the people in my time." Landry sat back and waited.

He roared with laughter, and he rubbed the tears from his eyes. "Did my friends put you up to this?" He stood up, searching the refectory. "Where are they?"

Landry raised her arm and with a shaking hand stretched out, turned her wrist towards Luke with the tattoo facing upwards. He froze, leaning forward to scrutinise it.

At the midland headquarters of Magera, a triple alarm sounded. Their data showed not one time-wave variation, but small spots of variation all moving rapidly to join one wave. The air was filled with panic and disbelief as Kyson and her operatives began trying to combat the wave that was racing through time towards them.

Luke spoke, "What is that? A tattoo?"

"No more than that." Landry placed the fingers from her left hand over it. "It's a key, but it also hides a Nanochip." She brushed her fingers over the tattoo, indicating for him to do the same. He tentatively placed his fingers against the chip, pressing lightly, "Press harder", She commanded, "Then you'll feel it." He followed her instruction.

"What is it?" he said.

She paused, "It's my Radan chip." She stopped to scrutinise his reaction. Confident that she had his attention, she continued, "It is my medi-support, it constantly checks my vital signs, blood pressure, level of white blood cells, temperature, my nutrient intake, the quality percentage of my lungs, liver and kidneys and much more." He drew his hand away and looked up at her.

"Is it doing it now?"

"No, I'm afraid not. It cannot sync with 21st-century networks, it's far too advanced a system."

She felt his cynicism rise.

"Look, this is hard for me. I'm breaking so many protocols just sitting here with you."

"How do you do it?" He interrupted, "how do you travel through time?"

"Look, I can't tell you how. I don't know myself, but I'll answer questions that you may have?"

"Prove it!" He exclaimed, "Prove it to me."

CHAPTER 30

LANDRY REAGAN

She scanned through the endless possibilities of what could be her next step. How could she prove it to him? From her training, they knew that sharing too much could severely affect the mental health of a past participant. She couldn't do that to him. She hadn't planned this part well relying upon her instinct once she had met Luke. Then it came to her like a shot from the blue. She had worn her graphene hooded clothing today; purely selfish comfort. She could show him the capabilities of her graphemo. She would show him in stages, hoping she wouldn't have to show him everything to convince him she was from the future. She tutted loudly and considered the Magera laws that she was breaking at this very moment.

"Ok then. Let's do this. Go get a knife, a sharp one."

He crossed the floor to the food providers, and then returned with a large knife. She had zipped up her hooded jacket to the neck. Pointing at her torso with her thumb, said, "Stab me."

"No, absolutely not." She was not surprised by his reaction, appreciating how vulnerable he must feel in his 21st century woven clothing. This graphemo technology had been a security mainstay for over one hundred years in her time.

"Ok then." She began removing the hooded jacket. "Just check the strength of the knife by slicing it into my paper pad." He followed her instruction and the knife, with little effort, sliced through the top five pages with ease. She spread her jacket onto the table, "Now cut my jacket." He hesitated.

"Don't worry- it's only a jacket. Press as hard as you can and cut it."

He placed his right hand flat against the collar and, using his left hand, pulled the knife blade across it. Landry watched as the blade made no indent or cut or even a mark as Luke attempted to cut the fabric.

He threw the knife down and looked up at her. "Specially treated hard resistant fabric. Maybe military strength. Are you from NASA? "

"No." She giggled at his naivety. Landry looked around the refectory. There were a few people still sat around but most were quite a distance away.

"Can the NASA fabrics do this?" She issued the command. "Colour change, lime green."

It rippled and the blue colour appeared to run off the jacket as it was replaced with a vivid shade of green. Luke jumped backwards in his chair, almost toppling it over. Landry was enjoying herself, "Colour change black with pink 1 cm spots." The jacket surface rippled as the green disappeared and became black and pink spots. "Tell me what colour you would like."

He considered for a moment, "red with red stripes of 2 cm and white stripes of 1cm." Landry repeated his request and the jacket change accordingly.

"It's bulletproofed, knife proof, as fine as silk but as strong as steel. It can change colour, thickness, even size." Landry sat back and waited. Surely, she had convinced him.

Neither spoke, and she watched as Luke's gaze fixed upon the red drinks can that she had so unceremoniously attempted to open earlier. She could feel his brain trying to take in what he was being told as he struggled with it.

Then Luke smiled. "Look, I cannot explain what just happened, but there is so much new technology out there that it could be a stupid stunt or what you are saying could be real. I really don't know what to believe, but I'm willing to stretch a little. So, you are telling me you can change what you are wearing to suit the social situation that you are in? Landry nodded but her smile faded. Her future had no socialising, no changing of clothes. That was all deemed non-essential. Survival – that was it. Just survive and be happy with that. Well, she wasn't satisfied with surviving – not anymore. She was running out of time. Her voice was now serious.

"Whether you believe me, it's the reason I'm here Luke. I came to visit you today, specifically you. I can't tell you anything about your future, and I don't want you to panic. But you must understand how crucial this is to the future of the entire human race."

Kyson, in the Magera midland headquarters, watched as an orb split away from the main timeline, now branching into multiple variations. The twenty orbs of variation were clumping together and shooting across the screen. A previously unrecorded event in the history of Magera. Kyson considered she could be watching the end of life itself.

Luke and Landry sat in 2018 oblivious to what was happening in 2188.

Luke swallowed hard, "Go ahead – I'm listening," he said.

"This Medical AI that you create, Radan is amazing. It changes the World - It helps so many people and it's everything that you described earlier. It can make judgements quickly and is so valuable that it..." Landry was careful not to scare Luke. "It helps governments in times of crisis. It is a great advisor." Luke was nodding, "However, it doesn't do what that doctor would do, it doesn't give 110% and never give up on life. Its algorithms consider only the quantity of lives saved, not the quality of their lives. I don't know what to do, but you need to account for the quality of a person's life as well. Otherwise, we end up with… what we end up with." Landry couldn't find the words.

Luke asked, "What do you end up with?"

Landry stopped, "I'm sorry Luke, I can't say." She placed her hand upon his. "You're clever. You've had your own doubts about the ethics of your initial programming. You know you have. Just find a way Luke. You're struggling with this too. In your heart, you know what you need to do. Find a way, please."

She watched as he stared, lost in his thoughts and she waited for him to speak.

"There are so many things I want to ask you, "He said softly, "but then I don't want to know."

Landry nodded, contemplating her next words carefully before speaking, "Just know this Luke White, your AI saves lives. It follows the programme that you have given it, it follows it well. It's a fine tool that you have created. Just know that all things can be improved, and this refinement could save even more lives. Luke, find a way, please."

Landry could see that his mind was going over the limitless algorithms, subroutines and objectives of his creation. He stood up suddenly, "We need to get started, I don't know how we're going to do this."

He looked at Landry and paused, "I think with your help we may make some subtle changes."

Landry slowly shook her head, "I am sorry Luke, but I cannot help you. I am just a messenger.

"Oh - I see." He paused. She could see him struggle with his words. "Will I see you again?"

Shrugging her shoulders, she shook her head then a broad smile filled her face, "That depends upon your success Luke. Put it this way, I hope to never have to return."

Her meaning was not lost on Luke, and he held out his hand. With great pleasure she shook it vigorously. "Thank you, Luke White." Landry could see that he was already lost in his algorithms. She watched as he ran through the door to the refectory. She hoped that she had done enough.

The orbs on the Kyson's screen began joining in one vast wave. It was what they at Magera had all feared. The multitude of small variations were now becoming one. One enormous time wave variation, possible a 2.0, so large that it was inconceivable that the consequences wouldn't be catastrophic. With all the minor variations that day, this was far and away the most terrifying. The operatives stopped looking at their screens and began looking around them. It was a moment in time they would never get back- their last moments. Kyson and the other operatives felt compelled to speak, "Good luck", "Goodbye", "we'll be ok", and then silence enveloped the group. Some got up and went to stand near to other colleagues, others sat, their thoughts elsewhere. Several people stayed at their stations bowing their heads.

When the wave hit, the force knocked some off their feet, others disappeared with a popping sound and others gripped onto their desks with all their might, attempting to keep themselves in that space and time. When the force swept through, so did their memories of what just happened. It was the same for Kyson. She transferred to the new timeline without a hitch. Her memory permanently altered, she adjusted her collar and continued as before, tapping the translucent screen in front of her and checking her data. The only way that anyone would know of the time variation was if they checked the historic data for that day. The timeline was complete. Whatever effects from the work of Karmal Ray, Wynter Lund, and Landry Reagan on that day had occurred, it was all done.

Landry walked out of Birmingham City University in 2018 under a brooding sky, her mind in turmoil. Forced to share the unthinkable, something she had sworn she would never do. She knew the risks of doing that. She knew that whatever happened, her future would not be the same as it was before. She reflected. Her memory didn't seem altered, which was a good omen. As she walked back to the Hippodrome Theatre, she considered the punishments she might receive if she had been unsuccessful. Or maybe worse, that they had made their future worse somehow. As she entered the theatre, she heard the lion king's roar echoing through the walls. Surely it couldn't be a worse future.

She reached the back of the stage, ten metres away from where the actors were performing. She felt ready. She would face whatever would be through the doorway. "End private mode." She commanded, waiting to feel the change in her auditorus. Pausing for a moment, she briefly considered staying in 2018. Should she stay and help Luke? No, she wanted to know, needed to know if they'd done it. Taking in a deep breath, she winced and closed her eyes as she placed her tattoo on the symbol at the edge of the wall. There was no ripple or change. She attempted it again, pressing her tattoo onto the Magera emblem. Landry placed her tattoo on the emblem again and again; nothing happened. Was this good or bad? Her Radan tattoo no longer opened the door.

She fought the initial panic then remembered the pre-Radan keypads. She knew where it was, inside the electrical box on the edge of the wall. She checked her date index three times and made sure it was correct: 05.08.2188.1800. She chose 6pm as she knew it would be after the timeline action by Wynter and Karmal. It was a relief when the blackness rippled, and the wall appeared liquid-like. The old symbol of ERA appeared. It was different and only had the Earth spinning. Landry's first thoughts were that it was because she had used the keypad or was it different? She cursed herself for her lack of attention previously.

Before stepping through the door, she prepared herself for the worst-case scenario. That she would step into complete nothingness because of their actions. The Earth may no longer exist in 2188. She could be attacked or arrested the minute she stepped through. Cowardice forced her once again to consider staying in 2018. This time was full of life, she could live a good life with these past participants. But knowing their future and not being able to do anything to stop it? She soon squashed those thoughts again. She wanted to get back to her family if they still existed; wanted to see her father again. With gritted teeth, she stepped through into blackness, thrusting her hands in front of her and finding the familiar flat surface. Sighing, she was relieved when she saw a small opening of light appear with the same symbol on the wall, ERA.

Kyson's voice was the first sound, "Welcome back Landry." And then her image appeared. Landry didn't know whether to be relieved or disappointed to see Kyson staring at her through the screen.

"Do you have a report to download?" Kyson asked.

Landry was flustered but kept her head, "No, it was a strange thing. My optic implants failed. I will have to write the report this evening."

Kyson acted as though this was nothing unusual, and Landry's confidence grew. Kyson spoke next, "I've got a date and time confirmation for you, 05/08/2188 and 1805 hours. "

Kyson was speaking, but Landry was not listening to anything she was saying. Kyson looked different. Her vitiligo seemed less pronounced, and she was smiling, jolly even. Landry could sense the happiness in her manner. Landry smiled back.

"Thank you, Kyson." She purposely spoke informally.

Kyson nodded, "I hope you found what you were looking for. I'll expect your report at say 0800hours tomorrow?"

Landry was quick to reply, "Oh yes, yes, thankyou Kyson."

Kyson looked up at the screen and smiled, "See you soon." And then the screen went blank.

Landry stepped out into the back wall of the theatre in 2188. She was disappointed. Nothing had changed. She was keen to see outside. She ran down the corridor and into the alley behind the theatre. The light wasn't good, the alley was in a dark shadow. Landry immediately looked towards Inge Street for some sign of change. Her shoulders slumped. It was quiet. The alley was still and silent as ever. She reviewed all their plans. How could they have no impact at all? Did history just right itself back on the same path?

The pressure of the past weeks engulfed Landry, and she felt the intense sorrow of their failure. Her hand pressed to her chest and large spots appeared on the floor in front of her as the tears ran down her face. Her naivety at thinking she could do it plagued her now, and she stood in the quiet sobbing softly.

Righting herself, she wiped the tears away. It wasn't over yet! Coming back through, she wasn't arrested, but Kyson seemed different somehow. Maybe it wasn't all bad?

As she moved towards Inge Street, she suddenly froze. Something moved across the corner of her optic, and again. They flew in small stuttering movements, small arcs up and down; a silent play circling each other and rising a falling like a beautiful dance. Landry stared, completely absorbed; it felt like they had chosen her. She saw that their wings were intricately detailed with shades of yellow and green. They were butterflies, she was sure that they were. Raising her hand to her mouth, she tried to contain a sob of joy that burst through, a triumphant cry. Butterflies in 2188 could mean only one thing. She didn't want to lose them. She ran with them trying to follow them, watching them dive and circle. Then was disappointed as they were lost to her over the alley wall.

Landry turned and looked up. There were shadows ahead and they were moving in the breeze. She set off stumbling, running up the incline, and as she reached the top, she saw that it was the dappled shade of the trees filling the walkway ahead. A city skyline came into view. A city changed. She squinted. In the foreground, shapes moved in the dapple sunshine. There were people. Groups of them. Some tall, some small. Are those children?

She stepped forward and the trees came into focus. Many trees, maybe hundreds, some glades together and some lining walkways where people walked, ran and jumped. The more she looked the more she saw. People sitting in large open green spaces filled with trees and fauna of all types and there was more. People sitting together and families she thought, being together in the outside. As she moved down the hillock she had been stood on, she began to make out the music of sound, laughter, joy, chatter. People were talking to each other…each other in one space.

Something made her stop as she reached the first trees and placing her hand on the rough bark, she heard it first. Birdsong. It was difficult as she desperately peered through the leaves and branches to find the source. And then she found it, a small sparrow on the branch above chirruping in what seemed to Landry as a song full of joy. She stood transfixed and then her heart faltered. Was she still in the past? She tapped her Radan tattoo and not giving it time to speak she commanded, "Confirm date and time."

The familiar voice came through loud and clear, "zero five, zero eight, twenty-one, ninety-eight at 1820 hours."

So, Radan was still being used for medical support but without the great fall hopefully that is as far as its influence went. Landry considered if Luke had made the changes. Whatever it was, the new future was dazzling!

Landry swallowed and she felt the corners of her lips widen into the greatest and largest of smiles as her throat constricted and the tears began to fall. They had done it! They had changed the future. Had they turned back the clock on the climate for the World? They must have. There was only one explanation for what Landry was seeing. There it was, a World full of life, a World not blighted by a changed climate.

Epilogue

She noticed that she was staring at her. A young girl sat on a bench at the end of Inge Street was studying her.

Landry continued to take in her surroundings and study the bushes and trees and sky in the hope of seeing more. The lady must have moved forward because Landry only saw her when she was right beside her, almost touching.

"Are you Landry Reagan?" She spoke.

"Yes."

Smiling broadly, "I'm amazed that this has actually worked." She cleared her throat and stated formally, "Landry Reagan, I am Landry Sanchez, the 4 times great grandchild of Wynter Sanchez and strangely, she asked us to give you this. She held out an envelope. I say us because I never knew her, but her story has been told throughout my family history and I am very proud of her legacy. This date and time was stated by Wynter Sanchez as an important event in our family's future. Someone had to come to this exact location on this exact day in the hope of seeing you and here you are. I cannot believe that everything that we have been told is true."

She stood holding out the envelope. Today's date was scrawled across the top and a small note underneath it. *Wait by the Hippodrome theatre, Birmingham from around 1700 hrs.*

"You wouldn't believe how over the years my descendants have wanted to open this envelope and see what is inside, but we made a promise and so … here it is. It's yours Landry Reagan."

Landry took the envelope and was immediately shocked at how fragile it was. Her own thoughts were of Wynter as she realised that this came from the past and that they could never meet again. Never share the success of their endeavours. Landry faced the sad truth that Wynter had to have died many years before. How strange that she had only been speaking to her two days ago. The young lady turned to go, "My task is complete and that's all I must do but I'm intrigued. Can I connect communicate with you and we could contact each other?"

Landry found her voice, "Oh yes. I'd like that. Yes of course." They hovered their tattoos close together, and both stated "Connect "in unison. There was a bong in their auditorus a signal that they were now connected.

Wynter's relative stood quietly and then turned to go. "I really hope that you do contact me. I've heard that Wynter Sanchez was an interesting person. I need to add to the story for my own children."

Landry's eyes shining with unshed tears, she gushed, "Oh it's a truly great story. "Landry smiled, "And yes, she was an inspiration. A great friend."

Wynter´s relative looked up quizzically and then turned and walked towards a gentleman standing near to a tree not far away playing with a small boy.

Landry watched her go and then found a bench for herself dappled in the shade of an oak tree.

The letter read,

Dear Landry,

It is 2095. It's hard to write this as I am coming to the end of my life, but I wanted and hoped that this letter may be delivered somehow to you. I cannot write much as I am very old, but I wanted you to know that I think we did it! I don't know for certain of course because I stayed in 2033. I couldn't return in case we were unsuccessful.

I know that it was wrong, but I carried a data storage device back with me with research on the dates, and landmark events for climate change and I know from that, that the timeline changed. I really hope that it was because of what we did.

Wow- what a life I have had Landry. I found my calling fighting for SAM. We knocked the socks off the predictions, and I really think that SAM made a difference in the end. I kept my eye on BUFR for you and they had great successes in their research. I live in a BUFR neighbourhood now where trees outnumber tarmac, and houses are all self-sufficient. Zero carbon footprints. Can you believe that?

But Landry I found love too. I knew that the connection with Robert was something I had never experienced before, and our friendship became much more very quickly. It took some adjusting to 21st century but he helped me every step of the way.

We have had a wonderful life Landry. Four children, 6 grandchildren and 2 great grandchildren already. I have no regrets about anything in my life. I have experienced so much joy and had so many adventures, I would love to tell you more. But as my life is reaching its end, my thoughts turn to you.

I know that if this letter gets to you, you will have just returned from 2018 to 2188 and I will be long gone.

But know this. I hope with all my heart that the world in 2188 is changed and that the great fall never happened. My predictions are that you did it because I know how determined you were and all signs in this time now are looking good. The London flooding hasn't happened, and it should have done by now. So, I'm optimistic for you.

Go on Landry. I hope you find your family and live the life you wanted and that your father is alive and well.

Love and regards,

Wynter

P:S I have included an obituary for one Karmal Rahman. Enjoy reading this also. He got it Land. He got the life he was searching for. How many other lives did we change for the better Land?

Now go and get what you deserve too.

Folding the letter carefully, Landry turned and walked slowly through the tree-lines avenue taking it all in. There was one last assignment. To try to find Roan and her family.

About the Author

Linda Bishop bade farewell to her distinguished teaching and leadership career in 2018, poised to embark on new endeavours.

A native of Redditch, Linda's educational journey led her to various corners of the globe, where she imparted her passion for learning.

This debut novel serves as a tribute to her former pupils' dedication to environmental stewardship and their collective concern for the planet. Now residing in sunny Spain with her husband Rob, she continues to cultivate her creative pursuits, immerse herself in the vibrant local culture, and advocate for a more sustainable world.

Printed in Great Britain
by Amazon